THE STRANGEST THING JUST HAPPENED.

Having just finished my journal—an entry of such length that my hand still aches from detailing it—I drifted to sleep, only to awaken and discover myself being watched by an odd boy.

I would have taken him to be a slave or servant, but he was wearing the crest of Cameliard indicating one of higher rank. I have ne'er seen his like. Pale skin like death, hair near as white.

His eyes provided the only color in his face at all; they were an amazing pale blue. It was hard to determine his age, although he was clearly nowhere near manhood. Seven years, perhaps eight at most. He was dressed in black and crouched near me, tilting his head slightly, like a dog. His nostrils flared, adding to the canine feel of his presence.

"Who are you?" I whispered, not wishing to awaken any of the other servants sleeping nearby.

He said nothing. Instead he stepped back and into the shadows. I clambered to my feet and went to the wall.

He was gone.

I write this down so I will not forget, although I am uncertain even now if what I witnessed was a dream. I have thought Castle Camelot many things, but haunted was never one I suspected.

An ill omen, at the very least, whate'er it was.

The Camelot Papers

Being the Shocking True History of Arthur's Acclaimed Table

As Recounted by Viviana, Royal Historian

To their Majesties Arthur and Guinevere

Adapted by Peter David

CRAZY 8 PRESS

To Mike Friedman, who is the reason you're reading this

Foreword by Professors Eugene Bronte, Dean of History, and Fletcher Hodges, Faculty chair of Anthropology, Golden Bough University

WE CANNOT BEGIN TO CONVEY the excitement in the academic world when Professor R. K. Simpson, possibly the most renowned expert in the realm of mythic historical studies, presented to our board what is thought to be the long-believed-lost journals of the fabled Viviana.

Viviana (also known as "Vivian" and assorted other variations) has been a long-standing "character" in Arthurian mythos, but depicted in a variety of manners. Some describe her as a disciple of Merlin's, others as a high priestess. Some have considered her interchangeable with the Lady of the Lake. But there remains a small percentage of historians, striving to separate Arthurian fact from fiction, who contend that—unlike such obviously mythical constructs as the aforementioned Lady of the Lake—Viviana was a very real individual. Now Professor Simpson has found the support that those academics have long sought.

As most of you know, the Professor virtually invented the study of what he calls "mythic history"—tales believed by many to be myth, but are actually anchored in fact. We at

G.B.U. believe that his most recent find may well surpass all his previous endeavors in importance simply because of the many iterations of the Arthurian legends. To finally know the real story from a woman who was there is an opportunity over which any true Arthurian enthusiast can only salivate.

Viviana, thanks to her varied incarnations in Arthurian tales, is considered by many in our field to be little more than myth herself. A woman capable of reading and writing, a rare enough commodity at that time in and of itself. But the things that she accomplished, especially when one considers the circumstances from which she came, and the environment in which she fought to survive, simply boggle the mind.

And now, at last, through the good offices of Professor Simpson, we have her actual journals, the authenticity of which we have established to our satisfaction. If we had not done so, we would not be sharing them with the reading public.

The papers present a virtual treasure trove of answers to historians who are obsessed with the apparent contradictions in the extant tales of Arthur and his knights. Picking one example: the status or even existence of Lancelot du Lac has been a subject of lively controversy. There is no mention whatsoever of Lancelot in the earlier recitations of the deeds of Arthur's knights. He does not make an appearance in any text until several centuries later, at which time he takes center stage at Camelot. This delay has prompted a number of scholars to postulate that Lancelot was entirely a fictitious individual. It is easy to understand how such a conclusion could be reached. Lancelot is presented as the best and boldest knight who had ever lived, a Frenchman so formidable and irresistible that even the queen succumbed to his charms and cuckolded her husband for him. Since the first poets to write of him were themselves French, the theory was that he was nothing more than a wish-fulfillment construct.

Yet now, thanks to Viviana's papers, the truth becomes clearer. Lancelot does not appear in the earliest poems because he was, in fact, a rather brutal and disreputable sort who did not fit in with the idealized world that earlier writers desired to present. Plus, to be candid, there was certainly no love lost between the English and the French. Hence Lancelot's omission from the earlier tales, and the obvious desire of later French writers to rectify that omission by elevating the very flawed Frenchman to idealized status.

And that is merely one example of the various revelations that Viviana provides us.

Professor Simpson, as he did previously with the Atlantis chronicles, has worked closely with fantasist Peter David to cull the narrative into a more manageable size for the general public and David adapted the language to something more palatable for modern audiences. Although scholars will wish to scrutinize every page of the originals (secured in the Golden Bough University Library and available for accredited researchers), the average layman would likely find much of Viviana's writings redundant or even uninteresting, detailing as they do her daily life, particularly when many of those days were mind-numbingly dull. Mr. David and Professor Simpson have therefore presented for this volume a structure—a story, if you will—that will answer all the questions that the more aggressive Arthurian fans have sent to G.B.U. since the discovery of Viviana's journals was announced. An unabridged edition will be made available next year, although the projected cover price of $275 will likely limit its sale to select libraries.

Step back in time, then, to a medieval era, and prepare to have many of your illusions dashed.

—Eugene Bronte, Fletcher Hodges
G.B.U., April, 2011

Day the First

MY FIRST SIGHT OF THE castle filled me with nothing but a deep and abiding anger. I looked upon it and all I could think was that it was populated by pampered creatures that cared only for themselves and stepped on the backs of people like me on their way to achieving their "great and glorious" destinies. Actually, in truth they did not even consider those like me to be "people." We were just things. I was a thing, a possession, no different than a table or chair, aside from the fact that they likely cared more about tables and chairs than for someone like me.

The lash fell heavily across my back as it typically did when I allowed myself to pause even for a heartbeat. The assistant slave master screamed in my ear, "Keep moving! Keep moving, you mindless cow!"

As I did as instructed, I allowed for the thought that the castle itself was somewhat beautiful; far more majestic than any I had ever seen. And I had seen quite a few in my years.

I have honestly lost track of how many years that might be. Birth dates are the sorts of things that mean a great deal to a free woman and little to a woman who is a slave like me. When your life is not your own but instead the property of others, you have only a passing interest in it. I believe I recall sixteen summers clearly, and so fancy I am somewhere less than my twentieth year. But I could well be wrong a few years either way.

At least this slave master did not have chains 'round my ankles. I despise those. The manacles weigh heavily upon me and always rub my skin raw to bleeding. They rob my legs of any feeling and then always leave me making a bad impression on whoever my new master might be, for I cannot move quickly enough to suit his or her fancy. This particular slaver, whose name was Lucius, settled for simple ropes that served more for guidance than imprisonment. Lucius told me, calm as you please, that ropes would suffice if I did not make any sort of attempt to flee. Were I to do so, he warned, then he would turn his dogs upon my trail and hunt me down and then the bonding would be far more severe.

He was doubtless trying to present himself as a man of compassion for some reason that suited his vanity. I am sure the truth of it was that he simply had no desire to diminish my resale value. In any event I agreed not to make any try at escaping and had been true to my word.

The spires of the outer wall of Camelot stretched so high that I thought they were like to touch the sky. Flags fluttered from the highest points, displaying a rendering of a fearsome dragon entwined around a sword. The wind was coming in steadily from the east.

The small procession of slaves, with Lucius in the lead, crossed the drawbridge that lay open over the moat. I glanced into the moat, curious to see if any strange or exotic animals resided therein. There appeared to be none. I was disappointed. I had heard tales of fearsome monstrous lizards that swam within some moats, capable of devouring anyone foolish enough to cross. Never had I actually seen such creatures. The only monsters I had ever encountered resided within the walls of castles.

Once across the drawbridge, we entered the main square of the keep. Camelot itself was a standard sized gated community, with the primary road stretching from the drawbridge through to the heart of a bustling marketplace. I watched sellers going about their business: farmers hawking their wares; butchers displaying the carcasses of recently deceased chickens. Every so often I would spot someone who was, like me, trapped in servitude. Sometimes our eyes would meet and the reactions were always different. They might nod in silent acknowledgment, keep their gazes locked upon me as if to say, Wait. Just wait. Our time will come.

Or else they might see me and just as quickly lower their eyes, as if considering anything other than their chores and duty to their master would be sufficient to warrant a flogging.

Honestly, I do not know for whom I felt more sorry: the ones who still bristled with hope never to be fulfilled or the ones who dreamt of nothing more than their current state since they had given up all hope.

Beggar children approached the small wagon that Lucius's horse was pulling, with Lucius leading the horse. Lucius snarled out curses at the children and gestured for them to go back whence they'd come. Seeing that they would obtain nothing from him, they started to approach me. Then they took a close look at me, with the bonds on my hands, the burlap clothes I wore that looked as if they were made of old potato sacks— which they were—and the thick, matted, unwashed black hair that hung lifelessly around my face like so much kelp. The two other slaves who walked behind me did not seem much more appealing. The children turned away.

It tells you something about your status in life when you are not even worth a beggar's time.

The portcullis that guarded the main entrance to the castle was old and rusty but looked sturdy nonetheless. As for the castle itself, it was the largest I had ever seen. As opposed to other castles that were little more than piles of stone, the outsides of Castle Camelot were made of varied colored stones that formed amazing mosaics. They displayed men at arms locked in battle with powerful mythic creatures, dragons and griffins and phoenixes. And the tiled mosaics stretched dozens of feet high, perhaps hundreds. It was so much to absorb that I stopped where I was just so I could take it in.

That was when I felt the lash across my back and the bellow from the assistant slaver to keep moving. It hurt as much as it always did and I sank to my knees, startled, gasping. I did not cry out, not wanting to give the bastard the satisfaction, but it was a near thing.

"Get up!" he practically shouted in my ear, which was ironic since I would not have been down had he not struck me.

He appeared ready to bring the lash across my back yet

again, and this time Lucius interceded, pushing him back and scolding him for his over-enthusiasm. "We want her at her best!" Lucius said. "Not beaten half to death! What sort of price do you think we'll get for her then, eh?"

"Pardons, sir," said his assistant whose name I had never even bothered to learn.

Lucius put out a hand and helped me to my feet. He spoke not a word to me, but there appeared to be the slightest hint of apology in his eyes. It was more than I expected and probably insincere.

We were brought through the main entrance to the castle. The hooves of the horse pulling Lucius' wagon clopped away on the paved entrance. The weather was tepid but a blast of cool air struck me as soon as we crossed the threshold. The more fanciful aspects of my personality made me think that it was an ill omen, a physical representation of a certain chilly reception, or perhaps simply an indicator that the master of the castle had all the warmth of a winter storm.

We passed servants going about their business, and children scampering around, stopped in their activities to point and laugh. One youth who was holding a roll saw us, drew back his arm, and slung it. I do not think he was aiming it at any of us particularly, but it bounded off my head. This sight was greeted with snickers from the children. Seeing the bread at my feet, I cared not for its origins or the disdain with which it was thrown. I tried to grab for it but as I did the rope 'round my wrist was yanked tight and I was pulled forward. The slave behind me snatched it up and crammed the entire piece into his mouth. He looked at me challengingly as if daring that I demand a share. I said nothing.

"Halt!"

We stopped upon the shouted order. A squat, swaggering man approached us. He was wearing a stained white tunic and seemed thoroughly unpleasant. "Is this the lot?"

"Yes, milord."

"Do I look like a lord?" said the man contemptuously. He had a point.

He walked past us, looking us up and down. He stopped when he saw the small burlap sack slung over my shoulder. "What is that?" he said.

"It is . . ." I began to respond out of reflex, more fool I. His hand swung and took me in the face. I swayed, staggered but did not fall.

"I wasn't asking you!" he bellowed in my face.

"It is her possessions," Lucius said.

"Possessions? A slave with possessions?" He grabbed the sack away from me, which was unnecessary since all he needed to do was ask. He pulled open the sack, looked inside and then frowned in confusion. "Why do you have this?"

Afraid to speak, I simply shrugged.

"Answer me!"

"My father gave it to me."

"Your father is a fool."

I said nothing. It seemed the safest course.

Obviously feeling the contents of my sack warranted no further interest on his part, he shoved it back at me. I clutched it to my bosom, taking care not to say "Thank you" or even make eye contact. Once upon a time it would have been the sort of situation that would have prompted me to start crying. That had not happened in a long, a very long, time. I was bereft of tears, having shed them all when my status in life had been transformed from free woman into slave.

He shoved a small sack of coins into Lucius' hand and said, "This should serve you for the lot of them." I could see by Lucius' expression that he felt the sum was inadequate. Instead he said nothing. Lucius was a free man and yet, in his own way, he lived in as much fear as I. He bowed his head in submission and pulled the horse's reins. Lucius cast one final glance in my direction and, although I may well have imagined it, it seemed tinged with regret. Then he turned the horse around and beast and master—each slaves in their own way—walked out of Castle Camelot.

A wizened woman had appeared at the side of the castle's slavemaster. He pointed at the slave to my right and said, "This one for the stables," and then to my left and said, "This one for the laundry." Finally he looked at me. He took my chin in one rough hand and pulled my head left, then right. Then he examined my teeth as if I was a mare. "The king will vet you personally."

"Vet me?" I should not have echoed his words, but they slipped out. I braced myself for the inevitable blow that would surely follow. None came.

"The king," he said, "inspects each comely female slave personally."

Ah.

Then I understood.

It was not the first time. It would not be the last. I had learned long ago, a lifetime ago it seemed, that a slave's body is not her own. That lesson, hammered home enough times, was the reason my store of tears had dried up.

The other slaves did not cast a glance my way as the slave master led me through the maze of corridors that constituted Castle Camelot. I had heard many things about the castle's fabled ruler. None of them had been especially flattering. Even less flattering were the rumors about his son, reputed by many to be an evil bastard, although a few whispered that he was simply a buffoon.

We passed men whom I took to be knights by their attire. Most apparently gave me no thought, although some seemed to feel I was worth a quick glance before going about their business. The master brought me to a large pair of doors and thrust them wide. They opened onto an impressive room, lined with all manner of weapons mounted upon the wall. There were also several mounted animal heads looking at me in a bewildered fashion.

"Wait here," he said as if I had a choice. Then he noticed that my hands were still tied. He pulled a knife from his belt and sliced through the bonds in one quick movement. "Do not," he warned, "even think of trying to escape."

I did not see how anyone could reasonably control one's thoughts, but I did not point that out as it seemed a futile thing to do.

He nodded once as if approving the sound of his own voice and then turned and left the room, pulling the doors shut loudly behind him.

I waited. I did not have to do so for long.

There was a smaller door at the far end of the room and a great bearded man entered through it. It was as if, in his very presence, he occupied the entire chamber. He was magnificently dressed, but my attention was drawn to his fingertips. They were thickly stained with what I knew to be dried blood, having seeped so thoroughly into his skin that his hands had become permanently discolored. That told me all I needed to know of him.

He took a deep drink from a silver chalice he was holding. He then extended it to me in what I imagine he thought to be a gesture of hospitality. My impulse was to decline, but I was so hungry and thirsty that my hands moved of their own volition. He looked down at me—he was at least a head and a half taller than I—as I gulped down the fiery liquid. I had no idea what it was. I did not care. In the worst case, it would numb me or even kill me, and thus relieve me of what was to come.

"I am Pendragon," he said.

I did not volunteer my name. He did not ask. I had learned in such circumstances that they typically did not wish to know. Knowing my name would bring me that much closer to being viewed as a human, and he might not be able to treat me like a sack of meat and bones suited only for his pumping pleasure.

"Put down the sack," he said, expressing no interest in its

contents. I dropped it onto the floor. Then he inspected my face in the exact same manner as the other man had. He brushed my hair back, ran his fingers through it. They snarled on tangles therein and he pulled the fingers through. It hurt like the devil but I bit tightly on my lower lip.

"You will do," he said, which for a man like Pendragon was about as close to words of romance as he was going to get.

I was hoping I would, at the very least, get a preparatory bath out of the bargain, but he had no such interests. Instead he threw me down upon the bed. I lay there for a moment and then said, as respectfully as I could, "Highness . . . I am dirty and disgusting from the road."

"I prefer dirty and disgusting," he said. "My wife, primped and perfumed within an inch of her life . . . it makes me sick to think of it. You are what a real woman should be."

"Filthy?"

"To engage in filthy activities, yes. Absolutely. On your stomach," he said.

I obeyed. I had no other choice. In days past, I had fought. And fought. Sufficient blows to the head and face and body will cure one of such resistance.

He approached me, grabbed my hips roughly. I closed my eyes and prayed that he wound up severely chafed.

That was when the far doors opened.

A servant entered. He had a round, open face and a confused expression. His long brown hair was tied off in the back to keep it out of his face, and his manner was bewildered. "I . . . am sorry, highness. Is this a bad time?"

The Camelot Papers   11

"Is this a . . . ?" Pendragon clearly could not believe the question.

The servant approached me and smiled vacantly. "Hello. Are you new here? What is your name?"

Unable to believe the circumstances facing me, I still found enough wits to say, "Viviana."

"Hullo, Viviana," he said.

"Hello, Viviana!" Pendragon thundered. He yanked himself off me, for which I breathed a sigh of relief. My emotions were long dead within me, but the man was damned heavy and uncomfortable. I should have been thankful that he had not had his way with me; instead I was just happy that he had not destroyed my back. "How many times have I told you to knock? In fact . . . how many times have I told you to leave me alone!?"

The servant's legs quivered as Pendragon approached him. His feet were rooted to the spot. He tried to put up his hands to avoid the inevitable fist but failed as Pendragon cuffed him soundly. The servant went down, his eyes spinning.

I wanted to do something but obviously could not. Pendragon could easily have broken me in half with one swing of his fist; he was that formidable looking. He was paying me no mind, however. He appeared focused on the servant whose very presence seemed to enrage him. He kicked the poor servant once, twice, thrice, and the servant begged for mercy and pleaded that he would try to do better and endeavor to remember to knock or, even better, never bother him at all.

Tiring of abusing the poor creature, Pendragon stepped back and said with a snarl, "What did you want, anyway?"

"I forget," the servant whimpered.

Pendragon let out a frustrated roar. "Get out of here!" He gestured toward me. "And take this with you! You disrupted my good humor and I will likely not recapture it for hours."

"Yes, highness. At once, highness." Nursing the places where he had been kicked, the servant took a few steps toward me and then winced. Even walking appeared to pain him. He gestured to me. I slid off the bed, pausing only to grab the small sack with my belongings. I ran to his side and he said, "Where shall I take her, highness, if you do not mind my asking?"

If Pendragon had minded his asking, I suspected the response would have been more abuse. But Pendragon sat on the edge of the bed, gestured vaguely, and said, "The kitchen. Bring her to the kitchen."

The servant bobbed his head, took me by the elbow and hustled me out the door. The moment we were in the corridor, he sagged against the wall and let out a low, pained moan.

"Are you all right?" I said.

I knew it was a stupid question the moment it had escaped my lips. Curiously, he did not seem to realize just how stupid it was. "Let me check," he said. He opened his palm and spit into it, then studied the spit. "No blood. That's a good sign. Right? Is that not a good sign?"

I had to think that he had been struck in the head quite a few times in his life to appear that disconnected. He even managed a smile although it seemed more of a lackwit smirk than a true smile. His eyes continued to have that vacant, empty look, as if his brain was functioning but only with sufficient energy to ensure his ability to talk, see, and walk without falling. "That is a very good sign," I said.

He took heart in that, told me he would walk me to the kitchen, and proceeded to escort me. "What is your name?" he said.

Clearly he was so addled that he could not recall I had told him moments earlier. Little surprise. Pendragon had likely knocked the memory right out of his head. "Viviana," I said again.

"Viviana. Nice name. Welcome to Camelot."

"Yes. What a wonderful welcome," I said humorlessly.

Considering he appeared to have no grasp of subtleties, it was impressive that he managed to discern what I was not saying. "Do not concern yourself about the king."

"'Tis easy for you to say. He is not interested in having his way with you." Then I paused and added curiously, "Is he?"

He blinked. "Not to my knowledge. God, I hope not. Anyway, he will forget all about you in short order."

I was not sure how to respond to that. The concept should have filled me with relief but I was unclear as to what the servant was saying. "Am I that unmemorable?"

"What? Oh . . . no. It is just that the king tends to . . . forget things. It has worsened lately. If matters proceed as they often have, then by supper tonight he will no longer recall there was a new serving wench in Camelot. You will be just another one of the servants beneath his notice."

It might have sounded insulting in other circumstances, but I knew he spoke aright. Lords and ladies, highborn of all manner, tend to look right through slaves and servants. If Pendragon had no recollection of me as an individual, he would certainly not discern me once I was one of the throng. Besides, better beneath his notice than beneath his body.

I allowed myself to feel some relief. As detached as I might be from the abuse to which others subjected my body, it did not mean I was desirous of such activities. I was glad that the brutish king would not, apparently, be requiring my "services" in that regard.

"Viviana." The servant frowned thoughtfully. "That is a French name, is it not?"

"In my case, Italian. Named for my mother."

"Italian. That is not the same as French?"

I did everything I could not to react to his stupidity. As much as Pendragon had abused him, I was starting to think uncharitable thoughts, such as that it was amazing Pendragon had not simply slain him out of annoyance long before this. "No. Two languages, spoken in two different countries."

"Ah." He took that information in stride but did not seem inclined to ask after it further. Instead, as if the subject of other countries bored him, he said, "I hope you will not judge the king too harshly by what you saw."

"How else am I to judge other than by what I see?"

"A bad impression, is what I am saying. It could be misinterpreted."

"He wanted to ravage me."

"Well, yes, but what king would not?"

Bizarre as it sounded, I believed the servant actually intended that as a compliment. I could not bring myself, however, to thank him for it. Instead I said, "Many a king, I should hope. His actions were . . ." I searched for the least inflammatory word I could devise. ". . . uncharitable."

"One hopes you will be here long enough to change your mind. Here is the kitchen."

Through a creaking wooden door I heard the sounds of utensils being sharpened and meat being chopped. Simple-minded he may have been, but at least he did not get lost in his own castle. I glanced right and left, wanting to make certain no one overheard, for slaves cannot be too careful, and I said, "Truthfully, I do not know why you defend him. We both know he is a brute. I understand you feel a duty as his servant, but still . . ."

"Servant?" He seemed most amused by that. "I am not a servant."

"Then who are you?"

"I am his son. Arthur."

I stared at him, terrified. "You . . . are the son of Uther Pendragon?"

"Aye."

Instantly I dropped to my knees, clutching at his breeches. "Forgive me, sire. I should not have spoken so out of turn, I . . . please do not have me executed . . ."

"Executed?" He stared at me in wonderment. "If I had everyone who said nasty things about my father or me executed, the castle would be nigh unto empty . . . as would the countryside, I daresay. No, no, do not you worry your little head about a thing. Just go about your business."

He walked away from me then, his hands draped behind his back, swaying slightly as he did so. "Everything is fine. Everything is perfectly fine."

Arthur Pendragon. Arthur, son of Uther. Future lord of Camelot.

This was no evil, conniving threat. This man, the one his father treated no better than a slave, was a simple-minded buffoon. An idiot, despised by his father, perhaps because he was clearly unfit to assume the throne upon Uther's passing.

Fortunately enough, it was none of my concern. I did not expect to be a permanent resident of Camelot; slaves have a way of being passed around. Instead it brought me a degree of grim pleasure, knowing that at some point in the future, those who had smirked at me or tormented me upon my arrival would find their fates in the hands of an incompetent boob. They would be depending upon him to defend them from their enemies and, frankly, it boded well for the enemies.

Day the Third

I DREAMT OF MY FATHER last night.

Sometimes I wish I would dream of my mother. My mind does not let me. I think on some level I resent her more than I do my father. That is so odd. It was not as if her leaving me was voluntary. She died. She died with so many regrets. The way she looked at me just before the angel of death took her spirit . . . did she know? Did she have some sort of last moment insight into what my fate would be and feel a swell of regret over it?

Father was the one who truly betrayed me. But is that betrayal mitigated by all the good he did for me as well? I do not know. Perhaps I shall never know.

My dream . . .

Father was here. He, rather than that harridan, Rowena, was overseeing the running of the kitchen. As is typically the case with dreams, I did not find his presence puzzling. Instead I accepted it readily and was eager to please him. I was cooking food rather than scouring plates, as is my typical job. He sampled a broth I was preparing. I waited with breathless anticipation. He held the liquid in his mouth for a moment and then spit it out. He told me I had failed him. Then he picked me up and thrust me bodily, head first, into the pot filled with scalding liquid. He slammed the lid down atop the pot. I was unable to move it. I tried to cry out but my lungs were filling with broth. Then I heard a scuffling, shouting, and suddenly the lid was removed. I broke the surface, gasping for air, and a hand was extended to me. I looked up and there he was . . . my knight . . .

Galahad.

Galahad, my ideal.

So perfect. So pure. So exquisitely wonderful.

I gripped his hand and he pulled me from the broth. I should have been dripping wet. I was not. My father's unconscious—dead?—body should have been lying there. It was not. All the other kitchen and scullery workers had disappeared.

It was just Galahad and me.

He drew me toward him. He kissed me.

I felt impure thoughts.

God chose to save me from those thoughts by having Rowena shake me awake. She scowled down upon me and told me to stop moaning like a harlot and get to work.

I did as she ordered.

Day the Seventh

Ran into Arthur today in a most unexpected place.

I was curled up in my corner of the servant's quarters—if "quarters" can possibly be used to describe the large and mostly empty room in which our simple beds of hay are sprawled—and I was writing in my journal. The other servants disliked when I did so. They found it confusing or daunting or bewildering. At least one murmured that I was likely a witch or demon of some sort, engaging in such activities that were the province of men and only learned ones at that. This concerned me a bit since, if she really thought me to be evil, she might feel justified in splitting my head open with a skillet whilst I slept. But I did not think she really had the nerve to do so. At least I hoped not.

Caught up in my scribbling, I was unaware of Arthur's standing there until he cleared his throat. I looked up and gasped.

"Hullo," he said with that same vacant, vaguely pleasant look I had come to know. The bruises he had sustained from his father's battering some days ago had vanished. He looked ready for more abuse. "May I see that?"

I had no desire to present it to him, for the sentiments I had expressed about him were less than flattering. But his outstretched hand left no other option. I handed him the journal. He flipped through it. "These are your thoughts?" he said.

"My . . . personal, private thoughts, sire," I said, keeping my gaze properly averted. "Not meant for others to read."

"How fortunate I am illiterate," he said. "I find it odd, though, that a slave would be allowed to have possessions."

"It is a book, sire. A book and writing utensils. If it were something of value then it would likely have been taken from me along the way," I said with a trace of bitterness. "But its value is only to me."

"Pity you are not a monk or a clerk. I hear they fancy such things."

"Yes. A pity."

"Or a historian. There is an official historian for Camelot. He writes, too. At least I think he does."

"It would seem logical, sire."

He pointed to an arbitrary point in my journal. "What does this say?"

Slowly I raised my eyes to see where he was indicating. "It says 'Day One.'"

"But . . . it is not the first entry, is it? I see much more before it."

"Yes, that is . . . sire is very observant," I said. "I always write 'Day One' when I arrive at a new place. I like to . . ." My voice trailed off, feeling that I was over-speaking. He gestured for me to continue and I said, "I like to pretend that each new place represents a new start. Starting fresh helps to erase what has gone before."

"If you wish to forget what has gone before, why do you write it all down?"

"That . . . is a very good question, sire."

"Is it?" He seemed genuinely surprised. Then he smiled affably. "Well . . . pay it no mind. I do not present good questions frequently enough for it to be a bother to anyone. Is there an answer to it?"

"None that readily comes to mind, sire."

"I have stumped the woman who reads and writes. How very epic of me. You will make a point of writing down that I did so, will you not?"

"If you wish it, sire." He was an idiot, but an amusing one, I give him that.

"I do. It is . . . pleasing . . . to think that somebody somewhere would find something that I do worthy of being made permanent. Or as permanent as these things are, at any rate."

Feeling emboldened, although perhaps I should not have, I said, "Sire, if it is not too forward . . . why are you here? This is no place for . . . for . . ."

"The prince?" He shrugged. "I was bored. No one else is around."

"Where be they?"

"At war," he said, sounding bored at the notion. "Old King Leodegrass is mounting an offensive to the west. Father mustered his knights and has ridden off to settle the matter once and for all."

"You mean Leodegrance? Of Cameliaid?"

"Right. Him. I can never remember his name properly. Too damned long."

"He is said to be most formidable."

"So is my father." He spoke with clear pride. It would have been touching if Pendragon did not so clearly despise his offspring. "I should like to be by his side, but . . ."

"But he feels the king and his heir should not risk their lives simultaneously, lest the kingdom be endangered should both fall?"

"Hmm? Oh . . . no. No, it is because he says having me near him angers him so that he cannot concentrate on what needs be done." He sounded so straightforward about it that it was clear he did not take offense at this notion. That he considered it the norm. I suppose if such attitudes from one's father is all one knows in one's upbringing, then it is the norm.

"Sire . . . may I . . . ?" Very tentatively, I indicated that I should like the return of my journal.

He did not understand at first but then he said, "Oh," and handed it back. It almost seemed he did so with reluctance. Wistfully, he said, "Learning to read might be nice. Pity I could never do so."

"Anyone can learn to read, sire."

"Are you saying you could teach me?"

I said nothing, but instead merely shrugged.

And then he laughed at the notion. Laughed loud and long.

"Ahhh, the reaction of my father if I acquired such a talent. I can just hear him. 'Do you think yourself a monk? A clerk? An historian? Idiot. Reading is beneath the attention of leaders.'"

"Clearly," I said boldly—for one can afford to be bold when one has little to lose—"you have your father's voice down quite well, sire. But have you a voice of your own?"

He shrugged. "Wherefore? Are we not what our fathers make us?"

I considered that. It brought my mind whirling back to days gone by, with my father sitting next to me and patiently teaching me the letters of the alphabet . . . smiling encouragement as I carefully reproduced the letters on precious pieces of parchment.

"I suppose there is much wisdom in your words, sire."

"Zounds," he said, impressed. "All this flattery will turn my head, woman. Have a care."

"Yes, sire."

He had been crouched upon the floor. Now he rose and headed for the door. Then he paused, turned and said to me, "Viviana."

"Yes, sire?"

"I was just trying to remember your name. Viviana, correct?"

"Oh. Yes, sire."

"French?"

"Italian."

"I knew it was something like that," said Arthur.

He walked out and, seconds later, Rowena bustled in. She was a Moor with the general build of a toadstool and much the same personality. She looked around and then, clearly bewildered as to how I could be the sole occupant of the room, said harshly, "Why was the prince here?"

"God as my witness, I have no idea," I said, and it was true.

She scowled fiercely. At least I believe she did. Her face was such a perpetual scowl that it was difficult to be certain. "Witch," she breathed, making a sign of the cross. "I'm going to tell." She then backed out of the room as if afraid to turn away from me for even a moment, lest I cast a spell upon her and transform her into a newt.

I had no idea whom she would tell. It worried me slightly. On the other hand, seeing the head of the kitchen treating me with respect bordering on fear was rather uplifting, so I suppose it balanced out.

Day the Eleventh

THE IRONS WEIGHED HEAVILY ON me today.

Some days I am able to ignore them. I have become so used to them that occasionally I do not even notice they are there.

But today I had an itch.

What a stupid, pathetic, utterly mundane thing to have to contend with. Yet there it was: an itch under the manacle on my left arm.

The iron cuff runs from just below my elbow down to my wrist. One on my right arm matches it and there is the iron collar around my neck.

It is, of course, how slaves are maintained and monitored. If we had shackles around our legs to impede our movement, it would reduce our efficiency in doing our tasks. So instead we are fitted with extremely conspicuous "bracelets," plus the collar. Impossible to have removed, save by a blacksmith or a slaver possessing the skeleton key provided by the slavers guild.

If slaves should attempt to run away, the irons mark them as property as surely as a brand on the forehead. They are far too large to conceal with clothing, no matter how diligently one may try. No slaver will aid a runaway by providing a key and every blacksmith in the land knows of the rewards available for returning a fleeing slave, as well as the penalties for aiding one that seeks to escape. I confess, were I in the position of a blacksmith, and I was given the choice, I would probably turn myself in.

Today I developed some sort of rash under the left one. It happens sometimes. Sweat can cause excruciating rashes to develop. This was one such. I tried everything I could do to get at it, but I could not fit my fingers down to scratch, nor could I find a piece of wood thin enough to slide under the metal to provide relief. Finally, in pure fury, I started banging it against the wall, howling my frustration.

Rowena informed the castle slave master, who had me taken out of the kitchen, tied to a stake, and given five lashes. Rowena watched from some feet away and cackled dementedly with pleasure. I fired a look at her and muttered a curse in gibberish. It meant nothing, but the fact that she could not comprehend it frightened her all the more. Probably thinking I had put a hex upon her, she ran from the spot.

I must be cautious. Let her have her unfounded suspicions all she wishes. But if she manages to convince the wrong people I am a true practitioner of black arts, she can make quite a bit of mischief for me.

At least the stinging I now feel in my back manages to distract me from the irritation under my shackle.

When one is a slave, one must find the positives wherever one can.

Day the Twentieth

EVERYTHING CAME TO A HEAD today.

I offer no excuse for my actions. All I can say is that the many tragedies that are my life piled upon my back until it broke under the strain.

I was working in the kitchen, the same as always. I had been charged with preparing beef broth for the king. It was a simple assignment, one that I had performed before. The recipe was a standard one and I was expected to follow it.

This particular day, though, the beef broth tasted flat and uninteresting. Perhaps it was that the meat bone I had used in the making was of insufficient quality. Impossible to say. Whatever the reason, I felt it needed something more in order to improve its taste. Deciding that some spices were in order, I went to the spice cabinet, pulled several out, and added them to the mixture.

Honestly, I did not care about improving the taste of the soup insofar as Uther and his ilk were concerned. They could choke on it for all I cared. But cooking brings back pleasant memories—among the few that I have—of a happier time with my father. So upon encountering something as unimpressive, taste-wise, as the broth was, I felt constrained to try and amend the situation. I did it for myself, not for them.

A shriek like unto the damned then erupted behind me. I turned and saw Rowena standing there, her face purpling, her hands gesturing wildly. "What do you think you're doing!?" Then, before I could even frame a reply, she howled, "Witch! Traitor!"

"What are you blathering about?" I said. I had been having foul dreams of late. Deprived of the balm of a good night's sleep for nigh unto a week, I was not in the best disposition to begin with.

"I saw you! I saw you put something in the broth!"

"I wished to improve the taste . . ."

"You wished to poison the king! Witch! Demon! Trollop!"

She advanced on me, waving her finger in my face, howling like a banshee. Every word was like a knife into my head. "Get away from me," I said, backing up. She continued to come at me, bellowing accusations. Every eye in the kitchen was upon me although no one was offering to intervene on my behalf. I bumped up against the wall, unable to retreat any further. She waggled her hands in my face and one of her long fingernails nicked my cheek.

I struck her.

In all my years as a slave, I had never raised a hand to anyone. That might well be because for most of a slave's life, we are treated with indifference. But Rowena's needless belligerence, her accusations, everything about her actions, had piled upon me until I could endure it no longer. I almost think that she may have provoked it, hoping to land me in even greater trouble. If that was the case, I could not have done more to accommodate her.

As if it moved on its own, my hand swung and the palm cracked across her face. Her head snapped around and she staggered back, eyes wide. I swept my hand back in the other direction, nearly blinded with fury. This time the back of my hand caught her and the added force of my knuckles knocked her clear off her feet. She came down hard on her backside. Total silence hung in the kitchen for an awful moment and then she began to spew a barrage of words so fast and furious that I could not make out a single thing she was saying. Truthfully I know not if she was saying anything coherent at all.

Then she was on her feet, grabbing a ladle from nearby and swinging it at me. A good and proper slave would have accepted the beating, but something within me revolted over the prospect of enduring further punishment from the harridan. I sidestepped her. She missed me and my fist connected with her chin. We both cried out in pain as she fell over again. I shook out my fist, extending the fingers and looking at them in dismay. I was sure that a couple of them were already swelling.

This time Rowena did not bound to her feet. Instead she lay there, stunned. I was not the only one with bruising. A dark spot was appearing on the underside of her jaw. I would have taken pleasure in it were I not in pain, plus anticipating that more pain in the form of lashings and beatings was in my immediate future.

"What in hell goes on in here?"

It was a man's voice, unfamiliar to me.

I turned and saw the owner of the voice. He was an older gentleman, with a short white beard, ruddy face, and wearing loose-fitting black robes that marked him as an apothecary. But there was more to him than that. He seemed to radiate authority and, even more, everyone in the kitchen—every servant, every scullery maid, and most certainly Rowena—clearly feared him.

Nevertheless, Rowena raised a trembling finger and pointed at me. "The witch was trying to poison the king! Putting a curse upon the broth!"

"Was she?" He did not seem convinced, but nevertheless turned his baleful glare upon me. "How now, woman? What did you to the broth?"

I bowed my head and, staring intently at the floor, said, "Naught but try to improve its flavor, sir."

"She strives to flavor it with death, I will warrant!" said Rowena.

"Have done, woman, or I will flavor it with your empty head!" said the apothecary. Rowena promptly backed down and he looked back at me. "Flavoring it, eh? Taste it, then."

"Taste it?"

"Do you fear to do so?"

I shrugged, shook my head I then went to the broth, withdrew a small amount and sipped it. I savored it for a moment and then signaled approval.

"Have more," he said.

I did so. I poured myself an entire bowl and downed it

quickly, greedily, hungrily. The simple gruel that was the staple of a slave's food paled in comparison to the quality of the broth. I smacked my lips, which I should not have done, but I was unable to help myself. Then I actually met the apothecary's eyes silently.

He had watched me drink the contents of the bowl without comment. He watched for long moments and then said, "Know you why I had you do that?"

"To see if 'twas poisoned, sir."

He nodded. Then he crossed to the broth, stuck in a finger, withdrew it and ran his tongue experimentally across the finger. "Spices, you say?"

"Oregano, mostly."

"Good for coughs. The king has been coughing a bit lately. Anything else?"

"Dash of paprika."

"I will try to remember that. Is that it?"

"A few other things, sir. I could write it down for you if—"

I caught myself, hoping he had not heard what I had said, but my hope was in vain. Nothing eluded him, it seemed. His face became a question as he said, "A kitchen slave who writes? I have never heard of such a thing."

Suddenly my legs were trembling almost of their own accord and I had no idea why.

"Come with me," he said abruptly.

Rowena chose that moment to find her voice. "But milord Merlin, she is needed here to—"

"You shall have her back, woman, now be silent!" said Merlin, and she instantly did as she was bade. He walked out of the kitchen and I trailed after him, my head swirling with uncertainty and confusion.

As we moved through the corridors, I could not help but notice that anyone who saw Merlin coming made a point of stepping out of his way to give him a wide berth. Some murmured greetings. He ignored all of them. Instead he said, as if talking to himself, "The king is very particular about his food. He lives in fear of poisoners. That is why I generate all recipes for how his meals are to be prepared. Do you understand now why Rowena acted the way she did in response to your tampering?"

"Yes."

"But you do not care."

"It is not for me to care or not care, sir, if it pleases y—"

"Cease that mealy mouthed slave talk before I have you flogged. Answer the damned question. Do you care why Rowena reacted the way she did?"

I glanced at my fingers, which were showing further signs of inflammation. "Not in the least, sir."

"Good. That is a start. Here."

I walked into what I assumed was his study. There were rolled scrolls of parchment all over. His desk was covered with them. I doubt I was able to keep the excitement from my eyes, seeing all that writing in one place.

He handed me a blank piece of parchment, then slid over a bottle of ink and a quill. "Write it down. What you did. Precisely the ingredients and in what measure."

There was unmistakable challenge in his voice. Fortunately I had struck Rowena with the opposite hand of my writing hand, else I do not know that I could have held the quill. I jotted down the specifics as he requested. He watched me with interest and slowly nodded. "So Rowena claims you to be a witch."

"Aye, sir."

"I hear claims that I am a wizard. People are superstitious fools. Still, how came you to write and read?"

"My father, a merchant, taught me."

He regarded me thoughtfully for a moment, stroking his beard. "A merchant who fell into debt and sold you into slavery in order to clear that debt."

I was taken aback. Momentarily falling into formal highspeak, I said, "Didst thou read my mind, sirrah?"

"Of course not, girl. Do not fall victim to the same stupidity as fools who call me magician simply because I pay attention to the world."

"My apologies, sir."

My apology clearly meant less than nothing to him. Studying the parchment with my specifics for improved beef broth upon them, he observed, "You have tidy handwriting. Quite flowing, in fact. Easy to read."

"Thank you, sir."

"It was no compliment, but merely observation."

I could think of no response to that, and so made none.

"You may leave now. I shall send word to Rowena that to inflict punishment upon you is to court my wrath. She will restrain herself."

I curtsied and then headed for the door.

"What is your name, girl?"

I paused, my hand resting on the door handle, and said, "Viviana, sir."

His eyebrows knit as he said, "Viviana. Viviana, the literate slave girl. It is a strange world, is it not, literate slave girl?"

"It is not for me to judge the world, sir. It is for me to survive in it."

"I thought I told you to give me answers, not mealy-mouthed slave talk."

"With respect, sir," and I squared my shoulders and raised my chin in a manner that I imagined to be proud, "that is my philosophy. I cling to it in order to survive. I find it more palatable than the thought that God permits my existence to be one long, unending misery because He has some higher purpose to which I am not privy."

Merlin considered that and then said, "A fair point. Go to, Mistress Viviana."

None had called me "mistress" since my days working in my father's shop. It brought back such pleasant memories that my eyes stung, which was the closest I was able to come to tears. Nevertheless, upon my return to the kitchen, Rowena looked at my red-rimmed eyes, nodded in approval and chortled, "So the old wizard reduced you to blubbering, did he? Ye had it coming, so ye did," and she waddled away chuckling to herself over what she fancied to be my just desserts.

Day the Twenty-Second

I SNUCK UP TO THE high tower today. It is the highest point in Castle Camelot. I have never had cause to go up there before. Truthfully, I did not have cause this time, either. But I knew it was there and I was desirous to see the view. I suppose I could have been punished over it, but my back has developed a thick hide to lashings and so I decided to avail myself of the opportunity when I was between chores.

It was a narrow, winding tower. The steps became progressively more angled the higher up I went.

The high tower had been designed by Uther himself and constructed under his personal guidance. The women in the kitchen laughed coarsely about it to each other, claiming that a vastly tall upright projection this big was designed for the purpose of compensating for other shortcomings. Fortunately, thanks to Arthur's timely interruption and Uther's failing memory, I had never had the opportunity to learn first hand if that was true or not. Nevertheless, the notion of what the tower might represent filled me with a sense of uneasiness as I climbed its length. I disliked the symbolism. It was not enough to daunt me, however, in my determination to reach the top.

Finally I saw a bit of daylight filtering through and down into the gloomy interior. The stairs were so narrow by this point that I was moving sideways, one careful step at a time. There was a small landing, large enough to accommodate only one person. I had been briefly concerned that there might be some sort of lookout perched there, but it was vacant. That made sense. This tower was intended to be for Uther's use and, since he was still off fighting his war with Leodegrance, he was not in residence. There was not even a guard posted at the entrance, because who would be mad enough to tread on the private area of the king?

I noticed a splotch of dark red several steps down on the wall. It appeared to have been there for quite some time. Dried blood, by the look of it. I wondered how it got there.

I eased myself onto the landing and peered tentatively out the window. As soon as I did, I knew that the risk I had assumed coming up was worth it. It was a magnificent view, breathtaking.

The path that I had trod to come to the castle stretched away like a dusty brown snake. It ran into a forest that I recalled trudging through, my face and arms being scratched by brambles and branches. From this vantage, I was able to appreciate it for its verdant beauty. Beyond the forest was a vast plain, and beyond that a mountain range that stretched along the horizon as far as I could see in either direction.

I had no idea in what direction my original home lay. I had moved around too many different directions in my years as a slave to be certain. I thought that perhaps it lay far past the mountains. I stared off in that direction and fancied that my father was looking back and dwelling upon whatever had happened to me. I wondered if he thought of me. I wondered if he cared or loved me at all.

I wiped at my eyes. No tears came, as always.

Then I was startled as a handkerchief was held up in front of my face. I turned and gasped as I saw who was offering it.

"Sire!" I exclaimed and jumped to my feet. In doing so I forgot the confined surroundings and succeeded in cracking my skull against a low overhanging beam.

"Are you all right?" said Arthur, for it was indeed he who had come upon me. Either he had moved with amazing silence or else I was so preoccupied that I had simply failed to hear him. I could not determine which it was at that moment since I was too busy dealing with waves of pain ringing within my head.

"A thousand apologies, sire, I should not be here at all . . ." I tried to sidle past him, but there was no room on the cramped stairway.

He put a hand on my shoulder. I suddenly became aware of our proximity, but he made no aggressive movement. Instead he simply smiled in that same slightly vacant way he always displayed. "Pray, do not concern yourself. Stay. It is fine. Are you sure you wouldn't . . . ?" I shook my head and sighed, but the sigh came out as an unsteady trembling. He said, "What troubles you?"

"Nothing. It . . . is nothing."

"From my admittedly minimal experience with women, even I know that they do not cry for no reason. Honestly, Veronica, what ails you?"

"Viviana, sire."

"Viviana ails you?"

"No, sire, my name is Viviana."

"Is it?" He frowned. "Are you sure?"

"Quite sure, sire."

"And it is . . ." He hesitated and then said, ". . . Italian?" When I nodded, he beamed in triumph as if he had just ascertained the secret truths of the universe. "And not at all French."

"No, sire."

"Good." He frowned. "What was I asking about?" He stared at me and then his face cleared and he said, "Oh. Right. The tears."

I did not bother to point out to him that I remained dry-eyed. The poor sod was confused enough, nor did I wish to go into detail over how I was emotionally dead within. "I was . . . just thinking about my father, sire."

"The one who sold you into slavery. Were you thinking of how much you would like to see him dead?"

Having no idea how to react to that, I settled for horrified laughter. "No, sire! He . . . he did what he had to do."

"Really. If I had a daughter, I would not sell her into bondage no matter how dire my straits were."

"With respect, sire, it is easy to make such declarations when one will never be put in that position."

"True. How about you then, Viviana? If you were a free

woman and you had a daughter, would you ever do what your father did? Do not," he interrupted as I tried to reply, "think to lie to me, because I will know. Tell me truly. Would you?"

I tried to meet his gaze and could not. Instead, my shoulders slumping, I said in a voice barely above a whisper, "I would die first."

"Yet he lives. Your father lives."

"I do not know that of a certainty. He could be long dead by now. Dead of a broken heart."

"And would that please you?"

"Of course not. I want him to live a long and happy life."

"I do not think you do," said Arthur. His eyes flashed with challenge. "I think you would like to see him dead. I think you would like to see him suffer pain, humiliation and degradation in order to balance the scales for all the suffering that he has visited upon you."

"Are we speaking of my father or yours, sire?"

It was an incredibly bold and ill-advised thing for me to say and I regretted it the instant I said it. Arthur seemed taken aback. My hand flew to my mouth too late, obviously, to pull back the cursed words. "I . . . am sorry, sire. I have overstepped myself."

"I suppose you have." He did not sound outraged, though, as would have been appropriate. Instead he sounded almost indifferent, as if he were so disconnected from his emotions that nothing much mattered to him. It made a certain degree of sense to me. I had done much the same in my time. Built up a shell around myself, constructing a fortress around my heart so it could not be shattered. Perhaps Arthur sensed that at some level and thus felt as if he could talk to me. That I could . . . understand.

"Did you . . . follow me up here, sire?" I asked cautiously.

He shook his head. "No. Pure coincidence. I like to come here on occasion and try to think."

"Because the normal hustle and bustle of the castle makes it difficult to concentrate?"

"No, because thinking does not come easily to me, and here I do not have to worry about people watching me and judging me." He sighed heavily. "I cannot tell you how many times thoughts—deep thoughts, maybe even important ones—are just there, right in front of me, just beyond my grasp. And I cannot get to them. I cannot . . . make my brain function in that manner. I keep dwelling on the notion that if I only think long and hard enough, I could do some good. But then I get bored sooner or later and it all just flits out of my head."

"That . . . is a shame," I said, having no idea how I should respond to what he was telling me.

"My father is returning."

I looked out onto the vista, wondering if he was visible from our vantage.

He realized what I was doing and offered a clarification. "I have received advance word that he is returning. A messenger, an advance runner, said that Leodegrass . . ."

"Leodegrance, sire?"

"Yes, correct. Leodegrance has surrendered and is prepared to acknowledge Uther as his liege again."

"Again?"

"Oh yes. They used to be great allies, my father and Leodegrance. Great allies. We visited them on any number of occasions during the winter since Cameliard has warmer climes. During the summer they would come here since it was cooler."

"They?"

"Aye. Leodegrance, his lady wife, and their daughters, Guinevere and Morgan." There was something about the way he said the latter name that seemed to radiate pure pleasure. "Morgan was the eldest. Guinevere was her officious little sister, following us about whenever she could and lecturing about this, that or the other thing. You might well have liked her. She read a lot. Father always said she was proof of the danger of allowing females to read. Eventually their young cousin, Modred, joined them in their trips here."

I did not comment on Uther's assessment of literate females since I did not think it would lead anyplace useful. Instead I said, "So . . . what happened? With Uther and Leodegrance?"

Arthur shrugged. "They had a falling out."

"Over what?"

"I know not."

"Did you not ask?"

"Why would I? If father wanted me to know, he would tell me. The fact that he did not choose to do so more or less ends the matter."

"But . . ." I searched for the words. "Were you not . . . curious?"

"I find it best not to be curious about things to which you cannot know the answer. The results are never positive."

"Do you not believe that seeking of knowledge always entails worthwhile risk?"

"Seeking land, seeking riches, seeking power . . . the risks inherent in those endeavors are worthwhile. Knowledge? What use is that?"

"Knowledge is power."

"Armor is power. A good sword arm is power. Weapons are power. Knowledge is a luxury, and I have never been much for luxury."

Lord God, what a simpleton, I thought. "With respect, sire . . . I believe you are wrong."

"You say that quite often, I have noticed. 'With respect.' Tell me, Viviana: Do you truly respect the people to whom you are saying that? Or do you say that so that you can express opinions without having your head severed from your neck?"

"A . . . bit of both, sire, I should think."

"I think a good deal more of the second than the first. You cannot hide your feelings from me, Viviana. I know you think very little of me."

I was startled. I knew that I was far wiser than he and yet he seemed able to anticipate or perceive the very thoughts in my head. His ignorance was towering; he even seemed to cherish it. But his instincts were formidable. I protested in vain, "Sire, that is not true . . ."

He waved off my denial. "It is all right. Everyone here does. Merlin says that is not actually a bad thing. He says lowered expectations can be of benefit because once you begin to accomplish things, people will be more impressed than if they had higher expectations of you in the first place. He says I should do nothing to make people think I am anyone they should anticipate greatness from. So you see, there is very little reason for me to try and broaden my horizons." He shrugged and said wistfully, "There is no use to which I could reasonably put such broadening."

"What of the notion of knowledge for its own sake?"

He laughed. "I was right the first time. You and Guinevere would get along. She sat right where you were sitting, some years back, and we had a conversation that was startlingly similar to the one you and I are having now. And I said to her that I thought knowledge for its own sake was a quaint notion, fit for a girl but not for a man who has more important considerations to attend to."

"And what did she say in response?"

"Say? Nothing. Instead she kicked me in the face. I fell backwards and struck my head . . . right there," and he pointed at the darkened splotch on the wall, "and then rolled half a dozen steps before I caught myself. Had I not I probably would have shattered every bone in my body. As it was, I was rather badly injured."

"How terrible, sire!"

"Not so terrible. Morgan patched me up." He looked wistful. "She always had the touch for attending to my needs, dear Morgan."

He stared off into space. It was as if he had forgotten that

I was there. Deciding that it would be rude to interrupt his reveries, I eased my way past him, stepping over him as carefully as I could. As I started down the narrow steps, he spoke without looking at me:

"If you do not want your father dead for what he did to you . . . you are a better person than I."

Then he said nothing more, and I withdrew from the tower as quickly as I could.

Now as I sit here, inscribing the events of the day, I find myself wondering whether or not Arthur was right. Do I, deep down, resent my father for what he did? What he has put me through? I have spent my life convincing myself that I do not. But is that just so I have some morsel of happy memories to cling to, rather than endlessly dwelling upon the betrayal that was visited upon me?

Already my mental image of my father's smile is tainted and I see darkness that I had not seen before. Or perhaps it was there and I did not allow myself to see it.

Arthur Pendragon may well have just taken from me the one meager defense I have against total alienation from the world around me.

No doubt he meant well.

Gods, I am beginning to hate that man.

Day the Twenty-Fourth

THE KING RETURNED TO CAMELOT today. A carefully organized spontaneous outpouring of adoration was arranged to greet him.

As near as I can determine, Merlin was the one who attended to the actual organizing. He may wear the robes of an apothecary, but it is starting to seem to me that he is in charge of far more than the king's physical well being. Occasionally, as I go about my chores, I catch glimpses of him in deep conversation with various men of power and prestige. One would think that men of power would try to keep their private chats, well, private. But the fact is that such individuals tend not to notice servants at all. We are as invisible to them. They look right through us, even when we are standing several feet away. Oh, if we happen to be holding something they want, such as a towel when clambering out of a bath or food during a banquet, then they notice us well enough. Except it is not really us they are noticing, but instead merely whatever object it is we are providing them. Once they have obtained it, they go right back to not noticing us. That is why one should seek out servants or slaves if one wants to know what is really going on in any castle. We have all the true knowledge that the powerful and privileged seek to hide from each other.

Wherever the instigation for the reception originated, the result was that servants and townsfolk mingled within the mighty walls of the keep, shouting and rejoicing the return of Uther and his knights from their mighty battle against Leodegrance. Truth to tell, no one understood the reasons for the warfare and it did not have any real impact on the day to day lives of us "common folk." However, it was made clear to us that Uther's assault had been a major undertaking and should be celebrated, and so we did, because we knew that to refuse to do so would be unwise.

So when Uther's army emerged from the distant forest and started down the path to the castle, they were greeted with a fanfare of trumpets from the ramparts. A crowd had assembled outside the castle itself. There were slaves mixing with freemen, merchants rubbing elbows with lords and ladies. There is never a sense of class distinction in a crowd of well-wishers.

The men following Uther looked somewhat tired and haggard but Uther himself appeared to be reveling in the attention. He was astride a powerful white horse and, as he crossed the lowered drawbridge at the head of his army, the volume of cheers increased in response to his approach. He waved to us one and all and, after soaking in the adulation for some moments, gestured for us to silence. We immediately complied. His followers looked as if they wanted nothing more but to tumble off their horses or their sore feet (since many of them were walking), collapse and go to sleep for several days. Nevertheless they stood patiently and waited for their king to address them.

"The day is won!" declared Uther. "Leodegrance has surrendered and, in a week's time, will come here to Camelot to acknowledge my dominion over him and pledge his allegiance to me!" He paused and, sensing that we were supposed to offer up an assortment of "huzzahs," we instantly did so, and continued to do so until he gestured for silence once more. "I expect you, my people, to extend courtesy to our guest, and to be magnanimous in this triumph . . . a triumph that is not just mine but all of ours."

We paused and then, realizing that we were expected to do so, cheered yet again.

Uther nodded approvingly and then guided his horse toward the castle entrance. When the horse did not move quickly enough, he snapped the reins and yelled at the beast to attend to its master's wishes.

The horse abruptly reared up.

No one had expected it, least of all Uther. He grabbed at the reins, trying to hold his place, but was unable to do so. He tumbled backward from the saddle, his feet coming free from the stirrups, which was a lucky thing lest he break his legs. Uther hit the ground hard, his armor making a thunderous clanking like an entire tray of dishes clattering to the floor.

Uther lay there, showing as much mobility as a flipped turtle. Quickly several of his retainers sprang forward and helped him to his feet. With a roar of fury fueled by a deep sense of personal humiliation, Uther yanked out his sword, took two quick steps forward, swung the blade with all his formidable strength, and cleaved the horse's head from its body.

People screamed as one. The horse's body stood there for a moment as if requiring extra time to fully comprehend that its services would no longer be required, and then it tumbled over. A vast pool of blood seeped out from the poor beast's neck. The head lay to one side, just a few feet away from me, and I could have sworn it was making piteous attempts to neigh, although that was probably my imagination. At least I pray that it was. Please, God on high, let it be that the pathetic beast died instantly.

Seemingly believing that his pride had been salvaged, Uther said angrily to no one in specific, "Clean this mess up!" Then he turned away and stalked into the castle without giving anyone else so much as a backward glance.

I cleared away from the scene as quickly as I could, lest it be noticed that a palace slave was nearby and I be pressed into service to attend to the poor creature's corpse. Even the recounting of the incident has been difficult for me. The notion of having to haul the headless corpse to a ditch or pyre is more than I was willing to contemplate.

Some time later this evening, as I was heading from the kitchen to the meager quarters I shared with other slaves, my arm was grabbed as I passed a chamber. I yelped in shock and then saw Arthur's face from within the chamber. "Quickly," he said and hauled me in, closing the heavy door behind him.

For a moment I wondered if he was planning to have his way

with me. Why not? His father had endeavored to do so. As they say, the acorn does not fall far from the tree. Such things were nowhere near Arthur's mind, as it turned out. The chamber was little more than a storage closet, and I wondered why in the world Arthur had taken up residence therein. I suspected it was because he wished to avoid his father.

"You are a woman," he said.

Of all the things he could have said, certainly that was not what I was expecting. "Was there some uncertainty to that effect?" I said cautiously.

"I require a woman's opinion."

Madness. The prince was asking the opinion of a slave. It was tempting to laugh in his face, that he was so pathetic as to seek my counsel. I said nothing, not trusting myself to speak without derision.

He shifted uncomfortably from one foot to the other. "Do you think she will be upset? With me?"

"She who? Upset about what?"

"Morgan. My father conquered her father, and he will be coming here. It is entirely possible that she may accompany him. Do you think she will resent me because of my father's actions against Leodegrance?"

"I . . . honestly do not know, sire."

"Guess."

"I cannot guess, sire. I do not know the woman. I have no idea how she thinks."

Arthur looked genuinely surprised at the concept. "Do not all women think alike?"

I wanted to be insulted by the comment. I had not forgiven him for casting aspersions upon my feelings toward my father, and was seeking further reasons to despise him. But honestly, he had a look of such childlike credulity about him. He was not seeking to give offense. He genuinely was clueless.

"No, sire. We do not."

"Hunh." Clearly a novel notion had been introduced into his brain. "Well . . . all right. If you should, uhm . . . gain any insight . . ."

"I am not certain how I can do so, sire, but I shall certainly do my best."

"Well . . . maybe I can help you there."

I looked at him in confusion. "Help me, sire? How?"

"You let me worry about that, Veronica," he said, and then bolted from the closet before I could even correct him. Not that it would have made any difference, I suspect. I was starting to think that his father's memory lapses were not merely the result of old age, but instead a condition that could trace its roots to youth, if Arthur was any indication.

Day the Thirty-First

BECAUSE OF THE SIZE OF the banquet, everyone in the kitchen—including me—was pressed into service. It was Uther's desire that at no point would any of his guests be found wanting. Food and drink—especially drink—were to be kept readily available, and that required additional hands around the table. Mine were to be two of them.

Rowena continued to scowl at me. Let her. Ever since Merlin told her to keep her distance, she has not raised a hand to me. Her accusations of my being a witch or a whore now come only under her breath, which is where they belong.

The hunters labored mightily to provide the best foods available for the kitchen staff to prepare. So much venison was delivered up to the cooks for preparation that I swan the hunters must have slaughtered an entire herd of deer. Even as the deer were being cooked, another hunting party returned dirty and sweaty but triumphant, hauling two newly killed wild pigs with them. The cooks seemed ready to pull their hair out upon seeing yet more to prepare, but they quickly set to work.

I, along with several others, was dispatched to put out plates and utensils. I made certain there were settings at every place, but suspected many of them would not be used. The women would delicately cut their food, no doubt, but the men would probably just grab great slabs of meat in their hands and tear at them with their teeth. They seemed to believe that imitating animals made them manly.

Nobles have been arriving steadily over the past days. They are coming in far larger numbers than even the castle can accommodate, so many have been pitching large tents in the fields just outside the keep. Those of higher rank have rooms available in the castle. Retainers are living in the tents. I could observe them while looking out the castle windows. Entertainers were also arriving. I could see their carts. Jugglers, clowns, actors and assorted performers. Not welcome in the castle until the actual feast, they settled for entertaining the tented community. Even from the distance that I watched, laughter was able to float to my ears as the jugglers caused small sacks to jump between their hands like cloth birds while tricksters produced cards from the air. They earned applause and coins tossed to them by lower ranked nobles grateful for the diversion. I watched them and wistfully dreamed of having the freedom to go down there and see them and mingle with the free folk.

Leodegrance, however, had not yet turned up as of this morning. His prolonged absence was weighing heavily on Uther's mood, and everyone in the castle was feeling it. Uther had invited neighboring kings, warlords, princes and princesses, to Camelot in order to make certain they saw for themselves that Leodegrance was acknowledging his superiority. If Leodegrance then failed to show up as promised, Uther would have to assemble his troops and return to war, and this time there would likely be no peace treaty, no compromise. Uther's men would move across Cameliard, destroying everything in their path. The thought of what would happen to the women, the children . . .

I mean, the men would have brought it on themselves by swearing fealty to Leodegrance, I suppose, and to hell with them. The fewer men in this misbegotten world, the better. But for what reason should the women and children suffer?

Visions of what rapidly became to me the inevitable slaughter haunted me as I went about the chores assigned me. I have to think they hung like a shroud upon Uther as well, for his mood and temper were foul, even by his standards. He cuffed servants and even some of his peers at the slightest provocation and occasionally without provocation.

At one point I was carrying a stack of dishes and Uther brushed roughly past me before I could get out of his way. It caused me to drop the stack, and they clattered to the floor making an unholy racket. Uther rounded on me, his fist drawn back, and I knew I was for it. Then there was a loud clearing of a throat and Uther looked up. Merlin was standing at the far end of the hall, a scowl deep set upon him. "A herald of Leodegrance has just arrived," spake Merlin, "to inform us that his master had been delayed by a dilapidated bridge over a river. His party had to find an alternate means of crossing since the bridge would not bear the weight. The herald assures me that they will arrive anon." He paused and then added, "I am told he brings his daughters."

Uther lowered his fist, my high crime forgotten. "His daughters?" he said with a growl. "Morgan and Guinevere?"

"If he has others, I know not of them," said Merlin.

"Why bring them here?"

"The herald said not, but I suspect you know why, Highness. This development is not unexpected."

"No. No, it is not. And I must think on it. We must be ready."

Merlin simply nodded. Uther stalked away at that point, leaving me on the floor. Merlin looked at me with a curious cocking of his head. "Art injured, Viviana?"

"Nay, sir," I said, pulling myself to my feet. "But while on the floor, I did not draw the king's further notice."

The apothecary actually seemed to find that amusing. He chuckled softly and then said, "Viviana . . . attempt to avoid notice as much as you wish. However it is my suspicion that you will eventually attract notice whether you desire it or not."

"Why so, sir?"

He did not reply. Instead, with one more enigmatic chuckle, he turned and walked away with a swish of his robes. Interestingly, he never offered to help me to my feet. He likely felt that I needed no help.

Leodegrance arrived with much fanfare. When word spread that he was within sight of the castle, I was able to slip into the main courtyard to see him up close. There was a crush of people there, and my feet were stepped on a multitude of times as I endeavored to hold my place.

He was majestic, I have to say. With his graying hair swept back and his beard neatly trimmed, he carried himself more like a king than did Uther. He was riding a great black stallion, a most magnificent creature. Retainers followed close behind, tossing coins to the outstretched hands of the spectators. One landed in my palm. I held it, turning it over and over, considering what if anything I might be able to purchase with it. Then I saw a small beggar girl looking up at me with hopeless eyes. I sighed and handed it to her. She turned and ran without saying a word. Typical.

Riding some distance behind him were two young women. Because of what Merlin said I assumed that they were his daughters. They were astride matching white palfreys, but the girls themselves could not have been more different. One was a raven-tressed beauty, dressed in flowing green that matched her compelling eyes. There was a gentleness about her, a core goodness, and I think everyone could sense it. She rode sidesaddle.

The other had blonde hair cut short in an almost manly fashion. Her jaw was outthrust as if she were challenging someone to try and swing at it. Whereas the dark haired woman allowed her body to sway to the horse's cadence, the blonde girl sat stiffly with legs astride the horse, again like a man. She wore a long, white tunic and white leggings, appropriate to the manner in which she was riding a horse, I suppose, but surprising clothing for a young princess. Her eyes were a blue as steely as her gaze. She looked upon the crowd with what seemed to me barely controlled disdain. Yet she bore a smile and aimlessly tossed coins to the crowd as the retainers had done, thus instantly earning their adoration even though her contempt for them was apparent, at least to me.

As she rode past me, our gazes locked for just a moment. Perhaps it was because I was the only one not smiling or trying to grab at stray coins. She was fooling the others in the crowd with her obvious attempts at largesse, but not me, and I think she knew that. Still, I was nothing to her, merely a face in the crowd. She looked away from me then and, I supposed, promptly forgot all about me.

But she had a darkness about her that portended ill tides. I hoped that her stay at Camelot would be short, for I could not help but feel that she represented nothing but trouble for Arthur and his father.

Then I wondered why I should care about that. Whether Arthur and his father had problems or did not have problems, it was no concern of mine. Indeed, any troubles that they did encounter, they most assuredly brought upon themselves and I should have no sympathy for them.

Yet I kept going back to the sheer, needy helplessness that informed every aspect of Arthur. I had never encountered someone in more desperate need of guidance and, dare I say it, a friend.

Well, he was not going to find such in me. He was who he was, and I was what I was. We had no business being in each other's spheres, and the greater the distance I maintained from him, the better for all concerned, and most especially, for me.

The feast and celebration was as amazing as anything that ever I had witnessed.

The long tables were crowded to overflowing, with men seated on benches and jostling for position, some in a friendly manner, others less so. The women sat across from them and were a stark contrast in their conduct and demeanor, trying to maintain airs of polite amusement outwardly while inwardly, I should think, feeling mortified over the behavior of their men.

As I moved through the crowds of these "noble" knights, my buttocks no doubt turning black and blue from the continued pinching and slapping courtesy of the nobility, I held close to my heart my vision of Galahad. He existed nowhere save in my mind, but nevertheless the ideal of what a knight could and should be helped to give me strength. It helps to cling to a vision of what could be than dwell excessively on what is.

Uther was seated at one end of a lengthy table, eating in a manner that once again blurred the line between humans and animals. His wife, Queen Igraine, sat next to him. She did not look at him distastefully. She did not look at him at all. In my days and nights at the castle, I see very little of Igraine. She has her own servants and tends to keep to herself. She had a hollowed out, used look to her. It seemed to me that Igraine was watching her life pass from outside her body and couldn't quite understand why it was transpiring in that manner.

The Queen excused herself early on, claiming a headache. Uther waved her off with barely a glance. He seemed much more interested in Leodegrance, who sat at the far end of the table and actually appeared to be a most convivial guest. One would never have thought that the reason for his attendance was to acknowledge his defeat at the hands of Uther.

The way they behaved, it almost made it seem as if war was some sort of vast game to them. That they engaged in it with no more animosity than two opponents in a round of chess. It was probably of no relevance to them that the pieces they were using were human beings and, when they were removed from the board, they were not being lined up neatly to the side but instead left lying dead on the field of battle.

The daughters of Leodegrance sat to either side of him. I had no idea which one was Morgan and which Guinevere. Arthur was seated on the side of Uther opposite from where his mother had been. He smiled and nodded and laughed at what he must have fancied were all the right places, but Arthur still seemed most uncomfortable. He kept stealing glances toward Leodegrance's daughters. Neither of them looked in his direction, at least not openly. But I noticed that both of them, from time to time, were sneaking the subtlest of glances toward him. Or perhaps it was toward Uther, or maybe Merlin. It was impossible to tell.

The night had worn on for a bit. The jugglers had juggled, and a jester had spoken truths cloaked as falsehoods to the king, as was the custom. Then Leodegrance placed his hands down upon the table and pushed himself to standing. He raised his flagon and said in a hearty and formal voice, "I salute thee, Uther, king of Camelot, warlord of lands high and low. I rose up against thee and was smited by thy mighty hand. I come here now to offer up, in front of these noble lords and ladies, my fealty to my liege."

I was standing about five feet away from Uther, holding a wineskin. Uther lurched to his feet with markedly less poise than Leodegrance. He raised his chalice and then noticed it was empty. He looked to his left. I came in from the right and quickly filled it. He did not notice my presence, and so it was that when he looked back at his chalice he evinced open surprise. "God's blood!" he said. The reason for his shock was evident to all and elicited good-natured laughter. Hearing the laughter, he joined in, unaware that it was at his expense. Arthur, who was stone cold sober, covered his mouth with his hand so the king would not see his amusement. He raised the chalice, the wine sloshing over the sides. "I accept your oath in the spirit in which it is offered," he said to Leodegrance. "May you always be as kin to me."

"As a matter of fact, your highness anticipates my next words," said Leodegrance. "In order to unify our houses . . . I propose a marriage between your son, Arthur, and my eldest daughter, Morgan."

A roar of approval went up from the crowd. Why not? It was not their bachelorhood or maidenhead being offered up in the spirit of treaties.

Arthur looked startled at the suggestion, and his expression was mirrored in the face of his father. The princesses continued to look resolutely down at the table, but it seemed to me for very different reasons. The dark haired one looked shy; the blonde simply appeared irritated.

When Uther did not reply immediately, Leodegrance said grandly, "Morgan . . . stand up and let the denizens of Camelot feast their eyes upon their next princess."

There was a moment's hesitation, and then the dark haired one rose. She bobbed her head slightly and smiled as a cheer arose from the onlookers. A number of them began thumping their fists on the table in approval.

I shifted my attention back to Arthur. He was now looking openly at Morgan, and I remembered how he had spoken fondly of her in the past. That fondness did not appear to have diminished over time. For the first time since Morgan's arrival, she and Arthur looked at each other openly and the affection they felt for each other was palpable.

The other daughter, whom I took to be Guinevere, merely glowered and shook her head, making no attempt to hide clear disgust. Whether she was disgusted with her father, her sister, Arthur, Uther, the court of Camelot or perhaps the entirety of the world, I could not say.

I remembered Arthur's words from earlier, about how Guinevere and I would doubtless get on well. I was beginning to think there was merit in those words, for I saw in her sourness a mirror of my own general disgust for a world that had shaped the circumstances in which I lived.

Speaking as carefully as if he were treading upon a frozen lake where the ice was thin, Uther said, "Noble Leodegrance . . . certainly there are places more meet to discuss these matters than here . . ."

"Why not here, highness?" said Leodegrance. "This is

a mere formality, certainly. I would have thought that your having me here was a pretense to make such an arrangement." He spoke so calmly, so evenly, that it was impossible to tell whether he was trying to be challenging or sarcastic or simply open. "The fact is, Morgan is well into the marriageable age. I have been in no rush to entrust her to another, and that is, I suppose, a weakness as a father. But now I believe the time has come. I would think that you would readily agree."

Uther pulled at his beard thoughtfully and looked at Arthur. One could almost see the wheels spinning within Uther's head. Arthur's expression was vacuous. I found it hard to fathom. The young man's fate was being determined right in front of him, and he appeared disinclined to contribute to the proceedings.

And then Uther said two words that came near to exploding within the hall:

"Not Morgan."

There was a gasp followed by a stunned silence. The level of insult from such a pronouncement could not be calculated. The first daughter is always married first.

Morgan looked stunned, as if she had been punched in the face. Guinevere's reaction was far more curious. She smiled for the first time since entering Camelot. It was not a pleasant smile. It was more one that evinced amusement at her sister's shock. But at least she was capable of twisting the edges of her mouth upward, which I would not previously have thought possible.

I have to give credit to Leodegrance. Another father, another king, would have drawn his sword and leaped upon

Uther in a heartbeat. But his words were fraught with danger. "Is there . . . a problem . . . with my Morgan?" The insertion of "my" was a clear warning, underscoring that Uther was dealing with a prideful father and the ramifications of a wrong word could be monstrous. "She is sweet . . . kind . . . loving. It had been my impression that, if nothing else, Arthur found her . . . alluring . . ."

Leodegrance's hand was hovering near the hilt of his sword. The rules of hospitality are quite clear. It would have been an unthinkable breach of etiquette to raise arms against one's host. But the feelings of a father whose pride in his joy has been besmirched probably trumped such considerations. And even under the rules of hospitality, Uther would have been entitled to protect himself should a guest assail him.

I saw Uther's eyes narrow. He had spotted the proximity of Leodegrance's hand to his sword. If he had made a similar gesture, I have little doubt that Leodegrance would have drawn, and likewise Uther, and then God only knows what would have broken out in the great dining hall. But Uther, wisely, kept his hands straight down, making not the slightest offensive move against his guest. Uther had seemed somewhat inebriated to me earlier, but any trace of drunkenness was gone.

"I am aware of his interest in Morgan," said Uther, "and frankly, noble Leodegrance, that is part of the problem. My son has never known what is good for him. The fact that he fancies your daughter . . . that, right there . . . is a clear warning that she is not the right match for him."

"Is it?" Leodegrance seemed mildly confused, but was

clearly willing to listen further since Uther was not denigrating Morgan but instead his own son.

"You have said as much."

"Have I?"

Uther gestured toward Morgan, who was looking chagrined and mortified over the entire business. "None could quarrel with your description of your daughter: Sweet. Kind. Loving. Would that I could give my approval of such a union, but the fact is that my son does not need a wife who is sweet or kind or loving. There is nothing wrong with your daughter," he hastened to add, seeing the darkening of Leodegrance's face. "It is my son. Entirely my son."

"What is entirely me, father?" said Arthur. It was the first words he had spoken since the business began. He seemed hopelessly out of his depth.

Uther did not even deign to look upon him. Instead he continued to address his remarks to Leodegrance. "Arthur does not need a wife who will be sweet and kind to him. The boy is already of too gentle a nature, too mild a temperament. A warm and loving wife will simply reinforce aspects of his personality that are acceptable for a woman but unthinkable for a man in general and a future king in particular. He needs a woman who will whip him into shape, because God knows I have tried and his teachers have tried and none of us has succeeded."

They seemed such harsh words to me, but Arthur simply smiled and nodded as if everything his father was saying made perfect sense and was entirely reasonable, rather than insulting and demeaning to him before the whole of the court.

Then again, I was still a relatively recent arrival to Camelot. If Pendragon routinely spoke in such demeaning ways about his son, then the court was hearing nothing new.

Even Leodegrance was nodding. Upon seeing this, Uther thus emboldened said, "Frankly, noble Leodegrance, what Arthur needs is someone like . . . her."

He pointed straight at Guinevere.

Guinevere looked over her shoulder, apparently seeking the person whom Uther was indicating. When she realized that there were no maids directly behind her, she turned back to Uther. There was no hint of either amusement or disdain upon her face now. Instead she looked stunned, even appalled.

Leodegrance turned and looked at Guinevere as if seeing her for the first time. She saw the way he was looking at her, like a butcher sizing up a beast for slaughter. She tried to laugh but it was a feeble attempt. Perhaps that was because she was tense, or maybe she rarely tried to laugh and was thus inexperienced. "Father, you . . . you cannot . . ."

Of all the things a princess can say to her king father, "cannot" is likely the worst. Leodegrance looked at her with a fearsome expression and said, "I cannot . . . what?"

Guinevere rallied in the face of her father's disapproval. "He is for Morgan! Not me!"

"That, girl, is not your decision to make. It is mine." Leodegrance was taking firm charge of the situation.

"But Morgan is the elder!" she said desperately. "That is the custom—!"

"What matters custom to kings? Kings make customs,

not the other way 'round. Uther, if you are interested in my daughter, Guinevere, as a match for Arthur . . ."

"Most interested, noble Leodegrance."

"Father, no! I will not—"

Credit the girl more nerve than brains. To openly defy her father, a king, in such a manner . . . well, if she wanted to avoid marriage to Arthur, then certainly suicide was one manner in which to accomplish it and she was well on her way.

"You'll not?" thundered her father. "You will! I have put up with much from you, daughter. Your arrogance, your manly ways. At your mother's urging and begging and pleading, I have tolerated it and indulged it, and see the result!"

Guinevere's red lips shone brightly against the sudden paleness of her cheeks. She seemed to shrink in her chair, her bravado diminishing as quickly as her father's wrath soared.

Leodegrance turned back to Uther and said, "By heaven, Pendragon, I am thinking that it will be a beneficial match in both ways. Perhaps some of her manliness will rub off on your son, and perhaps some of his womanliness will rub off on her! God's blood, she is yours if you want her, and lord help you, Arthur, for I envy you not your wedding night. Bring armor to buttress your sword!"

With those words, the tension was broken, and a huge roar of laughter filled the hall, drowning out Guinevere's admittedly muted protestations.

Morgan had been standing the entire time. Now she sank into her chair. She looked neither left nor right. Leodegrance leaned over to her, resting his hand on her forearm and muttering something to her. I could not make out what it was. She nodded numbly in response.

Meantime Uther was on his feet and issuing a toast to the happy couple. Arthur looked tentatively toward Guinevere. She did not meet his gaze.

"My daughter's mug is empty!" Leodegrance bellowed. "She should be allowed to raise a glass to herself in toasting her own marriage!"

I hurried quickly toward her with the wine skin. I had to lean in close to her to get the lip to the mug.

She looked up at me without really seeing me, this princess, this learned young woman, and said, "My life is over. I have just been sold into slavery by my father."

Guinevere was not actually speaking to me, I do not think, as much as she was to herself. Nevertheless, speak she had, and in a voice so low that only she could hear, as the cheers of the lords and ladies resounded around us, I said to her, "As was I. Yet I have nothing and you are marrying a prince, and you do not hear me complaining my life is over."

She saw me truly for the first time then, and her pale cheeks flushed with . . . what? Embarrassment? Fury? "What is your name, wench?" she said.

"Viviana."

"Go to hell, Viviana."

"As you wish, milady," I said. Her drinking vessel full, I backed away from her and kept my head low. She did not look at me again.

The strangest thing just happened.

Having just finished my journal—an entry of such length that my hand still aches from detailing it—I drifted to sleep, only to awaken and discover myself being watched by an odd boy.

I would have taken him to be a slave or servant, but he was wearing the crest of Cameliard indicating one of higher rank. I have ne'er seen his like. Pale skin like death, hair near as white. His eyes provided the only color in his face at all; they were an amazing pale blue. It was hard to determine his age, although he was clearly nowhere near manhood. Seven years, perhaps eight at most. He was dressed in black and crouched near me, tilting his head slightly, like a dog. His nostrils flared, adding to the canine feel of his presence.

"Who are you?" I whispered, not wishing to awaken any of the other servants sleeping nearby.

He said nothing. Instead he stepped back and into the shadows. I clambered to my feet and went to the wall.

He was gone.

I write this down so I will not forget, although I am uncertain even now if what I witnessed was a dream. I have thought this castle many things, but haunted was never one I suspected.

An ill omen, at the very least, whate'er it was.

Day the Thirty-second

I WAS BUSY STOKING THE fire in the kitchen when Rowena waddled up to me and yanked on my sleeve. I looked at her, bewildered. It was early in the morning; I had been awake less than an hour. I could not fathom what I might have done to incur her wrath so quickly.

"You are to serve the lady Guinevere," she said.

I still did not understand. "Serve her what?"

"Serve her," she said slowly, as if addressing an idiot, which is what I felt like. "She has requested you as a servant. Attend to her."

"Requested . . . me?"

"'Request' may not be the best word. Ordered. Commanded. Take your pick. Just get yourself up there. I do not need to be suffering the wrath of those above me because you took your sweet time doing what you were told."

For once I could see reasons for Rowena's concerns. So I hied myself up to the chambers that had been given to Guinevere for the duration of her stay.

The princess was in her bath when I arrived, being attended

by two handmaidens. She looked at me coldly, as if annoyed that I had shown up even though it was at her behest. "Leave," she said brusquely. When I turned to go, she made an annoyed sound and said, "I meant them."

The handmaidens exchanged confused looks and then did as they were bidden. I stayed where I was as they pushed past me and out the door, looking relieved to be gone.

I felt uncomfortable standing there as she lay naked in the oversized wooden tub. On the other hand, at least it verified for me that over which I had some doubt. She was indeed female. I had heard of princes occasionally masquerading as females to avoid conscription into the army, so I had some lingering uncertainties on that score. They were misplaced; Guinevere may have been many things that were unwomanly, but the assets of our gender were all where they were supposed to be. I fancied that would save Arthur some embarrassment on their wedding night.

"I spoke of you to Arthur, about punishing you. He suggested I have you enter my service, claiming attending to me was punishment enough."

I considered Arthur's statement that he would find some way to "help" me. This newest development gave me insight into the prince's thought process. This was doubtless his idea of a solution.

"He spoke very highly of you. Too highly, in fact. It prompts my curiosity. Is he using you for sexual indulgences?"

My cheeks flushed slightly. "No, milady."

"If he asked you, would you accommodate him?"

"I do not know, milady. No one has ever done me the courtesy of asking. They just take."

There was something about the flatness in my voice that caught her attention. To my surprise, she lowered her eyes as if she were somehow responsible and said, "That is regrettable."

To me it simply was what it was. But I said nothing.

"Tell me about him," she said abruptly, as if we were in the middle of a conversation.

"Him? You mean Arthur?"

She made a rude noise. "Of course not. I know all I need to know of Arthur. I meant your father."

"Oh." I hesitated. "Why?"

Guinevere arched an eyebrow. "Customarily, when a noblewoman asks a question of a servant, it is answered without hesitation."

"Yes. Of . . . of course, milady." I have no idea why, but I curtsied slightly.

Then I told her what there was to tell.

She listened without interruption, although I could see disgust in her face when I spoke of the moment that my father sold me into slavery. Finally I fell silent.

"He sounds a beast," she said.

"You do not know him, nor will you ever, so I would thank you, milady, not to pass judgment upon him." But my protest was a bit more half-hearted than it once would have been. Damn Arthur anyway, for planting seeds of doubt within me.

She smiled. As opposed to what I saw last night, this one was genuine. When she did it, her face softened. She was actually quite attractive if she allowed herself to be seen as such.

"So. The hint of fire you displayed last night was not mere passing. You have genuine flame burning within you, Viviana. May I address you as such?"

"I serve you, milady. It is your prerogative to address me however you wish."

"True. That is true."

"Milady . . . may I ask a question?"

"Of course."

"Why am I here?" When she stared at me, not answering, I pressed on. "I mean . . . you have other servants. I do not understand why I would be needed . . ."

"They are my father's servants. They serve me, but they are his."

"Yes."

She rose from the tub and indicated the towels that lay stacked on the foot of the bed. I gathered them and brought them over to her. As I helped her step out of the tub, she said to me in a low voice, "There are matters that need to be discussed. Matters that you can be of use to me in . . . bastard!"

The abrupt change in tone caught me off guard. I looked to see what had prompted her wrath so and I gasped in shock.

The ghost had returned. There, in the light of day, he was standing just inside the door. I had not heard the door creak, and it was a great heavy thing, so it should not have been possible. But there he was, large as life, which was an interesting contradiction since he was clearly not alive. I was a bit surprised that Guinevere was even able to see him, since I was beginning to believe that he was a spectral vision only visible to mine eyes.

Guinevere clutched the towels around her and snarled, "Modred! How dare you—!"

The thing called Modred exited the room. I would have thought that he would pass spectrally through the door, but no, he yanked it open and darted through just as any mortal might.

"Find him, Viviana!" Guinevere shouted. "Find him and drag him back to my thrice-damned sister and tell her what he was up to! Then bring him to me for punishment!"

My mind was swirling with questions, but a naked, dripping and outraged princess was clearly not going to be the source of answers. I hurried out the door after the fleeing pale lad, taking care to secure it behind me. I did not think that passersby ogling the nude noblewoman would do much to improve her disposition.

I looked left and right, unsure of which way Modred had gone. I was still trying to adjust to the notion that the pallid child was flesh and bone. Taking a guess, I headed to the left and hoped that I had guessed correctly, since Guinevere seemed in no mood for my telling her that I had failed in my task.

Quick questioning of people that I passed verified that I was heading in the right direction. Children of Modred's description tended to leave an impression.

I ran through the hallways and then, from ahead, I heard laughter. Childish laughter. It was not the pleasant type that brings a smile to one's lips. It was the mean, nasty sort that makes one recall just how truly cruel youngsters can be. It was a leap of intuition, but I had to suspect that Modred was the subject of the laughter.

Then came the screaming.

I rounded the corner in front of me, which opened out onto a landing.

I saw four boys of varying ages, a mix of the young sons of knights and nobles. They were in training for knighthood, which I was able to tell because they had wooden swords tucked into their belts. Two were pointing and shouting, one was lying on the floor shrieking and clutching the side of his head, and the fourth was pummeling Modred.

Perhaps the most bizarre aspect of this entire demented scenario was that Modred was deathly silent. Most youngsters would be crying for mercy or just crying. Not Modred. He remained silent as the grave, even as blood gushed from his nose. He was tightlipped and there was not the slightest hint of discomfort in those eerily pale blue eyes. It was as if he had taken his mind elsewhere and the damage being done to his body was of no consequence, for he was not there to experience it.

I did not hesitate. I ran to the boy who was beating Modred, grabbed him from behind, and lifted him bodily. I am hardly a warrior born, but I have spent my life engaged in hard labor and am not exactly lacking in strength. The boy let out a startled yelp as I tossed him aside. He landed on his back, looked up and saw me. His eyes widened as he realized a female, and a slave at that, had just manhandled him. "How dare you!" he howled.

"Shut up," I said, in no mood to bandy words. I was on

a mission assigned me by a princess and the future queen of Camelot, so I was reasonably sure that would afford me all the protection I needed from possible recriminations. My response was so forceful that it startled the lad into silence. His companions simply stood there looking stupid.

As much as I may feel impatience and disgust with royals and those who look down upon such as me, I have to admit that the power that comes with operating on their behalf can be heady.

I went to Modred, ignoring the wailing of the boy who had his hand clasped to the side of his head. The blood was continuing to pour from Modred's nose. His lips remained tightly sealed, so much so that it caught my attention. "What have you got in your mouth?" I said. "Show me."

With what could only be described as perverse pride, Modred did as he was told. I did not know what it was at first. It appeared to be a small piece of meat. Had Modred stolen someone's lunch? Then, with a wave of nausea, I realized. It was a lump of flesh, the bloodied outer section of an ear.

Which naturally explained the boy who was still sobbing and clutching the side of his head. Looking more closely, I now saw that his fingers were tinged with red, stopping the blood seeping from where the remains of his ruined ear were still attached to his skull.

Modred, by contrast, still had not stopped bleeding. It was everywhere. The lower half of his face was covered with it. He looked like an unshaven man with a crimson shadow where beard stubble would have been. It was on his clothes, on the floor.

And he was smiling. Combined with the sallow condition of his skin, he looked like some sort of demented harlequin.

I removed my apron and pushed it hard against his nostrils, trying to stanch the flow. The boy on the floor was screaming,"He bit off my ear!"

"Just part of it!" I shouted back, which struck me as a response that was in keeping with the insanity of the moment.

"What the bloody hell is going on here!"

The timing could not have been worse. It was Uther, having walked in on what could only be described as a complete disaster. I now had some idea of what my expression must have looked like upon coming onto the scene, because that shock was reflected upon the face of the king.

The boy whom I had dragged off Modred pointed at the bleeding, pale-skinned creature and said, "He's a monster! A demon! Kill him, your majesty, kill him now!"

"Do you truly think the king takes orders from snot-nosed brats such as yourself?" said Uther. "Perhaps I will kill you now for your insolence, boy, and who would there be to gainsay me, eh?"

That silenced the boy quickly enough.

"You, wench," Uther said to me. "Who have you there?"

He had not been able to see the identity of the bleeder since I had his head tilted back and my apron pressed hard against his nose. The bleeding was slowing but still not stopping. Nevertheless I angled his head so that the king could see him more clearly.

The king's spine stiffened. He seemed ready to say half a

dozen things all at once and instead settled simply for, "Modred. I might have known."

I began to speak. "Highness, I came upon—"

But Uther waved me off. "No need to tell me, woman. I will tell you. These boys opted to torment Modred because of his appearance. Modred leaped upon one of them and, by the looks of it, bit off a piece of his ear. Whereupon this hardy lad decided to start pounding on a boy half his height. Is that about the size of it? Well?" he said with growing anger when no response from any of them was forthcoming. "I said, is that the size of it? I am unaccustomed to repeating myself, God's blood, and you are well advised not to necessitate it!"

The boys promptly nodded.

"As I thought." He surveyed the sorry mess and then said, "You. Woman. Return the boy to Morgan. You," and he pointed at the lad with the diminished ear, "get yourself fixed up."

"He bit off my ear," the boy said with a whine.

Clearly in no mood for it, the king said, "Say that again and I will bite off the other and feed it to you. Understood?"

He did, as did the others. I headed in one direction, keeping Modred's head tilted back and my apron upon his face. They headed in the other.

I guided the lad to Morgan's chambers. He said nothing the entire time. I was beginning to think that he was dumb.

Rapping on the door, I then pushed it open without waiting for it to be answered. Morgan was there, seated in front of a mirror, brushing her hair. She looked up, a question on her lips, and then it froze when she saw the bloody disaster that was Modred.

"Oh my God!" she said. It was the first time I had heard her voice; it sounded musical even under circumstances such as these. She dropped her hairbrush and ran to him, taking the apron from me without another word and applying pressure.

"I have been trying to stop it," I said, feeling helpless.

She nodded distractedly. "He bleeds easily and profusely. He always has." She added in what seemed a gentle aside to him, "I keep telling him that royal blood is best kept inside the body rather than outside. Tell me what happened."

I reconstructed for her the events as I had witnessed them. When she heard how it all began, she scowled disapprovingly at him. "Modred! Spying on Guinevere in her bath? For shame. For shame."

He did not appear any too shamed. Instead he was looking at me. They were unnerving, those eyes.

"Milady, if you do not mind my asking . . . who is he?"

"Modred is my young cousin," said Morgan. "From a distant branch of the family. He lives with us. His parents were . . . unable . . . to keep him."

Then Modred spoke for the first time in my hearing, and what he said surprised me mightily:

"She gave a coin to a beggar girl."

"What?" said Morgan.

"She gave a coin to a beggar girl."

"I heard you, Modred. I just do not understand. Who . . . ?"

"I . . . believe he is referring to me, milady," I said, scarcely able to credit it. She looked at me, clearly awaiting further explanation. I cleared my throat uncomfortably. "I was in the crowd upon your arrival and coins were being tossed. I caught one and handed it to a beggar girl." I paused and then shrugged. "She did not thank me."

"I see. Well . . . that was considerate of you, to do that."

"But . . ." I looked at Modred. "I am . . . I am amazed that he saw that. Was he riding with you . . . ?"

"Modred tends to stay to himself." She looked at him with genuine affection. "When he is outside, the sun is unkind to him. He goes cloaked and somehow just tends to avoid being noticed."

"Well . . . even so," I said, "he must have formidable vision to have picked me out in that crowd."

"Actually, no. Modred's vision is somewhat lacking."

Modred smiled. It looked a bit eerie when he did so. "I see half as well as anyone else, so I watch twice as carefully to compensate." Then he turned back to Morgan. "Boys were beating me up. She saved me. Pulled them off me. Threw one of them around."

"Did she? Did you?" she said to me. She had settled Modred into a chair and came to me, taking my hand in hers. "That was so kind of you. I am in your debt."

"No, you most certainly are not," I assured her. "I saw him being bullied and, well . . . anyone would have done the same."

"You are wrong," she said. "I would be lying if I said there had not been previous incidents, and others were not quick to come to Modred's rescue."

Modred spoke again. His voice was flat and emotionless and chilling. "I was exposed at birth."

Morgan rolled her eyes. "Modred, that is just an old tale . . ."

"I was. I remember it." Modred's pale eyes glittered. "I was laid out on a hill and the wolves came and then turned away . . ."

"Modred, stop it," Morgan said.

". . . and then Death came and looked upon me, and would not have me as well . . ."

"I said stop it!"

She crossed the room quickly, her face twisted in agonized rage, and she stood over him with her hand drawn back and poised to strike. He looked up at her impassively. Her hand trembled and then she dropped to the ground with a sob.

I had no idea what I should do. I had no business being there. These were the affairs of royals, not slaves or servants. Feeling that some sort of action on my part was required, I offered her a cloth. She took it and looked up at me with such gratitude that I almost felt guilty over feeling nothing for her plight.

"I am sorry," she said, composing herself. She forced a smile that was a stark contrast to the misery in her eyes. "It has . . . been a difficult time."

"I would think so."

"Being rejected in front of an entire court . . ."

"I did not see it as you being rejected, milady," I said. "I saw it more as men simply showing once again that they never know what is good for them."

Morgan actually laughed at that. It was soft and ladylike. "That is very kind of you to say. And I suppose I have no business feeling sorry for myself. It is Arthur who most deserves pity. He is such a gentle soul and I fear for what my sister will do to him."

"Perhaps it will work out," I said. Searching for something to say, I said—without meaning it—"Arthur has hidden strengths . . ."

She looked at me oddly. "Do you know him well? Are you his servant?"

"I . . . would not say 'well,'" I said hastily, not wishing to give any wrong impressions. "We have spoken from time to time, which is, I admit, a bit unusual. For a prince to speak to a servant . . ."

"We live in changing times," said Morgan. "Many of the old rules are being set aside, and perhaps they were never wise rules to begin with. Did Arthur . . . ?" She hesitated.

"Did he what, highness?"

She rested her hand upon my shoulder. It was a very intimate gesture, one that bridged the gap between servant and lady. "Did he speak of me? In your conversations with him, I mean."

"Oh. Yes. Fondly."

"Well," she said with a smile and a sigh as if that settled the matter, and she squeezed my shoulder affectionately, "then I guess we should be grateful for that at least, eh? Modred, did you thank the young lady for aiding you?"

"Thank you, Viviana, " said Modred politely.

I was surprised. "How did you know my name?"

"I heard Guinevere shout it when you chased after me. Her voice carries."

"Viviana," Morgan said thoughtfully. "An unusual name. French?"

"Italian," I said.

"Ah. I always confuse those two."

I had to think that she would indeed have been a good match for Arthur at that.

Leaving the boy in the care of his cousin, I realized abruptly that I had failed in the mission that Guinevere had given me, namely to return the boy to her for chastisement.

Guinevere was dressed by the time I returned to her. She was wearing a simple blue and white frock and was standing in front of a mirror, looking this way and that at herself. "They will likely expect me to wear dresses more often as a queen," she said. "Terribly uncomfortable things. They make one feel more vulnerable, do you not agree?"

"I have never worn anything but skirts or dresses, milady, so I have nothing to compare it to."

"Take my word for it then." Her face twisted in disgust as she continued to study her new ensemble. "To hell with what they expect. I shall dress in the manner that pleases me, and the rest of them will just have to endure the sight." Then she turned from her reflection and glanced behind me. Seeing no sign of Modred, her eyebrows knit and she said, "Where is the little monster?"

I told her what had transpired. She listened and nodded and then said, "Well . . . I suppose there was some measure of punishment upon him for his effrontery, administered by the hand of divine retribution. And you spoke to my sister, I imagine."

Something in her voice indicated disapproval. "Is . . . there a problem with my having done so, milady?"

Guinevere tilted her head and regarded me with curiosity. I felt as if I were being tested in some manner. "What do you think of her?"

"I fail to understand why my opinion of your sister matters, milady."

"It does because I say it does."

"Well . . . she seemed very nice. Sweet. Considerate and compassionate . . ." I stopped speaking, for Guinevere was shaking her head with what seemed weariness.

"You too, eh?"

"Me too what, milady?"

"You seem a bright woman, Viviana. There are not many of us about, and I had hoped that your intelligence would see through my sister's façade."

"Façade?" I hated that I kept echoing her last words but I could not help myself. "I do not understand."

"Did she weep?"

"Well . . . a bit, yes."

"Mmmm," said Guinevere. "She does that. And she smiles and she sweet talks, and she does this." She rested her hand on my shoulder as Morgan had done, and then added, "And then, to show just how much she adores you, she does this," and she squeezed my shoulder. "Did she do all that with you?"

"Yes," I said. "But honestly, milady, I am not entirely certain what any of that indicates."

"My sister desires power, Viviana," Guinevere said patiently, as if explaining to a child. "That is all she has ever sought. She believes, however, that the only way she will attain it is through a man whom she can control. She has felt that Arthur represented such a 'catch,' and has eyed him for some time. The fact that Uther refused the union is a blow to her, and she will have to try and recover and come up with new plans, new allies."

"But milady, I am no ally of worth. I am no one of power who can serve any ends she desires."

"If you believe that, then I have overestimated you, Viviana," she said severely. "Servants have far more power than you seem to believe. The servants, the peasants, the serfs . . . if the lot of you organized yourselves and made demands of the nobility, we would have no choice but to do whatever we could to accommodate you. Instead you allow yourselves to be downtrodden and to believe that you are without either power or worth. You allow yourself to be helpless."

Her words stung. Tossing aside the caution that I by rights should have exhibited, I said with genuine heat in my words, "I allow myself to be helpless, milady, in the same way and with the same enthusiasm that you allow yourself to become affianced to Arthur."

The edges of her mouth twitched and then she nodded. "And now I think that perhaps my original estimation of you was not, in fact, 'over,' but rather right on target."

I spent the rest of the day with Guinevere. She spoke of a great many things, most of them having to do with politics and the various machinations of the men who controlled our lives.

For the most part, I listened. I must admit I was fascinated by her worldview in that she actually had a worldview. My anger was mostly localized in terms of how matters impacted upon me. Guinevere seemed concerned about everyone in terms of their wants and needs, and she even spoke of how royalty had failed to create any sort of equity between the great and small. I was, frankly, amazed. I was unaware that anyone in her station thought that way. It made me feel limited in my own perceptions.

I realize now that she said very little about herself. She enjoyed talking about everyone but herself, actually, remaining guarded as to her own hopes, dreams and aspirations. I could tell, though, that whatever those might have been, none of them involved Arthur or even marrying. In our walks around the castle and our varied activities, we encountered Arthur several times and Uther once. Guinevere remained polite but distant, and neither man seemed to know quite how to approach her. Igraine's lady in waiting, an older and very experienced woman named Eowyn, endeavored to ask Guinevere several times about her preferences for wedding specifics since Eowyn had been charged with preparing it. Guinevere declined to engage in discussion, citing a headache. Oddly, the affliction only seemed to bother her when Eowyn was around. The rest of the time, she was in perfectly fine fettle.

At the end of the day, Guinevere said, "We shall go for a ride tomorrow morning, Viviana, shortly after I break fast. I anticipate that it will be a bit of a journey, so dress accordingly."

Since I had little in the way of varied clothing, I simply

nodded as if I had a variety of options to pursue, and then said hesitantly, "We are to leave the castle, milady?"

"I think that riding horses down the main corridor would be problematic, do you not? Why? Does departing the castle present a problem?"

"No, milady," I said.

"Do you ride?"

"I am not what I would call an accomplished horsewoman, but I will not fall off a reasonably well-behaved mount."

She nodded. Apparently she found that response adequate.

I returned to my humble scrap of floor off the kitchen, crammed in with the other servants, and I reflected on the day. In some respects it made little sense to me. What was it about me that royals such as Guinevere and Morgan and even Arthur did not hesitate to unburden themselves to me? Despite Guinevere's high-flown assessment of me, I was nothing.

Then I decided that perhaps that might well have been the reason for it. Speaking to a servant was like unto speaking to a corpse or the wind. They could unburden themselves and since I had no social standing, no status or rank of any kind, the confessions and honesty carried with it no consequences. I could not hurt them. Even in Guinevere's description of a world in which those who labored below wielded considerable power over whose above, such influence required considerable numbers of the likes of me, banded together in order to accomplish our goals. I was but one person. What could I do to them? Nothing. With whom would I share the personal information that I gleaned from the nobility? No one. I had made no secret of the fact that I was isolated from the rest of the servants and slaves. None of them trusted me or wanted to have anything to do with me, particularly if they happened to learn I could read.

Perhaps the nobles would not have been quite so forthcoming had they known that Merlin had taken an interest in me. But something compelled me to keep that piece of information to myself. It would seem that I am learning quickly, becoming as secretive as the nobles. I wish I knew whether that was a good thing or a bad thing.

Day the Thirty-Third

I WAS HEADING TO GUINEVERE'S chambers this morning when I discovered Merlin in my path. I curtsied and was about to explain to him that I was hastening this morning to attend to my duties for her highness, but Merlin silenced me by merely crooking his finger to indicate that I should follow. I did as he bade and we stepped into a small alcove.

He smiled pleasantly but he appeared to have something on his mind. "How now this lovely morning, Mistress Viviana?" he said. *"Quo vadis?"*

"To milady Guinevere."

"Heading out and about, are you?"

I nodded.

"I had a feeling."

The way he said it suggested that he had feelings about other matters as well. I did not press him for specifics. Truthfully, there was still much about him that made me nervous and I would just as soon have limited my interaction with him.

"And where, precisely, are you heading out and about to?"

"I know not, milord. Milady Guinevere did not feel the need

to be specific. I thought . . . well, it was my impression that she merely desired to explore the immediate area."

"And she gave no indication of any interest other than that?" I shook my head. He seemed amused, or at least his expression appeared to find something funny, but there was nothing in his tone of voice that matched it. "It would be most unfortunate if she did not return."

"What?" I was not certain I understood what he was talking about. "Why would she not—?"

"I do not know why she would not. After all, she is affianced to Arthur, whom she despises, in an arrangement made by her father, for whom she also has no great love. What possible reason could she have to flee?"

I said nothing except, "Oh." The apothecary was making his point quite clearly.

"If she were to run off, or attempt to do so, the consequences would be," and he shook his head and spoke with great sadness, "most dire. Most dire indeed. Why, I tremble even to contemplate it."

"What . . . manner of consequences?"

"Well, first of all, Leodegrance would die, surely. Oh, not while he is in Camelot. Uther will attend to the rules of hospitality. But I would not wager a shilling's purchase on the odds of Leodegrance making it home to Cameliard. Not Leodegrance, nor his fetching Morgan. Uther has extremely formidable woodsmen at his command; Leodegrance will never make it out of the forest. He and all his retainers would die without ever seeing their attackers. Then Uther will gather his army, march upon Cameliard, and . . ." Merlin shuddered, although I suspect that it was a mere display of dread over the prospect he described rather than actual concern. "All those people suffering because of the impetuous act of one young girl."

"But . . . milord, if that is truly a concern, then would it not make sense to refuse to allow Guinevere to depart at all? Or to recommend that armed men be sent along with her so she could not flee?"

"You mean treat the future queen as if she is a prisoner here? No, no, Mistress Viviana. That would never do," and he made a "tsk" noise as if the notion was absurd. "The queen must be trustworthy. She must be beyond reproach. She must know early on that she is trusted, or else how can she possibly serve the needs of the people of Camelot?"

"So . . ." I hesitated. "What want you of me, then, milord?"

"Why, Mistress Viviana . . . I want nothing more of you than for you to do what is expected of you, as you always have."

"It might help if I knew what that was, milord."

"Yes. It would."

My head was spinning. "Milord, why are you speaking to me of this? I am a slave. A slave. Why do I feel as if I am being drawn into the murky world of court intrigues? Why do I suddenly feel as if the future is being dropped onto my shoulders?"

"The future is on all our shoulders, Mistress Viviana. The question is whether we choose to carry our share of the load."

"I believe I am carrying more than my share, milord," I said.

"Far more than those who have been accorded more benefits in life than I. The fact is that, in the grand scheme of things, I am no one."

"Is that who you believe yourself to be? Or are you allowing yourself to be defined by others?"

I held up my manacles. "These define me well enough."

"The shackles on your wrists and your throat are not your greatest problem, Viviana. It is the shackles upon your mind that are holding you back."

"I do not understand what you mean, milord."

"Aye. You do. Sooner or later, Viviana, you ought to start thinking of someone beside yourself. And I believe you will. The only question is whether you will do so in time to make a difference to the lives of all those who will be harmed if the queen-to-be does something foolish. Or do you not give any more of a damn about their lives than you do about your own?"

With that pronouncement, he went on his way.

I could not believe the temerity of the man. He did not know me. Who was he to render such judgments upon me? I resolved at that point to do nothing save what was expected of me as a slave. That would show him.

Guinevere was wearing her riding clothes when I arrived at her chambers. She looked me up and down and seemed to shrug mentally. Her other servants were standing there, glowering at me. Perhaps they saw me as some sort of threat. I have no idea why. I certainly did not think of myself as such.

I followed Guinevere out. She was wearing a satchel slung over her back, as if she were preparing to carry messages to someone. I did not ask about the contents since I did not see it as my place to do so.

Guinevere's white palfrey was brought to her and I was provided a brown jennet. The horse looked up at me wistfully. I was sympathetic to her. We were both, in our own way, prisoners of circumstance.

I sat astride the jennet and Guinevere glanced approvingly at me.

We started off on our jaunt.

Guinevere said very little. We exited through the main gate of the keep and rode past the array of tents within which the rank and file was residing. The jennet kept up easily with the palfrey, although I made certain to maintain a respectful distance. Every so often Guinevere would glance back at me, presumably to make certain that I was keeping up with her. People waved at her or cheered as we passed. Guinevere acknowledged them with a cursory wave of her hand, but she did not seem particularly pleased to see them.

Before too long we had left the temporary village of tents behind and reached the perimeter of the forest. If the forest had a name, I had not learned what it was, nor had I thought to ask. A path wound through the forest. It was rough and uneven and not accommodating to carts, but it was passable enough. Guinevere kept the palfrey going at a steady gait and the jennet and I kept up.

Finally, unable to restrain myself any longer, I said tentatively, "Milady? If it is not too forward of me . . . where might we be going?"

"We might be going wherever the road may lead."

"I see." I considered that for a short time and then said, "And how far do you intend that we go on this road, wherever it may lead?"

"I had not really given it all that much thought."

"I believe you have, highness."

She reined up her horse and turned it so that it was facing us. She looked at me imperiously. "You are bold this morning, Viviana."

"I thought you found that an attractive trait in me, milady."

"I do indeed. For boldness shall be a requisite this day. You see, Viviana," and she dropped her voice to a confidential tone, "we are not going to be returning to castle Camelot."

"Are we not?"

Guinevere shook her head and her face darkened with indignation. "I am a princess and I will not be bartered by my father like . . . like . . ."

"I was?"

She nodded at that. "It is for that reason that I have accorded you the honor of accompanying me."

"It is an honor I have not sought, milady, nor is it one that I may opt to pursue. Lest you have forgotten," and I held up the tell-tale manacles upon my wrists, "I am a slave."

She gestured dismissively. "That is of no consequence. I release you."

"The sentiment is appreciated, milady, but only Uther Pendragon has that right."

"Do you want to be a slave?"

"No, milady. But what I want does not enter into it."

"It most certainly does," said Guinevere.

"Would that that were true. Yet it is not, and the proof of that is that, sooner or later, someone will spot the bonds upon my wrist, or upon my throat, and I will be turned over to authorities and returned to Camelot. And the punishment will be . . ." I shuddered, not wishing to speak of such matters.

"Freedom," Guinevere said airily, "is not achieved without risk."

Her attitude was beginning to irk me somewhat. "It is easy to say that when you have not spent a day of your life enslaved."

"If I attend to my father's wishes, I will spend the rest of my life in that state. I refuse to do so."

"You cannot refuse."

That was clearly the very worst thing I could have said to her. By her bearing and attitude and words, Guinevere was unaccustomed to anyone telling her that she could not do anything. "I can refuse . . . and I will. And I would have liked to have a servant by my side to attend to my needs. If you do not wish to fulfill that role then I will embark upon my endeavors by myself."

She turned the palfrey around, making ready to ride off. I thought of the things Merlin had said. Most particularly, I remembered what he had said about having men vastly experienced in woodcraft, so much so that they could easily blend into a forest without being seen. I felt as if they were surrounding us right then, their eyes boring into us.

And despite my best resolve not to allow it, the words

of Merlin came back to me. Telling me how I could make a difference; that the choices I made were important. That there was a world beyond my own concerns.

It was a world that had treated me with either cruelty or indifference. But there were others out there like me—slaves, or women or children—who would suffer if the actions of Guinevere triggered a full-blown, earth-scorching war. Damn Merlin for making me feel as if all their eyes were upon me, silently pleading with me to do something, anything to avert a terrible fate.

"And have you considered the consequences of your actions?" I said.

Guinevere halted the palfrey before it could move forward as she glanced back at me. "Consequences?"

"Do you truly believe that Uther will not react to your desertion? He will see it as a personal affront. He will vent his wrath against your people. Is that what they would want?"

"I can tell you what my people would not want. They would not want a princess of the realm to be trapped in an unhappy arranged marriage. They would not want that sort of life for me."

"Honestly, milady? I think most of them do not care in the least about your life. They care about their own." I knew I certainly felt that way, and doubted I was alone. "And if their lives are forfeit so that you may indulge your desires, I doubt they would hesitate in choosing their interests over yours every time."

Guinevere simply stared at me as if I were some sort of

offal upon the sole of her shoe. It was clear to me what was transpiring: She considered me an intelligent woman, which was flattering enough, I suppose. And she likewise considered herself to be intelligent. On that basis, she likely anticipated that we would be in accord on all the important matters. That was not happening and I do not believe she knew quite how to react.

"Stay here if you wish," she finally said. "All I ask is that you take your time returning to the castle. Tell them . . ." She considered it and then shrugged. "Tell them whatever you want. Bandits took me. Or I knocked you unconscious and, when you returned to wakefulness, I was gone. Tell them that or something else; it matters not to me."

"And what of Arthur?"

"Tell him anything you want as well."

"But what of his feelings? You are rejecting him—!"

"As his father rejected Morgan. The scales are balanced as far as I am concerned."

She snapped the reins and the palfrey started off at a fast trot.

I matched the action with my own reins. The jennet seemed surprised. That made sense. She was a fairly quiet horse, accustomed to toting around noblewomen and the like who put very few, if any, demands upon her. Here I was, insisting that she keep up with the majestic palfrey ahead of us. Credit the jennet for fortitude. She gamely increased her hoof speed so that she could keep up with the palfrey.

Guinevere looked down at me disdainfully. "You are

dismissed, Viviana. Return to the castle at once!"

"You are trying to flee from your responsibilities, milady, and I cannot allow—"

"You cannot? Allow?"

It was very likely the worst possible thing I could have said to her. She snapped her reins, cried "Yaaaaa" and the palfrey picked up speed.

I urged the jennet forward and she sprang into action. It was a formidable task. The jennet was half the size of the smallest of horses in the stables, but I admired her dedication. Her hooves flashed as she caught up with the palfrey.

The entire time I could not believe I was embarking on this mad action. Part of my motivation was having no desire to return to the castle and have to tell Arthur that his prospective wife had departed. I was not concerned over Arthur's reaction in that regard, but Uther might well look to punish the last person to see her for failing to restrain her. I had seen what he had done to a horse that offended him, and had no reason to think that he regarded me as highly. Less highly, in fact. Horses were more expensive.

Also, as much as I hated to admit it, Merlin's damnable voice had taken up residence within my head, filling my imagination with thoughts of dead bodies, stacked like cordwood. It would be a calamity that I could have stopped, or at least tried to stop.

Guinevere glanced back at us and she clearly realized that her sheer moral indignation was not going to carry the day. She dug her knees into the horse's side and the palfrey went from trot to gallop. Clods of dirt sprayed from beneath the horse's hooves as it carried Guinevere rapidly down the path at a faster speed than my jennet could possibly match.

That did not deter either the jennet or myself from trying. I urged the horse forward with all possible speed and the valiant beast did its level best. But the palfrey was just too quick. Guinevere was opening up distance between us with every moment, and my heart sank.

"Milady! Come back!" I shouted in desperation, not expecting for a moment that it would work and not even sure she could hear me over the pounding of the hooves.

Guinevere glanced back at me and smiled grimly.

That was when I spotted the large branch extending from a tree. It was directly in her path and she did not see it.

"Look out!" I cried.

She may well have thought I was trying to trick her, and so made no effort to look in front of her. That proved to be a costly blunder as she ran into the branch, which took her just above the breasts. Guinevere was knocked clear off her horse. She sailed backwards through the air and thudded to the ground directly in my path. The jennet whinnied loudly as I yanked hard on the reins lest the speeding horse run right over Guinevere, trampling the princess into the ground. I barely managed to avoid disaster as the jennet halted not five paces shy of the fallen noblewoman.

I dismounted and went to her. Guinevere was lying on her back, staring up at the latticework of branches overhead. The breath had been knocked out of her. I crouched next to her and said, "Speak not. Take time to recover yourself, milady."

She was looking in confusion at the branch. I followed her gaze and it was most passing strange, for the obstruction did not appear all that low. I was not quite certain how she had managed to run into it.

Guinevere pushed herself to a sitting posture, shaking off the effects of the blow. The palfrey was standing a few feet away, looking unaccountably apologetic.

"Get my horse," she finally managed to say.

Automatically I started to do as she commanded. Then I caught myself and looked down at her. "So you can flee again?"

"That is my intent, yes."

"You cannot. You must not."

"I can, and I must. I will not be dictated to, nor have my future decided for me by others. I am a princess . . ."

"Yes, you are." I took a breath and then spoke quickly and even angrily. "And you have benefited from that status your entire life. You have led a life of privilege, doing naught but what interested you. The sweat and efforts of hard-working people, be they servants who clothed you and bathed you or cooks who prepared your food for you or humble farmers who grew that food or hunters who trapped it . . . all those people worked to support and serve your needs. Now you are being asked to return that service, to balance the ledger in the only way that you can: accommodating the orders of your father, the king. If you do not do so, then those servants and cooks and farmers and hunters and artisans and laborers and whomever else there is in Cameliard whose names you do not know, although they most assuredly know yours . . . all of them will suffer the consequences of your actions. Because as surely as night follows day, war will follow your departure, and those people will suffer and many of them will die cursing your name."

"What care I over when or how they speak my name?" said Guinevere defiantly. But her voice was wavering and there was an odd expression on her face that I realized, to my surprise, was uncertainty.

"You care. You know that you care. You may well wish that you did not, but you do." I paused and then slowly, carefully, said, "And what of your father and your sister? Do you despise them so, that you would sign their death warrants with your departure?"

"I do not despise them." Her temper flared. "How dare you insinuate such a thing? They are my family."

"Then honor them by doing that which your station in life demands."

"By condemning myself to a loveless marriage?"

"That depends," I said, "on what you love."

"Not Arthur."

"What of freedom? You love that. Power provides freedom, and if you are queen, then you will have considerable amounts of both. And . . . as for Arthur, well . . . perhaps you will learn to love him after a time . . . and after a fashion."

Guinevere stared at me, and for the first time I saw hints of genuine vulnerability in her eyes. "It is easy for you to say," she told me. "You are not being asked to give up your maidenhead in a marriage of convenience."

"Would that I had been," I said, "rather than ordered to do so by a cruel master who saw me as nothing more than chattel."

She opened her mouth and then shut it again. "Oh," was all she said for a time, and then in a low voice she added, "Yes, I had . . . forgotten about that . . ."

We remained there in silence for a time, Guinevere still seated upon the ground, me leaning back against a tree. Finally she said to me, "How did you not allow it to break your spirit?"

"By knowing that others could control my body no matter what my desires might be, but none could control my mind. This," and I plucked at the skin on my forearm, "this mere flesh . . . this is not who we are. It is just what others see. Who we are is within, and that no master has ever been able to touch, no matter how he may paw or molest my body."

Guinevere smiled at that. "How you talk, Viviana. How you do talk." She finally got to her feet then, brushing the dirt from her clothes. "I suppose that Arthur is a rather comely individual."

"He is, rather," I said.

"And easily malleable."

"Very much so."

"I could mold him, I suppose. Shape him into something useful and not too horrible."

"And he would be thanking you the entire time for doing so. As would the kingdom," I said. "For he will be king one day, and there will be many people here who will serve you and accommodate you in exactly the same way as all those people of Cameliard have done your entire life. And they could use a king who is wise and strong . . ."

"Rather than a vacuous oaf?"

"I did not say that."

"You did not have to."

Honestly, I thought she was being a bit too hard on Arthur. Still, this was not the time to mount a strident defense.

She touched her right hip tenderly and winced. "Damnation," she said, and then limped carefully toward her horse. She did not bound onto the palfrey as she had earlier; instead she tried to pull herself up and winced once more. I went over to her, cupping my hands, and providing her additional leverage to mount the horse. She looked down at me from atop the horse and said, "How do you know I will not ride away again?"

"I do not know," I said. "I can merely hope. One never gives up hope."

"No. I suppose one never does," she said. She inclined her head toward the jennet. "Well? Mount up. It is a long ride back to the castle."

"Yes, milady," I said, trying to sound as humble and subservient as I could.

We rode slowly back toward the castle. The jennet appeared relieved not to have to sprint in futility after the palfrey. The palfrey seemed indifferent to the whole matter.

Guinevere said not much of anything on the trip back, but my mind was racing over all that had transpired and I was coming to conclusions. Upon our return, I went straight to Merlin's study. I did not do so lightly. There was much about the apothecary that I still found daunting. Nevertheless I needed to speak to him.

I found him there, studying scrolls that were laid out upon a reading table before him. He looked mildly surprised when I entered. He said nothing; merely cocked an eyebrow and waited for me to speak.

"I hate you," I announced.

He did not seem put off. "That is only because you do not yet know me well. Once you do, you will grow to loathe me."

"It was your doing," I said.

"Very likely it was," he said. He paused and then added, "What are we talking about?"

"Guinevere tried to flee through the woods."

"Ah."

"On horseback."

"That would be the way to do it."

"And a branch knocked her off her horse."

"Did it knock some sense into her as well?"

I advanced upon him. My legs were trembling but I felt compelled to confront him. "You spoke of how you had woodsmen at your command. I think one of them was up in the tree and applied force to the branch, bending it so that it was in her path when she rode into it and was thrown off her mount."

"Is that what you think?"

"Yes. So why did you need me? If you already had your woodsmen in position, then Guinevere's failure to escape was already assured. Why were my futile endeavors to prevent her leaving required?"

"Mistress Viviana, has it occurred to you that I cannot keep an eye on the queen every hour of the day? So I must recruit others to attend to it if, and when, I cannot. Allowing for the notion, of course, that what you said happened represents the truth. I do not necessarily admit that that is what happened."

"Well?" I prompted. "Is that what happened?"

Merlin carefully rolled up the scroll that he had been reading and placed it into a leather tube. "You will find as you go through life, Mistress Viviana, that if you can prompt people to think that matters transpired in a certain way, then the actuality of what happened is irrelevant. One might even go so far as to say that there is no such thing as reality; merely perceptions of reality. History is not fact. History is shaped by those who describe it."

"That is not true," I said. "Things happen in a certain way. Varying descriptions do not change the actuality of the events."

"What does actuality matter? Only the impact that the events have on those who learn of it matters. And they learn of it through historians. As a budding historian, Mistress Viviana, I would have thought you would know that."

"Milord, I—"

"Quiet." He raised a finger and I immediately fell silent.

Merlin got up from his table and walked over to the nearby shelves. He pushed aside rolls of parchment containers and I saw there, much to my surprise, a large assortment of books. I had seen very few books in my time, and never so many together. He studied them for a moment and then withdrew one from the shelf. It was sizable but not extraordinarily heavy.

He brought it back to me and handed it to me. I stared at the cover in reverence. Then I slowly placed the book on the table and opened it gingerly. The pages were crisp and crackled with authority as I turned them. A smell of must and wisdom rose from them. I looked at the title.

"*Aesop's Fables?*" I said.

He nodded. "They are short tales. Morality plays, if you will. They are, each and every one, fiction. Yet they mold and shape the way that others perceive the world. There is more truth in those fictions than there is in truth. Read them. Read the lessons therein. Learn from them. Then return the book to me. Once you have done so, I will lend you a book of writings by a Greek named Plutarch. He was a historian . . . much as you are, even if you do not willingly acknowledge it yet. In this particular history, Plutarch spent time detailing the lives of various noblemen. I believe you will find it educational."

"Why . . . why are you . . . ?"

"Why am I doing this?" I nodded. "Because, Mistress Viviana, I find you interesting. And I believe you could be of use to me. The simplest way to ensure that is for me to be of use to you. Fair exchange for fair value. You have the potential to make a lasting contribution to the human condition."

I laughed at that. "That is nonsense, sir. I am a slave."

"So was Aesop. Yet his words have crossed the centuries to wind up in your hands. Who is to say you cannot accomplish the same for others, centuries hence? Not I, certainly. It is for you to say, Mistress Viviana. Only you."

He turned away from me then, the audience clearly ended. I

left his chambers, clutching the book to my breast and bringing it with me down to the section of floor near the hearth that was my home. It was not until much later, when I was deeply engrossed in a tale involving some sour grapes, that I realized I had totally forgotten my anger with Merlin that had compelled me to seek him out in the first place.

Perhaps he was the wizard that people claimed him to be after all.

Day the Thirty-Fourth

ROWENA AWAKENED ME RUDELY THIS morning, shouting at me
in a most accusatory nature. I was groggy at first but I came
fully awake when I saw that she was waving about the book of
fables. "Whence did you steal this, girl? Answer me!" she fairly
snarled.

"I did not steal it! It was given me by Merlin!"

"He did no such thing and I have had a bellyful of you,
missy!" She waggled her finger at me as if I was a child, and her
face purpled with rage. "But I have you now, I surely do!"

"Fine," I said, my conscience clear. "Let us go to Merlin
then and ask him."

"We will go nowhere. But you will."

Suddenly I was grabbed by either arm. I looked around
in confusion and saw several other women were holding me
tightly. I knew I had earned myself no friends in my stay
there but—fool that I was—I had no clue that others of my
station bore such ill will toward me. In retrospect, I suppose
I should have seen it coming, but I did not. I may be an
acute observer of other people's lives, yet it would seem I am

depressingly blind to my own.

"Take her down to the stables," she said. "Give her to the stable master."

"Even better," chortled one of the women, "give her to the mute. He hasn't had a woman in some time."

"I don't know that even she deserves that," said Rowena.

I had no idea to whom she was referring. I had been down to the stables but seen no one who was mute. Nor, from their description, was I especially eager to meet him.

I pulled fiercely at the women who were holding me but they were too strong. I opened my mouth to offer protest, but a gag was already being drawn over my mouth. "I am wise to your ways," Rowena said. "Even the most talented of witches cannot cast spells if she cannot speak."

"Release her."

Rowena gasped, startled at the unexpected voice that seemed to materialize at her right elbow. She looked down and there was Modred. His pale complexion emphasized his eerie demeanor. What was even more disconcerting was that Rowena was facing the main door to the room and Modred had not entered that way. She jumped a good foot or so in the air. "What . . . how did . . . ?" She seemed unable to complete a sentence.

"I said . . . release her." He turned to the women who were on either side of me. They were no longer pulling at me. They seemed spellbound by him. One of them was actually trembling; I could feel it. "Are you deaf as well as stupid?"

"How . . . how dare . . ." Rowena made another valiant

attempt to string words together.

Modred turned his pale blue eyes upon her. He spoke with the voice of a child but the dangerous intonations of a most threatening adult. "I," he said, "do not need my mouth to cast spells. All I have to do is think, and so mote it be. Would you like to know what I am thinking right now? It involves you, so you would probably be best served to know precisely what—"

"Release her!" Rowena said, gesturing frantically for them to let go my arms.

The women did so, transfixed by Modred's stare. It was at that point I realized that, since arriving in the kitchen moments earlier, he had yet to blink.

"That was very wise," said Modred. He never spoke above a low tone. He stood perfectly still, like a tree, his hands at his sides. He shifted his gaze to me. "Viviana, gather your things; you are leaving here. Morgan and Guinevere have requested that you become a permanent part of our retinue. I was sent to fetch you."

All I could do was nod. I quickly gathered my bag, making certain that my writing utensils were within. I faced Rowena and put my hand out expectantly. She hesitated, then growled and handed me the book of fables. "To hell with you. Now you can be somebody else's problem." She spat on the floor directly in front of my feet.

I looked at the small puddle of spittle and said, "I pity whomever you will order to clean that up." I flashed a quick smile, then turned and followed Modred out the door. The other women stepped aside as I went, glaring at me. I did not care. Let them all rot in hell.

I followed Modred down a corridor. There were still bruises on his face from when the boys had beaten him, and they stood out in stark contrast to his pale skin. I noticed that people who saw him coming tended to step out of his way. They cast nervous glances toward me as well, as if concerned that I was being led off to be made a human sacrifice or some such. It was a ridiculous worry. I hoped that they did not in fact have a reason for it.

He stopped in front of a hanging tapestry that depicted a unicorn being savaged by a couple of hunting dogs. I knew how the mythical beast felt. Modred glanced around, apparently to make certain that we were unobserved, and then he said conspiratorially, "Would you care to see something?"

"All . . . all right," I said. I had no idea what to expect.

He pulled the tapestry aside and then pushed on the wall. To my shock a section of it swung inward, revealing some sort of hidden passage. "Quickly," he said.

By all rights, I should have declined the invitation. Instead I stepped through. Moments later Modred had moved in behind me and slid the wall shut. We were enfolded in darkness.

Modred's head seemed to float disembodied near me, the rest of his body obscured by the blackness of his attire. "What is this place?" I whispered. I have no idea why I lowered my voice. It just seemed the correct thing to do.

"Come this way," he said rather than answer.

His hand folded around mine. It was cold, unnaturally so. I shuddered inwardly; it was as if a corpse had reached up from the grave and taken my hand. Modred guided me through the darkness. My eyes slowly began to adjust. I could make out vague shapes. Then I yelped as my toe struck what turned out to be a stair. It was the bottom of a staircase and I followed Modred as he pulled me through.

"Stop," he said softly. I did as he instructed. He moved aside a brick, leaving a small hole in the wall, and then indicated that I should look through. I did so and gasped.

I was looking straight into Arthur's bedchamber. Arthur was still abed. He was lying on his back. His eyes were open and he had a blissful expression on his face. His hand was moving up and down beneath the sheet in a curious manner. Then I realized.

"My God," I blurted out, and then yanked my head away from the hole.

In the darkness, Modred showed his teeth in a mirthless smile. From the other side of the wall I heard Arthur call out, "Who's there? Where are you?" I clapped my hands over my mouth. Even though a wall separated us, I was terrified to make the slightest noise. My own heart sounded deafening as the blood pounded against my ears.

Long moments passed and then the rhythmic rustling of the sheet recommenced.

Almost stumbling, I headed up the narrow passageway that stretched away from us. Modred replaced the brick and followed.

I kept going, as if I could somehow leave that awful image behind me. As a result, since my eyes had still not fully adjusted to the darkness, I ran headlong into an unmoving wall. I almost fell backwards except Modred was behind me, putting a hand in the small of my back to stop me. I leaned forward and, to my surprise, the entire wall swung open. Light flooded the passageway. I took a tentative step forward and emerged into familiar surroundings: the high tower where I had talked with Arthur. I was amazed, having not had the slightest idea that this means of egress existed.

Modred stepped in behind me. He flinched back from the pool of light filtered through the window, stepping delicately around it as if it was something virulent. He took a place several steps up and then simply sat there and stared at me.

"Was that not interesting?" he said.

"Interesting?" My stomach heaved and it was only then that I remembered I had eaten nothing yet that morning. I had never been quite so grateful for extending my fast. "That was horrid. Invasive. I feel terrible."

"What was he doing?"

"What do you mean? Did you not see?"

"Yes. But I am not sure I understand. Why was he smiling like such a fool?"

I looked at him, thinking that he was making some sort of jest. I realized then that he was not. "I . . ." My lips were suddenly dry. I licked them and said, "I . . . honestly do not know. I . . . believe he was having a pleasant dream."

"Then why was it invasive and horrid?"

"Well, because . . ." I cleared my throat and forced a smile. "Because it is not appropriate to spy on people when they are dreaming."

"Oh."

I was not sure if that explanation satisfied him. I doubted very much that it did. There seemed to be so much going on in Modred's head at any given moment that it was difficult to determine what he was thinking about anything.

"What . . . are these?" I said, pointing in the direction of the hidden passage, the entranceway to which was still open.

"Secret ways through the wall. Built into the castle when it was first constructed. I am not sure that anyone recalls that they were put here in the first place. But I found them when I first came here. I was perhaps four summers old," he said with a touch of pride. "I looked closely, as I always do. Saw a brick in the wall that was half the size of all the ones around it. I pushed on it and found an entrance. They go all through the castle. There are other entrances as well. Through a bookshelf. A fireplace. Now that you know this is here, you can find them as well."

"I very much doubt that I will be using these passages."

"Yes, you will. You will not be able to help yourself."

I could not help but wonder if he had a point. As awful as I felt about having espied Arthur during such an inopportune time, there was something terribly attractive about the notion of being able to watch people during their unguarded moments. At my core, I am an observer of those around me, and an advantage I have always had as a slave is that people tend not to put on airs or pretend to be aught but what they are when I am around. As a servant and slave, I am a non-entity. Still, the prospect of being able to watch what went on behind closed doors . . .

I shuddered then. It seemed such a terrible thing to contemplate. What would that make me, if I were to stoop to such behavior? I thought of the things Merlin had said to me. But even if I fancied myself an historian, how much could really be excused in the pursuit of recording history?

Modred appeared to have lost interest in me. Instead he stared balefully at the pool of sunlight inches from his feet. "Why did you stop those boys from hurting me?"

"It is as I told your cousin. I could not simply stand by and allow them to hurt you."

"Yes. You could have. You chose not to. Why?"

"I do not know."

"I think you do."

I considered it for a time. He did not look away from me. He continued not to blink. I do not believe there has ever been a boy so casually disturbing as Modred.

"Those boys," I said at last, "would be knights. But knights should aspire to an ideal of behavior. Those boys were, in their actions toward you, not chivalrous. That . . . offended me, I suppose."

"So it was not as much about me as it was about them."

"It was both, I imagine."

"Knights are brutes."

I gave him a scolding look. "Only the brutish ones are. The good knights, though, the great knights . . ."

"Such as who? Name one."

"Galahad," I said instantly, and regretted having done so, for I knew that I had committed myself to a path that would only make me sound foolish to the boy.

His eyebrows, as white as the rest of him, arched. "Who?"

"He is no one."

Modred would have none of my retractions. "You brought him up. Who is he?"

I rolled my eyes, feeling unaccountably foolish. "He is no one, literally. He is someone I made up."

"Made up?"

"Fabricated. I . . . ." I tried to determine the best way to explain it to him. "My life is not always easy. I am sure that you can sympathize." He nodded and I went on. "When I am faced with the casual cruelties that life has to offer, I like to . . . to . . ."

"Take your mind elsewhere?"

I was amazed that this child had summarized it so well. He seemed far older than his years. "Yes. That is exactly right. It is a means of escape, I know, but one does what one must to survive, I suppose. And when I do take my mind away . . . Galahad is there." I stopped and laughed softly. "I cannot believe I am telling you of this. I have never told anyone."

"Did anyone ever ask?"

"No," I admitted.

He leaned back and said, "Tell me about Galahad."

"Well . . . he is . . . he is strong. And brave." I began to warm to the subject. "Very tall, with broad shoulders and a soul as pure as a nun's prayers. He is kind to all and uses the great skills God has provided him to help those weaker than he."

"Does he have adventures?"

"Of course. What great knight would not have adventures?"

"Tell me one."

Truly, for the first time, Modred seemed to be acting his age. He no longer seemed a ghost or a foreboding figure, but merely a boy who desired to be entertained.

So I told him. I told him of how Galahad had first sojourned to a great court overseen by a great king, and several of the mighty feats of generosity and heroism that he performed en route. And how the court of the great king was wracked with dissent and frustration because they were laboring under a great curse, a curse that condemned them to endless fighting and warfare and could only be broken by the finding of a pure vessel called the Holy Grail. And that a great hero would arrive to fulfill the quest, and he would be known because he would sit in a chair called the Siege Perilous that killed lesser men, but not him. And Galahad arrived in the court, and it was deserted, and footsore and weary, Galahad sat in the chair without realizing what it was.

"And nothing happened to him," said Modred.

I nodded approvingly. "That is correct."

"And did he find the Holy Grail?"

"I do not know."

"How can you not know?"

"Because I have not figured that out yet. Galahad only exists in my imagination, Modred. That is part of what makes him so special."

For a moment I thought he was going to petulantly insist that I figure out the story of the Holy Grail right then and there. Instead he appeared to give the matter some thought. Finally he said, "When you do know, will you tell me?"

"You will be the very first I inform."

"Have you written it down?"

I blinked in surprise at the notion. "No, I . . . had not. Which is odd, I suppose. I write down everything else."

"I would like you to write down what you know of him for me, so that I can read it whenever I wish. I would provide you the paper you need to do so."

I tried not to laugh. "Is that a command?"

His expression did not change but his pale blue eyes seemed to harden. "If that is what is necessary. I should hope it would not be."

I was taken aback by the change in his voice but tried not to show it. It seemed to me, though, that Modred was a most difficult lad to pin down. There was so much going through his mind that it threatened to overwhelm him.

I hope that it does not tear him apart someday.

"Very well," I said cautiously. "Tonight, if you wish, I will—"

"Now," he said.

"All . . . all right. Now, then."

We reentered the hidden walkways of the castle. My eyes were adjusting more quickly, and I found that I could guide myself with more confidence by trailing my hands along the wall. Modred took us off a different path than that which we had followed before, for which I was relieved. I had no desire to pass near Arthur's chambers anytime soon.

Modred pushed aside the wall and stepped through, and I followed. I was surprised—although I suppose I should not have been—to find myself in Morgan's chambers.

"Wait here," said Modred. I did as he bade and he returned minutes later with pen and paper. I only realize now, belatedly, as I pen these words, that it never occurred to me to ask how Modred knew that I was literate. Yet now that the thought crosses my mind, perhaps it is preferable that I did not inquire. I might not have liked the answer, assuming that I received an answer at all.

I began to write down all that I "knew" about Galahad. I discovered in doing so that it was actually enjoyable. I had never written down anything except the things that had happened to me in my day-to-day life. It had literally never occurred to me to inscribe things that were false. It lent permanence to fabrications and that did not seem right to me somehow. It was the equivalent of elevating lies to truth and might even have been considered sinful. But as I scribbled Galahad's adventures for Modred's entertainment, I realized that if the Greek slave, Aesop, had likewise confined his fables to oral tradition, then I would not have been exposed to them centuries later.

Modred took each sheet of parchment as I finished filling it with words and read it eagerly, nodding on occasion, smiling on others. I kept stealing glances toward him to see his reactions. Once again he seemed more like a boy than before. Perhaps he could not decide what he was supposed to be and therein lay his problem.

I finally finished the last of what I knew of Galahad and handed it to Modred. As I did so, the chamber door opened and Morgan walked in. She seemed lost in thought and so stepped back, startled, when she saw me. "Viviana," she said after a moment, looking from me to Modred and back to me again. I lay down the quill and the gesture caught her attention. She saw the black smudges of fresh ink on my hands and fingers. "How now?"

"With respect, milady . . . Modred informed me that I was to serve you from now on."

Morgan looked quite surprised. "Me? No. I put in no such request. I am not in need of another servant."

My heart sank. I was not enamored of the prospect of returning to the kitchen. If my life was hellish before, I did not even want to contemplate what it would become thanks to my leave taking of Rowena. I looked to Modred. His face was devoid of any childish airs. It was back to being a slate as blank of expression as his skin was of color. He was gently waving the last parchment back and forth to expedite its drying.

"Morgan!"

It was the sharp voice of Guinevere. She entered the room, looking most put out. "You cannot simply walk away when we are in the midst of . . ." Her voice trailed off when she saw me. "What are you doing here, Viviana?"

I suddenly saw a way out of my situation. "The lady Morgan was just discussing the prospect of adding me to her serving staff," I said. "It would, of course, be a great honor . . ."

"How dare you!" said Guinevere, turning to Morgan, her temper flaring. "I went riding with her yesterday and suddenly you wish to snatch her away?"

"I wish no such thing," said Morgan, looking bewildered.

"Do not lie to me, Morgan." Guinevere shook a scolding finger at her. "You may be able to fool others, but not me. Never me."

"I was not trying to . . ." Then she ceased endeavoring to gainsay Guinevere and shrugged. "Very well. Whatever you say, dear sister."

Guinevere gave her a poisonous look and then said, "You can have my two ladies in waiting." Morgan started to offer up protest, but Guinevere continued, "I know they serve as spies for you or our father. Let them be your problem then. And do not think we are finished discussing the . . . other matter. Come, Viviana," she said, gesturing commandingly.

I followed her, looking as docile as I could. I cast one quick glance behind me. Morgan looked puzzled as if she was still trying to figure out what happened. Modred was busy reading the pages I had just finished writing.

Guinevere went straight back to her chambers where—as good as her word—she informed her ladies in waiting that they would be henceforth attending to Morgan's needs. They scowled at me in a manner that I assume they thought was fearsome. Compared to what I had endured from individuals ranging from slave masters to Rowena, they were amateurs. "Thank you, milady," I began to say after they departed, "I—"

"Quiet."

I silenced myself immediately.

She walked up to me and studied me up and down. "Let us come to an understanding, you and I. I think you are presumptuous . . . exceedingly so for one of your station. You had the temerity to lecture me in the woods and I took great offense at that."

"You hid your anger well, milady."

"I am trained to keep my emotions hidden."

If that happened to be the case, then I could not help but think that whoever trained her had performed miserably in their task, for Guinevere was a remarkably easy woman to read. She hid her emotions the way that a woman nine months heavy with child concealed her belly. I think she simply regretted that she had allowed herself to lower her guard with me and would be damned if she would admit it now.

She walked back and forth in front of me. "I had been considering dispensing with my family's spies and am now taking the opportunity to do so. You are to answer to me and only to me. You are not to have congress with Morgan or Modred or even my father. Anything that you witness, you are not to repeat to anyone. I do not need to concern myself that you are going to serve as eyes or ears for those who would do me ill. Do you understand all of that?"

"Yes, milady."

"Good. Also, I desire one other thing of you."

"Yes, milady?"

"Speak honestly to me."

I did not quite understand. "About what, milady?"

"About whatever seems relevant to a conversation. They," and she nodded disdainfully in the direction of the departed handmaidens, "would simply smile and say, 'Yes, milady' and 'no milady.' It annoyed me mightily."

"But . . . they were handmaidens. Were they not simply serving their function?"

"It is not a function that is of interest to me."

"What would you then, milady? To be attended by people whom you actively dislike and will speak their mind knowing that it could well annoy you?"

"Yes."

"Oh," I said. "Then . . . this should work out, I suppose."

I remained with her the rest of the day and in the evening was assigned simple quarters that were directly adjacent to her chambers. It was cramped, not much larger than a stable, with a straw mattress on the floor. But it was mine, all mine.

As I recount the events of this day, I am moved to wonder whether, in doing so, I am violating the promise I made to Guinevere. It could be argued that I should not be keeping a record of these events. When I contemplate ceasing keeping my journal, however, I find I simply cannot do it. There is too much of me invested in these pages. Besides, I am not "repeating" anything to anyone, as she said. I am merely recording my own observations for my private reading.

That is certainly a very different thing. However I think I shall keep the fact of my diary to myself, lest lady Guinevere disagree.

Day the Thirty-Sixth

I SAW THE MUTE TODAY.

We were down in the stable. I was aiding Guinevere in grooming her horse. She says she trusts no one else to do it.

As she brushed out the palfrey's mane, I asked her if she was at all interested in telling me what she had been arguing with Morgan about the previous day. She simply stared at me and shook her head. I stepped back and then spotted a figure hovering in the corner of the stables. From the way he was lurking about, for a moment I thought it was Modred. Then I realized that he was not simply lurking, but was mucking out one of the stables. He had stopped in his endeavors and was staring right at me.

He was rather awful to look at. His face and arms were covered with grime, and his long brown hair was rat-tailed and hanging in his face. A smell wafted from him that was forceful and nearly overpowering. "Hello," I called to him tentatively. "Is there a problem?"

Guinevere noticed and stepped by my side to see better who I was looking at. Her noise wrinkled as she detected the same aroma I did. "You," she said. "A woman has spoken to you. It is customary to answer; whether you are of noble or ignoble birth, it matters not."

He did not reply. Instead he simply continued to stare.

"Ye'll get no answer from him, yer worship." The head groomer, a squat fellow with a belly hanging over his breeches, approached us and chucked a thumb toward the unspeaking man. "He's a mute."

"Is he? Tongue cut out?" Guinevere did not seem appalled by the notion; just curious.

"Do not rightly know, yer worship. He always just has been, long as he's been here, since he was a young'un. Says nothing. Just mucks out the stables, does as he's told. Never asked more of 'im than that."

"I suppose not. Well, mute, if you're not deaf as well as dumb, I suggest you go about your business."

He did not respond, which should not have been all that surprising for a mute. But the way he was continuing to stare at me . . . it might well have been my imagination, but I felt as if he was imagining me unclothed. Without even thinking about it, I put one arm across my breast and the other hand in front of my nether regions. Then I realized I was doing it and, feeling foolish, let my hands drop to my side.

"I said," Guinevere repeated, anger lacing her voice, "that you should—"

He did not wait for her to complete her sentence. Instead he turned his back to her and returned to mucking out the stables.

I remembered how the kitchen servants, when Rowena had them manhandling me, spoke gleefully of turning me over to the mute down in the stables. Obviously this was he of whom they had spoken. How many mutes in the stables could there possibly be, if one did not count the horses? A shudder went through me as I imagined being subjected to his . . . attentions.

Still, I asked the groomsman, "What is his name?"

"Don't rightly know. He never said."

"He is a mute. He could not possibly tell you."

"Yeah. I know," said the groomsman and then brayed laughter like a mule, which indicated to me that perhaps he was spending far too much time in the stables.

Day the Thirty-Seventh

ARTHUR STOPPED BY GUINEVERE'S CHAMBERS today.

Guinevere was not there, for her father desired to speak to her privately. So, having naught else to attend to, I was reading more of the Greek slave's morality tales when I looked up and Arthur was standing there with that same sheepish expression he typically bore. "Greetings . . ." He paused, frowning.

"Viviana," I said.

"Right. Viviana. Greetings. Is Guinevere about?"

I explained that she was not and where she was. I was having difficulty holding his gaze, for my thoughts were upon what I had accidentally witnessed the other day and I was shamed to look him in the eye. "Is something amiss?" he said.

"What? No. No, sire, not at all."

"Well . . . good." He seemed quite satisfied with my less-than-convincing protest of all being right. "You will tell the lady that I came by, will you not?"

"Of course."

I rather expected him to leave at that point. He did not. Instead he stood there for a moment, as if caught in an internal struggle, and then he turned and shut the heavy door behind him. I was puzzled but said nothing.

"What does she think of me?" said Arthur.

I was taken aback by the question. "That . . . is not for me to say, sire."

"It actually is, if I so ask. I am, after all, heir to the throne." There was something in his voice that had not been present in the previous times that we had spoken. There was an edge, and perhaps even a hint of desperation that he was barely able to contain. "If I ask a question of you, you are bound to answer."

"With respect, sire, replying that it is not for me to say is an answer. It is simply not an answer you like."

Abruptly he drew back his hand and for half a heartbeat he looked ready to strike me. I flinched, my eyes wide.

Arthur froze that way and then stared at his hand as if it belonged to someone else. Then slowly he lowered it. We stood there a moment, unspeaking. He did not apologize. Someone in his position could not. That was understood without having to be said. The closest he came was saying, "I have been under a good deal of strain lately."

"I can imagine."

"Can you?"

I considered it and said "Probably not."

"Tell me this, then, if you cannot speak of that which you know of a certainty . . . tell me instead of your speculation. Do you think she could come to love me?"

"I do not know, sire."

"I am not asking what you know. I am asking what you think."

"I think that the human heart cannot be predicted, nor can a woman's mind."

"Thus am I doubly damned." He sighed. "Not that marriage need be about love. Most of the time it is not, really. True?"

"Well . . . not necessarily, sire. Many peasants, servants . . . they marry out of love. Out of a desire to be together."

"People who have nothing, in other words."

"In a world where they have nothing, I suppose having each other is important." I looked at his face. It was the first time I was able to look directly at him since he had walked into the room. "You . . . find that amusing, sire?"

"More ironic, I suppose. People at my level rarely marry for love, but rather to establish treaties or create alliances between powerful families. Those at the level just below us marry for financial gain. It is only the poor who have the luxury of marrying for love since they have nothing else of value."

"Perhaps love is the most valuable thing of all, sire?"

"Love does not provide food for the table, clothes for the back, or a roof over one's head."

"Granted. But if you did not consider it important, you would not have come here asking about it."

"I never said it was not important. It simply has little practicality. Nevertheless . . ." He shrugged. "I was just . . . curious. A foolish thing to be curious about, I suppose. But my father never tires of telling me what a foolish creature I am, so I suppose there is something to be said for consistency."

The door swung open and Guinevere entered. She stopped and looked momentarily surprised when she saw Arthur and me standing there. "Oh. Speak of the devil," she said.

"Were you speaking of me?" he said.

She explained that she had indeed been speaking of him, to her father. That her father had informed her that plans for the wedding appeared to be dragging and the principle reason for that was the bride and groom. Neither seemed especially interested in expediting the process, and Leodegrance was apparently getting pressure from Uther who now seemed rather determined to make certain that Arthur and Guinevere were bonded. Treaties and kingdoms, it seemed, were tottering on the outcome, and neither king was interested in waiting any longer to get matters sorted out.

Once Guinevere finished informing Arthur of all this, the two of them then faced each other in uncomfortable silence. I was unsure of what I should do. It seemed intrusive that I was there at such a personal time but Guinevere had not indicated that I should depart.

I said nothing. It was not my place.

"Do you want to marry me?" Arthur said finally.

Guinevere appeared surprised that he would even ask. "I was led to believe that what I want or do not want is of little importance," she said.

"Not to me. I mean," he amended upon realizing his meaning wasn't clear, "it is not of little importance to me."

"That is not the impression I had from the evening when our marriage was arranged. Rather it was my impression that you would do whatever your father ordered you to do."

"I am obliged to obey him, but not because he is my father," said Arthur quietly. "I am obliged to obey him because he is my king. If I, who am to be king, do not respect the importance of fealty to one's monarch, then who can be expected to?"

"Then you admit that my own concerns are of no importance."

Arthur rubbed his temples, looking as if he were developing an ill humor. "I suppose you are right. I just did not wish to admit it. You are far smarter than I, Guinevere. We both know that. You always have been. I suppose that is why you have always despised me."

"I have never despised you, Arthur," she said. "Why do people keep accusing me of despising others?" This remark was aimed at me, obviously. "I just . . . well . . . you always seemed more suited for Morgan, and she for you. And besides, truth be told, I never saw myself as the marrying sort. Still . . ." and now she cast a quick glance in my direction, "I suppose there is some matter of obligation upon me in exchange for the years of privilege I have enjoyed."

"I do not wish to have a woman marry me out of obligation," said Arthur.

"Perhaps not, Arthur, but let us be realistic. It is very likely the only way a woman will marry you."

"Now wait a minute!" Arthur seemed rather irked, and I could not blame him. "I am going to be a king, you know! Someday! And I am not entirely without attractive aspects! I am . . . I mean, I have been told that I am not terrible to look upon."

"No, you are not," she made the admission. It could have

been my imagination, but she seemed amused at Arthur's annoyance with her.

"And I am a rather decent fellow. I try not to hurt anyone. I can be a pleasant conversationalist, so they say. And . . ."

"What do you believe in?"

Arthur appeared taken aback by the question. "Pardon?"

"It is a simple enough question. What do you believe in? If you were king, or I should say, when you become king, what do you wish to do? What do you want to accomplish? What is your guiding goal and philosophy? Who and what, in short, will you be?"

He thought about that for a very, very long time. He even looked to me for help, but I offered none.

Finally he gave a long, heavy sigh and said, "I have nary the faintest idea."

To his astonishment, and mine, Guinevere smiled, then leaned forward and kissed him chastely on the cheek.

"I believe I can work with that," she said.

He looked with concern at her outfit, the long tunic and leggings that she preferred. "Will you start wearing dresses?"

"On formal occasions, perhaps. Otherwise, no."

"I believe I can work with that," he said.

And so did Arthur and Guinevere become engaged.

Day the Forty-Seventh

THE GUESTS ARE BEGINNING TO gather at Camelot for the marriage ceremony.

The first to arrive was Guinevere's mother, Sirona. She looked like an older version of Guinevere, but more put upon, even tired. That could have been from the trip, though. Guinevere greeted her with a distant politeness, as did Uther Pendragon. Her face was expressionless when she saw Uther. I do not think she liked him much, or he her. Then again, neither of them was marrying each other, so that should not have posed too much of a problem.

Knights were showing up, and kings. I did not know who most of them were, nor did anyone bother to introduce me to them because, really, why would they? I heard that King Lot of Lothan was there, as was Melwas of the Summer Country and King Hoel of Brittainy and King Pellinore of the Isles and his sons, Sir Tor and Sir Percival. And Maleagant was in attendance—the Great Stone Warlord, as he was called, for his fabled strength and endurance. He purportedly had little love for Uther or Arthur but did not have the following to do anything about it. Other knights, such as Sirs Dinadan and Gawain were also said to have arrived, and also Sir Palamedes the Saracin. I hoped to catch a glimpse of him since I had never seen a Saracin and they were reputed to be most exotic looking individuals.

I have been most busy aiding Eowyn in preparing Guinevere for the wedding. The dress that is being crafted for her is nothing short of magnificent. Guinevere appears to be settling nicely into the role of bride to be. She is actually even smiling on a regular basis. However the other day I caught her looking in a mirror, practicing that selfsame smile. So that would seem to indicate that it is manufactured rather than genuine. Then again, it is hard ever to be fully certain as far as Guinevere is concerned.

I have only encountered one knight definitively whose identity I learned, and I very much wish I had not. His name is Lancelot du Lac. He is the most obnoxious Frenchman I have ever met, and that is saying something because I have met more than my share of Frenchmen.

Eowyn had brought me down to the wine cellar to help her survey the casks and barrels, to make certain that there would be sufficient stores for the wedding and subsequent celebration. She had me keeping count with an abacus as to how many casks were filled. I did not inform her that I could write and keep detailed records using quill and paper. I was already uncomfortable with the number of people who were aware of that fact.

"And this one," she said, but then rapped on it with her

knuckles. A hollow sound came back to her and she frowned. "This one should be full. Someone has been at the casks. Any ideas as to identity, Viviana?"

"None, mistress."

"We shall have to send word to the winery to . . ."

Her voice trailed off as she looked at something behind me. I turned to see what she was staring at.

It was Lancelot du Lac, although I did not yet know him by that name. He was tall and lean, his black hair was cut very short, and there was nobility to his features that was not reflected in his bearing. He was wearing a white surcoat with a red eagle emblazoned upon it, but the way he leaned forward gave him more the appearance of a hungry vulture. Indeed, he studied us as if we were the carrion upon which he was planning to feast.

He was holding a wine sack in his hand. How appropriate considering he was little more than a walking wine sack himself. He upended it to display that it was empty. "If you will excuse me, madam . . . mad'moiselle," he said to Eowyn and me respectively, "I wish to replenish." His thick Gaulois accent betrayed his origins.

Eowyn spoke carefully, for this man was clearly a knight and also a guest within Camelot, so full attention to decorum had to be paid. "With all respect, sir knight, I would ask you to refrain at this time. We must husband the current resources of wine available to us for the upcoming celebration."

"Do you truly think," he said, "that the amount I might imbibe would possibly make that significant a difference to your stores?"

I could tell by the look on Eowyn's face that she was thinking the exact same thing that I was. That this man could probably decimate the wine supply singlehandedly.

"That is not the point, sir," Eowyn said as delicately as she could. "The point actually is that—"

"The point, madam," said the knight, wavering unsteadily on his feet, "is that I am Sir Lancelot du Lac of Joyous Guard, and a guest of Uther Pendragon, and you will get the hell out of my way!"

Credit Eowyn that she did not back down in the face of such behavior. "And I, sir, am Eowyn, without any sort of joyful guards, and this is Viviana, and we are in the employ of Uther Pendragon and charged with making certain that all aspects of this affair are attended to in an orderly manner. And you, sir, are behaving in a most disorderly manner, and I will thank you to sleep off the considerable amounts that you have clearly already imbibed before you drain further of our stores!"

This speech did not go over well with Lancelot du Lac.

"How dare you!" he thundered. He reached around to his back and produced a short sword that neither Eowyn nor I had seen, because if we had, I am reasonably sure that Eowyn would never have considered gainsaying him. Whether you are king or cook, thwarting the will of an armed drunken man is an unwise course of action.

Eowyn's eyes widened in alarm and she took a step back, trying to say things to placate Lancelot. None of them appeared to have the slightest effect. Truthfully, I could not even tell if he heard what she was saying. Instead he advanced upon her, wavering but no less dangerous. He went right past me, paying me no mind, his focus entirely on Eowyn. She screamed, but we were down in the wine cellar and the odds were that her voice would not carry to anyone who could provide succor in time.

I did the only thing I could with what I had on hand. As Lancelot passed me, I swung the abacus with as much force as I could muster. It slammed against the back of his head and shattered, beads spilling everywhere. Lancelot staggered, turned, and glowered at me, his eyes red rimmed and angry. I backed up, holding only a few splintered shards of the abacus.

"You . . ." he said with a snarl, and came right at me, his short sword extended. There was nowhere for me to go to avoid it.

"Beware, Viviana!" Eowyn cried out rather unnecessarily.

Then his feet hit the beads that were scattered on the floor. He let out a startled yell and clawed at thin air, trying to keep his balance, but did not succeed. His feet went flying out from under him. Lancelot fell sideways, shouting a string of what I imagined were Gaulois profanities as he did so, and then he struck his head on the nearest cask of wine. The sound of crunching was so calamitous that, despite the fact that he had just been trying to kill us, I shuddered upon hearing it. Lancelot slumped to the floor. He tried to rise, but then I watched his eyes roll up into his head and he passed out.

Eowyn was gasping, trying to catch her breath out of sheer terror over what had just transpired. Then her fear turned to rage and she stepped forward and gave the unconscious knight several savage kicks to the midsection. I shouted her name and she recovered her senses.

"Get this French bastard out of here!" she said. "Now!"

He was far too heavy for me to lift, particularly in his drunken state. I hurried out of the wine cellar and encountered, luckily enough, Leodegrance and told him what had transpired. Leodegrance quickly dispatched several of his men to accompany me back to the wine cellar. I noticed that Lancelot seemed to have a few more footprints on his surcoat than had been there when I had left, leading me to suspect that Eowyn had kicked him several more times in my absence. It seemed beneath her somehow but I supposed I could not blame her for her ire. The man had terrified her.

"Go with them," Eowyn said to me. "Make certain that he is returned to wherever the hell he is staying."

I did as she bade, of course. I accompanied the guards as they hauled the insensate knight through the corridors of the castle. What annoyed me the most was that, as we passed other knights or lords, they glanced at Lancelot and smiled or laughed or otherwise did not take seriously his inebriated state. And there was no questioning that state, for the smell of liquor rose from him like stink off a privy. How, I wondered, could they find it at all amusing? I knew that Galahad was a figment of my imagination, meant to be an idealized knight rather than an incarnation of an actual one. But did there have to be that much of a gap between the fantasy and the reality?

There was a woman waiting in Lancelot's chambers. She was wasp-waisted and possessed a vague prettiness, and wore concern like a veil. I saw her pacing as we entered, her hands moving in vague, fluttery ways. When she saw us, she let out a sigh of relief that was tempered with chagrin over Lancelot's condition. "Over there," she said in a businesslike manner, as if directing movers to put a chest someplace. She pointed toward a large wooden chair. The guards obediently placed him in it. He slumped over, snorted several times like a goat, but otherwise showed no signs of life.

"Did he get into trouble?" she said to the guards. The guards shrugged, not having been present during Lancelot's ill-advised assault. She turned to me with the same question hanging in the air.

In as straightforward a manner as I could, I told her precisely what had transpired. She gave no reaction to my litany of events, but instead just nodded and took it all in. When I was finished, she said, "Please tell your lady Eowyn that Lancelot's wife, Iblis, tenders her most extreme regrets." Her accent was likewise French, but softer, less harsh than Lancelot's own.

"I will do so, milady," I said.

I left her then as she just stood there, staring at her besotted knight. I wondered if perhaps she had had her own vision of what an idealized knight would be like when she had married Lancelot. For that matter, had he once been that knight himself and fallen from grace? How far a fall that must have been, and what a resounding crash it would have made when he landed.

Day the Forty-Eighth

GUINEVERE SENT ME TO GET some apples for her for she was desirous of fresh fruit. I returned to her chambers bearing a small basket of them, only to hear an unholy row coming from within. Several voices were raised in anger. I could not make out what they were saying, but the fury was palpable. I did not know what to do. It was certainly not the time to enter the room. So I remained where I was, standing just outside the door, straining to hear and feeling guilty while doing so.

The door was abruptly thrown open. Leodegrance stormed out. He shoved right past me and knocked me to the ground without even noticing I was there. I dropped the basket and the apples rolled all over. He crushed one beneath his feet as he passed and left a trail of apple bits and juice on the floor behind him. I gathered the scattered fruit as quickly as I could, polishing them with a cloth to get the dirt from them. Then, tentatively, I entered the chambers.

Guinevere and Morgan were there and, to my astonishment, the sisters were standing with their arms draped around each other. They were looking toward the floor as if unable or unwilling to meet each other's gaze. Sirona was there as well, seated nearby, her face ashen. She was staring off into space, saying nothing.

I wanted to ask what had happened but naturally could not.

I lay the apples down in front of Guinevere. She nodded in a vague manner and gestured for me to depart.

I went to my small chambers and sat on the straw mattress because there was nowhere else to sit, really.

Sometime later, there was a footfall behind me. I turned and saw Modred standing there, leaning against the wall. I did not question how he had suddenly turned up there. For that matter, I suspect the only reason I heard him was because he allowed me to do so.

I should not have asked, really. I know that. My overwhelming curiosity is my greatest fault. There are many, many things that I should not be sticking my nose into, and yet I cannot help myself. My father used to say that it would be the death of me someday and I have no reason to doubt it.

"Do you know what happened?"

He nodded.

I waited.

He said nothing.

"Are you going to tell me?" I said finally.

He shook his head.

"Why not?"

"Where would be the fun in that?"

With that comment, the eerie child walked out of my quarters. I wondered what in the world he had been on about, and began to think that maybe it was better that I did not, in fact, know. Indeed, sometimes I think there is already too much knowledge of things banging around in my head, and naught good will come from it.

Day the Forty-Ninth

MY HAND IS TREMBLING. I have never had so much difficulty writing as I do this day. It began so gloriously and I had such high hopes that all would turn out all right. But then the disaster happened and the accusations that flew . . .

I cannot help but think that I have been present at a defining moment that will begin the fall of Camelot as we have always known it to be.

Calm yourself, Viviana. Steady your hand. Write of that which you have witnessed.

The wedding was as opulent as anything I have ever seen.

Guinevere walked up the aisle in a magnificently gorgeous dress. It would not have surprised me if there had been droplets of blood in the lacing, courtesy of the seamstresses who sewed their fingers into bloody stumps in order to get the dress done on time. I noticed with curiosity that she was not wearing a veil. I suppose I should not have been surprised at that. She was hardly a demure woman and covering her face was not something she would readily have done. Besides, knowing Uther, he might have been suspicious that Leodegrance would try to substitute Morgan at the last moment.

It was a baseless concern, particularly since Morgan was serving as maid of honor. I would have thought that Modred would be the ring bearer, but instead another young boy performed that service. Modred was nowhere to be seen, which was typical of him.

She did not appear to be the least bit nervous. That was fine, for Arthur was easily more than nervous enough for the both of them. His knees were not knocking or any such thing, but I thought his face appeared a bit sallow, and he was biting his lower lip a good deal. The high priest waited for Guinevere at the altar, Arthur standing to his right while Uther and Leodegrance were off to the left watching the proceedings. Arthur was attired in finery of deep purples and blues. Sirona was seated in the front row. I noticed that Merlin was there, not remaining stationary, but instead in constant motion, moving around the vast hall with its cathedral ceilings as if he were afraid that remaining in one place for too long would make him a target.

I was standing off to the side. As a mere slave and servant, naturally I was not entitled to a seat on any of the wide benches. I found my eye drawn, not to Guinevere, but to Morgan. If she was upset over any of what was transpiring, she was doing a superb job of keeping her feelings to herself. She kept her chin pointed and her focus entirely upon Guinevere as her sister approached. I wonder now if that had anything to do with the shouted "discussion" that transpired in Guinevere's chambers the other day. Perhaps Leodegrance had loudly informed his family that no displays of disloyalty or resistance would be tolerated. If that were the case, then his words had certainly sunk in. Morgan's emotions were fully contained.

I suppose that could be seen as a positive. Then again, it has been my experience that feelings, when suppressed, do not dissipate. Instead they build up until they can no longer be held in, at which point they explode with far greater force and dire consequences than if they had simply been indulged all along.

Guinevere reached Arthur and they smiled shyly at each other. It may well have been the most genuine exchange of undisguised emotion between the two of them that I, or anyone, had ever witnessed. They both knelt before the high priest and he performed the ceremony. I found it interesting that the words spoken were the same whether they were for kings or commoners. We are all the same in the eyes of God, for He created us all and He will gather us all back as He sees fit.

The ceremony was completed. Arthur turned his face up to hers and kissed her gently. She leaned in toward him, which I fancied a positive sign. Honestly, I had been concerned she would turn her lips from him and permit him only to kiss her on the cheek, or maybe even pull away entirely.

There was much cheering and swelling of organ music followed them as they strode down the main aisle, husband and wife, future king and queen.

Morgan watched them go. Her face could have been carved from marble. I noticed Leodegrance put a hand on Morgan's shoulder and she shrugged it off. That did not bode well, I thought.

Some time later the banquet hall was alive with celebration. Minstrels moved through the crowd, playing sprightly tunes. It was not dissimilar to the festival that was put on when Leodegrance first showed up in Camelot, but it was minus the air of submission that was implicit on that occasion.

As Guinevere's handmaiden, it was my responsibility to stay as near to her as possible and make certain that all her needs were attended to. What that meant, in effect, was that I was to supervise the very kitchen wenches who had once tried to manhandle me. Even better, I was to supervise Rowena. It is uncharitable of me to admit just how much I enjoyed informing Rowena that the princess felt her leg of mutton had been undercooked and to set matters to right immediately lest Hell itself demand compensation. If glares could kill, yesterday's entry in my journal would have been my last.

I did not share in the repast beyond the small bits of food that I was able to grab and eat while attending to Guinevere's needs. Even so, that was more than enough to satisfy me. I have become accustomed to functioning on far less food than I consumed during the feast while others were shoveling food into their faces as if there was a famine expected within the hour.

Uther was in a particularly expansive mood. He actually went so far as to pat Arthur on the shoulder in a paternal manner and made several references to "my son" that were not patronizing. Guinevere looked on and smiled that exact same smile I had seen her practicing in the mirror.

Uther's food tasters were particularly busy. As I had learned rather brutally when I first arrived, Uther was very particular about anything he ate, always fearing poisoning. Hardly the mark of a confident king, but there it is. In a banquet situation such as this, however, such control was problematic at best, impossible at worst. So Uther made certain that his official taster, a poor, put-upon devil named Roderick, was sampling everything before he himself consumed it. Roderick was certainly enjoying more of the food than I was, but given the opportunity, I doubt I would have been willing to trade jobs with him.

The guests appeared to be having a marvelous time. The only one who did not seem to be enjoying the festivities was Maleagant, the Great Stone Warlord. He seemed bound and determined to talk with Uther, although naturally I could not determine what the specifics might be. He drew close to the king, speaking emphatically about something, but Uther did not appear interested in listening. He waved Maleagant off dismissively while Uther's wife, queen Igraine, looked on with faint concern. With a face as immobile as his sobriquet, Maleagant turned and walked away.

Various kings and guests brought forward gifts one by one for the newly wedded couple. Some was livestock, which was quickly taken away to the livestock master for use either in the royal farmlands or else to the butcher. Some were various articles of ornate clothing such as capes, tiaras, and such.

The one that drew the strongest reaction was presented by the Lady Iblis, wife of Lancelot du Lac. It was a broadsword that she bore, holding it carefully in its scabbard. Her husband, who

I noticed was drinking far less than he had the other day, sat and watched with an impassive expression. Perhaps he simply could not enjoy himself if he were not drinking himself into a stupor.

She presented the sword to Arthur. I do not claim to be terribly knowledgeable about weapons. However the collective gasp from the assemblage when the blade was pulled free of its sheathe verified for me from experts what my untrained eye could readily discern. It was a magnificent weapon. I do not exaggerate when I say that it almost seemed to sing when Arthur withdrew it from its scabbard. The hilt was golden, and the pommel was large and round and had the crest of a sun inscribed upon it. The blade itself gleamed. The metal picked up the reflections of the torches that illuminated the room, almost giving the blade the appearance of being on fire.

"The greatest sword artisans of du Lac labored over it for a year. It was intended to be a gift for my father, but he passed away before it could be completed. I think he would have been proud to know that you will wield it. I named it for him: 'Escalibor.' Your highness, of course, can call it whatever he wishes . . ."

"It would honor me to continue to call it by the name of the man for whom it was originally conceived," Arthur said. "I thank you, Lady du Lac, for such a magnificent gift."

I saw that Lancelot's face was darkening, and immediately intuited why. He had desired the blade for himself. He was dissatisfied with his wife's decision. Good. Anything that irritated that lout was pleasing to me.

Shortly after the last of the gifts had been presented, Uther stood and raised his flagon high. Upon seeing this gesture, everyone else got to his or her feet as well. Uther's crown, which he tended to wear only on formal occasions, was tilted on his head, indicating that Uther had already imbibed quite a bit. Not surprising: Uther's reputation for being able to consume ale, mead, wine . . . any spirits, really . . . was legendary.

"My friends . . . and the rest of you bloody bastards, and you know who you are," said Uther, an opening salvo that generated much goodly laughter. "We are here to celebrate the joining of my son, Arthur, to one of the two superb daughters of King Leodegrance." I saw Morgan nod her head slightly as if acknowledging the attempt at a compliment. "I truly believe that in the joining of these two kingdoms—the largest in the realm—we are ensuring peace throughout the land for generations to come. To Arthur and Guinevere . . . to the sons that their union will produce . . . and to a long and glorious reign on the part of my son . . . although let us hope it does not begin too soon, eh?" This prompted a roar of laughter from the assemblage, followed by choruses of "To Arthur and Guinevere!"

They drank deeply, and then there was a loud clatter as the flagon slipped out of Uther's hand. Uther began to sway. This drew laughter from several of the onlookers, for it seemed that even the mighty Uther had finally found the limit to his ability to drink. But Igraine looked sore afraid, and Arthur concerned, and suddenly Uther—who had been standing—fell forward, slamming hard and face down onto the table. Any further laughter the sight might have generated was instantly quelled by the scream from Igraine. The crown toppled from his head and rolled away.

Arthur was instantly on his feet, grabbing his father and hauling him upright. He shouted Uther's name and cried out for a physician moments later. Uther's eyes were open, but they had rolled up into his head. His tongue was hanging out and his lips appeared to be turning blue.

"Someone help him!" shouted Arthur.

Merlin appeared at his side, pulling Arthur's clasping hands from Uther's tunic and easing the king back into his seat. Then Merlin produced a small vial and held it under Uther's nostrils. I do not know what effect he hoped would result from it, but nothing did. Uther simply sat there, his head lolling to one side. Merlin placed his fingers against Uther's throat. Long moments passed.

Then he reached for Escalibor and pulled it from its sheathe before Arthur could ask why. He held the gleaming, polished blade directly in front of Uther's face and instantly we all understood. He was looking for some trace of breath.

I was not close enough to see the result but the outcome was evident in Merlin's reaction. Slowly he lay the blade down.

A deathly silence had fallen upon the assemblage.

"The king is dead," Merlin intoned.

There were gasps of shock and cries and a low sustained moan from Igraine . . .

. . . and a grim smile from Sirona, which I may well have been the only person in the hall who noticed.

Then Merlin called out loudly, "Long live the king!"

"Long live the king!" others shouted, but not everyone, and not in chorus.

And Arthur, God save him, poor Arthur, looked for all the world as if he wanted to crawl off into a corner and join his father in death.

That was when a cold voice, cold as stone, cold as death, said, "That would be me."

Maleagant had placed the fallen crown upon his head.

"Are you insane?" King Lot called out, and cries of protest came from King Pellinore and his sons as well. But others were not so quick to raise their voice against the concept.

"Insane?" Maleagant's voice rose above them all and seemed to pound through the great hall like a surf. "Is it not far more insane a prospect to have a nattering fool such as the son succeed the father? Say what you will of Uther Pendragon, but at least he was formidable! A force to be reckoned with! His contempt for his own son was well known, and now we are expected to follow him?"

"How dare you!" Guinevere said, on her feet. But Sirona, seated next to her, grabbed her by the forearm and slammed her forcefully back down into her seat.

Arthur still had said nothing. He merely stood there with a stunned and stupid expression on his face.

"I regret the timing of this as much as any here," said Maleagant, and he was walking in a large circle. He did so with a confident swagger that caused his sword to slap against his leg.

"Regret it?" shouted King Lot. "You fairly revel in it! Uther's body is not even cold, and you have the effrontery to claim Pendragon's crown?"

"If you are all bellowing 'long live the king,' you do not exactly put me in a position wherein I can afford to wait, now, do you? Besides, the crown rolled to my feet! If that is not a sign of—"

"It was you!" Merlin had spoken. He strode toward Maleagant, pointing a finger in an accusing manner, fairly trembling with rage. "You poisoned the king's wine!"

"You accuse me of regicide?"

"You seek to benefit from a tragedy! Does it not make sense that you instigated it specifically so that you could capitalize upon it?"

"That is nonsense."

"Yet you do not deny it!"

An ugly smiled played across Maleagant's lips. "Prove it, Merlin. Prove it, master manipulator, whom some are credulous enough to call wizard. Proof your calumny, or withdraw it."

"Your actions and prevarication are proof enough for me, and I withdraw nothing."

"Then I withdraw this!"

With those words, Maleagant yanked his sword from his scabbard. He was vastly outnumbered purely in terms of bodies to stand in opposition to him, but there was no consensus that everyone present desired to do so. There were shouts and arguing, some taking his side, some in opposition . . .

Suddenly the main table was upended. Heads snapped around in time to see Arthur overturning the table, sending plates, food, flagons and wine scattering every which way. He stepped through them all, Escalibor gripped tightly in his hand. His face was pale, his breathing heavy. "Answer the damned question," he said, and he pointed the mighty sword at Maleagant. "Did you, or did you not, slay my father, the king?"

"If I answered in the affirmative, would it cause you to grow a set of manly endowments?" said Maleagant. "Certainly your pretty new wife would thank me for doing so, eh? Very well. Yes, then, if it will make you enough of a man to—"

Arthur did not wait for him to complete the sentence. He came straight at Maleagant, and a howl of the damned was ripped from his throat as he brought Escalibor screaming around.

Maleagant, even though his sword was already out, barely brought it up to defend himself in time. Escalibor struck it hard, and although Maleagant was the stronger and more experienced by far, astonishment and something akin to fear appeared in his face.

Maleagant rallied then and roared a battle cry. I think he believed it would startle Arthur, cause him to back off, enable Maleagant to regroup. It did just the opposite. It enraged him and Arthur stepped up his attack. The Escalibor moved so quickly that it was little more than a blur, and that same singing noise could be heard as the blade whipped through the air. As assorted knights and kings shouted encouragement to both of the combatants, and Guinevere sat there with the pinkness of her cheeks flushing brightly against her face, and Morgan looking genuinely excited by the display, Arthur pounded

Maleagant back and back. Maleagant banged up against a table at the far end, momentarily halting his retreat, and he attempted to take back the offensive. He thrust forward with the sword, overbalanced himself, and Arthur shoved Escalibor in under Maleagant's guard. Maleagant let out a startled gasp that was echoed by most of the witnesses as Escalibor drove in through Maleagant's chest and out the back.

The Stone Warlord stood there for a long moment, transfixed, and then Arthur yanked the sword from him. Maleagant clutched at his chest, looking down in stupid surprise as blood bubbled up between his fingers. Then he looked up and, of all things, laughed. The laugh was choked with the life fluids that were doubtless filling up his lungs.

"This would probably be a bad time . . . to tell you . . . I am innocent . . ." said Maleagant, and then he fell like a towering oak, crashing to the floor. A thick red pool spread from beneath him.

For a heartbeat there was no sound, and then a chorus of cheers and huzzahs went up, singing the praises of Arthur Rex and shouting that justice had been properly meted out in the death of Uther Pendragon.

A crush of people crowded forward to hail Arthur, congratulate him, give thanks that he had seized control of the situation and acted in a manner that would have honored his late father. Servants gathered up the body of Maleagant, moving so quickly that they had his corpse cleared away before anyone could check to ascertain whether he was genuinely dead. This was and is of concern to me, for Maleagant has the capacity to be a formidable opponent. For my own peace of mind, I would just as soon have seen Arthur cleave his head from his shoulders in order to finalize his status.

It took many hours for matters to calm down. Everyone was talking with or to or at everyone else. It was all we humble servants could do to be there when we were needed and vanish into the background when we were not. I learned that the coronation would be the next day, to be followed by the internment of Uther Pendragon. My mind whirled in sympathy with Arthur: to acquire a wife, lose a father, gain a kingship all within a matter of hours. How difficult it must have been for him, I reasoned, with the ground shifting beneath his feet as if the earth was buckling from a quake.

I saw Guinevere to the royal bedchamber where she was to await the arrival of her husband, the king. I wanted to ask her if she was nervous or concerned or anything of the sort, but she offered no insight into her state of mind. That did not surprise me. In the end, I was not her mother nor sister nor even her conscience, but simply a servant.

But then she did surprise me when, just as I was preparing to depart the bedchamber, she rested a hand on my shoulder. I turned and looked at her, thinking that she had forgotten something and needed me to fetch it for her.

"Will it hurt?" she said.

I blinked in confusion, not realizing what she meant at first, but then I did. "Oh. It."

"Yes."

"Well," I said honestly, "it always has for me. But I have

never had the opportunity to engage in the act where love or tenderness was involved."

"Will it be that way here, do you think? I mean . . . you saw him. As filled with rage and vengeance and brutality as any other man."

"That is true, majesty, he did display those traits. However it took the death of a father to bring them out. And I am certain the love of a wife can prompt other traits."

"So I would have to bear love for him then."

"It would certainly facilitate matters."

"I shall see what I can do," Guinevere said, sounding uncertain but determined.

I left her there then and retired to the chambers that she had been occupying earlier. There was naught for me to do there. I started to head for my small and unimpressive quarters, but then realized that her far more majestic bed was unoccupied and inviting. It called temptingly to me. I knew it would be a violation of etiquette, but as I ran my hands enviously over the mattress, thoughts of proper behavior dissipated. I was overcome by the image of myself lying upon the bed, reclining comfortably and reading a book.

It was at that point I remembered that I had finished the book of fables and that Merlin had promised to provide me the history book in exchange for it. I gathered up the fables penned by the Greek slave and hurried down the hallways to Merlin's study, hoping that he would be there.

Truthfully, I wanted to discuss many of the aspects of the day with him. When I tried to contemplate all that had transpired,

I thought my head was going to explode from trying to contain it all. I had come to respect his wisdom and understanding of the paths of history; paths that seemed indistinct to me but abundantly clear to him. The future of Camelot seemed a blank wall to me. I was certain that one of Merlin's knowledge would be able to use his understanding of the past to give me at least a glimpse of what was to come.

I knocked on the door to his study. There was no answer. By all rules of proper procedure, I should have simply turned and left it for another day. My curiosity got the better of me, though. I hoped to trade out the book now. I was certain that Merlin would not mind. He had seemed supportive and friendly enough, if a bit daunting in the way he presented himself.

I entered his study and went straight to the bookshelf from which he had withdrawn the tales of Aesop. I began to study the bookshelves to see where the book by Plutarch was. I was not entirely certain that I had the nerve to remove it from the study, but at the very least I could sit there and skim through it.

The bookshelves stretched around a corner in the room into an alcove. I followed them around, my gaze gliding over the assorted volumes. I did not know where to look first.

I reached for the closest one, and suddenly the door slammed open. Since I was in the alcove, I could not see who it was. But I could hear right enough; it was Merlin, and he was seized with a fury that I would not have thought possible. It was a stark contrast to the avuncular manner that he customarily displayed.

He was bellowing at someone and I was relieved not to

be the subject of his wrath. Then it occurred to me that, if he found me there, I might very well be. What had seemed a harmless pursuing of his earlier hospitality now seemed to be a reckless intrusion, one that would not be generously greeted.

I reasoned that I could simply try to hide in the alcove, but it was visible to the back half of the chamber. If his path carried him down there, as it invariably would, he would see me. I looked around desperately to see if there was somewhere I could secret myself, and my eyes fell upon the far wall.

There was a brick there half the size of the rest.

I immediately moved toward it, placed my hand against it, and pushed. I heard a soft click from the other side and the wall swiveled inward, revealing a narrow passageway. I stepped into it and, just as I did, I heard Merlin say, "Wait . . . what was that?" Quickly, my heart pounding, I pulled on the wall. It stuck and for a moment I was visible and exposed. Then the wall moved and blocked the passageway from view. Darkness enveloped me.

If I had the slightest bit of sense, I would have fled at that point. But I spotted a narrow slit in the wall, just wide enough to peer through. I did so and found myself staring straight at Merlin, who in turn was staring at me, or at least in my direction. He was not in the alcove, but rather in the main chamber. But he was gazing into the alcove with a suspicious expression.

"What is bothering you now, you madman?" came a second voice, and with a deep sense of shock I recognized it as belonging to Guinevere.

"I thought I heard something. I could have sworn . . ." He

took a few steps in my direction.

The other speaker stepped into view and it was indeed Guinevere. She was wearing a white robe and her short hair was disheveled. "'Tis not enough that you have courted disaster by snatching me from my wedding bedchamber? Now you waste my time with delusions? When Arthur arrives and discovers that I am gone, he . . ."

"Will wait for you," said Merlin, casting one final look in my direction before returning his attention to her. "I very much doubt he will start without you."

"You have utterly lost your mind. I am the queen, you . . . you poseur. You nothing . . ."

"How did you do it?"

She blinked in confusion. "Do what? What are you going on about?"

"Do you believe that you could fool me? That I would be oblivious to your plots?" He grabbed her by the shoulders then, and I gasped at the temerity, but fortunately he did not hear me. "The others may be too blind to see your hand behind it, but I cannot be deceived."

Guinevere pulled away from him. "I still have no idea what you are—"

"Lie to me again and you shall awaken as a newt!"

She laughed at that. "Save the stories of your wizardry for the suspicious masses. They impress me not. Now speak plainly and have done with vague accusations."

"You despise vagueness? Very well." He paused for a moment in what was either high dudgeon or an attempt to achieve dramatic effect. "I know you are responsible for Uther's death."

I could not believe what Merlin was saying. Neither, apparently, could Guinevere. She tried to reply and was at first unable to. Finally she found her voice: "I called you 'madman' before, and now I see I spoke more truly than e'er I could have suspected."

"You deny it then?"

"Of course I deny it! How can you even think it . . . ?"

"How can I not? Who benefits more from Uther's demise?" He walked in a circle around her. "You resented him because he demanded that you, rather than your sister, marry Arthur. A marriage that you neither expected nor desired. And now, rather than merely a princess in waiting, you are a queen in fact, ascending to the throne alongside your husband. You gain both vengeance and power. What better motivation? And you were seated close enough to him to poison him . . ."

"If I poisoned him, then why was the man who sampled his food not dead?"

For the first time, Merlin seemed momentarily stumped. Guinevere seized the opportunity and said, "You have as much to gain from Uther's demise as I, mage."

"I?" He appeared thunderstruck at the notion.

"Yes, you. I know your kind, manipulator. You thrive on control as a fish does water, and you were never able to be more than an advisor to Uther. He did as he desired. Everyone knows that."

"Be wary of what everyone knows, young queen. For you

will find that that which everyone knows, nobody understands."
He took a step closer to her. She did not step back but instead
held her ground. "Uther was my king."

"And he was the father of my husband. If you do not
think I would honor that status, then you, Merlin, for all your
purported wisdom, are ignorant of the woman that I am."

"I do not pretend to understand women in general, much
less you in particular," said Merlin. "What I understand are
grabs for power, and shuffling Uther off this mortal coil gives
you far more power than you had before."

"As it does you. We both know that Arthur will look to you
for advice. You will have his ear."

"And you will have the rest of him."

"Well then," said Guinevere mirthlessly, "perhaps we would
be better advised to work in concert with each other rather
than hurl accusations."

I hate to say that I felt a twinge of pride in the way Guinevere
was handling herself. Merlin appeared to consider a number of
responses before he said, "Perhaps we would at that. But be
aware, young queen, that I will be keeping a close eye on you.
My suspicions of your complicity in Uther's demise are not
allayed."

"Nor are mine of yours. Except . . . if you suspected me, then
why did you accuse Maleagant? Was he not responsible . . . ?"

Merlin snorted contemptuously. "That fool? He is a
formidable killing machine, granted, with a sort of fundamental
resourcefulness when it comes to warfare. But he would not
have the wit or the nerve to dispatch Uther."

"Then I do not understand . . ." Then she paused and said, "No. I do understand. He provided a convenient scapegoat. Someone to foist blame on to so that no one would suspect you . . ."

"Or you," said Merlin.

". . . of doing the deed. If the hunt for Uther's killer had consumed a great deal of time—or, worse, had proven inconclusive—it would have made Arthur look weak. Perhaps even contributed to a power struggle."

"You learn very quickly, young queen. Since Maleagant was courteous enough, not to mention witless enough, to stick his head into the noose, I felt justified in knocking the stool out from under his feet and leave him dangling."

"But how did you know that Arthur would attack him? Kill him?"

"I did not know," said Merlin. "I had no blessed idea how Arthur would react. For all I knew, Arthur would walk forward, shake his hand, thank him for dispatching the cold-hearted bastard and turn the kingdom over to him."

"He would never have done such a thing," said Guinevere. "Not to the slayer of his father."

Merlin regarded her with curiosity. "You defend him."

"I am his wife."

"Not by choice."

"Perhaps not. But by circumstance. And I am bound by matters of honor to live up to the obligations that my new status entails. Now if you will excuse me, mage," and she curtsied slightly, "I have other responsibilities as well. The king awaits."

"I would think he does. Treat him well, young queen. And enjoy your time together while you can. I very much suspect the travails awaiting you will be most daunting."

"I suspect you are right. And mage . . ." Her voice became harsh. "Never again drag me away to your chambers to hurl accusations at me. Call me 'young queen' all you wish, but queen I am, and will be treated as such, lest you suffer the consequences. Is that understood?"

"Yes, highness, as long as you understand that I have considerable resources at my command, and that I can and will be pivotal in shaping the way in which the kingdom regards the king."

"The king's own actions will attend to that, I should think."

Merlin shook his head, his beard swaying from side to side. "You display your naiveté. Actions themselves mean nothing. The best intended actions can be seen as executed with the worst intent. It is not enough for the king to do things. They must be seen as being done for the right reasons. We must sell his actions to the people—commoners and nobility alike—so that they will support him."

"He is their king. They will support him because of who he is."

"Tell that to Uther's corpse," said Merlin.

Guinevere hesitated and then bowed her head slightly. "Valid point, mage. You do your job then, and I will do mine. With any luck, Arthur will avoid the fate of his father."

"We can only hope as much," said Merlin.

She departed Merlin's chambers then, leaving Merlin

looking pensive. He wandered toward the alcove then and looked down. I realized to my horror that I had left the book of fables lying out on the table. He picked it up, stared at it, and then I could have sworn he looked directly into my eyes. We both remained frozen for a time and then he turned away. With a sweep of his robes, he walked out of my field of vision. It was at that point that I finally let out a sigh. I have no idea how long I had held my breath; an age, it seemed.

I made my way through the hidden passages in the walls. As I glided past various rooms like a ghost, I heard snatches of conversations, whispers, laughter, sobs. All the typical congress of human interaction. But I could have observed them while unobserved myself. From the point of view of an historian, it was a remarkable, unique situation to be in.

Except that is a ridiculous thing to think. Despite what Merlin said, how can I think of myself as an historian? Yes, the Greek storyteller was a slave, but still, that was in olden days, not modern times.

Besides, why should I care about the lives of others? They care not a wit for me.

Except . . .

As I lie here, alone with my thoughts, I am ashamed to admit that the notion of spying upon people both repulses me and excites me. Especially if I am doing so in the pursuit of something so grand and noble as documenting living history. That I would be seeking the truth, if such a concept as truth actually exists, rather than simply different shadings of lies and self-serving attitudes.

For most of my life, the world has treated me shabbily. How delectable it would be to turn light upon that same world and immortalize it so that future generations would know of the ugliness and cruelty that constitutes it.

The unused bed of Guinevere beckons to me. She in turn is on her honeymoon bed.

As soon as I finish writing, I am going to stretch out on the bed of my mistress.

I will be ashamed of myself for doing so. But not so ashamed that I will not sleep well and deeply, and dream of a world where I can perhaps achieve some measure of lasting revenge with the aid of a quill pen and paper.

Day the Fiftieth

ARTHUR WAS OFFICIALLY CROWNED KING of Camelot today.

It was a somber occasion. We had barely had time to adjust to the passing of Uther, who is currently lying in state. And now we must accustom ourselves to the rise of a new king.

The high priest, who had performed the marriage barely the day before, placed the crown upon Arthur's head in a ceremony that was widely attended. Arthur's face was impassive. I wondered what was going through his mind. Was he brimming with anticipation? Was he terrified? There was no way for me to know. I wished that I could have asked him but I was hardly in a position to do so. I had felt uncomfortable enough in the casual relationship we'd earlier enjoyed when he was merely a prince who was held in open contempt by his father. Now he was king, the anointed of God. He had a queen wife, he had advisors. He had been elevated to an entirely different level.

As for me, I was still to be a servant to the queen, a handmaiden. It was preferable to working in the kitchen, that much was certain.

Morgan was to attend her as her lady of the privy chamber.

I found this an odd choice for Guinevere to make. It is not unusual—indeed, it is customary—for a sister to serve as that highest rank of lady-in-waiting, the lady of the privy chamber. But there was no love lost between Guinevere and Morgan, and Guinevere had even made a point of making clear to me how little she trusted Morgan. That she was certain that Morgan would serve as a direct siphon of information back to her father. Why place a woman whom you believed to be a spy at your right arm?

The only rationalization I can think of is that Guinevere sees Morgan's presence as an opportunity to control the flow of what is being reported back to her father. Plus, considering that Leodegrance will be returning to Cameliard while Morgan naturally remains in Camelot, it could be that Guinevere does not see leaked confidences as such an immediate threat.

It is my further surmise that, by keeping Morgan here, she hopes that Morgan will be introduced to, and married off to, an available king or duke or other person of nobility. Morgan will, after all, have the opportunity to meet many other interesting men here in Camelot than she would if she returned to Cameliard. If Morgan marries, then she becomes the concern of her husband and no longer a factor for Guinevere to have to contend with.

Uther will be interred within the next few days. Arthur will hold his first court at that point.

Guinevere created a major stir at the coronation. She showed up wearing, not a gown, but a white and purple surcoat, with a white gambeson underneath that had long, flowing sleeves. She sported black chauses to cover her legs. It was all very formal and regal looking, and similar to what the men were wearing, but on a woman it was unthinkable. There was much muttering over her attire, but Arthur seemed to pay no attention. His mind was elsewhere, for which I suppose he could not be faulted. But many were wondering aloud how he could possibly be a ruler of men when he could not even keep his woman in check. None could fathom why Guinevere insisted on wearing such manly raiment. Her ready and simple answer that she found them more comfortable did nothing to still the wagging tongues or assuage the feelings of concern nursed by so many.

There are days I have no clue what goes through that woman's head. It seems ridiculous to think that a monarchy could be threatened by a queen's choice of attire, but certainly stranger things have happened throughout the course of history. I should know; I have been reading about them.

Day the Fifty-First

IT IS BECOMING INCREASINGLY EVIDENT that Arthur is simply not up for the demands of the job that has been thrust upon him.

Guinevere returned to her chambers today. She continues to dress in mannish fashion. I wonder if she is going to continue to do so until she brings the full wrath of the court down upon her. I had assumed, foolishly I suppose, that the king and queen would share living accommodations. Such is not the case, apparently. They maintain separate living quarters, and only intend to share a bed when other activities will be in order. Morgan informed me that this is very much standard for royalty. Indeed, she said, that is the case with her parents. Nevertheless it seems odd to me. Had I a husband, I would be so grateful for the companionship that I would want to be with him every hour of every day, sleeping or awake. I suppose it is because I am a slave and have no life or property of my own, save these writing utensils, that I possess such a narrow view of the world.

She seemed concerned, upset. Morgan asked her what ailed her, but Guinevere was not forthcoming. Morgan was worried that Arthur had not performed his manly duty by her, but Guinevere insisted that he had indeed done so, and I learned from the laundress that there were indeed telltale stains upon the sheet. Multiple such, in fact, which was the source of amusement from some of the women who were impressed by the queen's virginity and the king's potency. Still, Guinevere was clearly worried and unable to mask it even in the slightest.

The queen decided that she wished to get some distance from the castle, so we repaired to the gardens. It was the three of us, Morgan, Guinevere and myself, although naturally I remained a respectful distance behind.

We wandered into the hedge maze. As mazes went, it was not really all that much of a challenge. If one knew to stay perpetually to the left, it was difficult to become truly lost. Plus it was convenient in that it shielded one from prying eyes.

They could not have been more a study in contrast, Morgan in her feminine finery and Guinevere in her tunic and leggings. They even walked differently, Morgan with small, mincing steps, and Guinevere with a distinct swagger that would have done any man proud.

"I know we have not always been the closest of sisters," Morgan said to her once we were within. "But the fact that you have appointed me your lady of the privy chamber says to me that you are trying to bridge the gap between us . . . a gap that I have never understood and always regretted."

"How you speak such sweet things," said Guinevere. She sounded darkly amused.

Morgan stopped walking and turned to face her sister.

When she spoke her tone of voice dropped and a good deal of the sweetness seemed to dissipate. "I am aware of what you think of me. That I am some sort of villainess, carefully cloaking my true personality behind a veneer of charm. Perhaps you think Modred is my henchman, performing my evil deeds while I hide behind him as the manipulator. I tell you now and for all time, Guinevere, that it is all in your head. I cannot help it if . . ."

She stopped and looked at me. I realized immediately that she wished to say something and was daunted by my presence. But Guinevere, realizing, said dismissively, "You need not concern yourself in front of Viviana. She will repeat nothing that is said. If naught else, she has no one to repeat them to. True, Viviana?"

"That is true, highness. All the other slaves and servants despise me." I did not exaggerate. The kitchen staff whence I came loathed me, and the former attendants to the queen similarly disliked me since I had effectively replaced them weeks earlier.

"Good," said Guinevere. She looked to Morgan then, her face a question.

"I cannot help it," Morgan said slowly, "if you feel as if you are sleeping with my leftovers."

"Oh, is that how I feel?"

"Nor can I help it if every man that we ever encountered was attracted to me and not you."

"That," Guinevere said fiercely, "is not true."

"It is, and you know it is, and frankly, dear sister, you have no one to blame for that but yourself. You, with your mannish ways and belligerent attitude. What did you expect, truly? What did you expect save that every man, beginning with Arthur, would find me preferable?" Her voice rose as her anger, which I suspect was long suppressed, began to bubble forth. "To be blunt, your highness, my assumption had always been that you had no interest in men, and appreciated the fact that they typically preferred me. It relieved you of having to pretend that you find them attractive."

"If that is what you believe, then you know nothing of me," said Guinevere.

"Do I not? Is it that I know as little of you as you know of me? Or is it that I know more of you than you find desirable? I have ne'er sought to be anything but your friend, Guinevere. Keep me at a distance or embrace me, it is entirely up to you. But I am reaching the point where I am beyond caring."

With that she turned away and headed off into the maze. Guinevere did not follow her. Naturally since the queen remained where she was, so did I.

"Much of what she said had no merit," Guinevere finally said.

"Meaning that a small amount of it did?"

Guinevere did not appear to hear me. If she did, she chose to ignore it.

Then her shoulders suddenly began to shake. She turned away from me and put her hands over her face.

"Highness?" I said softly with great concern. Guinevere may well have been one of the strongest women I had ever encountered. Seeing her thus, fighting back tears, caused my gizzard to twist into knots.

She sank to the ground as if her legs were no longer strong enough to support her. I immediately dropped with her so that I was lower than her eye level. "Highness . . . if there is anything that I can . . ."

"This is all your fault," she said.

I was taken aback. "My fault, highness? What is—?"

"It would have been better had I fled. That day in the woods, and your pretty words of responsibility and the outcome of what would transpire if I departed . . . that would been preferable to this." She uncovered her face and looked straight at me, her eyes red rimmed, her cheeks stained. "The circumstances would not have arisen that would have allowed Maleagant to poison Uther, and we would not be in this situation."

I found it interesting that she was subscribing to the public perception of Maleagant's treachery, particularly in light of what I knew of her encounter with Merlin. I said nothing of it, since I was not about to reveal my presence at that supposedly private discussion. Instead I said, "I still do not understand what you mean by 'this situation,' highness."

"Arthur . . ." She took in a deep breath and then let it out slowly. When she spoke again it was in an even softer, lower voice than before, as if she were concerned that we were being watched. Considering my own activities in the realm of secretive observation, I had to appreciate the caution. "Arthur is not ready for the job that awaits him. Not remotely."

"How now, highness?"

"He has not the stomach for it."

"So you say, but I am sure that others perceive it differently. He slew Maleagant without hesitation."

"He cried."

I was confused. "Who cried?"

"Arthur. On our wedding night. After we . . . after he performed his husbandly duties. He cried tears, womanly tears, and I begged him to tell me what was wrong. And he said he was wracked with guilt over having slain Maleagant."

"Guilt? Why guilt? He believed Maleagant to have slain his father. Blood for blood . . ."

"But Arthur had never spilled blood."

"Never?" I was astounded, but only briefly. Then I remembered that Uther, in his disdain for his son, had kept him out of war. The foolishness of his decision was becoming more and more evident. Arthur had been schooled in the art of war right enough. He was formidable with a blade, as we all had seen. But all the training in the world could not ovecome his soft-hearted, inoffensive nature. That was what Uther had seen in him that raised such contempt for him.

"He is a gentle soul. A gentle soul trapped in a man who must take up the mantle of warrior king. He sobbed over the moral burden of taking another man's life. And other men will see that softness in him, Viviana. They will see that he is weak. And they will feast on his heart for it."

"Possibly not," I said, trying to cast a hopeful light upon matters. Yet I knew she had a point. If Uther had perceived it, then how would others react if they did likewise? The council of kings would be convening within the next day or so, and Arthur would need to rise to their expectations. If they thought him weak, despite the display that they had seen at the wedding, then there was every possibility that they would try to make a move against him. Men will not follow a man whom they believe womanly.

Guinevere steadied herself and then looked shamed that she had allowed her emotions to get the better of her. Squaring her jaw, she said, "Possibly not, yes. But not likely. I will need to bolster his resolve."

"I believe you are more than up to the challenge."

"Your confidence is appreciated, Viviana. Although you seem to have a question on your mind."

Slowly I nodded. "That is true enough. It's just . . . you've made no secret of your dislike for Arthur and for your personal situation. You seem prepared to simply make the best of it."

"I suppose that is true. But that is not a question; merely a statement."

"My question, highness, is . . . do you want to help Arthur out of wifely devotion? Out of concern for Camelot? Or do you, maybe, love him?"

She stared at me for a time and then said, "Viviana . . . just how well do you know Arthur, anyway?"

"If you are implying what I think you are, highness, the answer is not at all. But I like him and I care about him. And it would be nice to know that his fate is in the hands of someone who is like minded, rather than simply tolerating him or using him." I looked down.

Guinevere appeared to think long and hard about her answer and then she gave one of her rare smiles. "He has a certain . . . charm. And sweetness. And I have shared my body with him and it was far more pleasant than I thought it would be. And his vulnerability initially was off putting, but when one considers the brute that was his father, I am rather grateful that he does not emulate his father in that regard. I think I could come to love him, Viviana. I think I am well on my way, and I think we could make a great team. I want to help him because failure would crush him and I would not want to see that for all the world. Does that answer your question?"

"I believe it does, highness."

She then rose. "Come," she said. "Let us go find Morgan."

We made our way through the maze and then, ahead of us, heard voices. One of them was Morgan's, and she sounded irritated and put out. Another was a male voice, and I recognized it immediately. Guinevere did not. I informed her that I believed Morgan to be in the company of none other than Lancelot.

As we rounded a corner we discovered that I had been, in fact, correct. Lancelot was there, and he was moving in a manner that I expect he believed to be playful. Morgan was endeavoring to step around him, and he would move from one side to the other, obstructing her path. He was swaying slightly, so I had a feeling that he had once again imbibed more than he really should have. Then again, being French, he no doubt believed that he could drink as much as he wished with impunity.

"Sir knight," Guinevere said sharply, and the harshness of her tone immediately cut through whatever haze might have settled upon his brain. "How now?"

Lancelot apparently did not recognize Guinevere at first. "How dare a squire address me without—" Then he squinted and realization came to him. He did not, however, seem especially daunted by the fact that the queen was standing before him and was clearly annoyed with his conduct. "Greetings, majesty," he said. "Apologies for the confusion, although you must admit it is understandable. Are you enjoying your day?"

"I was, until I discovered you importuning my sister."

"Is this magnificent creature your sister?"

Guinevere shifted her attention from Lancelot to Morgan. "Morgan? What transpires here?"

"I do not wish for there to be difficulty," said Morgan.

"Very commendable. But I would still enjoy a response to my question."

"I was walking," she said hesitantly. "And I encountered Sir Lancelot, who was wandering about . . . a bit lost, it appears. And, uhm . . ."

I realized at that point that Lancelot was staring at me. "You look familiar to me," he said. "Have we encountered each other before?"

I somehow felt that informing him that I had knocked him senseless with an abacus would do nothing to placate matters. Furthermore, he was wearing a short sword on his hip. Formidable I may have been against a drunken man while standing behind him, but I had no desire to brave him face to face.

Fortunately Guinevere interceded. "Do not address my

servants when the queen is standing directly in front of you, demanding answers," she said.

Lancelot swerved his unwanted attentions from me back to Guinevere. "Your sister appeared attracted to me. So I suggested we explore that attraction."

Morgan's face colored. "I am no such thing, sir knight, and your 'suggestion' was neither encouraged nor appreciated. Need I remind you that you are married?"

"Trust me, ma'amselle, I am reminded of that fact every blessed day. But that does not mean that we cannot in turn—"

"Yes, it does mean precisely that," said Guinevere. She stepped between Lancelot and Morgan. "A lady in waiting to the queen of Camelot, particularly one as highly ranked as the lady of the privy chamber, is not to be considered a potential mistress for a knight. Is that understood? For if it is not, I can certainly arrange to have the king explain it to you."

"The king." Lancelot smirked. "The king himself, eh? That would be . . . interesting."

"What do you mean by that?"

"I mean I care that," and he snapped his fingers, "for the wrath of your king, who unfairly wields the sword that should have been put into my hand. I am a grown man and milady Morgan here a grown woman. If she does not welcome my advances, well, that is her loss. I need not force myself upon any woman, for there are many out there who would not be opposed to my attentions. But do not seek to threaten me, highness, with the prospect of King Arthur," he said with a sneer, "coming down upon me like the right hand of God. That is not a threat. That is a grand jest."

With that, he bowed mockingly and then walked away.

Guinevere said nothing to either Morgan or myself, but she gave me a look that spoke volumes.

Arthur was in trouble.

Day the Fifty-Second

THE COUNCIL SUMMIT HAS BEEN delayed, which does not bode
well. The delay has been caused by the most absurd of problems:
disputes over seating. Merlin, acting on Arthur's behalf, has
asserted that Arthur should be seated at the head of the table
since he is hosting the gathering. King Lot believes that the
lord of the largest kingdom should sit at the head, which by
startling coincidence would be he himself. King Pellinore
advocates that the oldest ruler, by right of seniority, should be
at the head. In what should be an unsurprising coincidence,
he is the oldest. Leodegrance, the only one not taking a selfish
stand, claims that the head chair should remain vacant in
order to honor the departure of one of their own. Then again,
perhaps Leodegrance simply wishes to make sure that anyone
but Arthur is seated there. When all is said and done, Uther
did force Leodegrance to bow to his will. Mayhap he seeks a
measure of revenge, however spiteful, on the son of his enemy
since the father is beyond his ability to attack.

Although now that I think on it, who is to say that
Leodegrance did not have a hand in sending Uther to the

beyond, thus exacting revenge directly?

That is not a notion I dare suggest to Guinevere. I think she would take great umbrage were I to do so.

In any event, I think all this arguing is ridiculous. Why do they need a table at all? Why not simply pull all the chairs into a large circle and sit in that manner? It would solve innumerable problems.

Meantime, I believe that I have discovered that Rowena is up to some mischief. If I am correct in my surmise, then I can cause her no end of grief. It will be, at the very least, some measure of payback for the aggravation that she caused me.

I was in the market square, running an errand for the queen. She desired bath lotions that were only available from one particular source and dispatched me to obtain them. Having done so, I had tucked them into my basket and was on my way back to the castle when I spotted Rowena hurrying along as quickly as her stubby legs would allow her to go. She was carrying a sizable basket with a cloth over it. But I saw a sausage tumble out of it, all unnoticed, and surmised that the basket contained food. Moreover, I quickly reasoned that it was food cribbed from the castle's stores. Rowena, it appears, is a thief.

Desirous to see where she was absconding to with the food, I hung back until I was certain that she had not noticed me. Then I followed her, keeping my distance. The marketplace was bustling, so I was easily able to blend in with the crowd so that she noticed me not. Nor did she make eluding her notice an easy matter. She continually glanced around in a most guilty manner. Obviously she wanted to make certain she was unobserved, thus confirming my suspicions that she was either up to no good or very little good.

I did not have to follow her for very long. She went straight to the royal stables. The stable master was standing in the door and he grinned lopsidedly when he saw her. He shooed her in, glanced around himself to make certain they were unobserved—a task he obviously did not accomplish very well since he did not see me standing perhaps twenty feet away— and then hurriedly closed the creaky doors. I heard the sliding of a wooden bolt, indicating that they had fastened it closed.

Apparently Rowena was having some sort of illicit encounter with the stable master. They would stuff their faces with food that she had swiped from the castle larder, and then . . . well, I shudder even to picture such an assignation.

Or perhaps it is something even more criminal. Perhaps she is bringing him food that he is turning around and selling to others for a pretty penny. That makes sense as well. The quality of food that one could acquire from the castle is substantially superior to that which is available to the common throng.

I waited for a time to see what would happen while I tried to figure out who at the castle I should report Rowena's activities to. I was becoming impatient and suspected the queen would likewise be waiting in ill temper since I was taking far longer than originally anticipated. But as I was about to leave, I heard the bolt withdrawn and Rowena emerged. The basket was devoid of the supplies she had carried. The stable master hung in the doorway and watched her go, waving to her cheerily.

He was about to close the door when he just happened to

turn and look in my direction. He saw me and we locked eyes. His face paled as he realized I had seen Rowena emerge. Nor did he know how long I had been there, or what I had seen. I said nothing, did nothing, made no move. I just tried to give him my most fierce glare. Hastily he slammed shut the door, so hard in fact that it bounced open and I saw his comical expression as he grabbed for it and pulled it closed once more.

Smiling in satisfaction, I headed back to the castle.

Obviously he was able to get word to Rowena very quickly, for it was barely a few hours later that she accosted me in the corridors. Credit her with nerve: caught red-handed, she nevertheless tried to act as if I was in the wrong. "Why were you lurking about outside the stables?" she demanded. "Are you spying on me?"

I opted to offer no defense of my presence. Instead I drew myself up and looked down upon her coolly. "I need not explain my reasons to you. You, however, will have to explain your reasons for your actions."

"Whatever you think you know of this—"

I did not permit her to finish. "I know your illicit little secret, Rowena, lurking about in the stables."

"It is none of your business!" she said, but I saw her trembling, her dark skin flushed.

"Really. Well, we shall let the queen decide that." The truth was that I had no intention of mentioning it to Guinevere because I did not truly think she would care overmuch. Her thoughts were far more filled with concerns about Arthur and his place in the council. If I were to go to anyone, it would be Eowyn, who would likely have some harsh words for Rowena.

I began to turn away and was stunned when Rowena grabbed my hand. I turned back to her to pull it away and saw genuine fear and even vulnerability upon her face. "How long have you known?" she whispered.

I should have felt smug satisfaction at the clear terror she was displaying, but instead, much to my annoyance, I almost felt sorry for her. "Long enough," I said.

"Please," she said. "I beg of you. Say nothing. He needs me."

It was hard to believe the stable master was that desperate. All I could say was, "Oh, does he?"

She nodded so vehemently I thought her head was like to topple from her shoulders. "Tell me what you require. Please. There must be something . . ."

I so very much wanted to laugh in her face or turn from her and walk away, leaving her begging in futility. I certainly had no desire to be her accomplice in theft. At the same time, I considered the prospect of running to Eowyn and telling her what I had seen and now knew to be fact. Somehow it seemed petty. Beneath me. The sort of thing that Rowena herself might do. Was I so desperate for a measure of vengeance against her that I would lower myself to her level?

At last I said to her, "Know this, Rowena: I will take steps to make certain that the knowledge I have of this affair is provided to select confidantes. They will guard it with their lives . . . but should something happen to me . . ."

"You fear for your life, thinking that I would murder you

to keep my secrets? Just because I . . ." Her voice trailed off, and then she said fervently, "Your life will be sacrosanct, miss. I swear on my life . . . and on his."

"Then we will consider the matter closed for the nonce," I said in my most imperious manner.

I could not have been more shocked when Rowena sank to her knees, grabbed the hem of my skirt and kissed it fervently. "Thank you, miss," she said, clutching it as if it were a prayer shawl.

Carefully, and not a little disdainfully, I pulled the cloth free of her fingers and walked away. When I glanced over my shoulder to see what she was up to, I saw that she was no longer there.

I hope I am not making a calamitous mistake. I shall indeed have to keep to my word and tell someone of what I know, because I still do not trust Rowena not to try and arrange for an "accident" to befall me. Should that occur, someone in a position of power will need to know who the likely culprit is and avenge me.

Day the Fifty-Third

I SHOULD HAVE KNOWN. I should have known that this day would end in disaster, because it began with Modred. I am beginning to think that any time that child is involved, trouble follows him as certainly as winter follows autumn.

I was in the midst of a quite normal conversation with Eowyn, who was all in a tizzy over dining arrangements for the assembled kings and needed, I think, someone to vent her spleen unto. Eowyn abruptly appeared startled, and I turned and jumped slightly as well. Modred had appeared as if by dark magic at my elbow, as was not unusual for him. I swear that shadows make more noise in their passing than that lad.

"Morgan has need of you," he said calmly.

I immediately assumed that Morgan requested my presence in connection with something that Guinevere required or would require in the future. "Is she with the queen?" I said.

He shook his head. "In her own chambers. She was quite insistent, Viviana. I would make haste, were I thee."

"Thank you, young sir," I said. How friendly was I. How foolish as well.

Taking a hurried leave of Eowyn, I hied myself to Morgan's chambers. I pushed in through the door with only a hurried knock, and only as I entered did I belatedly realize that I had heard some sort of scuffling noise from within.

I began to ask Morgan how I might serve her, but the words died in my throat as I saw Morgan pushed back upon the bed and Lancelot atop her. Her skirts were hiked high and I could not for the life of me determine whether it was at her preference or displeasure.

That question was instantly settled as Lancelot, who was clearly preparing to unleash his manhood from his breeches, looked toward me and frowned at my intrusion. Morgan took the opportunity to sit up violently and shoved Lancelot back as hard as she could. Lancelot fell backwards off the bed and landed heavily upon the floor.

"Viviana!' Morgan cried out. "Fetch the guards! Fetch Arthur! Fetch—"

Lancelot scrambled to his feet and looked angrily at Morgan. "What are you on about?" he said. "You . . ." Then he abruptly reacted, as if the words she had spoken had taken a few moments to work their way through to his brain. "Viviana . . . ?" he echoed. "I know that name. I . . ." His eyes widened and recollection flooded back to him. "You! You were there in the cellar! You were the one who struck me from behind with a mace and near to killed me!"

"I wish she had succeeded! I wish she had taken your fool head off!" said Morgan.

I did not bother to point out that I had in fact used an

abacus, not a mace, and he had done more damage to himself than I had when he had slipped, fallen, and knocked himself unconscious courtesy of the fallen beads.

Lancelot's sword belt was upon the floor. He grabbed it up and yanked the short sword from its sheathe. Morgan grabbed at his arm, ordering him to stay clear of me, but Lancelot pushed her hard and she fell backwards upon the bed. He was clearly not drunk this time, and I disliked the odds of my survival.

I should have run, but I was literally paralyzed with fear. Would that this had been a story in my imaginings. Were it so, Galahad would have arrived in the nick of time and rescued me.

Lancelot advanced upon me and the motion snapped me from my paralysis. I turned and bolted for the door, but I had waited too long. Lancelot, far faster than I would have thought possible, was across the room and he slammed the door shut before I could reach it. In doing so he nearly caught my fingers in the jam. I yanked them away to avoid their being crushed.

"Leave her alone, du Lac!" shouted Morgan.

"Worry not," said Lancelot. "She shall live. But she shall carry upon her pretty face my mark, so that all will know the folly of—"

The door swung open and Arthur was revealed in the doorway. I saw instantly that he was unarmed. Not only that but, of all things, he was carrying a bouquet of lilies. "How now, sweet Morgan?" said Arthur with a broad smile upon his face, and then the bouquet fell from his fingers as he saw the display within.

By all rights, he should have shouted for his guards. Instead, to my shock, he entered the room and closed the door behind himself. "What transpires here?" he said. I expected him to be angry. Instead he appeared puzzled.

"I might ask the same of you, majesty," said Lancelot, eyeing the flowers upon the floor. He had sheathed his short sword by this point.

"Yes, you might. But I am not obliged to answer. You, on the other hand, are."

"Very well," Lancelot said and he fired me a furious look. "I was about to discipline this slave for illegally assaulting me several days ago."

"Illegally . . . ?" I said.

"I was protected under the rules of hospitality, woman, and you recklessly attacked me. I could demand your life and the king would be helpless to say otherwise."

"But you were—"

"Silence, woman," said Arthur, and I was so taken aback at being addressed by him in that manner that I instantly fell silent as he bade. Arthur looked straight through me. Instead his gaze was upon Morgan. "Speak to me, Morgan. What transpires here?"

Morgan spoke quickly, the words tumbling one over the other. She spoke of how Lancelot had burst in, how he had tried to have his way with her, and that he would like to have succeeded if I had not arrived when I did.

Lancelot laughed contemptuously at her recitation and responded that he was there at Morgan's invitation, and that his attentions that he had paid to her had been encouraged and welcome, and that she was now lying in order to maintain her own reputation. Morgan protested roundly at this characterization and Lancelot continued to laugh as if the entire matter were too ridiculous to discuss further.

Arthur considered everything that was said to him and then he said to Lancelot, "Extend your apologies to the lady Morgan."

The laughter stopped. The Frenchman drew himself up stiffly and said, "I will do no such thing."

"I am afraid, sir knight, that I must insist."

"And I am afraid, majesty, that I must refuse."

"Then," Arthur said easily, "we are at an impasse."

There was a moment of terrible silence and then Lancelot said, very slowly and very dangerously, "Majesty . . . do not force me to—"

"To what? I am unarmed," said Arthur, spreading wide his hands. "Kingship aside . . . you would attack an unarmed man?"

"Any man who insults me should take care to arm himself before doing so."

"Have I offered insult?"

"It is borderline, I admit," Lancelot admitted, "but—"

"Well then," said Arthur, "let us not allow any uncertainties to exist."

Arthur stepped forward then and his hand flew. His open palm cracked across Lancelot's cheek. The Frenchman took a step back, shock upon his face.

"Unleash your fury, sir knight," said Arthur. I scarcely recognized his voice. It was low and gravelly and not at all the gentle and even befuddled tone I had come to know. "Employ your sword in a murderous manner if you have it within you to do so."

"You think I would not!" said Lancelot.

"I think I care not!" Arthur rejoined. He threw wide his arms, offering no defense. "Strike truly, if you wish! I shall not stop you! Do you think I find life pleasing? Do you think I am enjoying any of this? That I desired it? I was ill prepared for the challenges that face me and I have no stomach for learning how to cope with them! Strike and relieve me of this horrific burden called existence! Strike, if you be a man!"

Lancelot tried to stammer out a response and Arthur slapped him again, leaving a vicious redness on his cheek. "Strike I say!"

At that moment everything happened very quickly. Lancelot reached for his sword and for some mad reason, I thought that I could stop him from pulling it out. I had no desire to see him cut Arthur down, and Arthur was doing nothing to save his own life. Morgan cried out both their names. Lancelot unsheathed his sword with the same unexpected speed that had allowed him to reach the door before I had been able to. He swung the sword wide and backwards, preparing—I would assume—to thrust it forward at Arthur with maximum force. Instead he buried the blade in my bosom without even seeing me coming up behind him. Morgan let out a horrified shriek, and Lancelot turned to see what she was shrieking about and why his sword was suddenly impeded. He saw the point stuck in my chest, blood seeping from the wound.

He stared, not at me, but at the blood, and then his eyes rolled up into his head and Lancelot du Lac, the pride of Joyous Guard, collapsed in a swoon.

The moment he released it, the short sword slid out of me and clattered to the floor since it had not penetrated all that deeply. Nevertheless the wound was still both unexpected and grievous. I felt myself going weak in the knees and then Morgan caught me before I fell to the floor.

Arthur was leaning above me, and there were tears in his eyes. Morgan saw them, for she fairly snarled at him, "Stop that instantly! Thy tears are womanish and have no place in the eyes of a king! Be a man, for God's sake!" With the back of his hand, Arthur wiped the moisture away from his face.

That was the last I remembered of all that transpired in Morgan's chambers, for then I lapsed into unconsciousness.

When I awakened, I found myself back in Guinevere's chambers, save that I was lying on her bed rather than mine own. For a heartbeat I thought that perhaps I had simply fallen asleep and dreamt all that had transpired. Then I endeavored to sit upright and the sharp pain in my chest told me that quite the opposite was true.

Then a woman stepped into view with an aggrieved expression upon her face. As disoriented as I was, it took me a moment to realize that it was Iblis, Lancelot's wife. She called out, "Summon Merlin! Tell him she has awakened!" I heard a voice respond in the affirmative, some guardsman like as not, although I knew not his name.

I felt a deep, parched sensation and, as if she could read

my mind, the lady Iblis brought a water skin to my mouth and eased some down my throat. I nodded in gratitude. "Thank you, milady," I said.

"It is the least I can do, Viviana. That is your name? That is what I am told." I nodded. Her hands moved in vague, distressed patterns. "My husband is distraught over what transpired. He would never willingly take a blade to a woman."

"With respect, milady, mere moments before he stabbed me, he threatened to carve my face."

"He would ne'er have done so. He merely wished to frighten you. Not that I excuse the behavior, but I assure you that is as far as he would have taken it."

"Because he is such a lover of women?" I could not keep the sarcasm from my voice, although admittedly I made little effort to do so.

"Not that. Because . . ." She hesitated. There was something she wished to say and apparently she could not bring herself to do so. "I . . . that is to say, he . . . it is a great shame, his great shame, Mistress Viviana, particularly since he in fact is so filled with pride, and he would be so humiliated that I think he would never recover, which might not concern you overmuch but would devastate me, if . . ."

"Milady, I cannot pretend to understand—"

She dropped her voice to a whisper and said, "He faints at the sight of blood."

I thought she was jesting, but the seriousness of her demeanor precluded such an interpretation. Still, I had to say, "Speak you truly?"

"Every word. His reputation in the joust is well earned. In mock combat, not only is he formidable, he is unbeaten. But blood sickens him to such a degree that he cannot remain conscious whenever he sees it. That's why his threat to cut your face was groundless. You comprehend how—"

"Make way!"

It was the commanding voice of a herald announcing the arrival of a king. Not that there was actually anyone or anything impeding the king's path. It was merely the customary warning that was typically made.

To my surprise, King Lot strode in moments later, followed by King Pellinore. It was almost more than I could fathom, that such highly ranked monarchs would feel the need to see what had transpired with me.

"If you would be so kind, milady Iblis, to leave us with the slave for a time," said King Lot.

"With submission, majesty, I do not think, in the interest of health, she should be left unattended."

"It was not a request, milady," said King Lot stiffly.

Adopting a more mollifying tone, King Pellinore said, "Her color is a bit wan, which is to be expected from blood loss, but there is clearly no bleeding now, and her eyes look alert. I believe she can endure some minutes without your ministrations, milady."

"Yes, of course, majesty," said Iblis. She curtsied to them and left the room, although she cast one final, apprehensive glance to me before closing the door behind her.

"So . . . slave," said King Lot.

"Even slaves have names, Lot," Pellinore said with gentle admonishment. "Yours, child?"

"Viviana, majesty."

"Very well, Viviana," said Lot, displaying very little patience. "We wish to know what transpired in the chambers of the lady Morgan."

"Certainly the lady Morgan would have already told you, majesty."

"She has been less than forthcoming," Pellinore said, "and her father, King Leodegrance, has made it abundantly clear that he would prefer we not involve his daughter in this business. Politically, it would be simpler for us if you were to tell us what transpired."

"With all respect, majesty—and please, I beg you, forgive the impertinence of a slave—but may I ask why you must needs know?"

"It is indeed an impertinent question," Lot said, "but you are a handmaiden of the queen and therefore I will accommodate you. The simple fact, sla—Viviana—is that it is an incident involving a king who is new to our ranks."

"One about whom there have been . . ." Pellinore appeared to be searching for the right words.". . . whisperings," he said finally, "insofar as his suitability to the task ahead of him is concerned."

Lot drew closer to me and looked me fixedly in the eyes. It was like staring into the heart of a storm at sea. Immediately I endeavored to look down, but he said, "Look into the face of a king, girl. I command you." I did as I was bade. "My authority," he continued, "comes to me from God. You know that, girl, do you not?"

"Yes, majesty," I said, unable to keep my voice from trembling.

"So when you are looking into my face, you are looking at a direct conduit to the Almighty, and He is watching you, hearing you and, most importantly, judging you. If you lie to me, it is tantamount to lying to Him. And you will be smited for it, if not here in life, than by Him in the afterlife. Do you know that as well?"

I was so terrified by that point that I could not even find my voice and barely managed to nod my head.

"Then in the interest of preserving the fate of your immortal soul, speak to me now and tell me what transpired in that chamber."

I should have spoken immediately. After all, two kings were demanding that I speak to them. It was, so to speak, a command performance.

The truth beckoned to me, but all I could think of was how it was going to damage Arthur. Arthur, who had welcomed a killing stroke from Lancelot without offering up the slightest resistance, all the time claiming that the crown was too heavy for his head. How would this portrait of Arthur possibly serve to inspire confidence from such as Lot and Pellinore?

And what of Iblis? I hardly knew the woman, but she seemed inoffensive, and more, I felt sorry for her. Here she was, clearly dedicated to a husband who thought nothing of pursuing other women the moment she was not around. She was endeavoring to protect him from public scorn and humiliation. Obviously she had failed to hold his attention as a wife. If I were to inform them of not only Lancelot's boorish behavior, but his unmanly swooning whenever blood was present . . .

My words could destroy the reputations of two men. What in the name of God had the world come to, that a slave could wield that sort of power?

I wondered if either of the kings was able to see the degree to which I was trembling. I even contemplated God almighty looking through their eyes upon me, as Lot had claimed. How would He render His judgment, I wondered, if I should indeed lie to His face upon Earth? Would there come a great thunderbolt crashing down upon me? Or would His vengeance wait until I had departed this mortal coil to find myself writhing in damnation?

I kept thinking, *This is not your problem. None of this is your problem. Think of yourself.*

Except I had been thinking of myself and only myself for years, and honestly . . . where had it gotten me? Helpless and hopeless, entrenched in a life of slavery, always beholden to others. The books of Merlin's that I had been reading spoke of being beholden to something greater than other people, or even to oneself. Ideals of thought and aspirations to noble, altruistic purposes. Such words, written by great men who rose from circumstances as humble as mine own, made my own concerns seem petty. Made me seem petty.

I had longed for my circumstances to change, but I was starting to realize that nothing was going to change them for me. I was going to have to do it myself, and that might well mean taking some chances. Chances with kings, with my life, and even with my immortal soul.

"The king came to the lady Morgan's chambers," I said slowly, "to meet with her over matters pertaining to the queen. There he discovered Sir Lancelot in a . . . questionable . . . position with . . . a woman . . ."

"What woman?"

I took a deep breath and let it out. "Me, majesty."

"You?" Lot appeared astounded. "Are you claiming that Sir Lancelot was having an assignation with a slave girl?"

"He knew not that it was me. I had affected the dress and mannerisms of the lady Morgan and had obscured my features with a veil. It . . . was an evil thing, I know, but he is such a comely individual and I . . ." I lowered my head. "I am but a woman, and women are weak."

"That is true," said Pellinore, a bit too quickly for my taste.

Lot's jaw twitched as if he were literally chewing upon my words. "Very well," he said, looking none too pleased but unwilling to pursue the matter further. "What then?"

"King Arthur confronted Sir Lancelot, believing that Lancelot was forcing himself upon the lady Morgan, since he was convinced—quite rightly, of course—that the lady would never willingly make herself the lover of a married man. Not a lady of her station. I, afraid to reveal the depths of my imposture, said nothing."

"And what next ?"

I licked my lips, which were suddenly bone dry. "A mighty

battle ensued, milord. Both wielded their weapons, each ironically feeling that they were acting to protect the honor of the woman in question."

"So what happened?" said Lot.

"As I said, majesty, a mighty battle it was. They had at each other with their blades. Thunderously powerful were the blows that both laid one against the other. They might well have gone on for hours, neither yielding, and then I could no longer allow my sinful behavior to cause strife between these two great men. I endeavored to reveal myself to them, and a stray blade struck me and bit deeply. I collapsed. The two titans instantly realized their error and I must say, majesty, they would have been within their rights to slay me right there for my foolhardy actions. But they did not do so. Instead they displayed great mercy and sought medical aid for me."

"So ultimately," said Lot, "the only one who behaved in a dishonorable fashion was you, a slave, who by dint of your station in life has no true concept of honor in the first place."

"As you say, majesty."

"Look me in the eye once more and swear that this is true."

Steeling myself, I fixed my gaze upon him. "Every word, majesty."

Lot "harrumphed" in a manner that indicated he might not have fully accepted my tale, but Pellinore said, "You see, Lot? I told you it was very likely something along those lines."

"So you did. Then the only thing remaining is the nature of the girl's punishment."

I froze when I heard that. All the means by which they

could punish me for my "sins" flew through my mind, and I suddenly decided that this entire notion of trying to help others, and risk myself in so doing, might in fact have been the worst idea that ever I had had. It further occurred to me that my resolve might not be as steadfast as I had originally thought. Faced with punishment that entailed brutal torture or even the threat of death, I suddenly realized that I might well change my story and give up the true version of what had happened merely to save my own neck. Of course, in doing so, I would then be admitting that I had lied to a king, which in itself was punishable by death. So I had effectively doomed myself no matter what the outcome.

"I would think," said Pellinore, "that the creature has already suffered sufficiently for her transgressions. Ultimately it is not up to us to decide her fate, but personally, I would not blame King Arthur if he gave her no lashing more severe than that of his tongue. Come then, my good King Lot, let us away, and leave this pathetic creature to her well-deserved misery."

I sagged in relief and sank back onto the bed.

Once they were gone, the door slowly creaked open. I fully expected to see Lancelot's wife enter, and thus was startled to see instead the face of Merlin.

"How now, Mistress Viviana," said Merlin. He closed the door behind himself. I had a brief glimpse of Iblis's face, wrought with concern, and then the shutting door obscured it. "Gotten yourself into a pretty pickle, have you not."

"I did not do so without aid," I said somewhat heatedly. "Modred told me that my presence was required in Morgan's chambers. I arrived and found myself in the middle of . . . I know not what."

"An altercation between our king and a knight. One that ended badly for both. Yet that is not how the story will be told, is it."

"What do you know of it?"

He had moved across the chamber and reached down with the clear intention of pulling aside the clothing I was wearing. I flinched back, guarding my modesty. He gave me a pitying look. "Too late for blushes, young woman. Who do you think stitched you together like an old shirt after you sustained your wound?"

"You?"

"Who else? Now if you wish to cling to your modesty, by all means, do so. And if, days from now, you are dying of blood poisoning, seek not sympathy from me."

I hesitated and then pulled aside my robe. Merlin leaned in close, pushing aside the last covering of the cloth. I looked where he was studying and gasped, scarcely recognizing it as part of my own body. There was a deep gash in my upper chest that was held together with strands of catgut. The area surrounding it was bruised a deep black and blue. Merlin studied it with the air of an expert and then said approvingly, "No inflammation. No sign of ill humours. Obviously my potions and my surgical skills were up to the challenge. Consider yourself lucky that Lancelot's thrust missed any vital organs."

"You . . ." I paused. "You know the truth of what happened?"

"Of course I know. Arthur told me all. Arthur always tells

me all. If he tried to keep a secret from me, he would bleed out his eyes. It is my job to manipulate the truth of things in order to improve public perception of him, and I cannot do so if the truth is withheld. He told me, with great embarrassment, of his plea for a swift termination of his existence. He told me of Lancelot's swoon, and Iblis confessed the nature of his weakness to me, as I know she did to you."

"And do you also know of . . . ?"

"Of the yarn you spun for Lot and Pellinore? Aye. A most effective tale it was, and one that I much suspect they will be swallowing." He regarded me thoughtfully for a moment. "Why did you tell it?"

"For mine own reasons, sir."

"And they are . . . ?"

Truthfully, it was still difficult to articulate. I felt as if something long dormant within me was beginning to stir to life for the first time. I settled for saying, "Mine own, and such will they remain."

"Interesting." He smiled thinly. "I believe, Mistress Viviana, that you were concerned about the needs of the kingdom, which would be a most far reaching attitude for a slave to possess."

I did not know if that was indeed the case, but I did nothing to contradict him on his assertion. Instead I merely shrugged.

"We shall talk more anon. For the time being," he said ruefully, "believe it or not, I must needs deal with more arguments from the kings regarding their seating."

"Yes, I had heard about that. I had been wondering why they do not simply sit in a circle and be done with it."

Merlin started to laugh, but then he stopped. He looked most thoughtful. "Why not indeed?" he said. As if greatly distracted, he turned away from me at that point, pausing only to say, "Remain in bed until I instruct you otherwise. Is that understood?"

"Yes, sir, it is."

Once Merlin departed, Iblis entered once more. Apparently she had been listening along with Merlin, and she thanked me profusely for all that I had said to the kings, risking punishment, damnation, and whatever other penalties both life and afterlife offered. I told her it was nothing she need concern herself over and that her offers of reward were unnecessary.

"Want you nothing that I can provide you?"

"Can you provide me freedom?" I said.

"I can perhaps arrange for you to be purchased by my husband and brought to Joyous Guard. And from some point on, I could likely arrange for your freedom."

I was not especially tempted by the offer. There were far too many variables, and besides, the prospect of being the property of Lancelot du Lac was not an appealing one. I thanked her for her offer but politely declined, citing loyalty to the queen. I did, however, ask if she could grant me the boon of bringing my possessions to me from my small chamber, since Merlin had bade me remain where I was. She did so and I have spent the rest of the time since her departure writing in my journal.

I set it aside only when Guinevere came to me. I did not know what to expect of her. She seemed as if she had no idea how to react as well. She must have known by that point what

I had said to kings Lot and Pellinore, the lies that I had sewn together that would benefit her husband and, by extension, her.

She said nothing for a time. She simply stood at the foot of my bed.

Then, finally, she spoke.

"Do not feel the need to return to your duties until you are fully recovered. Is that understood?"

"Yes, highness."

She started to leave, then hesitated, and then turned back to me. Guinevere looked as if she were having difficulty preventing her chin from quivering. "The only reason," she said, in a voice husky with emotion, "that I am not giving you your freedom . . . is that I am concerned that you will leave me. And right now, I . . . do not care to risk that."

Uncertain of how to respond to that, I settled for a tentative, "Thank you, highness."

"You are welcome," said Guinevere. And she departed, leaving me alone with my thoughts.

Day the Fifty-Fourth

As I write these words, the sun has not yet risen. I must pinch myself to make certain that I am awake, since much of what I have already experienced in the few hours that have passed in this, my fifty-fourth day of residence, has the unreal aspect of a dream.

He came to me during the night. I suspect it was, appropriately enough, just past the witching hour. I awakened out of a sense of someone watching me, and sure enough, there he was, just like a ghost.

"You!" I said and snapped upward. Then I cried out, clutching at the pain in my chest that my precipitous movement had engendered. "'Tis you!"

"Of course 'tis. Who else would I be?" said Modred, sounding supernaturally calm.

"This is all your fault!"

"How do you determine that?"

"Because," I said, "this was your manipulation! You summoned me to Morgan's chamber. You summoned Arthur as well, and Lancelot too, I would warrant! You masterminded the entire confrontation like some master puppeteer!"

"To what end?"

"Am I supposed to know and understand the devious workings of your mind?"

"Why assume you that it is my mind at issue?" he said. "You do not allow for the possibility that I was, as I asserted, simply performing Morgan's bidding."

"Is that your claim now?"

"I make no claim, offer no explanations." He smiled, and it was an eerie thing to see.

Modred turned to leave then and suddenly I cried out, "Wait!" He stopped and looked back at me. He waited expectantly. "Tell me what transpired that day, when you and your cousins and Leodegrance and his queen gathered."

"Why do you wish to know?"

"Because I believe it to be important, especially in terms of how things subsequently transpired. You said I would know eventually, when it was time for me to. Is it that time?"

"Even if I told you, there is naught to assure that you would believe me, and everything to indicate you would not," said Modred reasonably, and I could not in honesty say he was wrong. "Speak not to me of it."

"Who then, if anyone?"

"Morgan."

"She will explain if I ask her?"

"Of course not." His usually impassive face took on an air of disgust. "I had no idea you were such a fool, Viviana. You disappoint me greatly."

I snapped. There is no other explanation for it. I simply snapped.

With a roar of fury I bounded from the bed. Pain shot through my chest yet again, but this time I forced myself to ignore it. Modred, for the first time since I had met him, actually looked startled. Even in the darkness of the room I was able to see that, courtesy of the moonlight. He backpedaled and bumped up against the far wall. As I suspect he would, he pushed against it and the wall swiveled inward.

"Oh no you do not!" I shouted.

He darted into the opening with such haste that he did not even bother to swing it shut. I staggered in after him, holding my hand tightly against my wound. Unlike his previous spectral passages, this time Modred was making a very earthly racket. He sprinted down the hidden corridor and I could tell whence the noise was coming. I lit off after him.

As God is my witness, I have no idea what was going through my head. I was too consumed with righteous anger, feeling as if I were merely the plaything of a crafty child. How long had he been manipulating the situation, manipulating me and Morgan and the rest of us? There might be schemes within schemes that had not even occurred to me. Perhaps even the passing of Uther could be laid at his door. I could rule out nothing. With Modred, all seemed possible.

I made my way through the passages as quickly as I could. The pain in my chest was increasing. I brought my hand to my wound and felt blood seeping through the stitches. Apparently Merlin had been quite right when he said that I should remain in bed. For a moment I considered giving up the chase, but my legs continued to move almost as if they were doing so of their own accord. I had no choice but to go where they took me. I shoved my hand against the wound and did my best to keep my blood inside my body.

Modred continued to sprint ahead of me. I became momentarily dizzy, came near to swooning, but I growled "Modred!" and the ferocity of my call to him spurred me onward.

It seemed to go on forever, the pursuit, and once or twice I nearly lost track of him. Whenever that happened, though, he slowed up just enough so that I was able to catch sight of him and keep going. As I write this now, I am amazed that I could have been so deluded. How could I not have seen that his masterful manipulation was continuing? How could I have thought for one moment that I was steering the boat of the situation rather than being caught up in a typhoon?

I saw a sliver of light ahead of me. Modred had opened a section of wall in a chamber and stepped through. In my foolishness, I thought he was being overhasty rather than that he was leading me. Instead of questioning, I bolted through the opening and into the chamber where it led.

I took a few steps forward and then stopped dead. My jaw dropped. It took my eyes a few moments to adjust to what I was seeing. It took my mind considerably longer.

I was in Morgan's chambers. Illumination was provided courtesy of numerous burning tapers. Morgan was stretched out on her bed, slumbering peacefully. She had one arm draped around her bedmate.

It was Lancelot.

They were covered with a sheet, but I could readily discern that they were both naked.

There was a loud noise from behind me. It was the wall slamming shut, moved with far greater of a racket than when it opened. The movement was undoubtedly deliberate on Modred's part, and it served its purpose. It awoke both Morgan and Lancelot.

"Who is there?" called Morgan groggily.

I stepped back, hoping to exit the chamber before I was perceived. Unfortunately, unlike Modred who customarily dressed in black, I was adorned in a white shift and stood out prominently.

Lancelot became fully aware of his surroundings much more quickly than did Morgan. His short sword was hanging from the bedpost in its scabbard. The instant he saw me, he let out an angry roar. He yanked the sheet clear of Morgan, denuding her, so that he could wrap it around himself in a manner similar to a toga. Then, as I stood rooted to the spot in terror, he yanked his sword from its sheath and advanced on me. "For this," he declared, "you will surely die, you—!"

I did the only thing I could think of. I help up my hand, palm facing him. It was covered in blood from where I had tried desperately to stanch the flow from the wound.

Lancelot stopped in his tracks, brandishing his sword but looking distinctly pale in the candlelight. His gaze flickered from my outstretched, crimson hand to the bloodstain on my shift that was very slowly spreading.

He stumbled backwards then, making soft "unnnnh" noises. Morgan, apparently uncaring of her nakedness, steadied him and eased him back onto the bed, saying, "Breathe, my dear. Breathe slowly." Lancelot did so and Morgan looked poisonously at me then. She strode across the room, ignoring scattered articles of clothing on the floor, and fetched herself a dressing gown. As she wrapped it around herself, she spoke to me in a tone utterly different from any she had used before. There was harshness to it, an edge, and all her previous gentle mannerisms were gone as if they had served their earlier purpose but would serve none here. "How dare you?"

I should have been thoroughly cowed. I was, after all, an intruder into her chamber. Instead I rallied. "How dare I? I was injured protecting you, I thought, from unwanted attentions from this . . . person. How dare you?"

"You speak so to me? Who do you think you are?"

"Who are you?" I said. "What has transpired to bring matters to such a pass? There are . . ." I hesitated. My strength and vigor appeared to be returning, perhaps because the bleeding was slowing, even stopping. "I have risked my life, my very soul, and am bound into your lies as surely as you. I should at least know the reason why."

"There is no earthly reason for me to tell you."

"You mean, aside from what I know now of you and Lancelot?"

"Knowledge," Lancelot spoke up, "that will die with you."

"I would not advise that."

It was not I who had spoken. It was Modred. I had no idea

that he was even still in the room. Apparently he had closed off the exit to protect knowledge of its existence, but he had remained behind, secreted in shadow as was his habit until he opted to make his presence known. Morgan gasped upon seeing him. Lancelot looked stunned stupid, although he managed to find enough voice to say, "How many damned people are in this damned chamber, anyway?"

Modred ignored him. Instead, speaking in a voice that sounded far older than his years, Modred said, "What she knows, I know, and I know far more than she. If anything should happen to her, then I will make certain that everyone knows. Do you truly desire that, Morgan? Or are you prepared to kill me as well?"

"I shall gladly attend to that," said Lancelot. Making certain not to look my way, he rose from the bed as if to advance upon Modred.

Morgan halted him with a sharp word. Brusquely she ordered him from her chamber. He offered some token resistance, but Morgan would not bend on the subject. He dressed himself hurriedly as I looked away, and moments later it was only Morgan, Modred and myself remaining.

"What would you?" said Morgan, her voice flat and detached.

"I would know what is unspoken," I said.

"It remains unspoken for a reason. If you know of it, there are responsibilities that come as part of that knowledge. You must speak of it to no one. If you do . . ." Her voice trailed off, but the threat was implicit.

I nodded. Modred watched me with those frightening pale eyes, and I realized at that moment that if I did reveal anything that was said to me, not only would Modred offer no protection or retribution for my untimely demise, but he might well be the instrument of it. I began to wonder what in the name of God I had thrust myself into and could not help but think that I was well out of my depth. Part of me desired to retreat from the room as quickly as I could and forget that I had ever been there. Unfortunately such was not possible. It was akin to staring into the face of the beast that's about to charge and suddenly deciding you would rather not have gone on the hunt.

"You appear slightly dizzy," Morgan said. "Blood loss, no doubt. Sit yourself, I pray."

I did so, more grateful for the invitation than I would have let on. The spectral form of Modred hovered nearby.

Morgan slowly walked across the room, her fingers steepled as if giving matters weighty consideration. "What know you," she said, "of Uther Pendragon?"

The question surprised me a bit. Then again, I suppose I should not have been surprised at anything by that point. "Beyond that he is dead? Well, he despised his son. And he . . ." I cleared my throat, glancing at Modred since I disliked referring to such matters in his presence. However adult a mind he may have had, he was still a child. "He attempted to assail me, as a man does a woman."

To my surprise, Morgan snorted as if it meant nothing. "You are a member of a singularly non-exclusive guild," said she.

"So I was given to believe. I was told he 'vetted' every comely slave personally."

"Comely had naught to do with it, nor slave. If it was female and possessed a pulse, it engendered Uther's interest. The man probably has more bastards walking around than you could possibly imagine."

"Was no one immune from his . . . passions?"

"No one." She paused and then said four words that changed everything: "Not even my mother."

It took me long moments to find words. "S . . . Sirona . . . ?"

"If I have another mother, it has not been brought to my attention," she said dryly.

"How is that possible . . . ?"

"One time when he came to visit. He and my father were once quite close, you know. There was much celebrating, and my mother was in a merry mood, and apparently, well . . ." She sighed. "Apparently he had long lusted after her, and my mother—then, as now—was not skilled in holding her liquor. Leodegrance was too under the influence to notice that Uther was escorting my tipsy mother back to her chambers, and there he took advantage of her. She awoke the following morning with only vague recollections of what had transpired the previous night. Unfortunately," and she paused and smiled ruefully, "nine months later, she was provided a permanent reminder."

I could not believe it. "You?" I whispered.

She nodded.

"And Leodegrance . . . did he know . . . ?"

"The king has very little understanding of the manner

in which a woman's body functions, save when it serves his purposes," said Morgan. "He kept not track of time, and so it never occurred to him that I was anything save his daughter. Nor did I know. Until . . ."

"Until the night before the wedding."

Slowly she nodded. "I was inconsolable," she said. "Uther's rejection of me in favor of Guinevere . . . I had tried to endure it, but with the wedding imminent, I was unable to maintain my emotional distance any longer. I was furious with Guinevere, feeling that she had somehow stolen Arthur from me. My parents intervened, emotions ran high. Truthfully, Leodegrance was still nursing fury over the rejection as well. He was prepared to go to Uther, to terminate the wedding, even risk war over it. My mother endured it all for as long as she could and then confessed to the true nature of my parentage."

"A truth," I slowly realized, "that she must have already revealed to Uther at some point."

"That is why," she said, "he passed me over for Guinevere. Because—"

"Because he knew that you and Arthur were brother and sister. And such a union would be an abomination . . . not to mention that it could likely produce off-spring replete with . . ."

My voice trailed off.

I turned and looked at Modred. He smiled.

"Oh my God," I said.

"Like father, like son," Morgan said.

Had I not been sitting, I likely would have fallen over. "You . . . and Arthur . . . ? He . . . he had said how fond he was of you . . .

spoke so highly . . . but he never said that you and he . . ."

"He was a teen who felt weighted by his virginity, and I was happy to relieve him of it during a time when my father— or at least the man who thought himself my father—brought us here for a holiday. When my belly began to swell and my father demanded in rage to know who had deflowered his loving daughter, I claimed the culprit was a young bravo in my father's ranks who had been considerate enough to fall off a horse several months earlier and crack open his skull like a melon. I was sent away to a convent before the swelling became too noticeable and widely discussed."

"Was . . ." I was feeling overwhelmed by all that I was being told. "Was Modred . . . truly exposed at birth?"

"Yes," Morgan said in a flat voice. "The mother superior declared him to be a demon child. While I lay there in bed, bleeding and exhausted, she gathered him up and took him away. I sobbed for an entire day and an entire night, and then to my shock the next morning he was returned to me. The nuns looked shaken, even terrified. Supposedly, so the story went, a wolf came upon him and, rather than devour him, picked him up in its jaws and returned him to the front door of the convent. Half of the order was convinced that it was the work of the devil; the other half thought it was the hand of God. Neither wished to take the chance of finding out definitively one way or the other. They conveyed news of the events to Leodegrance who had no desire to offend the wishes of either God or His darker counterpart." She smiled ruefully. "Thus did Modred become welcomed into Cameliard as the orphaned child of my mother's sister . . . who never actually existed, of course. That was how he was raised."

"And when did you tell him of his true parentage?"

"I never had to," she said, looking at him. "He simply knew. Figured it out all by himself."

"I paid attention," Modred said with that same sort of vacant tone that Morgan had displayed. I began to wonder if there were hidden passageways in castle Cameliard to which Modred had gained access. It would not have surprised me. Indeed, when it came to Modred, nothing surprised me.

"So . . . now you know," said Morgan. "Does that satisfy your curiosity? Does it answer the questions that appear to torment you so?"

Her voice was dripping with sarcasm. The truth was that it provided answers that I believe she was not even considering, but which I felt the need to voice. "Milady . . ."

"Considering the information I have just dispensed to you, certainly I think we are beyond honorifics. 'Morgan' will suffice."

"Morgan . . . consider the timing . . ."

"Timing?"

"I think it likely, when one considers the information that your mother imparted to you and Leodegrance, and what transpired shortly thereafter . . . surely, Morgan, you have to see the possibilities that—"

"She believes Leodegrance was responsible for the death of Uther," said Modred.

Morgan looked from me to Modred and back to me. "Truly?"

"How could it be otherwise?" I said. "Upon learning that years earlier, his wife had been dishonored by a man set to become an in-law . . . what husband would not seek vengeance against one who did such a thing? Vengeance swift and terrible and . . . and . . ."

"Deserved?"

"I . . ." I stopped. "I suppose it . . . could be argued . . . that there was a degree of justice involved, yes, but still . . ."

"The affairs of kings are not to be judged by such as we," said Morgan. "Personally I do not see how Leodegrance could have arranged for such a thing. He has no knowledge of poisons, nor any reason for knowing. If Leodegrance wants a man dead, he comes at him with sword in hand. Furthermore, he was in Camelot as a guest. He takes such matters extremely seriously. He would no sooner see harm come to his host than he would bring harm to a guest while a host himself."

"I understand that, but even so—"

"If you truly understood it, then you would not add qualifiers to the sentence. I do not consider it a possibility that Leodegrance murdered Uther. The manner and place in which he died would seem to undercut its likelihood. But if he acted in defiance of all expectations, well . . ."

"Then he murdered your father."

"My father is King Leodegrance, no matter what the happenstance of my conception is," said Morgan. "He . . ." She paused and there seemed to be a touch of genuine emotion working its way into her. "He came to me after my mother revealed the truth. And I was sore afraid that he would reject me utterly. Instead he took my face in his hands and told me when I was little, I was such a happy, dancing child that there were some who believed that I was not human but instead a changeling child left by the fairy folk. By the Fey. They called me Morgan the Fey. And he told me that whether I was sired by the Fey or by Uther Pendragon, I was still his daughter and none could take that from him, and that my true parentage did not matter. Was that not sweet of him to say?"

I had to admit that it was. It would not seem in character for a warrior king such as Leodegrance. For that matter, perhaps it was not meant to be. Perhaps it was intended to deflect suspicion on Morgan's part from any retribution that Leodegrance might take against the man he now knew to be her true father.

I tried not to think along those lines. I should have instead been appreciative of Leodegrance's attitude toward Morgan. But I was too filled with suspicions directed at him, and also at Morgan. How did I know of a certainty that Leodegrance had said what she claimed he had? How did I know about any of it? I did not know what to believe or whom to trust. I began to realize, though, that if I was going to survive—and I had to think that my very survival was indeed at stake—then I was going to have to believe everyone and no one, all at the same time.

We lapsed into silence then that was only broken when I said, "So . . . who did kill Uther Pendragon, if not Leodegrance?"

"I had thought that was settled, surely. Maleagant did the deed. He admitted to it. Certainly that should be the end of the matter, rather than hurling insinuations at Leodegrance."

"Yes. Yes, I suppose it should be at that," I said.

"So," Morgan said, and she rose from the edge of the bed where she had seated herself. She held her hands in front of her, interlacing her fingers. "We understand each other clearly now, I take it? You know what you wish to know, and bear the responsibility that such knowledge brings with it."

I assured her that I would live up to that responsibility.

"Yes," she said. "I am quite certain you will. And my sister is not to know of our little discussion."

"She will not learn it from me, Morgan."

"Good." She smiled. "You know . . . Guinevere told me that, upon having learned that I was in fact a bastard child conceived under less-than-delicate circumstances . . . for the first time in her life, she did not envy me. I did not know whether to feel pleased for myself or sorry for her. That is a sad way to exist, eating away oneself with envy. I think that has served to make Guinevere largely what she is, namely an angry, mannish woman."

"I do not see her that way at all."

"Then you see her generously." She gestured vaguely toward the door. "You may go now. I am fatigued and wish to return to the sleep you so ruthlessly snatched from me."

"Yes, Morgan." I bowed slightly and headed for the door, since I had no intention of showing her that I had entered through the wall. At the door I paused and said, "If I may ask . . . ?"

"Have you not had enough questions answered this night? Oh, very well. What?"

"Why Lancelot?"

"Why...? Oh." She glanced at her bed. "Boredom, I suppose. He is a rather pretty thing, his odd appetites notwithstanding. And being with a lover in a warm bed is preferable to being alone in a cold one, do you not agree?"

"I . . . would not know."

"You have never had a lover?"

"Does one consider men who have forced their way on me as lovers?"

"Of course not."

"Then no."

"That is a shame. You should endeavor to remedy that."

I did not say anything in response to that, for I could not think of what I possibly could say.

"Now answer one question for me, since I have supplied you with so many answers this evening."

"What would that be, Morgan?"

She said softly, "Is Guinevere . . . caring for Arthur? Is she being considerate of him? Or simply tolerating him?"

I was relieved in that I was able to answer truthfully, since I had had enough of speaking falsehoods to last me a lifetime. "I have watched her attitudes change toward him. I do not think she will ever be a passionate woman, but I believe she has come to love him in her fashion, and cares about his welfare."

"Good." Morgan sighed. "He deserves someone who cares for him. If I cannot be with him, then . . ." She allowed the thought to trail off. "You may leave now," said Morgan.

"I will walk you back to your room, Viviana," Modred said. His volunteering to do so surprised me, but I said nothing. We left Morgan's room behind and, as he walked alongside me, he said, "I told you I was doing her bidding."

"But why did she do that?" I said, mentally chastising myself that I had not asked her.

"You have a brain. Think about it. And write me more stories about Galahad. I like them."

"Do you?"

He nodded and then turned and walked away, leaving me to reach my chambers on my own.

Now, as I finish writing down all that transpired this morning, and with the sun just now beginning to creep up over the horizon, I ponder things as Modred bade me do. And all I can think of is that Morgan fancied Lancelot as she claimed, but she wanted to make Arthur jealous. And she wanted me there probably to be a witness to it all.

If I am right and that is the case, then she succeeded in all her schemes as I think Morgan the Fey typically does.

I had disregarded Guinevere's description of her sister as cynical and suspicious. Now I think that Guinevere may well be the only individual in her family, save for Modred, of course, who sees her sister truly.

As much as Modred frightens me, it behooves me to remain on his good side. He may well be the only thing that stands between the grave and me.

Day the Fifty-Seventh

GUINEVERE CAME TO ME TODAY with news that completely stunned me.

She arrived most solicitous, wanting to make certain that my condition was stable and that my wound was healing. I assured her that it was and that I would be able to return to my duties in short order.

She was also, however, brimming with news, and when she told me of the details, I could scarce credit that I was hearing her properly.

The council had finally met, and the reason they had done so—as Guinevere described it—was because Arthur had had the masterful notion of creating a round table. Thus all concerns over who would sit at the head became of no relevance. "Did Arthur truly conceive the plan," I said, "or was it Merlin?"

Guinevere shrugged. "I do not know, nor do I care. It is Arthur who has received the credit for it, and that is all that matters."

It was not all that mattered to me, but I held my tongue.

She went on then about how remarkably successful the

gathering had been. Having overcome the initial reticence and skepticism of the other kings, Arthur had found himself in his truest element. He had been affable, pleasant, outgoing. He had spoken in a confident and relaxed manner, oozing charm from every pore. Guinevere said that, to look at him, one would never have known that his knees were practically knocking shortly before the meeting began.

Apparently the encounter with Lancelot, as the story had been spread from Kings Lot and Pellinore to their brethren, combined with Arthur's actions and the slaying of Maleagant, had gone a long way toward cementing a positive view of Arthur's potential as king.

"The council has not only agreed to ally itself with Arthur," Guinevere continued, "but an assortment of prominent knights have sworn fealty to him and resolved to remain here in Camelot, to cement a sort of fellowship of the round table. That is what they are calling it."

"Are they now."

She did not notice the deep sense of irony I was endeavoring to convey. I suppose it was understandable. "If knights are united, Viviana, there is so much great good that can be accomplished."

"Are you certain, highness?"

Guinevere looked at me oddly. "Why do you say that?"

"Well . . . it has simply been my experience that knights gathered together for extended periods of time tend to engage more in mischief than great deeds."

"That," she said with confidence, "will not be the case here."

I very much wanted to believe her, but feared that I could not.

Some time later, Merlin came to me to check on the healing of my wound. He appeared taken aback, though, at the fearsome scowl I bore him. "You seem perturbed, Mistress Viviana."

"Perturbed? Aye, you might say that."

"Why would that be?"

"Because 'twas I who suggested the notion of the council meeting in the round. Yet now it is Arthur who is solely credited with the concept."

"You said nothing of a table, as I recall."

"No," I admitted, "but still . . ."

"But still nothing," said Merlin firmly. "Hear me well, mistress: I thought better of you than this. I thought you were starting to come around in your thinking. Moving toward your long-term potential rather than your short-term self-interest. Perhaps I overestimated you?"

I did not know what to say. Merlin did not wait for me to conceive something.

Instead he continued, "Should I really have advertised far and wide that the king was acting upon the advice of a slave? Do you truly believe that would have elevated the esteem in which the others hold him? What benefit would it have served, except to salve your ego that, frankly, I was unaware required salving. My God, woman . . ." He held up his hands. "These fingers stitched you back together. These fingers which previously only tended to the needs of kings and nobles. I would have thought that my personally taking the time to save your miserable life would be sufficient recompense for your efforts thus far. Was I wrong?"

"No, sir. You are not wrong," I said humbly. I felt contrite although honestly I have no idea why I did. It still rankled me somewhat that I received no credit for my ingenuity, but Merlin clearly had no sympathy to offer.

As if reading my mind—which, honestly, I would not have put beyond his capabilities—Merlin said, "'Twas I who combined your notion with the idea of a round table and brought the concept fully formed to Arthur. Do you see me taking credit for it? Do you?"

"Nay, sir, I do not."

"That is correct. Creatures such as you and I, Mistress Viviana, are meant to be behind the scenes, propelling great men forward. Rather than generate the light, we bask only in reflected glory while we manipulate the light to shine on those who most require it. In this case, that is King Arthur. Understand you what I am saying?"

"Aye, sir, I do."

"Never underestimate the power and influence that those who operate in shadow can exert upon the light."

I had the feeling that it was a lesson Modred had already learned, or perhaps had been born knowing. "Valuable words, sir. I shall attend to them."

"Good. That is good," he said approvingly. As we had been speaking, he had been inspecting my wound in a most clinical manner. "There has been some seepage. Were you moving about excessively or straining the stitches?"

"I was moving around, yes."

"Have a care with such activities. Still, I'd best remove the stitching since the skin may start to bond with it if I allow it to remain. The wound itself seems mostly healed, although I will keep it bandaged for another week."

It was the work of minutes for Merlin to cut the threads free. I bit upon my lower lip, wincing and trying not to cry out during the times when he was forced to tug a bit harder than either of us would have liked. Finally, though, the stitching was removed. I ran a finger tentatively across the scarring that had been left behind. The skin felt rough to my touch.

"I will inform the queen that you may return to your duties on a limited basis." He paused and then added, "She is quite fond of you, you know."

"Truthfully, sir, I am not entirely certain why."

"Because she feels she can trust you, I suppose. She sees you as the only individual within her circle that has naught to gain for herself. Whether Camelot stands or falls—whether it ends well or in flames—you are merely a slave. The outcome will have no more impact upon you than it would on the bed you lie upon."

"If it ends in flames, sir, and the bed is reduced to ashes, then I would have to say that is an impact."

"Fair enough," Merlin said with a small smile. He tilted his head slightly. "Would you care to see the table?"

"Table? You mean the round table?"

He nodded.

I realized that I did, in fact, want to see it. Merlin waited outside the room for me as I dressed hurriedly. Soon I was following him to a large chamber. It had served as a meeting room where Uther had welcomed various ambassadors and others of influence. There I stood, amazed, as Merlin gestured toward the vast table that now occupied most of the room.

It was large enough to accommodate twenty men, at least. It was not solid, as I would have initially suspected, but instead designed in the manner of an "O" with the middle empty. The image of a dragon had been carved into the surface of the table, with the lengthy serpent twisting its way completely around the table and coming full circle.

"The table does not truly have a head," said Merlin, "but Arthur positions himself to sit in front of where the dragon's head falls. Thus is the image of power imparted to him even though all are, in theory, equal."

"Ingenious. But how did you manage to craft the table so quickly?"

"You would be amazed, Mistress Viviana, what artisans can accomplish given the proper incentive."

"The promise of considerable fortune for succeeding?"

"The promise of a painful death for failing, actually. Threats are far more economical than rewards, do you not agree?"

I had to admit that I did. One could certainly not argue with the results.

"Would you care to sit at it?" he said.

I was taken aback by the notion. It seemed so presumptuous. At the same time, what a remarkable opportunity. "Dare I?"

He gestured toward the round table.

Slowly, feeling overwhelmed by the sense of history surrounding me, I walked to the table, slid out one of the chairs that was grouped around it, and sat myself down. It was a heady, almost intoxicating feeling. I rested my hands upon the table and imagined myself a ruler who had control of life and death over countless subjects. Even though it was mere fantasy, I still felt swollen with power. I even felt, I blush to say, a tingling in my loins. What an odd location on one's body to have a sense of power.

"And what goes on here?"

It was King Arthur. He had strolled into the room, his arms draped behind his back. Instantly I stood, far too quickly than I should have, knocking the chair backwards. It clattered to the floor and I nearly fell over it in my haste to right it.

"I . . . I am sorry, highness, I . . ." I could not get words out, I was stammering so.

Merlin, naturally, was completely at ease. "Mistress Viviana was curious to see what it would be like to sit at the round table, highness."

"Indeed. Are you planning to become a king, Viviana? Or a knight?"

"No, sire. I have neither the lineage nor the strength of character."

"Lineage is happenstance, while character . . ." Arthur shrugged. "There are so many kings and knights of varying character that I daresay you would not be worse at the endeavor than any other." He paused and then said, "How fares the injury?"

Merlin answered for me. "It is largely healed, highness. She will doubtless still feel twinges from time to time, but otherwise she is whole."

"That is good. I am pleased to hear it. A regrettable affair all around. Does the round table please you, Viviana?"

"It is most impressive, majesty. Most impressive."

"It is rather. It was all my idea, you know."

"Was it?" Merlin gave me a look that was fraught with warning, but I simply kept my face impassive as I continued, "May I ask how your majesty conceived it?"

"Honestly? It came to me without warning. I think mayhap it may have been Merlin who triggered the notion, now that I think upon it . . ."

"Not I, majesty," said Merlin. "If it was a brilliant idea, which I think we all agree it was, then surely it must have originated with you."

Arthur nodded and smiled vacuously. "I cannot argue with that logic, Merlin. You are right again. He is always right," Arthur said to me, indicating Merlin.

"That must be gratifying, to always be right," I said.

"It is a vast responsibility, but I endeavor to live up to it," Merlin said gravely.

In the distance, from down a corridor, I heard the clanging of swords. "Majesty? What is that?" said Merlin.

"Two knights fighting, I would expect," Arthur said carelessly. He even laughed. "They tend to do that. They have a good deal of energy. We shall have to find things to keep them busy. I shall put my mind to it. And you, Merlin, can put your mind to it on my behalf."

"Yes, majesty, at once. And perhaps you might wish to intercede in the . . ." He gestured toward the sounds of battle.

"Hmmm?" said Arthur, and then realized what Merlin was referring to. "Ah. Yes. Of course. Quite right, quite right," and he headed off toward where the unknown knights were having at it.

I said nothing to Guinevere of the skirmish that Arthur needed to involve himself with. Perhaps I should, but her mood is sufficiently cheered that I am loath to say anything that will dispirit her. Arthur, for his part, spoke not to me about the truth of what happened. It may have been that he was too grateful for my intercession to express himself, or else too mortified to admit to his self-destructive weakness. I suppose I understand, although a royal "thank you" might have been gratifying.

Day the Seventy-Third

HE TOUCHED MY HAND. THE mute touched my hand.

I am not a romantic fool. There is no way that I could possibly be. Still, when he lay his hand upon mine . . . and it was not a random gesture, not a happenstance, I am sure of it . . .

And when he did . . .

I am blathering, getting ahead of myself. I must organize my thoughts and produce these things in the proper order.

Guinevere is continuing to stir up consternation in the court. Not enough that she continues to dress in a mannish fashion which others find off putting. She also continues to insist on making forays into the neighboring countryside to speak to the people as if she were one of them. None of them know what to make of her. If only she dressed in a manner resembling a woman, she might engender at least a modicum of trust. Instead, in her intransigence, she challenges people to come to her on her terms, and they are disinclined to do so.

Today was her third outing in the last several weeks, and whenever she returns the result is sustained arguments 'tween herself and Arthur, and it is always over the same thing: The living conditions of the villagers. Guinevere has become obsessed with it as of late. Arthur is convinced that it has become of such importance to her so that she can feel as if she has something to do, some personal cause of her own. Honestly, I cannot say that he is wrong in his thinking.

"Why can you not be focusing on something else that matters!" he had said to her in exasperation at one point.

"Something else like what?"

"Like providing me an heir! I am certainly giving you enough opportunities," he had added with a smirk that quickly disappeared when she didn't smile back. "As queen, that should be your focus."

"I think as queen my focus should be on whatever I wish it to be," she had said. "Truthfully, Arthur, producing offspring is nothing I am eager to embrace. But I would do naught to forestall it. If we are to have children, then nature will attend to it, and nothing you can do will speed it any more than anything I can say or do will prevent it. If it is all the same to you, however, I would occupy my mind while you attend to my body."

"I can live with that," Arthur had said.

Guinevere's own Cameliard, for which her father and mother departed yesterday thus ending what Guinevere privately referred to as their "endless stay," is a smaller realm than Camelot, and on the whole a wealthier one. That is to say, there are fewer people in residence and those that are, are reasonably well off. At least that is what she tells me, and I am taking her word for it having never been there myself. The same cannot be said for Camelot, and it is weighing heavily on

Guinevere, which in turn means that Arthur is going to feel the weight of it as well.

She has discovered that the merchants in the vicinity are eking out a living, but that as soon as one wanders beyond the immediate town into outside villages, it is a very different story. Farmers, workers, even owners of taverns and other smaller businesses, barely have two coins to rub together. Nor have matters been helped by the taxes that have been levied against them. The taxes have gone toward supporting the lifestyle to which Uther and now Arthur have become accustomed, but it has not come without a price. And that price, unfortunately, is the ability of the peasants to feel any measure of comfort or financial security.

Guinevere is also horrified by the medical situation. The mortality rate of children is at an all time high. Families have been countering this in the traditional manner, namely having as many children as possible and hoping that a significant portion survive. But either alternative is unpleasant. Either mothers are forced to bury the bodies of their young dead and mourn their passing, with little pieces of themselves dying along with their offspring. Or else the children are discourteous enough to survive, thus ensuring the household has more mouths than it can readily feed.

I have watched Guinevere move through the countryside, talking to the peasants and trying to assure them that she is going to make certain that matters improve. What I see, which she does not appear to, is that the peasants are regarding her with extreme suspicion. Her attire is just the beginning of their distrust. Ultimately, they are accustomed to a monarchy that does not especially care about them. It is the way that they understand the world to exist. As well intentioned as Guinevere's plans may be, it could well result in the populace thinking about things that, well, that they should not really be thinking about.

As we were heading for the stables this morning to go on yet another excursion, I voiced my concerns to Guinevere. She merely laughed, not in a contemptuous way, but a little sadly, as if I had disappointed her somehow. "I am simply endeavoring to anticipate future problems, Viviana," she said to me. "Sooner or later, the peasantry will grow frustrated with the vast gap between the way we live and the way they live. It can lead to revolution. By sharing the wealth with them, we would forestall that."

"But is it also not possible, highness, that once we begin to share with them, they will need more than we can provide?"

"If they need more, we provide more. It is our duty to care for the poor."

"Is it?" It was a novel concept to me.

Guinevere, pulling on her riding gloves, looked at me in surprise. "How could it not be? How could it not be the job of those who are in a position of power to serve those who are not? As I recall, Viviana, you yourself spoke of the responsibilities I must needs fulfill because of my station. Are you now saying that it is otherwise?"

"No. I am simply saying that efforts to change the status quo can often be met with suspicion."

"Suspicion? How so?"

"Because it is human nature to wonder why someone is doing something."

"Could not the answer simply be out of a sense of altruism?"

"Not in my experience, highness, no."

Her eyes darkened. "Do you mock my motives? Question them?"

"No, highness, I do not. Others, however, will. They will not understand why one who is privileged will selflessly endeavor to help those who are not. They will seek to discern what your 'true' motive might be. When it is not readily apparent, they will come up with their own theories for your motivation, and I fear they will not be flattering theories."

"I believe you are overthinking matters, Viviana. I believe that when offered kindness, people will simply accept it graciously and not question it."

"The story goes that the residents of a great walled city did precisely that centuries ago when they accepted the gift of a gigantic wooden horse. It led to the sacking and downfall of their city. Since then people tend to be a bit more skeptical when presented with a gift horse."

Guinevere merely shook her head. "Such cynicism in one so young is truly discouraging to see, Viviana. If the people of the realm were to be suspicious, it would only be because they do not know me. So it only behooves us all the more to meet as many of them as possible. Thus, we shall continue on our current path of endeavors." We had arrived at the stables and she gestured for me to enter. "Go now in and fetch us horses.

Our escorts should be here presently."

I did as she instructed.

The stable master glowered at me as he typically did these days. Although he did not speak of it, there was no doubt in my mind that Rowena had told him of my discovery and he was not appreciative of my interfering in his little arrangements. I did not care. I had matters of far greater weight to concern myself about.

He gestured toward the far end of the stable and there I saw that the mute stable boy was busy grooming a horse. As always he seemed covered head to toe in muck. His long, stringy hair obscured his face. He did not seem to care. Instead he was entirely focused on stroking out the horse's mane. A pity, I thought, that he could not bother to attend to his own grooming with the same enthusiasm that he provided the horse.

I walked over to him and told him that the queen desired her mount.

He turned and looked at me without saying a word, of course. I found myself recalling how I had had the feeling previously that he was imagining me unclothed. It was a disconcerting sensation. "Give me the palfrey, if you please," I said firmly, endeavoring to show him just exactly and precisely who was in charge.

The horse's bridle was already upon it. The mute took the horse's reins and offered them to me. I took them.

That was when he placed his hand upon mine.

I cannot begin to explain what passed between us at that moment. It was as if lightning had struck me. I believe I even gasped aloud. There was no reaction upon his face as I did so, but his eyes were fixed upon me. I realized for the first time how deep set they were, and there was a quiet ferocity within them, as if there was so much he wanted to say and burned with frustration over being unable to do so.

There was a loud clearing of throat that caught my attention, snatching me from my reverie, and it was at that moment that I realized I had lost track of how long we had been standing there with his hand upon mine. Guinevere was standing not far away, her arms folded, a bemused expression upon her face. "Are we waiting for something, Viviana?" she said impatiently.

"My apologies, highness," I said quickly as the mute removed his hand from mine. I led the palfrey over to her and then automatically rubbed the back of my hand against my dress in order to clean it. I said nothing further to her as I hurried for my jennet and, moments later, we were riding away from the stables. The customary squad of knights to guard us accompanied us as we rode at a leisurely pace down the highway referred to simply as the King's Road.

"Did mine eyes deceive me?" she said in a low voice lest our escort overhear. "Or were you sharing a private moment with the stable hand . . . and the hand of the stable hand."

"'Twas meaningless, highness," I assured her. "That muck encrusted creature? The notion that he and I . . ." I shuddered, or should say I made a grand gesture of shuddering.

"I should hope not," Guinevere said primly. "You are a handmaiden of the queen, Viviana. One would hope that you have some standards."

"Yes, highness."

Nevertheless, as we rode off, I cast a quick glance behind myself. The mute was gone from sight. That was a relief. If he had been standing there, watching me depart, that would have said something to me. The fact that he did not bother to do so told me that whatever I was imagining when he laid his hand upon mine, it was just that: my imagining.

Sometimes I think the tales of Galahad that I have been writing for Modred have sent my imagination off in directions that it would behoove me not to allow it to go.

We rode further than we had in previous weeks, to smaller and even more outlying villages. Guinevere went from hovel to hovel, speaking with the residents who regarded her with a combination of awe, fear and suspicion. Describing their environs as "humble" would be to understate matters. There was dirt everywhere, along with the stench of human waste that had not been properly disposed of. Insects darted about, and I swatted at them as aggressively as I could to keep them out of the queen's face.

Every peasant had much the same story: that times were difficult, particularly due to the considerable tax levies that had been foisted upon them.

I noticed that our escort guards kept giving each other nervous glances as the peasants spoke of their frustrations and difficulties. None of the valiant knights truly desired to hear about the difficulties that the poor were experiencing. Guinevere seemed oblivious to the knights' discomfiture. Her focus was entirely upon the people.

As we rode back to Camelot, Guinevere kept saying, "The king shall hear of this," and variations of that sentiment. The knights continued to give each other silent, concerned looks. Once we returned to the castle, I advised Guinevere of what I had witnessed. She did not appear concerned in the least. "They are resistant to new ideas," said Guinevere.

"What new ideas did her highness have in mind, if I might ask?"

"The idea that the nobility has an obligation to ensure the betterment of the underclasses. The knights feel no sense of obligation to any except themselves. That is going to change. I am going to make certain it changes, with Arthur's help, of course."

"Of course," I said.

Just how much of Arthur's help she expected became evident at supper. Arthur had done away with the entire notion of a food taster. He said that he did not wish to live with being afraid to trust even the food that was provided him. He also pointed out that a food taster had not prevented death from claiming his father. The taster had suffered no ill effects from the food, so the theory was that—if Uther truly had been poisoned—Maleagant had administered it through some other means. Perhaps a poison ring that he had brushed against the king's skin in passing or some other means of disposing of him had been utilized. I was attending to the queen's needs as was my responsibility as a handmaiden. Servants had provided the food and had subtly withdrawn, as they typically did, and would return within an hour to remove the plates and leftovers. Arthur was munching on a shank bone when Guinevere brought up the topic of her latest excursions.

Arthur forced a smile and said, "Yes, I had been meaning to speak to you on that. It is quite the talk among the knights and nobles, this interest that you have taken in the peasantry."

"And what did you mean to say, in speaking to me of it?" There was a hint of warning in her voice that I think went completely past Arthur.

"Well . . . they are saying that these are matters over which you need not be concerning yourself."

"So they are not worried about the state of the peasantry?"

"Not as such, no."

"And are you?"

Arthur smiled. "Of course I am, my dear. As king, I worry about the needs of all my subjects, whatever their status."

"Perhaps. But it seems to me that those who have the least require more concern than those who have the most."

Arthur leaned back in his chair and lay down the shank bone. He scratched his beard thoughtfully. "I suppose there is something to be said for that," he said, sounding guarded, as if worried that he was conceding a point that he was ill-advised to concede.

Guinevere appeared to sense that, and leaned forward eagerly. "You have it within your power to set matters right. To better the lives of those below."

"How so?"

"Reverse the flow of taxes. Tax the nobility and siphon the money back down to the peasantry."

He blinked. "Are you serious?"

"Absolutely."

"Just . . . give money to the peasants? They will misuse it! Spend it on frivolous things!"

"Like food and clothing?" she said with no trace of humor in her voice.

"Yes, like . . . no! Not that. On . . . what I said. Frivolous things. There would be no means of control, no way of administering . . ."

"Then set one up. Create some manner of central fund through which money could be administered and dispensed to those most in need."

"It is not the job of the monarchy to aid the poor in that manner!"

"Well, if not your job, then whose?" Guinevere said in exasperation. "Who is going to help them?"

"They can help themselves!"

"And what purpose do we serve, then?"

"We provide them something to aspire to. We provide them a symbol of—"

"Of everything they cannot have, simply because an accident of birth placed us in a position of authority and them in a position of helplessness? Arthur, do not you see?" and her tone changed to one of imploring. "We have vast power. But what is the point of that power if we do not use it for the welfare of others?"

"I was not aware that power required a point. I thought it was more an end unto itself."

Guinevere flopped back in her chair and rubbed her face with her hands. "Are you hearing a word I say?"

"I hear every word, Guinevere. And I hear the words that others say as well. The words about you and me." His voice rose in anger, speaking over Guinevere's attempts to interrupt him. "The way they say that a man is running this kingdom, but there is uncertainty whether that man is you or me. There are some who claim that I should start wearing frocks since you have so many nice ones that are going to waste!"

"Arthur, such cruel japes are nothing you need concern yourself ab—"

He slammed his fist upon the table, causing Guinevere to jump in surprise as he bellowed, "I will decide what I need concern myself about, woman! Yes, *woman*! That is what you are, and it would be damned nice if you occasionally acted as such!"

She spoke back, her voice flat and even. "I cannot be other than who I am, Arthur. Even if you do not love who I am, I thought you at least liked it."

"Who said I do not love you! Who—oh, never mind."

He stared at her for a long moment and then slumped back in his chair, his ire seemingly spent. Arthur was not one to remain angry with Guinevere for long. Whether that was a true measure of his love for her, or his inability to sustain such an intense emotion, I could not say. With a heavy sigh, he returned to the previous subject. "I just do not see how this . . . this 'welfare' plan of yours . . . can possibly work. If nothing else, it would require the cooperation of the nobles, and I honestly do not see why they would provide it. I would be asking them to contribute money to help others with no benefit to them."

"The benefit is obvious, Arthur. The peasantry, the commoners, are the foundation upon which our society is built. Improving their lot in life makes the foundation stronger. That can only serve to benefit the nobility in the long run."

"I fear they are concerned merely about the short run."

"Then it will be your job to convince them otherwise, Arthur. You have considerable charm and personal charisma. You could sell boots to a hawk."

He stared at her, confused. "What would a hawk need with boots? A hawk flies; it does not walk."

"That is exactly right."

"And how would the hawk purchase the boots? A hawk has no currency . . ."

"Arthur!"

Arthur was startled by her abrupt outburst. Guinevere appeared as if she wished to speak again, but instead looked to me with helpless frustration.

"I believe, majesty," I said, "that her highness was speaking metaphorically to indicate that you can be extremely persuasive if you put your mind to it."

"Oh." His eyebrows knit and then his face brightened. "Oh! Yes. I understand."

"Good," said Guinevere. She reached across the table and laid a hand upon his. "I believe you can accomplish this, Arthur. I believe it is a worthy goal."

"Perhaps it is," Arthur said. "Perhaps it is." He did not

sound certain. I hope that his lack of resolve does not defeat the notion before it has the opportunity to reach fruition.

And then, very softly, she said, "You do love me?"

"As much as I can. You make it a trial sometimes."

"I know." She squeezed the hand that was under hers. "I know."

As I write this entry, I find my thoughts drifting back to the mute. There is something about it that I cannot quite pinpoint. Part of me thinks that I must give him much greater thought, while another part suggests that I would be well-advised to cease thinking of him at all.

Day the Seventy-Fourth

MERLIN IS NOT HAPPY WITH Guinevere.

Apparently Arthur has indeed been speaking with the nobles, and the nobles are not especially pleased with what they are hearing. Arthur is contending that he has developed the notion entirely on his own, but no one seems to believe it. Merlin has learned of it, either witnessing it firsthand or having heard about it after the fact. Either way he is unhappy. He burst into Guinevere's sitting room today in a greater state of ire than I have seen him in before. "You little fool!" he snapped.

Both Morgan and I were there. Morgan was immediately on her feet, and she said angrily, "How dare you trespass here so, unannounced and uninvited! The queen has not granted you an audience!"

"The queen can go to hell, and I will happily send her there myself!" Merlin said heatedly. "And if you wish to complain of me, feel free to do so to Arthur. I doubt he will attend you."

"Go and fetch Arthur," Guinevere said icily. When Morgan offered protest, Guinevere said, "I said go, sister." Morgan did as she was instructed, leaving the queen and myself alone with the mage. Guinevere did not seem concerned with the mage's outrage. "You should have a care, Merlin. A man of your advanced years would do well not to overexcite yourself."

"Are you endeavoring to destroy Arthur's kingship before it can even get solid footing?" he demanded. "Bad enough that you offend sensibilities with your deportment. Now you seek to sow discord with your actions? Why not just . . . just have an affair with a knight while you are at it!"

Guinevere made a face. "Why on earth would I do such a thing?"

"I have no idea! I have no idea why you do anything that you do! This taxation business, this program designed for the welfare of the commoners . . . this is your doing! It has to be!"

"What if it is?"

Merlin was pacing furiously, and he brought himself to a halt with what seemed supreme effort. "Arthur has been endorsed by the council of kings, true. And through his actions and his own natural charm, he has created the beginnings of a circle of supporters. Also true. But many a thing can and will go wrong in the building of any coalition. If you had introduced this notion a year, two years . . . even better, five years from now, it might stand a chance of garnering support . . ."

"And how many commoners will lose their homes or suffer hunger and deprivation in one or two years? How many children will die in five? If Arthur is to effect change, he should do so early in his reign, when it is possible to set a tone for what is to come. If he simply continues with matters the way they have always been, then it will make it that much harder to effect changes later on."

"Matters were proceeding smoothly and without difficulty for years," said Merlin.

"Really." Guinevere seemed unimpressed. "Tell that to Uther. Except, of course, you cannot, since he was murdered."

"And would you have the same fate for Arthur?"

Guinevere's body stiffened. "Of course not," she said. "I would rather have him avoid such a fate, obviously."

"How?"

"By being loved and appreciated by all his subjects, nobles and peasants alike."

"That is problematic, if not impossible," said Merlin. "Uther, dead as he may be, ruled well during his time. He did so by being feared."

"Arthur does not have the temperament to be feared. Even if he can generate such emotions for a short time, they will not sustain."

"Fear will get him further than love."

"I do not believe that," Guinevere said firmly.

"Then, highness, I believe that you are going to be faced with a rude awakening," said Merlin.

Abruptly there was a pounding on the closed door, and it flew open a moment later to reveal Arthur standing there. He was out of breath, clearly having run from wherever he was to this place. He looked in bewilderment from Guinevere to Merlin. "How now?" he said when he had sufficiently gathered his wind. "Morgan said that something was amiss and my presence was required forthwith."

"A discussion of the future of Camelot between myself and your queen, majesty. Nothing more than that," Merlin said.

"Oh." Arthur processed that and then said, "Does the discussion require my presence?"

"I do not see why it would."

Arthur looked back to Guinevere. "Does it, my dear?"

"Apparently not."

"Excellent." He clapped his hands together and rubbed them briskly. "Then I am off to talk to Palamedes. You will be interested to know, my dear, that he finds this entire welfare business most intriguing. Here is hoping for good things!" With that cheery comment, he walked away.

"There. You see?" said Guinevere.

"Sir Palamedes," said Merlin with great patience, "inevitably takes the contrary position to the opinion held by the majority. Part of his Saracin sensibilities, I would warrant. Were Palamedes in opposition, you could take heart. With him on your side . . ." He shrugged, allowing the statement to die there, and departed.

Guinevere was silent for a long moment. Cautiously I said to her, "Is there anything you require, highness?"

"A crystal ball," she said ruefully, "so I can have some instinct of how all this will end."

My instinct was that it would end badly, but that is only because that is always my instinct as to how things will end.

Day the Seventy-Sixth

THE LADY IGRAINE IS NOT well.

Indeed, it is said she has not been herself since the passing of Uther. She has wandered aimlessly around the castle, scarcely talking to anyone. When I have passed her in her perambulations, she has nodded to me indifferently, and in such a way that I cannot be entirely certain whether she truly sees me or not. Eowyn has been fussing over her, and informed all of the ladies in waiting and handmaidens that we should attend to whatever the lady Igraine may need at all times. How fortunate that the ruling of Camelot passes along from ruler to child. If, with Uther's passing, she had retained the title of "queen" and was responsible for the throne, Camelot would have been extremely vulnerable.

I ran into her in the corridors today. She was not moving. She was simply standing there, staring off into space. I was about to pass her by, but her demeanor made it seem as if she were in need of assistance. "Milady?" I said softly. "Do you require anything?"

"Where is Uther?" she said.

I certainly did not like the sound of that. I hesitated and then ventured, "He is . . . not about. I believe your son is, though. Perhaps I should fetch him for you?"

"My son?" Her voice sounded more like a passing breeze than anything uttered by a human. "Yes. Yes . . . fetch Arthur. That would be pleasurable, to see him."

I immediately did so.

It took me some minutes to locate Arthur. I found him in the main study, engrossed in conversation with Palamedes and Sir Percival, one of Pellinore's sons. They looked up upon my entrance and, after begging their pardon for the intrusion, I alerted Arthur to his mother's confused state. He excused himself and followed me. Igraine was precisely where I had left her. She looked distantly at Arthur and when he spoke softly her name, she merely stared at him blankly. "What do you wish, sirrah?" she said.

Arthur was startled to be addressed in so dismissive a manner. "I thought . . . I was given to believe you required assistance, Mother."

Igraine glanced over her shoulder as if under the impression that Arthur was addressing someone behind her. When she realized there was none such, she turned and looked back at him in bemusement. "Who are you?"

"I am Arthur. Your son."

She laughed merrily as if it were a grand jest. "Arthur? My Arthur is but a youngster. Such a wretched little thing he is. You remind me of him in a sort of distant manner—that same sort of empty smile, I think. As if he makes the gesture with his mouth because he believes it is expected, but does not truly have the inner spirit to connect with it."

Arthur did not provide any visible reaction to what she said. It was as if he simply refused to acknowledge that she had spoken. He took her hand gently in his. She seemed politely bewildered but did not pull away. "Let us look around and see if he is about," he said.

"As you wish. You seem a kindly young man." She smiled and patted his face. "Your mother must be proud of you."

"I should very much like that if that were the case," said Arthur, and he led her away, presumably to Eowyn. I watched them go and felt a great sadness as I did so.

What use is our lives if we do not remember them? Igraine's life was slipping away from her and Arthur was helpless to do anything to prevent it. And, worst of all, it was not as if she were prostrate on a bed with her heartbeat creeping to a halt. She was experiencing a sort of living death, leaving her loved ones behind while remaining at the same time. It was truly tragic, and I wondered just how much tragedy Arthur was yet going to have to endure.

Day the Seventy-Eighth

MERLIN'S CONCERNS MAY HAVE PROVEN to be prescient.

Arthur is not only encountering resistance to his "welfare plan," as it is being termed, but the disagreement is splintering the denizens of the Round Table. Palamedes has a number of Saracin followers—the most sizable retinue of any of the knights—and naturally they are lining up behind him. Percival has likewise definitively come to Arthur's side. But Tor is stridently against it, which is a harsh outcome for Tor's brother, Percival. Dinadan is also in opposition to it, as is Gawain and quite a few others. Almost all of the others, in fact.

I have been told, however, by Guinevere, that Lancelot can still be swayed.

As little use as I have for Lancelot, he inexplicably remains respected by the other knights. I have to think that it is because of his prowess as a warrior . . . a prowess that means little when coupled with his terminal distaste for the sight of blood. But that weakness of his remains a closely held secret.

Guinevere, hoping to work behind the scenes, summoned Lancelot's wife, Iblis, to her, and asked her to speak to her husband on behalf of the welfare plan. Iblis said naught at first, and then suggested, in a voice that was stiff and formal, "Mayhap you would be well-advised to ask your sister. I am sure that, as of late, she is in a superior position to ask a boon of my husband than I am."

Guinevere was obviously confused. "My sister? Morgan?"

"Have you another?"

"Not to my knowledge, but I do not understand . . ."

"Then, highness," said Iblis with that same formality of tone, "you are even more naïve than the court already believes you to be. May I have leave to depart?"

Still completely bewildered, Guinevere gave her leave as requested. She looked to me then, and I feared that she would ask me what Iblis was going on about. Had she done so, I would have been honor bound to tell her, for I was already feeling uncomfortable over not being fully forthcoming with my queen. The only excuse I had made for myself was that since she had not asked me anything directly, I had not lied. A pathetic excuse, I know, but one thinks what one must in order to survive these little crises of conscience.

It turned out to be unnecessary, for I suddenly saw understanding dawning in Guinevere's eyes. Immediately she was on her feet and she said stiffly, "I need to speak to my sister."

"Shall I bring her—?"

"No. That will not be necessary." With that ominous pronouncement, she walked quickly out of the room.

I knew precisely where she was going, of course. By all rights of decency, I should have remained where I was, waiting for her to return. Yet, even as my mind screamed at me that I was doing the wrong thing and would likely be punished for it somehow—in the afterlife if not in the current one—I ran to the section of wall in the chamber that I knew moved. I tripped the latch, shoved it open, and stepped through into the hidden passages that ran through the walls.

Quickly I made my way through the walls to Morgan's chambers. If that was not where Guinevere was going, then I was wasting my time. It was, however, my time to waste. Guinevere had issued me no orders to remain where I was, and since she had also not commanded me to attend to her, then I could do as I wished. That, at least, was how I was justifying my actions. The fact was that I was being invasive and evil and a bad person, but I could not help myself. I had to see what was to happen next, as if I were a fictional creature caught up in one of the Galahad tales of my own design.

I approached the section of wall that I knew provided a view of Morgan's chambers, and then drew back and nearly yelped, which would have proven a cataclysmically wretched move that would certainly have given me away. The reason for my being startled was that one of the shadows just ahead of me had moved, had risen to greet me. It took a moment to register upon me that it was Modred. I have no idea whether he was spying on Guinevere and me and then went on ahead to Morgan's in anticipation, or if he just happened to be there.

Upon seeing me, he smiled. Really smiled. It was a terrible and frightening thing to see. It was as if he was silently welcoming me into his world of darkness wherein I had become a willing co-conspirator. My instinct was to take this as the final proof that I should be anywhere save for where I was. Instead, to my eternal shame, I leaned forward so that I could better hear what was being said.

It was not all that difficult, for Guinevere had arrived before I had managed to get there. She was already in the process of haranguing Morgan, and Morgan had yet to get out a word as near as I could determine. That, however, was about to change.

"Are you through?" Morgan demanded. "Or are you simply taking a breath?"

"Why Lancelot?" Guinevere said. "What possible reason—?"

"I need not explain myself to you, sister dear. Nor do I understand why it concerns you so. Unless . . ." She paused and then laughed. "Unless you are interested in him yourself."

"That is ridiculous."

"Is it?"

"Yes."

"Then I do not see what else remains to be discussed here. A lady in waiting, even she of the privy chamber, retains the right to a private life. That being the case, what more is there to say?" When Guinevere did not immediately respond, Morgan said, "Well?"

"I need your help," said Guinevere. She did not do so easily or lightly. Indeed, she sounded as if she were choking on the sentence. "Arthur requires Lancelot's support on a project that will help the common folk."

"And of what moment is that to me?"

"It is of moment to me. That should suffice."

"One would think that, wouldn't one?" Morgan did not immediately continue after that. I could not see her face from where I was secreted, but the pause spoke volumes. "Speak to me of this project."

Guinevere did so, outlining the details of it as quickly and efficiently as she could. Morgan listened without comment or interruption. When Guinevere finished, Morgan still said nothing. Time seemed to drag on with excruciating sluggishness until finally Guinevere was moved to say, "Well?"

"Naturally I shall talk to him," said Morgan. "I shall convince him of the wisdom of the plan. He will offer his full allegiance to Arthur on this matter. And he will bring the others into line. Indeed, why should they not be brought into line? Arthur is their king. They have taken oaths to serve him. How dare they, the ingrates," and her voice rose in ire, although it was difficult for me to tell if she was mocking the situation or being serious. "How dare they offer any response to a scheme of their king's other than undiluted support? As far as I am concerned, Arthur should take a blade to any who stand opposed to him. He would be well quit of them."

"I do not think that plan of action would be a particularly prudent one, Morgan."

She appeared to consider it. "Perhaps you are right at that. In any event, although I can guarantee nothing, I am quite certain I can convince du Lac to cooperate."

"And what will you demand in return?"

"Return?" Morgan sounded puzzled and, yet again, I could not determine if she was genuine in her meaning. "Why would I seek anything in return?"

"Because that is the way of humans, Morgan. And it is certainly your way. No one does anything without desiring something for themselves."

"Is that a fact? That is a rather shocking sentiment to be expressed by one purporting to begin a program of welfare for the underclass, ostensibly for no other reason than generosity and caring about her fellow creatures. Pray tell me, Guinevere: How do you expect the populace to greet your good intentions with open arms and open hearts, when you are incapable of accepting a boon from your own sister?"

Guinevere did not answer immediately, and when she did, it was with a lack of conviction that was a stark contrast to her typical manner. "I . . . admit there is a certain . . . validity . . . to that concern. You pose an interesting question."

"I typically do. It is simply that, more often than not, you have no interest in attending to what I have to say. You wish to know what I could hope to gain on a personal basis? Very well: your trust."

"My trust?"

"Yes. If I do you this service, I am asking that you accord me some modicum of trust, as befits a younger sister to her elder. My position as your highest ranked lady in waiting is meaningless if you do not offer me your hand in trust, and you have yet to do so. Since you insist on wishing to know what my reward is simply for accommodating my sister and queen, then accept this as payment on your part for services rendered. In all future dealings, when I speak to you of something, you must accept my word as the unvarnished truth."

"And if I cannot promise you that boon?"

"Well, then," Morgan said readily, "you are cordially invited to seek out Lancelot du Lac and approach him yourself . I suspect, however, that you will find his demands for cooperation to be a bit . . . stiffer . . . than mine."

Modred found that hilarious and clapped both his hands over his mouth in order to suppress laughter . I had no difficulty keeping my mouth shut. I simply bit the inside of my cheek as hard as I could. I did so with such force that I can even now still taste my own blood between my teeth.

After a time, Guinevere finally said, "You are asking me to set aside a lifetime of enmity through sheer power of will."

"Indeed. But that is the only way you ever will be able to set it aside, considering that I have never been anything but kind and cordial to you, whereas your antagonism toward me stems entirely from your belief that you can see through a façade that exists not."

I knew that they were pretty words, but just words. That Morgan was indeed as manipulating and cunning as Guinevere had originally perceived her to be. But I had said naught to Guinevere of it, lest I put my own life at risk through revenge Morgan might direct at me. I prayed silently to Guinevere that she hold true to her suspicions, make no bargains with this devil incarnate, and instead find some other means to accomplish her ends.

My silent prayers to Guinevere had as much impact as my silent prayers to God typically did, so I blame the lack of efficacy on the means of transmission rather than the recipient. I angled myself forward so that I could see out the small view hole. Modred leaned back in order to accommodate me.

"Very well, Morgan," Guinevere said. She extended a hand in a formal handshake. "You have my trust."

Morgan smiled and said, "A hand? Please." She walked over to Guinevere and embraced her. The gesture chilled me and I cursed myself for my cowardice and elevating my concerns over my own life above my obligations to my queen.

I tried to tell myself that perhaps I was being far too negative. I supposed it was possible that Morgan was genuinely interested in finding a way to connect with her sister. That however manipulative and cunning Morgan might be in other matters, some part of her genuinely wanted a sororal bond. I very much wanted to believe that. It would certainly make it easier to feel decent about myself. Yet there I was again, placing personal considerations above considerations for the welfare of others.

I noticed that Modred was staring at me with those pale blue eyes. He crooked his finger, indicating that I should lean in toward him. I did so, my own thoughts in turmoil. He brought his lips to my ear and whispered, "You owe her nothing. She would not give you your freedom for her own selfish reasons."

Once again it was as if Modred had a window into my head. I did not question how he knew of the conversation that Guinevere had with me. He had likely been watching from one of his vantage points, a practice I could no longer hold him in contempt for considering where I was. By this point I had come to assume that Modred was always watching, which was why I had not only plugged the viewing hole that I knew opened to my own chamber, but had taken to bathing and getting dressed and undressed in darkness, just in case.

I said nothing in response to him, but instead merely scowled and then turned away.

Still, the icy tendrils of his comments had already insinuated themselves into my consciousness.

I returned to my chambers, but Guinevere did not. I had to assume that she had gone to Arthur to tell him what she had been up to. Or I suppose she might have simply gone to him to be with him, as a wife is with a husband. And I certainly did not wish to dwell on what Morgan was up to with Lancelot, although I yet again felt pity for Iblis, who was becoming more and more the tragic figure to me.

The hell of it was that Modred had a point. Guinevere could have given me my freedom. She chose not to do so for eminently selfish reasons. I believe that on some level she felt she was complimenting me, forcing me to remain in servitude so that she could be assured of my companionship. Insanely enough, to some degree I was flattered. Still, what it came down to was that Queen Guinevere was expressing more concern about the welfare of random peasants than she was about her own handmaiden. Her interest in the well-being of others, it appeared, ceased when such priorities conflicted with her own considerations.

I tried to tell myself that I was being uncharitable. Yet it continued to rankle within me, and that in and of itself was irritating because I was aware that the seed had been planted by Modred and I was allowing it to blossom. I knew he was a master puppeteer and I could see the strings that he was pulling on me. I was allowing it to happen all the same.

I should speak to Guinevere of it. I should tell her all, tell her everything. But I know that I am not going to do that, and this knowledge makes me even more ashamed of myself. It seems that I am more than merely a slave to others. I am a slave to my own fears.

Damn my weakness. I wish I had never come to this miserable place.

Day the Eightieth

I AM SLOWLY BECOMING CONVINCED that men are insane. They have no idea how to sort out quarrels or reasonably come to any manner of decision without involving violent means.

Madmen, the lot of them.

While taking her evening bath, Guinevere related to me what happened at a gathering of the round table earlier today, having been told in turn by her husband. Lancelot, to the surprise of a number of the knights, came out in favor of the king's proposal for taxation on behalf of welfare for the commoners. This prompted a furious dispute amongst the knights. Arthur tried to keep matters in check, but failed spectacularly. Insults were hurled, and then several knights set upon Lancelot.

Because I have seen Lancelot dispatched by something as common as an abacus and become weak-kneed and womanly at the sight of blood, it is easy to overlook his considerable fighting skills.

"He was nothing short of astounding, according to Arthur," Guinevere said with wonderment in her voice. "Four men launched themselves at him and he took them down almost simultaneously, with both his hands and his feet. His feet, of all things."

"His feet?" I could not keep the distaste from my voice. "You mean kicking? That does not seem very sportsmanlike."

"He did not merely kick. He used his feet as weapons, like . . . like this," and she swept her leg up high.

"I have never seen the like," I marveled.

"Nor have I, nor had Arthur. Lancelot told him that it was a technique he learned from sailors in the port city of Marseille. It is called . . ." She hesitated, endeavoring to pronounce the foreign word properly.". . . *chausson.*"

"Amazing."

"It indeed was. It all happened so quickly that the last man was knocked unconscious ere the first one had finished hitting the ground."

"So no swords were drawn then."

"No. It merely came to blows, not lethal force."

"That is a relief," I said.

"Indeed. I must ask him to teach me the techniques. There are worse things I could do than learn means of defending myself."

Considering the amount of resentment she was building within the court, I had to agree. Then I asked, "So . . . so what happened? Did they discuss the specifics of the plan?"

"They never got to it, actually. There was a great deal of acrimony over the subject, but on the other hand, they were vastly impressed by Lancelot's prowess. So they decided on jousts."

"Wait . . ." I blinked repeatedly as if trying to clear my head. "They decided on jousts?"

"Yes."

"Why? To what end?"

"To determine what is to be done regarding the matter of taxation."

"But I do not understand. What does one have to do with the other?"

She slid underwater and for a moment I thought she was drowning in the tub. Then she surfaced and wiped the water from her face. "Honestly? Not a damned thing. But this is the way men operate. They decide matters not through rational discourse, but through force of arms."

"Not all men, surely."

"Most of the ones I've met do. The most persuasive arguments are made with the sharpness of a man's sword than through the sharpness of his mind."

"So those who subscribe to Arthur's proposals are going to engage in mock combat with those who are opposed. And whoever triumphs will carry the day, and the proposals will stand or fall based on that."

Guinevere nodded. "Correct. Plus it will be a superb day of entertainment for the common folk. They love a good joust."

"But are the common folk going to know what is truly at stake?"

"No, of course not. They never know."

"Never? You mean this has happened before?"

"It happens all the time," said Guinevere. She ran her fingers through her sodden hair, straightening out the knots. "It is the reason most such tournaments are held. I am not speaking of the more base entertainments provided by traveling hedge knights, mind you. I am speaking of royal jousts. The typical motivation for them is to settle disputes."

I shook my head in frustration. "I still do not see how whether one man is capable of knocking another man off a horse at full gallop decides the merits of an argument."

"It does not. It decides which man can force the other to bend to his will."

"But should not ideas stand or fall on the merits of the ideas alone?"

"Yes. They should. Unfortunately, they do not. That is simply the way things are done."

"Then, with all respect, highness, it should be done differently."

"Granted. And if women ran the world, I believe it would be. Unfortunately it is run by men, and we are merely left shaking our heads at their thunderous stupidity. That, and manipulating what men do from behind the scenes. The conjugal bed can be as formidable a weapon, in its own way, as a sword or lance. Nations have risen or fallen based upon what is said in the afterglow of lovemaking." She saw the way I was looking at her and sat up in the bath. "Speak your mind, Viviana. Something is on it, I am quite sure."

"It is just that . . ." I shifted my feet uncomfortably. "Truth to tell, I am uncertain whether I am hearing Queen Guinevere speaking now . . . or if it is the sentiments of your sister being expressed."

Guinevere seemed to consider my words. "I suppose," she said after a time, "that even my sister is entitled to be correct now and again. Oh . . . she suggests that I begin wearing dresses more often than not. I despise the notion. What think you?"

I thought Morgan was absolutely right, but instead I said, "You must do what is right for yourself, highness."

"Yes. So I should."

The door to her private chambers opened. Guinevere gasped and sank lower in the tub at the unexpected interruption. Automatically I stood between her and the door, holding wide a towel in order to block uninvited views. To my surprise, the lady Igraine was standing there. She looked as confused to see us as we were to see her.

"Milady?" said Guinevere, peeking from behind me.

Igraine focused on Guinevere and then said something most puzzling: "Why came I here?"

"I . . . do not know," said Guinevere. "You were not expected."

"There was . . ." She scratched the side of her head. "There was something I wished to discuss with you."

"If you wish to come in, by all means, milady, do so. But please close the door in any event, for you are creating a draft, and the queen is hardly in an appropriate state to be subjected to it."

"Oh. Yes, of course. Quite right," said Igraine, whereupon she closed the door with herself on the outside.

Guinevere and I exchanged confused looks. Quickly I proffered her a robe and as she pulled it on, I walked to the door and opened it.

Igraine was gone. Presumably she had wandered off.

"If I am blessed with children," Guinevere said, "I pray they are girls, despite whatever Arthur may wish for an heir. By all evidence, being the mother of sons can drive you insane."

I could not disagree.

Day the Eighty-First

NOTHING GOOD EVER COMES FROM violence. Nothing. Not violence created in the interest of sporting ventures. Not violence performed as a means of determining who is right and who is wrong. Certainly not violence for the purpose of bringing war on another. If I had ever doubted the truth of any of these precepts, those doubts were erased by the events of this day, the darkest day that I have ever experienced since I set foot in this cursed place called Camelot.

One would never have been able to foresee the turn that this day would take based upon the weather. It was glorious, with nary a cloud to be seen against an azure sky. Her highness awoke in a fine mood, brimming with confidence that the outcome of today's joust would more than meet her expectations. She claimed that she was fortified by the simple conviction that her cause was just. That, indeed, the justness of the cause would bring about the hoped for outcome simply because . . . I do not know. Because God willed it that way, I suppose. As for myself, I had to think it dangerously prideful to assume that God felt a certain way about a concept simply because one felt that way oneself. It has been my experience that God has His own priorities, steeped in unknowable motivations that border on cruelty. Did I say "border?" Nay, many has been the time that God has crossed the border and cavalierly sojourned through vast tracts of wickedness and mayhem. If His actions were pursued by a mortal man, he would likely be considered the cruelest creature ever to walk the earth. As it is, it is impossible to argue with God. I should know, having attempted it often enough over the years and seen my efforts come to naught.

But Guinevere was confident that God was aligned with her interests and thus would ensure triumph in order to better the lives of peasants. I was motivated to wonder why, if God was so concerned about peasants, He allowed them to be peasants in the first place instead of simply elevating them with a wave of His hand. Certainly a being that can create vast storms or cause the ground to tremble can see fit to toss a few more coins their way.

I had never been to the jousting field before. A long rail ran down the middle, which I assumed was to serve as a guide for men on horseback charging each other with lances. There were men with rakes smoothing down the dirt on the field. I learned later they were combing it out for random stones to try and ensure smooth approaches for horses. I seriously doubted that the outcome of a charge would be determined by a horse getting a pebble lodged in its hoof, but I suppose one cannot be too careful.

Guinevere sent me on ahead to make certain that the royal box in which she and Arthur would be sitting would be sufficiently commodious to accommodate her, the king, and their respective retinues (of which I was to be a member, of course.) I climbed up into the box, which was mounted in the middle of the grand stands. It certainly seemed spacious enough. Even luxurious, particularly in comparison to the quality of the seats designed for the commoners, which were little more than elevated benches.

Even though the joust would not be held for several hours, people were already gathering and seeking out seats. Having made my way down from the royal box, I gave ear to the sentiments of the crowd, curious to see if they were as enthused about the coming entertainment as Guinevere thought they would be.

Apparently that was not the case.

The children were excited, I will admit that. But the adults were cynical, suspicious. They spoke of how this was merely some grand gesture to try and distract them from the miserable quality of their lives. That Arthur was obviously a far weaker king than Uther, and he was putting on this display of strength to try and convince everyone that it was otherwise. That the money being spent to put on the joust would be better served being disbursed to the poor. One even joked that the kingdom would be well-served if Arthur spent the money to buy his wife a proper dress, and that provoked much merriment.

I have to admit that the observation about helping the poor was particularly galling since I knew the reasons behind the joust. I wanted to shout at them, "Fools! This is being held for your benefit!" But they would not have believed me, and even if they had, I was not convinced that the revelation would reflect well upon the round table. The notion of fighting to determine the winner of a political argument had seemed absurd to me on its face. How then to convince others that it was not, particularly since I did not believe that to be so?

It made me start to think, though, that Merlin had yet again made a salient point. Human nature was to be suspicious of anything, no matter what the intent. It would seem that, as a race, we are untrustworthy ourselves and therefore do not trust others because of that shortcoming we all share. It is a terrible thing to believe, and would that I did not. But the longer I am here, the more I start to think that it might be so. There is no gesture that the king and queen can make that is not going to be subject to scrutiny and suspicion, and no action they could take that would not be found wanting in some manner. Sometimes I think that if Arthur walked on water, he would be accused of being disrespectful to ducks.

The populace did not behave in that manner with Uther. Then again, the man hacked off the head of a horse with his sword simply because the beast irritated him. Uther did not give a damn if people loved him or not, which seems to be Arthur's main concern. Yet I would believe that love is a far preferable emotional state to fear. So I do not know what to think at this point.

As I prepared to depart the jousting arena, I noticed that the horses were already being brought to the holding pens. And there was the mute. I realized I had never seen him in the light of day, and even now he was trying to stay out of it, staying to the sides of the horses and tending to them. He was as dirty and disgusting as ever. I could scarce stand to look at him, and yet I did. I have to think that it was the same compulsion that causes one to stare in fascination at open sores or the rotting corpse of a dog.

Somehow the mute sensed that I was looking at him, for he shifted his gaze toward me. His eyes peered out from between filthy strands of hair hanging in his face. I looked away immediately. When I glanced back, he had returned his attention to the horses. I quickly withdrew.

Upon returning to Guinevere, I was stunned to see that she was attired in a very attractive dress. She was studying herself in the mirror, turning this way and that, and she looked grim but determined. Morgan was adjusting some ties on it, and when Guinevere saw me enter, she turned stiffly and said, "What do you think? Be honest."

Honestly, I thought she looked uncomfortable and out of place, and should switch to her more accustomed attire immediately. But Morgan fired me a warning look. I cleared my throat, smiled and said, "Words fail me, highness."

"How sweet of you to say."

Inwardly I breathed a sigh of relief as I assured her that the box would indeed be spacious enough. I also told her what I had heard the peasantry muttering. I thought she would be disturbed by it, but she simply shrugged and said, "They will come around. When Arthur improves their lot in life, things will change."

I hoped she was right, feared she was wrong, and said

nothing further on the matter.

I have to admit that, once the pageantry of the joust commenced, my misgivings began to melt away. And the throngs that, prior to the festivities, had been sour and suspicious, nevertheless cheered and shouted and applauded as loudly as one could have hoped. I began to think that Guinevere might have had the correct attitude, not to worry so much upon what the people had been saying to each other. It appeared they had exceedingly transient memories.

When the crowd saw the queen dressed as they imagined a queen should be, there were collective murmurs and even applause. She curtsied, even affecting a shy look that I had noticed her practicing in the mirror before our arrival. I would have liked to think that the common folk have matters of greater weight on their minds than how royalty dresses, but apparently that is not the case. Or perhaps they simply like to dwell on such things because it takes their minds off their more serious problems. Nobility as diversion.

I have never been to a joust and I have to say that it certainly gets the blood flowing. And I mean that in a positive manner— the blood within you, not the blood without. The knights rode on their horses in a slow circle around the ring, holding their lances aloft to salute the king and queen. Arthur and Guinevere waved or nodded acknowledgment, even to those knights who I knew were in opposition to the king's proposed policies.

The greatest cheers and, interestingly, boos, all came for Lancelot. It appeared that Lancelot was developing something of a reputation in the village. He was hard drinking and free spending, which most of the men appreciated, but he was also extremely "attentive" to the more comely women, which the men most definitely did not appreciate. So Lancelot had gotten into not a few scuffles, although nothing that had been too difficult for the knight to handle. And after he had laid out an opponent, he would turn around and buy the man and his friends drinks, which immediately made him popular all over again. I believe that, as long as I live, I will never understand how men's minds work, or even if they work at all.

Arthur applauded, as did Guinevere. Also in the royal box were Igraine, who watched the proceedings with a detached air, and myself, and Morgan as well. She, naturally, was watching Lancelot with eagerness, and applauded robustly when he passed. I noticed that Arthur was regarding Morgan with what appeared to be resignation.

Damn the man, he still loved her. I had no doubt that he had fully committed his emotions and devotions to Guinevere, but he could not take his mind off Morgan. Still, I suppose that as long as he has done nothing to act upon those feelings, one cannot condemn another simply because of thoughts that pass through his head.

I noticed that Igraine was muttering softly to herself. She kept glancing at Arthur, then at Guinevere, and then shaking her head. Concerned, I moved toward her and murmured, "Are you in need of something, milady?"

"He was watching me," said Igraine. "When we came in. Uther. His eyes were upon me. Did you not see him?"

I had to admit that I did not, and could not, for he was dead and buried and lived only in our memories.

"I can show him to you," she offered.

"Show who, mother?" said Arthur, who had noticed that we were talking and leaned over from his throne to hear what we were on about.

She smiled and looked at him in a vague, blank manner. "I do not remember," she said, and it was impossible for me to determine whether she honestly did not recall or simply had no desire to discuss the matter with her son. Whichever one it was, her noncommittal response was sufficient for Arthur to nod and turn away from her, shifting his attention back to the field.

The afternoon progressed as did the assorted battles. The knights were both armored and padded to minimize any chance of any catastrophic damage. This, of course, served Lancelot extremely well, since it did not seem likely there would be any major gashes or wounds that would result in blood flow which would in turn result in his reacting in his customary manner.

It was the first opportunity I had to observe Lancelot in full combat situations. I have to say, it was impressive. None were able to stand against him for long. One, two passes upon horseback at most, and then Lancelot's lance would find a weak point and unhorse his opponent. Man after man was sent clattering to the ground.

And after every encounter, Lancelot would dismount, walk up to his fallen adversary, extend a hand to help him up and then embrace him as one would a long-lost brother. It was an exciting and astounding display. Lancelot was easily the most formidable knight there, and I could only thank the stars that he was allied with Arthur at this particular point. If he had been in opposition to the king's wishes and fighting on the other side of the issue, the welfare of the poor would have had no chance.

Morgan and Guinevere applauded loudly and long after each man was unhorsed. Sisters they were, united for once in mutual interest. My response was politely enthused but muted, for there was still much about Lancelot that I disliked. Then again, it is hard to feel much affection for one who has jabbed a sword into you.

I kept glancing back at Igraine. None were paying her much mind, and it seemed to me that she was becoming increasingly agitated, muttering to herself and looking more and more concerned. I had no desire to distract Arthur from the proceedings nor did I want him distracted by his mother's state of mind. Instead I leaned in close to Guinevere and whispered to her my worries about Igraine.

Guinevere looked to see the source of my concerns. Arthur was caught up in the joust, which had moved from horseback confrontations to man-to-man battles. At that moment Lancelot was busy pounding Sir Tor into submission with a broadsword. Taking the opportunity, Guinevere moved from her seat over to Igraine, who was positioned toward the back of the royal box. Igraine appeared gratified to see her and appreciative of the attention. She started speaking animatedly to Guinevere. The queen listened, her face becoming more and more concerned. Then Igraine, who had been seated, rose and began to head for the back of the royal box toward the exit. Guinevere followed her, and I naturally went right after Guinevere. Morgan noticed our departure and started to rise, but Guinevere gestured for her to remain where she was and Morgan sat once more.

"How now, highness?" I said as we moved to the rear of the box. There was a narrow set of steps that led from the box to the ground. "Is something wrong?"

"The lady Igraine insists that she has seen Uther," said Guinevere. "Between this and her confusion some days ago, I think it best to humor her."

"Perhaps I should accompany you."

Guinevere nodded and together the three of us descended from the back of the royal box. Arthur, still fascinated by the battles before him, did not notice.

Considering how many people were in attendance, it was amazing how relatively isolated we were. Typically whenever the queen goes anywhere, an escort accompanies her. Guinevere has little patience for such perpetual care but accepts it as a necessary evil. In this instance, the three of us were relatively alone.

Cheers arose from behind us as we moved along the outer perimeter of the stands. Igraine seemed to know precisely where she was going and we had no choice but to follow her.

She led us to the far end of the arena, gesturing eagerly anytime we slowed. Guinevere's dress was far too ornate for easy running, but she did the best she could to stay close behind Igraine. We passed a couple of stragglers whose eyes widened when they realized who was moving among them, and promptly dropped to their knees. Guinevere waved in passing and kept going, and I hurried to catch up.

I could not imagine where Igraine was bringing us. The smell of horses wafted toward me; handlers were in the process of returning them to the stables, since the part of the program involving horses had been concluded.

Then I saw four men with cloaks, two of them with hoods pulled up, directly in our path. There were looks of clear surprise upon their faces as if they could not believe that they were seeing us. It was a look I was not unaccustomed to. People were always surprised to see royalty standing directly in front of them.

But then I saw something upon their faces that was not typical: the cruel look of men about to seize an opportunity.

They advanced upon us quickly, and I saw swords dangling off their hips under their cloaks. "God is with us, gentlemen," said one of them. "Here we thought we'd have to go to a deal of trouble, and she is delivered unto us . . . with the king mother tossed in for good measure."

Instantly it was evident to all of us that we were in dire straits, and that these men meant us nothing but ill-will. Guinevere was not one to back down. Were she armed, I believe she would have given a good accounting of herself. Unarmed, she still did not brook their insolence. "Stay your distance, sirrah," she said archly, "in the name of King Arthur."

"I think not, highness . . . in the name of Maleagant."

The name froze us where we stood, as if spears of ice had transfixed us. And then the men descended upon us with a triumphant roar. My instinct was to back up, to flee, yet for some demented reason I placed myself between them and the queen, calling out, "Run, your highness!" I swung a foot at the closest one, hoping to strike him in his privy parts, but he brought his leg up and my foot bounced harmlessly off his hip. I saw there was a large burlap sack in his hands, and then it was over my head. My vision obscured, I tried to struggle, but the sack was drawn down over my arms, restricting my movements. He slammed me face first to the ground and within seconds, with terrifying expertise, he had bound both my hands and my feet. I was helpless.

"This one's a slave," called the one who had bound me. "We might be able to make a tidy profit off her. How fares the queen?"

"Fighting like a hellcat, but secured! The mother is—"

"Damnation!" I heard the third one shout. "She's slippery as an eel, this one! She—hey! Who are you? Get away! Put that shovel down, you—"

Then I heard a sound such as I shall never forget. It was the sound of metal striking what sounded like a melon, but I realized quickly it was a human head. And it crunched, God in heaven, it crunched, and I knew even though I could not see it that whoever had been struck by the shovel was a dead man. From the immediate sounds of confusion and shouting, I intuited that the dead man had not been whoever the newcomer was.

Then came the sounds of swords being drawn, and more shouting, and more cutting and clanging and hideous sounds of huge metal things connecting with bone and muscle, and then something warm and moist struck me in the back of the head, or rather where the back of my head was within the burlap sack. Something had been sent flying across the space. I very much suspected that it had been something that had previously either been inside a human body or, at the very least, attached to it. I wretched and snapped my head to one side, trying to get it off me, but I did not have much mobility, tied up as I was.

And then I heard one of the men shout, "Get away, you freak! Put it down or I swear this dagger goes into her heart!" and then another voice, milady Igraine's, and she cried out defiantly, "No one threatens me!" and there was a noise that sounded horrifically similar to the one I had heard that night when Lancelot's blade had buried itself in my chest. Then I heard a horrified scream that was interrupted, truncated, and something hit the ground with a sound like a large heavy ball.

There was a long moment of silence, and then it was broken by the soft moaning of a female voice. Then something cut me loose from my bonds. Frantically I pulled my hands free, sat up, and yanked the sack from over my head.

I could not believe what I was looking at.

Standing a few feet away, staring at me in his customary silence, was the mute. He was holding a sword that he had undoubtedly taken away from one of the attackers. In his other hand he was clutching a shovel, brown from manure but now tinted with dripping red. His face was impassive save for his eyes, which blazed with ferocity. Then the mute threw down the sword, gripped his shovel with both hands, and turned away.

"Wait!" I called out, but seconds later he had fled.

My instinct was to go after him, but I realized I had more pressing matters to attend to. Guinevere was lying several feet away, tied up within a bag as I had been. Of greater and more immediate concern was Igraine. She had a dagger buried in her chest.

Strewn all about were the bodies of our attackers. They were all dead, their heads crushed in or their chests run through.

There were alarmed shrieks from nearby. A couple of harlots had come across the scene. Their faces had gone pale, a stark contrast to the fiery red of their colored hair. "Summon the king!" I shouted. "Hurry! Hurry!" They ran off to do my bidding, probably the only time in their lives that they had done what they were told without someone thrusting money into their hands to compel them.

Quickly I freed the queen and yanked the sack from off her head. There was no fear on her face when I uncovered it, which was likely a stark contrast to the way I must have looked. "Where are they!? They are dead men!" she bellowed.

"Aye, they are, but look to Igraine," I said.

Guinevere was startled as she saw the carnage around her, but then her attention rightly focused itself upon where I had directed, namely the fallen Igraine. She was lying upon the ground, staring at nothing, and she was saying in bewilderment, "Uther . . . where did Uther go . . . ?"

The fact was that Uther was dead, as all save Igraine seemed to know, and she was about to join him. "The bastards stabbed her," said Guinevere to me as if I was unaware of what had transpired.

As it turned out I was indeed unaware, for Igraine said fiercely and with sudden lucidity, "Like hell. The cretin pointed a dagger at me, threatened to take my life. I will end my life on my own schedule. I thrust myself forward onto the dagger, not the other way around. Such as he will never slay me. I would sooner kill myself."

Indeed she had. In her increasing dementia, somehow she considered that a good thing. Guinevere choked back a sob, her hand hovering over the dagger, unsure of what to do. Pulling it out would unleash a torrent of blood, but it looked ghastly sticking out of her in that manner.

And then Igraine looked up at Guinevere and her eyes cleared. As if seeing her for the first time in a long while, she said, "I just remembered what I wanted to tell you. 'Tis very important."

"What is it, milady?"

"I warned him. I warned him his appetites would be the death of him someday."

"Warned who? Uther? What about his appetites?"

Then Igraine's eyes glassed over, and she smiled softly and said, "Oh. There he is."

By the time Arthur arrived, crying out his mother's name, the lady Igraine was gone.

Day the Eighty-Second

Camelot is in mourning and in shock and in so many other states of emotion that I scarcely know where to begin.

Arthur went into seclusion with the death of his mother. He did not do so immediately. The first thing he did was spend an inordinate amount of time asking Guinevere what she had seen and heard in the course of the attack. He was stoic as she told him that the attackers had declared they were acting in the name of Maleagant. It seemed impossible, and yet the fact remained that Maleagant's body had vanished under mysterious circumstances in the confusion following Arthur's assault upon him. Arthur turned to me then as Merlin looked on and asked me the same questions that he had asked Guinevere. I answered them to the best of my ability, asserting that Guinevere had heard our attackers correctly.

"But how is it possible that he survived?" Guinevere said.

"Obviously he did," said Arthur. His voice was distant, as if he were speaking but the voice had little relevance to him. "He survived . . . and his warriors are acting upon his orders. And my mother is dead because of it, and they would likely have taken my queen if it had not been for . . ." Then his voice trailed off, and he and Merlin exchanged looks.

"That remains a point of confusion," said Merlin when Arthur seemed at a loss for something to say. "Obviously you ladies were not responsible for the carnage that resulted from the abortive attempt upon you. Who, then, was?"

"I saw nothing until Viviana freed me from the bonds that Maleagant's men put upon me," said Guinevere.

All eyes turned to me. They waited for me to speak.

I was about to tell them all. To tell them of the mute who had somehow dispatched our assailants with little more than skill and a shovel.

I have no idea what halted my tongue. This was my king and queen, and Merlin was . . . well, I have no idea what he was to me, but he intimidated me a'right, and lying to him was not an endeavor upon which I would lightly embark.

It occurred to me then that I did not, in fact, have to lie. I could speak the truth and it would still provide no clue as to the identity of our rescuer.

"I heard battle," I said. "Then someone cut loose my bonds. By the time I removed the sack obscuring my vision, it was all over. The 'somone' ran off."

"I see," said Arthur. "So you do not know definitively who was involved in the rescue."

"I assume that he wished to remain anonymous, your majesty." I bowed my head in deference to him and then glanced toward Merlin. He remained inscrutable.

"Very well," Arthur said finally. "I bring this to the round table then. Guinevere . . . Viviana . . . you shall accompany me, and you shall tell them what you witnessed."

"Tell them, majesty?" I said, and I think my voice went up slightly as I spoke. "Is . . . is that truly necessary?"

"I want them to hear first-hand what happened," said Arthur, and his voice was shaking with fury. "I tell you that this bloody business will not go unavenged."

"Of course it will not, my love," said Guinevere. I silently bobbed my head in agreement. I think it was the first time she had ever called him "my love" in public. Perhaps even in private.

"My mother's life will not have been lost in vain. She . . ." His voice trailed off and I could see his eyes welling with tears. "And Guinevere . . . when we go before the table, wear a damned dress. I wish to underscore the vulnerability of my queen."

"You want me to appear weak so that I will seem more sympathetic? Is that what you are say—!"

"Yes!" thundered Arthur, "and this is the wrong time to ignore my wishes, woman! Is that clear?"

I held my breath, uncertain of how Guinevere would respond. She seemed to be contemplating a variety of responses, but finally she simply nodded her head and said, "Yes, my husband."

I saw Merlin mutter *Thank God* to himself.

Hastily Guinevere turned to Merlin and me and bid us excuse ourselves, stating that she and the king required some time in seclusion. We both bowed and took our leaves. The moment we were outside the door of the chamber, in the anteroom, Merlin gazed at me levelly and said, "You had quite a scare, Mistress Viviana."

"Aye, sir, I did."

"Interesting," he said slowly, "that you spoke of your rescuer as 'he.' One would reasonably have thought that it would have taken several men to save you from multiple assailants. Yet you spoke with confidence of a single rescuer . . . except you likewise claimed that you did not actually see who was the author of your salvation. I find that odd."

I licked my lips, which had suddenly gone dry under Merlin's soft-spoken but very direct probing. "I . . . suppose it is odd, sir. I just assumed, I suppose, that it was the one man, but I suppose it could have been more. In . . . in fact maybe it was—"

He raised a finger, silencing me. There was still much about him that I found unnerving. "Do not," he said slowly, "start changing your story now. For better or worse, you have said what you have said, and now you will maintain it. Do you understand, girl?"

I nodded.

He leaned in toward me and said softly, "You have no comprehension of what this can and will lead to. People are going to be hurt. People are going to die. We have two imperatives from this point on: to make certain it all benefits Arthur, and to make certain that we ourselves are not amongst the corpses. Do you understand that as well?"

Again I nodded.

Merlin seemed satisfied with that, but before he departed the antechamber, he said, "Never forget, Mistress Viviana:

When the horses of war have been unleashed, that is not the time to ride sidesaddle. Do you see what I am saying?"

I did not, but I nodded as if I did. It seemed hard to go wrong with nodding where Merlin was concerned. That philosophy served me well as Merlin departed without another word, leaving me behind trembling.

Arthur took no time at all arranging for the gathering. An armed escort marched me in and I saw arrayed before me the knights seated around the table. I had seen the table before, but never with the participants in attendance. It was a moment of staggering power for me, so much so that I felt my legs going weak. Seemingly sensing my moment of faintness, my escorts on either side of me supported me by the elbows. A small chair was brought out for me and I was seated in it. Guinevere was seated in a chair to the right of, and behind, Arthur. Apparently the queen did not rank highly enough to sit at the grand table itself. Nor was Merlin seated; instead he wandered the perimeter, as he typically seemed to do at gatherings, like an oversize cat stalking prey.

"We have heard the words of the queen," Arthur said. "Now we will hear yours, handmaiden."

I cast only the briefest glance in Merlin's direction and then repeated, word for word, what I had told Arthur. I hesitated only a moment before saying "he," hoping and praying that no one at the table would notice the use of the single pronoun. If they did, I was ready to try and allow for the idea that there had indeed been others and I had merely misspoken. Certainly they would accept such a notion; I was a "mere woman," after all, in the presence of great men, and could easily be forgiven a few oral blunders.

It turned out to be unnecessary. None of them noticed the slip that Merlin had so easily detected. Instead they accepted my story without reservation, not even asking any questions. Of course, they might well have already asked the questions of the queen and did not require answers of me.

"Somehow," Gawain said, "Maleagant managed to survive. And now he sends warriors to operate on behalf of his insidious desires."

"We do not know that of a certainty," said Percival from across the table. "Remember, they said they were operating in his name only. It could be that his followers are bandying about his name for their own purposes while Maleagant's body lies moldering in the ground somewhere."

There was a deal of back and forth at that point, some knights arguing that Maleagant had to be dead, simply had to, for none could have survived such a smiting as the king had lain upon him. Others advocated that, short of having Maleagant's head upon a pike, there was no final proof of his demise and he remained a threat.

Some advocated caution, others a rush into battle.

"Dare we take that chance that Maleagant is dead?" Gawain was saying, and then Lancelot spoke up very sharply and said, "No. We do not."

All eyes and attention turned to him in a manner that had not existed when the other knights had spoken. It was clear from their reaction and demeanor that Lancelot had come to be considered a first among equals. As ludicrous as it might have seemed, his ability to physically overwhelm any man who faced him somehow lent disproportionate weight to his words. The priorities of men have been, and likely always will continue to be, a mystery to me.

"We do not dare take that chance," Lancelot continued. "These warriors of Maleagant's desires are a very real and very credible threat to king and country." His fingers curled into a fist and he slammed the fist down on the table for emphasis. "We must dedicate all our resources into finding these warriors of Maleagant's desires. They must be tracked down, they must be dispatched, lest these acts of terrorism against us be allowed to continue."

As other knights began to swing over to Lancelot's point of view, that same phrase kept being repeated: warriors of Maleagant's desires. I could understand why. It was stirring and exciting and frightening, all at the same time. Warriors of Maleagant's desires. It spoke of a vast army conspiring to bring down everything that the knights loved and protected. They had already struck and would no doubt strike again unless we struck back, quickly and immediately and with every resource that Arthur had at his command.

It was resolved right then and there: Camelot would marshal its forces and move against Maleagant.

Maleagant was no king, but a warlord. As such, he had no set residence, but instead simply areas of territory that he patrolled and held sway over. Some claimed that he had a stronghold in Glastonbury. Others asserted that Cumberland was where he preferred to reside, particularly if he was in hiding. Arthur and his knights resolved to set out first for the former and then, if unable to track down Maleagant, head for the latter, and further seek out any sympathetic hamlets or individuals who might provide care and support for the warlord.

They began slamming their fists rhythmically on the table as they spoke of the war and carnage and vengeance that would be spread throughout Britain against any who dared to stand on Maleagant's behalf. I found the display daunting, intimidating, even frightening. Dozens of men, who between them commanded hundreds of soldiers, slaves and vassals, swearing to dedicate their combined forces to seek out and destroy the warriors of Maleagant's desires.

And the most disturbing thing of all was that, as Merlin beheld the display, he smiled broadly as if war was not a bloody and unwanted necessity but instead a joyous achievement worth celebrating.

I am becoming more and more convinced that dark times await us all.

Day the Eighty-Third

I HAD TO FIND HIM today. As much as he frightens me, as off-putting as I consider him to be, I had to go to the mute stable hand. I owed him my life.

I tried to think of something I could bring him to tender him as a gift of thanks. Some small foodstuffs or something like that. It was not as if I had the resources to purchase him anything of great monetary value. Ultimately I could not think of anything that did not seem trite and absurd. "Here. You have saved my life, and so in appreciation I present you with this crumpet."

I made my way down to the stables. The stable master glared at me upon seeing me. Obviously he was still smarting over my having terminated his tawdry affairs with Rowena. In retrospect, I suppose it might have been a cruelty to him that he suffered merely because I wished some bit of revenge upon Rowena for her treatment of me. Perhaps I should have felt badly about it. Unfortunately, I did not.

The stable master turned and walked away from me without saying a word, leaving the stables abandoned save for myself and, presumably, the mute. I did not see him at first but then I heard the sound of hay being rustled toward the back. I moved toward it, squinting in the dimness, and found him mucking out one of the stables. The aroma of horse manure hung pungently all about him. He did not appear to notice it or, for that matter, me. He was wielding a pitchfork and when I cleared my throat loudly to gain his attention, he reflexively brought the pitchfork up as if meaning to wield it in a lethal manner. I jumped back slightly and let out a startled cry, my hand fluttering to my breast. The mute immediately realized his error and slowly he lowered the pitchfork.

We stood there for a time staring at each other, myself as wordless as he. The awkwardness of our situation became progressively more evident.

I felt as if his eyes were devouring me. No one had ever looked at me that way, with such . . . intensity. It was most unnerving.

"I . . ." My voice cracked unexpectedly. "I know it was you. That rescued the queen."

There was a flicker of concern on his face and he tilted his head slightly in what I interpreted to be the general direction of the castle.

I have no idea how I knew what he was thinking, but I did. "No. I did not tell them. They know nothing of your participation. I said nothing because I believed that, had you desired credit for your actions, you would have remained on the scene to receive it. Your hasty departure told me that you desired it not."

His body sagged slightly and I realized that he was sighing with relief. I had clearly made the correct interpretation. But knowing the truth of it did not answer the why. I stepped closer to him, staring at him quizzically. "I respected that wish because I owed you . . . owe you . . . my life. Nevertheless, it is strange to . . . I do not understand. You would be hailed a hero. All would sing your praises. And . . . and your fighting skills! The way you dispatched them, you against all those men and you did not flinch. Unless 'twas not you who did the deed, but somebody else . . ."

He shook his head and thumped his chest. I was relieved to see him responding so to questions in direct address. I had not been entirely certain until that moment that his muteness did not stem from some lack of wits. Clearly that was not the case. He understood everything that I said and responded in a reasonable, if silent, manner. "Ah. So 'twas you," I said. He nodded in confirmation. "Then still I do not understand. Why not accept the accolades, the rewards that would rightly be yours for your valiant actions."

He shrugged and shook his head slightly. His gaze never left me.

What a puzzle this man was.

"Well," I said, "whatever the reason, know you that I have kept your secret out of gratitude. But you have my thanks. It is a small and useless thing, I know, but 'tis all I have to give. My hands may be empty, but my heart is full of appreciation for your . . ."

My voice trailed off.

He continued to look at me.

The manner in which the girls in the kitchen had spoken of throwing me to the mute implied that he was a creature with terrible and brutal carnal appetites. I had not considered their words in quite some time, but they came roaring back to me now and I felt the skin crawling on the back of my neck.

And yet . . . as shamed as I am to say it . . . I felt intrigued. He had such an aura of . . . of strength about him, and even a crude nobility buried beneath the muck.

He walked slowly toward me. I remained rooted to the spot. The way he looked at me gave me the strangest feeling, as if we had met somewhere before. I knew that we had not; I was certain of it. And yet there was this sense that we were connected in some way. There are those who speak fancifully of souls reuniting, having known each other in previous lives. But I tend to restrict my fancies to my imaginings of good and valiant knights, such as my idealized Galahad, and do not for a moment think that such things exist in real life.

Yet how then to explain the strange sense of knowing the mute from elsewhere? I could not, nor am I entirely certain that I wish to.

He stood only a few inches from me. I did not move or flinch. He seemed almost to be testing me, to see how close he could come to me before I withdrew. He reached out toward me and I could not help myself: I stepped back. He looked momentarily surprised, and that reaction made him seem—I do not know—more human somehow, rather than a manure-encrusted creature.

I looked down, feeling ashamed. "I . . . am sorry. You are just so . . . so filthy. Your hands . . . they . . . I am sorry . . ."

Were he the brutish, unthinking creature that the kitchen wenches portrayed him as, I doubt anything I would have said would have elicited a response. In fact, he likely would have ignored it and instead come at me, shoved me down onto the hay, perhaps even brutalized me. Yet he did nothing, and of course said nothing. Instead he simply stood there, and for a heartbeat I thought I saw genuine hurt in his eyes. Just that quickly, though, he masked it. Instead he turned and walked away from me.

"I . . . I am sorry," I said. "I did not mean to—"

He looked back at me. His silence was painful to behold, as was the unspoken accusation in his eyes.

What had he expected? That he had rescued me and therefore I was to show my gratitude in physical repayment? Was that his intention all along? That he found me attractive, wanted me, and hoped to thus make me beholden to him?

But it made no sense. I was a slave and he was a stable hand. If he fell upon me, wantoned me, what standing would I have to make complaint? Then again, I was a handmaiden to the queen. Certainly he would be taking a risk. If she took umbrage at having one of her servants manhandled in such a way, her vengeance could be formidable.

No. No, I could not accept any of that. He had seen Maleagant's men fall upon us and had been moved to rescue us for no other reason than that he saw we were in distress. For that matter, when he had come upon the scene my features were obscured, so he could not possibly have been certain who was involved. He had seen women who needed help and had responded quickly and brutally.

And now . . . now, as I write this, I wonder if that was the true reason that I stepped back from him. Not the filth that covered his hands, for God knew that I had been filthy myself many a time, existing in squalor not much better than what the mute had to endure. No, it was that I had witnessed the carnage that those hands had been capable of inflicting. Someone capable of such brutal actions, even in the service of the queen and in the name of women who required rescuing . . . what could such as he know of tenderness or compassion?

Then again, what do I know of such things? I have never experienced it personally. I am told it exists, but I have witnessed precious little of it in my time. Harshness and self-interest and calculating manipulation, these things have I seen aplenty. But tenderness, compassion, nobility and pureness of heart? These things have remained the province of my imagination and my more fanciful writings.

I walked across the stable to him and lay a hand on his upper arm. I was startled by how rock-hard it was. He did not seem overlarge, but the muscle beneath his sleeve was impressive. "I did not mean to offend you. I . . ."

He pulled away from me. He reached for his pitchfork, keeping his back to me, and then returned to mucking out the stables. No words were required to convey to me his desire. He wanted me to leave so that he could return to his normal pursuits.

I backed up and almost slid, reaching out for an upright beam and grabbing it to right myself. I had slipped in manure. There was, I had to think, some measure of dark justice in there. I hastened from the stables and, once outside and breathing the relatively fresh air, I wiped my shoe clean of the horse offal.

I made my way back to the castle, my thoughts whirling. Upon returning to the queen, she asked where I had been and why I smelled like horses. I explained that I had gone down to the stables to check on her palfrey. She seemed mildly puzzled that I had done so, but then thanked me for my attention to such details. She said that I should feel free to make certain regularly that her horse was being well-treated, and then she dropped her voice to a whisper as if we were being watched (which, considering the passages that lay within the castle walls, I could not say of a certainty that we were not) and said, "I am not certain I trust that mute stable hand. There is something about him that I find most invidious. Do you not agree?"

I did not know if I did, mostly because I was uncertain of the meaning of "invidious," but I played it safe and nodded which, in the end, is all that she typically requires of me.

She sat by the window then, staring out at nothing in particular. "I did a terrible thing, Viviana."

"Did you? When?"

"When those men tried to take me, I was so furious, so filled with anger . . . my pride was so wounded . . ."

Her voice trailed off and I waited. I saw no reason to prompt her; she would say what she needed to say.

"Arthur is going to war because of me," she said finally.

"Surely not, highness! I mean, yes, the attack on you and the death of his mother were naturally the precipitating events, but that hardly places the responsibility on you . . ."

"There's no reason for this. After all, the men who assaulted me, killed Arthur's mother, they have been slain, so their punishment was final. Other of Arthur's advisers were suggesting that he allow small groups of men to run inspections, searching for actual proof of Maleagant's handiwork before committing our full forces. But I, motivated by personal outrage and humiliation over being handled so . . . I was the one who told him in no uncertain terms that, if he were to be a man, then he must act like one. Arthur is very easily manipulated, Viviana. I have much influence over him and here I had been attempting to use it in a positive manner. Instead I allowed myself to be driven by my own anger and impelled him on an unwise course that will lead to great tragedy. Don't think for a moment that it will not. Whatever the knights may say now, once in the field, they will not distinguish between innocents and enemies. All will be suspect and harmless citizens who have done nothing wrong will know torture and death. I had such lofty intentions for what I could accomplish with Arthur and the very first opportunity I had, I tossed it all away because of personal pique."

"Seeking vengeance over an assault is hardly pique, highness."

"It doesn't matter," she said bleakly. "Whatever you would call it, I could have guided Arthur toward a reasonable path. Instead I have done the exact opposite and now it's too late to stop it. I was presumptuous, to think I was so much smarter than Arthur when all I've done is proven that I can act just as stupidly."

I had no idea what to say except for, "I have no doubt that you do your best, highness."

"I'm a queen," she said. "People die when my best isn't good enough."

I could not argue with that.

Day the Eighty-Fifth

KING ARTHUR AND HIS KNIGHTS set out for war today.

It was a great and majestic undertaking. It recalled for me the day when his father came home from war. It was a similar situation now, with the throngs lining the street as Arthur and his knights sat proudly astride their horses.

I had heard Guinevere's description of her own involvement in this passing and how she had influenced her husband. Now I wondered how Arthur himself felt about the endeavor. In fact, I was anxious to find out. I found myself missing the days past, before Arthur had been king. Back when he had been a vague, detached, pleasant sort of fellow who wished wistfully that his father would give him a chance to prove his worth, while simultaneously wondering if he really had any worth to prove.

I know not what prompted me to do so, but I found myself guided to the tower where I had encountered Arthur in the past. The morning sun had barely risen. I knew that Arthur and his knights were scheduled to depart today. I suspected that the crowds were already beginning to gather. Or, more likely, they were in the process of being gathered. Merlin would naturally make certain that his operatives would ensure Arthur had a send-off appropriate to a king embarking on a holy mission of vengeance.

I climbed up the narrow steps to the tower and then ahead of me I heard a familiar voice say, "Who approaches?" My instincts had clearly been spot on.

"Viviana, your majesty."

"Viviana. Ah." For the first time in a long time, he sounded a bit more like himself. That, naturally, assumed that the man I had met months ago was the "real" Arthur. "You may approach."

"Thank you, your majesty."

He was quite splendid to look upon. He sported a surcoat with an inspiring drawing of a poised lion upon it prepared to strike, and it was trimmed in regal purple.

He was sipping from a cup with steam rising from it in the cold morning air. Holding it up, Arthur said, "Just starting the day with tea. My father became enamored of it in his latter days, particularly with honey in it. Would you care for some?"

Well, when the king is offering to share his drink with you, one cannot reasonably say no. I took it gingerly. The warmth of the mug felt good against my hands. I sipped it and found that he was quite right; the taste of honey in it in particular was quite good. He watched me carefully for reaction and smiled when it was positive. "Did I not speak truly?"

"Aye, majesty, you did."

I handed it back to him. He looked down at it wistfully and said, "I love my wife dearly, you know. And my people. Yet, strangely, I think it will be the little things such as this I miss most of all during my absence. So," he said, taking another sip, "What brings you here, girl?"

Now that I was in his presence, I did not feel comfortable admitting that I had sought him out. "I was . . . simply looking for somewhere to think, majesty. And I remembered this place."

"Fondly, I should hope. You know," and he lowered his voice conspiratorially, "when it is just the two of us, it is really all right if you address me as 'Arthur.'"

I tried to. I honestly did. I wanted to say, "As you wish, Arthur," but could not manage it. Instead I admitted, "I . . . do not think it is, your majesty. 'All right,' I mean. You are who you are, and I am who I am, and whether we be in alone or in the midst of a crowd, that is not going to change."

"I suppose you are right," he said with a heavy sigh. He gazed out the window. I sat near him, perched on a step. "What matters of particular moment did you need to think about, if I may ask?"

"You are king, majesty. You may ask whatever you wish."

"Very well, then. Consider yourself asked."

Now, of course, I had to come up with something. I chided myself mentally for not having thought this out particularly well. I grabbed at the first thing that crossed my mind. "It . . . involves a man, your majesty."

"A man. How interesting." He actually seemed amused. "Have you developed a love life, Viviana?"

My cheeks flushed at the notion. "Nothing like that, your majesty."

"But you have been considering it?"

It did not occur to me that I even had. But the truth was that, since that day, I had been unable to expunge the mute's face from my mind. I found him both repulsive and alluring and felt my thoughts drawn to him with such ferocity that my body seemed inclined to follow.

"I . . . do not know what I am considering, majesty. It is complicated."

"Oh, such things need not be complicated," said Arthur easily. "Most things can be fairly simple if you try to think about then simply. Problems only become complicated when you complicate them."

I could not be sure whether Arthur had just said something absurdly profound, or profoundly absurd. So I settled for nodding my head as if I understood his meaning.

Arthur returned his gaze to the window. "My mother used to bring me up here when I was a lad," he said softly. "I wish you could have known her as I did. She was there for me when my father was not, which was most of the time. What Maleagant's people did to her . . . she did not deserve it, Viviana. I can think of so many people who deserved such a fate, but she was most certainly not one of them. And the hell of it is . . . it is my fault."

Considering the earlier conversation I'd had with his wife, I was amazed that there was this much blame to go around. "Yours, majesty? I do not follow . . ."

"'Tis not obvious? I failed to kill Maleagant. I thought I had succeeded, but obviously I did not. And now these warriors of Maleagant's desires have focused their attentions upon us, and I have to finish the job that, had I performed it properly, Igraine would still be alive. A fine king I am turning out to be."

"I believe you are the best king you can possibly be under the circumstances, majesty."

"That is very kind of you to say, Viviana, not to mention very delicately phrased. I appreciate both."

No words were spoken for long moments, and then Arthur slapped his thighs and said, "Well . . . time to be off."

"Arthur . . ."

I was as surprised to hear his first name roll off my tongue as he was to hear it. But he did not react other than to raise an eyebrow and say, "Yes, Viviana?"

I thought about what Guinevere had said, but I could not share those concerns with her husband. She counted on my discretion and it would be an utter betrayal to repeat her thoughts to her husband. So, fishing around for some means of perhaps averting a path that neither king nor queen was eager to tread, I said, "Are you sure?"

"Am I sure that you are Viviana? Reasonably so."

"No, I mean . . . are you sure about Maleagant? Really sure that he is directly involved in this business? You speak of vengeance for the death of Igraine . . . except those who were directly responsible for the deed have already been disposed of. So that is vengeance of an immediate nature. Do you truly think it wise to go to war when you are not absolutely certain of your facts?"

"Merlin is absolutely certain," said Arthur with touching confidence. "He is convinced Maleagant is still out there. He said that there have been rumors for some time, but nothing absolute. Well, Igraine's murder and the attempted kidnapping of my queen are certainly absolute enough for me."

So there was more to this than just Guinevere's instigation. That might ease her conscience somewhat, except that I couldn't think of any elegant way to tell her without further inflaming her, either toward me or Merlin or possibly both.

"But with respect . . . you still do not truly know. Would it not make sense to send an exploratory force first, to ferret out these warriors of Maleagant's desires? Perhaps work in closer conjunction with other kingdoms? Present a united front? Have you even spoken to other kings?"

"I have," said Arthur, sounding regretful. "They have, in fact, urged me not to send in forces. They claim that I am being precipitous."

"Is it possible they are right?"

"Anything is possible, Viviana, but I must make my decisions based upon what is probable. It is probable that Maleagant lives and his warriors of Maleagant's desires will make continued assaults on our way of life. I must strike first, preemptively. It is the only way to ensure the safety of my people and my kingdom."

"And if you are wrong? So many will die . . . our own warriors and civilians."

"It will be regrettable. But I do what must be done. What I am told must be done. There is nothing else for it, really."

"But you could—"

He placed his hands upon my shoulders and smiled sadly. "It is time for me to depart, Viviana. Will you be there to see me off?"

"Of course, majesty."

"Good. Good." He started down the steps, stopped, turned to me and said, "I have enjoyed our chats."

He left with the air of one who thought he might well not be returning. I could not say that he was wrong.

True to my word, I was among the assemblage when the brave knights departed. Women threw flowers in their paths and the men cried out shouts of justice in the name of Igraine. Everyone performed as they were supposed to. Arthur looked especially resplendent in his armor, glinting in the noonday sun. There was Lancelot, riding just behind him, and Gawain and Bors and the rest of them. Never had I seen anything quite as majestic as this procession.

A company of knights was being left behind to defend Camelot, just in case an enemy concocted the notion of assailing us whilst Arthur was engaged many leagues away. For the most part, though, the best and bravest of them were marching off to war with King Arthur. Maidens wept. Stalwart wives watched with various degrees of stoicism, some waving handkerchiefs, some blowing kisses, and some just staring as if they were watching the better parts of themselves head off to war.

No one knew what was to come and the fact that Arthur knew not any more than anyone else did not stir confidence in me. Nor was I enthused by the notion that Merlin had been spurring him on. If it had just been Guinevere's opinions, he might have been able to set them aside. But he held Merlin's word higher than he did anyone else's. Despite the kindnesses that Merlin had displayed toward me, I still did not trust him. I felt he had darker, self-serving motivations behind his actions. Yet there he was, riding in the rear of the procession, coming along to serve as Arthur's advisor. It was difficult to determine if he was smiling or not beneath his vast beard.

Something bumped up against me. This was not an unusual occurrence in a crowd of this size, but I instantly sensed it had been done with purpose. I turned and gasped. It was the mute. He said nothing, merely stared at me with those same smoldering eyes.

I retreated into the crowd and headed back for the castle, and was sure that I could feel his gaze upon me the entire time.

Day the Ninety-Second

WITH MERLIN DEPARTED I HAVE been quietly, during my own time, continuing to make use of his library. I do not think he would mind.

Just as he foretold, the histories that he has gathered are what intrigue me the most. I am currently reading the works of Pliny the Elder, beginning with his *Naturalis Historia*, which I have found fascinating. It is an amazing series of volumes discussing all aspects of the physical world. As I complete each volume, I take the time to sample other writings as well, such as those of Julius Caesar, Herodotus, dubbed the father of history, Xenophon who was himself a knight. No women, curiously, or at least none that I have found so far in Merlin's library. I cannot help but consider that a depressing omission. Certainly women endured the same trials and tribulations, victories and defeats, triumphs and tragedies that men experienced. Were their views not equally compelling and deserving of preservation?

I find myself wondering whether it truly is possible that at some point in the future, there will be a young woman like myself . . . a slave, or perhaps a free woman . . . living in a world that I cannot begin to imagine, reading the words that I am writing here and now. And she, in turn, may be motivated to write her own histories as a result. Here I am, someone who has lived her life in chains, and yet I may well be part of some great and more positive chain that binds me both to the past and to the future. I begin to wonder if I have here, in the quill between my fingers, more than a hobby or means of self-expression. I may in fact have a sacred responsibility that should be properly utilized, lest I be wasting a magnificent opportunity.

It is daunting to be thinking this way. Sometimes my head threatens to explode from all the new thoughts that it is being required to contain. I almost begin to miss the days when all I cared about was myself. I now find myself caring about everyone and everything else, which is madness since they care not for me.

Except . . . what if they did? What if the queen did? And Arthur? And even the mute? Cared for me, not as a slave to be their servant or a convenient sounding board, but someone they liked as an individual? Even loved?

Would I be expected to reciprocate? Am I even capable of it, after all this time of hollowness within?

I am almost afraid to find out.

Day the One Hundredth

WHAT IS THERE ABOUT CENTENNIAL days or anniversaries that prompt great expectations for such times? I cannot begin to imagine. It is just a day, with the numbering only having weight because we choose to accord it such. And yet . . .

I have written more Galahad adventures for Modred. He grabbed the sheets from me and read them so eagerly that it was hard for me to remind myself that he may well be the devil incarnated in a child. He smiled and nodded and said, "Yes. Yes, excellent. So heroic. So romantic a creation. You are to be commended, Viviana, truly."

"Thank you, young sir," and I curtsied.

And then, to my surprise, he said, "How long have you been here at this castle?"

"One hundred days, as a matter of fact."

"Ah," said Modred. "That certainly calls for some type of celebration, do you not think so?"

"No, Modred, I do not. Now if you will excuse me, I must tend to the queen . . ."

We were in Modred's chambers, Modred having been

sitting in an overlarge chair. He hopped off the chair as I started toward the door and said, "The queen is resting. She is, in fact, asleep. I suspect you know that."

The fact was that I did. That Modred knew should have been disconcerting to me, yet it was not. That simply indicated how accustomed I had become to the lad's uncanny knowledge of all that transpired in the castle.

I did not say anything. Truly, there seemed to be nothing that I could or should say under the circumstances.

Modred actually smiled, which was never a good thing. "I know exactly what you need. Come to the great meadow this evening, after supper."

"Modred, do not be absurd. I will do no such thing."

"Yes, you will."

That was all he said. Yes, you will.

The words stayed with me for the rest of the day. Guinevere, of course, was not remotely aware that today represented any sort of landmark. There was no reason she should be. She was instead busying herself with the duties incumbent upon the reigning queen. Most of the time seemed to be spent with the wives of departed knights, engaging them in such pastimes as needlework, embroidering banners and such. She maintained a steady stream of conversation, alternately sharing her own thoughts and listening patiently as they put forward theirs.

She was wearing dresses more often these days, but leggings beneath. An odd compromise, but one that seemed to fit her needs.

It would be understating matters to say that the interaction between Morgan, who was typically present, and Iblis, the wife of Lancelot, was brittle to say the least. They kept their discussion polite; achingly so, in fact. But the tension in the air could have been cut with Arthur's sword. I have to believe that they remained on their best behavior because they were in the presence of the queen. God only knows what would have happened between them were Guinevere not there.

All during the day, I kept returning to Modred's words. Such a pretentious child, and so insanely overconfident and full of himself. I could not understand what in the world made him think that I would go out to the great meadow, based purely upon his assertion that I would.

During supper, Guinevere noticed that I appeared distracted and asked if there were something on my mind. "Not at all, highness," I assured her.

"Are you quite certain?" she said. I told her I was but she did not appear satisfied. "Sometimes, Viviana," she said after some consideration, "I think you do not devote sufficient time to your own needs."

"That is very broad minded of you, highness," I said, and I meant it. It was atypical of mistresses or masters to be concerned about the personal needs of their slaves. In fact, I could not recall a time when Guinevere had voiced such worries.

"Well, frankly, Morgan said something to me about it."

Instantly the hairs went up on the back of my neck. "Morgan did?"

"Aye, she did. She whispered to me that you seemed preoccupied and perhaps you needed some time to yourself.

I admit," she said with a smile, "that I can be relentless in my demands."

"Not at all, your highness."

"Ah, now I know that something is wrong. I provide you an opening such as that to speak your mind and you do not seize upon it? I dismiss you for the night, Viviana . . . and for the next day and night as well. Take time for yourself as you see fit."

"But highness . . ."

"Are you challenging my will, Viviana?" She did not sound unfriendly, but there was the slightest hint of warning in her words.

I promptly looked to the floor, submissive. "No, highness."

"It is settled, then. Oh," she said as an afterthought, "it is lovely weather tonight, and I do not think you get out near enough. Why not take the air this evening?"

"The air, highness?"

"Yes. The great meadow is lovely during moonrise, especially under a full moon as we have this night."

Oh yes. This had Morgan's hand all over it.

I could not say that to Guinevere, of course. The queen would be furious if she thought she was being manipulated not only by her sister, but also by her insidious nephew. So I smiled and nodded and left her presence with absolutely no intention of going anywhere near the great meadow.

The more I dwelt on it, however, the angrier I became. My original intentions to try and aid Modred appeared to have rebounded upon me. His constant insinuation into every aspect of my life was becoming oppressive, and clearly he had recruited his mother into his endeavors. Why was she participating? Out of some intent to dispose of me? Or mayhap simply out of a perverse amusement in making merry sport with peoples' lives?

However I was not a person, was I. I was merely a slave, a piece of property, with no more rights than a stray dog.

For all I knew, someone was waiting out in the great meadow to ambush me. All manner of wild thoughts began to rampage through my mind. I considered the possibility that Morgan had herself been behind the attempted kidnapping of the queen. Why not? Did it not make perfect sense? If Guinevere were stolen away or, even simpler, disposed of, it would leave a clear path for Morgan to move in upon the grief-stricken Arthur. Arthur did not know of the incestuous relationship that would result, and if Morgan cared not—and I suspected that to be the case—he would be vulnerable to such machinations.

And now she was trying to arrange for me to go out to the great meadow alone, at night, all unsuspecting, or so she thought, so that I could be ambushed. Why? Because I knew her secret, and I represented a threat to her.

Yet if that were to be the case, then what were my options? To tell all to the queen? Make her believe that her sister had designs upon her life? What if I was wrong? I could launch a fatal feud between the sisters based purely upon suspicion and hunch.

And if I were to constantly concern myself that Morgan was actively seeking to entrap me in some manner, then what? Was I to spend the rest of my days perpetually watching my back, jumping at shadows, living in constant dread and not knowing when or whence the final assault would come? Even for a slave, the lowest of the low, that was no way to live.

I walked the halls of the castle, trying to find Modred. It seemed he was the key to all of this, but he was nowhere to be found. No surprise there; he was likely watching me from hiding, secreted behind a wall or perhaps dwelling in shadow so close to me that he could reach out and touch my elbow before I even saw him. I kept glancing around me to see if he was, in fact, in such close proximity to me.

With night's fingers caressing the land, I could not tolerate it anymore. My mind was running riot with possibilities, but I knew one thing of a certainty: I simply was not going to live the rest of my life in fear.

Defying my worst expectations, I strode from castle Camelot and headed for the great meadow.

The closer I drew to that vast expanse beyond the castle walls, where on pretty days children frolicked and occasional faires and festivities were held, the harder my heart began to beat. Part of me was certain that I was walking straight toward my death. Part of me did not care. It was not as if the life I had was so marvelous a thing. I had no desire to lose it, but if I was going to live it, it was going to be on my terms. Or at least as much terms as were available to one who had no free will and no control over her own destiny.

Except, mayhap I did at that. I could have cowered in the castle, waiting for some sort of plot to fall upon me. Instead, if I were to die, I was going to be looking my executioner straight in the eye and challenging him to take his best shot.

I was not wholly unprepared.

Within the folds of my simple dress, I had a knife concealed. Were someone to attack me, I would do my best to drive my blade into his heart. My life, as pathetic as it was, was not something I would willingly yield up without making my assailant feel the consequence of his attack.

I walked onto the great meadow. Its rolling hills stretched out before me. It seemed so innocent, with the vast stretch of grass spread and flowers dotting the landscape. Everything seemed so quiet. Would this be my resting place? Would this be where I would die? It seemed ludicrous to contemplate my assassination in such dispassionate terms, and yet I was. I tried to think if I had any regrets and realized, to my surprise, that my major regret was that I would be unable to continue my stories of Galahad. He would die along with me and none, aside from Modred, would ever know him. How foolish that seemed that I would expend such concerns upon someone who existed only within my head. I suppose what it came down to was that those who owned me could take from me my writing implements, the clothes on my back, my free will, my freedom, anything that they desired to snatch away . . . anything save my imagination. That remained solely mine, and since Galahad was the product of it, it made him more precious to me than anything that was real.

Something stirred on the meadow in front of me, just on the other side of one of the hillocks. It could have been anybody taking the night air, yet I was certain that whoever it was, they were in fact for me. He rose into view, and it was most definitely a he. I could not see him in detail at first for the shadows cloaked him and the full moon had taken refuge behind a cloud.

"Good evening," I said, surprised how calm I was managing to keep my voice. "May I help you?"

The figure moved toward me, slowly, steadily, with measured tread. And then, even in the darkness, I was able to discern who it was.

I froze. Any serenity that I was attempting to cling to dissolved immediately when I saw that it was the mute stable hand who was approaching me.

He had something in his hand that appeared to be a club of some sort, although it was hard to make out from that distance. The realization crashed down upon me that all of my worst suspicions had been correct. Modred and Morgan had conspired to plan my death and they had enlisted the mute to do the deed. He was naturally the ideal cat's-paw. Whom would he tell? Whom could he tell? Their vile secrets were safe with him.

I wanted to run, but I remained rooted to the spot, immobilized. I wanted to convince myself that I was dreaming, that this was all some nightmare scenario from which I would awaken before the climactic and dreaded moment arrived. Yet I knew this was not the case. It was all too real and within moments would prove all too fatal.

Then the clouds moved aside from the moon, illuming the meadow.

The mute raised the hand that held the club, except that

now that the full glowing orb in the sky was providing additional light, I was able to see more clearly what he was wielding.

It was a bouquet of flowers. Small purple flowers.

Relieved laughter choked in my chest, then fought its way up toward my mouth but got stuck in my throat. So all I was able to produce was a small strangled noise that sounded as if I had swallowed a mouse.

There in the darkness the mute drew close to me. He still smelled of stables and horses, but never had I welcomed that aroma the way I did at that moment. His hair was as disheveled as it ever was, and his clothes were rumpled and dirty. They were probably the only clothes he owned. Yet never had poor hair care and a filthy wardrobe been as welcome a sight.

He was wearing gloves, which surprised me. They were brown leather. For a moment some of the old fears came back to me. What if he was planning to strangle me and the gloves were to prevent him from getting blood on his hands?

The mute stopped about a foot away from me and proffered the bouquet. As speechless as the mute himself, I took them. Then he removed his gloves, first the left and then the right. I could not imagine what his purpose for doing so might be.

He held them up in the moonlight and I stared at them, goggle-eyed, not comprehending at first. But then I did, or at least thought I did. I gestured for him to bring them closer to me. He did so, tentatively, as if afraid that I would turn and bolt. I took his hands by the wrists and examined them in the moonlight.

They were clean. More than clean, in fact. He had scrubbed

them until the skin was practically raw and red. There was still dirt under his fingernails, but I suspect that nothing short of a torch could have scoured the filth out from under them. Nevertheless he, or whoever had aided him in the reclamation project that was his hands, had done a magnificent job.

I stared at the palms, and then turned them over and studied the backs. I stared up at him then and there was a look on his face such as I had never seen upon him. Instead of the surly and dangerous edge that I had come to associate with him, there was an almost boyish shyness and eagerness to please that reminded me somewhat of Arthur.

"They are beautiful," I said, and they were. Strong, manly hands, fingertips calloused from years of hard labor. The veins stood out against his wrists. The skin itself was rough overall, but I liked that in a man. Far better rough hands from a lifetime of honest labor than soft, effete hands belonging to a man who lived off the hard work of others.

He smiled and nodded in appreciation. Then, very gently, as if he were caressing an egg, his right hand wrapped tentatively around mine own. He gestured with a nod of his head toward the expanse of the meadow, a silent invitation to take a walk.

I accepted his invitation.

I did not bother to ask him how he had come to be at this place, or who had arranged it, for such would naturally have been a waste of time. I suspected I knew. Besides, it was not as if he could have responded.

I removed my footwear so that the cool grass massaged my feet and we walked across the meadow, basking in the moonlight, enjoying each other's company. So much of what I was experiencing seemed unreal, a waking dream. This was that same mute stable hand that the kitchen wenches had threatened to toss me to so that he would presumably do terrible things to me. What terrible things? Make me feel warm and special just with a gentle, even loving look?

It prompted me to ponder the importance of environment. The way in which I perceived the mute now was totally different from when he was in the stables, shoveling manure. Who would not be at less than his or her best in those sorts of circumstances?

I, of all people, had no right to judge others by their appearances.

He squeezed my hand once, a little tighter, but not harmfully or threateningly. I think he realized my mind was drifting and he wanted to return my thoughts to the moment. It was sweet, really. He wanted my attention.

We stood upon a hillock and he faced me. All trace of the brutish creature I had seen him to be had vanished. He was simply a young man now. If he had been properly bathed, given a haircut, he would be unrecognizable as the surly, filthy creature that dwelt in the stables. As it was, the real person beneath the muck was showing through to me. The person who had witnessed an abduction and, rather than stand aside and allow matters to progress, had leaped to the rescue.

"Thank you again," I said, "for saving the queen."

He shook his head. I frowned in confusion. "What do you mean, no? You saved the queen."

Again he shook his head and before I could inquire again what he meant, he extended a finger and gently tapped me on the chest. The silent gesture spoke volumes.

"You did it . . . to save me?"

Slowly he nodded and a smile spread across his face that seemed to light it up.

I had no idea what to say, rendered momentarily as mute as he. So he *had* known that it was me.

He leaned toward me, took my face gently in his clean hands, and tilted my head back. He brought his lips to mine. The kiss was gentle and loving. I had never known such, for all my previous congress with men had been brutal and uncaring.

He kissed me again, and a third time. The third time my body practically melted into his, my arms wrapped around him. I did not know how far he was going to take matters. He was far stronger than I, and I could not have stopped him if he pressed his desires. The thing was, and I blush even as I write this, I do not know that I would have wanted to stop him.

As it happened, I did not have to make the decision. He squeezed me tightly once more, and then with one arm draped protectively around me, walked me back the way we had come. We left the great meadow and he walked me all the way to the castle entrance. There, in the darkness, he took my hand, kissed my knuckles in a manner so gentlemanly that any gentleman would have envied the suavity, and then backed away and vanished into the shadows.

I wandered, dazed, through the castle corridors and, as I approached the queen's chambers wherein lay my humble quarters, a figure separated itself from the long shadows. It was Modred. He simply stood there and stared at me.

"Thank you," I said.

"You are welcome, Viviana," said Modred, and then the darkness enfolded him once more.

Day the One Hundred and Ninth

WORD IS BEGINNING TO FILTER from the front. Much of it is not positive.

Displaced villagers are moving north, coming in the general direction of Camelot but keeping themselves to the outlying areas. They have been telling horror stories of their experiences, and these stories are being told and retold by others. Tales have a tendency of doing that, spreading from hamlet to village to town with lightning speed.

And they were not pleasant.

I have to allow for the possibility of exaggeration. Things tend to become exaggerated through repetition, building and building as each person relates events and adds their own perceptions and their biases. Heroes become villains; acts of kindness can be misconstrued as acts of cruelty.

Yet even though I knew that people could be unfair, it was hard to dispute the possibility that all I was hearing was rooted in reality.

In their search for the warriors of Maleagant's desires, fired by their thirst for vengeance over the death of Igraine, Arthur and his knights—or at least Arthur's knights—apparently felt they had license to take whatever actions they believed necessary to accomplish their goals.

Before they departed Camelot, there was much shouting that nothing would stand in their way. Those are fine words when one is endeavoring to steel resolve. Unfortunately when taken literally, it is a license for immoral behavior.

The goals, as stated, were to find Maleagant and destroy any and all sympathizers, supporters or recruits to his cause. With such a broad based mandate, the knights were reputedly laying waste to villages and villagers. Everyone and anyone they encountered was considered a suspect and treated as such. People were being arrested, browbeaten, beaten down, or just simply beaten. They were flogged for information, or shoved headfirst into horse troughs and held there until they were willing to cooperate. Knights would torch villages and then celebrate, commending each other and claiming that they had rooted out yet another nest of Maleagant sympathizers.

The tragic circumstance of these tactics was that it was creating supporters for Maleagant where there had been few or none before. Many people, as I noted, fled and sought new places where they could reside and start life over. But others came together and formed roving bands whose entire purpose was to harass the knights in their pursuits. And since they knew the territories far better than the knights possibly could have, they had the advantage. They did not engage the knights openly. Instead they hid themselves, creating traps that the knights would unknowingly stumble into, and then lay waste to them with arrows fired from hiding. Arthur's knights would be injured or die without ever once seeing the face of an enemy.

As word of their heinous activities spread, the people of Camelot began to grumble to each other that this was not what they had supported. They were naturally irate about the death of Igraine, and they were also concerned for their own safety from Maleagant or his agents. But a month had passed since the assault on the queen, with not the slightest hint of any further violence against Camelot or its peoples.

Guinevere took the extreme action of holding meetings with townsfolk in their gathering places, making herself as accessible to the population as possible. Perhaps she thought that they would appreciate the queen bringing herself to their level. I am not entirely certain that they did. She tried to answer their questions and buoy their spirits.

"Have you not considered the likelihood," Guinevere would say, "that the reason we have experienced peace here in Camelot is because the king and his valiant knights are fighting against those who would bring terror to our lands? Stopping them from coming here by going there instead? And does not your king therefore deserve our respect and support in that endeavor because of it?"

Some listened. Some seemed moved. Some seemed persuaded. Many did not.

In private, however, Guinevere's attitude and reactions have been much different.

Upon returning to her chambers, she removed her bonnet and threw it across the room in anger. As I scurried to retrieve it, she stalked around the room like a caged animal, yanking herself free of her dress so that she could walk about in her more manly clothing. She lost any appearance of femininity, walking with a shoulder-swaying swagger. There was no hint in her bearing of the frustrated woman who had been taking the responsibility for this bellicose endeavor upon herself.

"How can he be putting me into this position?" she raged. "How can it be that he cannot even control his own men?"

"I am sure they are spread out and therefore it presents considerable, if not insurmountable, problems."

"Who asked you?"

I stood there with the bonnet in my hands, feeling the fool. Then I gathered up her fallen dress as I said, "I had thought you were asking, highness. I was unaware that the questions were rhetorical."

She fumed for a moment but then her mood softened ever so slightly. "No. They were not rhetorical, and shame be upon me for scolding you in so unwarranted a manner." She stopped short of offering an apology. She was, after all, the queen while I remained a slave. "What you say may have some merit. Still, it is a situation that he should have foreseen and allowed for."

I remembered something that I had read in one of the histories. "All plans for war work up until the moment when confronted with the war. None can foresee the unforeseeable."

"Mayhap. But he should have," said Guinevere. "Still, it is commendable, I suppose, that you defend him in his absence."

"As do you, highness, once we pass from behind these doors."

"Well, I am the queen," she said stiffly, "despite the fact that I feel these days like the court jester." She sagged down onto a sizable chair. "'Tis true, you know. They think me a joke."

"They?"

"The people."

"Oh, not at all, highness." I hung up the bonnet and went to help her remove her boots. "They respect you mightily. They appreciate both your support of the king and your stirring words." I was not entirely certain any of that was true, but it was what she needed to hear.

Guinevere was not stupid. She eyed me suspiciously and said, "Do you truly believe that, Viviana?"

I nodded. I was a facile enough liar, but I disliked doing it unless I absolutely had to. So I limited my response to an unspoken affirmation.

It appeared to be sufficient.

There was a knock at the door. "See who that is," the queen said. "And send them on their way. I am in no mood for visitors."

I went to the door and opened it slightly. To my surprise, Rowena was standing there. She was holding a steaming mug. I stepped through the door into the hallway and pulled it closed behind me. "The queen desires no visitors," I said sternly.

I expected hostility or some such response. There was, after all, no love lost between us. But Rowena, in a subdued voice, said, "I did not consider a humble creature as myself a visitor. I merely brought a refreshing beverage for the queen after a long day. It is a favorite of her husband's, so I thought she might likewise enjoy it."

I recognized it as the tea with honey that Arthur had been drinking. Nevertheless, I was suspicious. "She is not receiving."

"Very well." She took a step towards me and said in a lowered, confidential voice, "My support is meager and means nothing to one such as she, but I just want you to know that you have it nonetheless. What they did to Igraine is nothing less than an insult to Camelot and its people. Whatever measures are taken in order to exact some measure of retribution is just fine with me." She nodded once as if adding confirmation and then turned and began to walk away.

I felt the slightest twinge of guilt. Granted, the woman had treated me ill, but I had done no less by severing her relationship with the groomsman simply to satisfy my desire for petty revenge. "Rowena," I said. She stopped and looked at me with curiosity. "Might I . . . ?" I gestured toward the tea.

She smiled. She genuinely smiled. And who would have known that she had a smile that was actually sweet? In her haggard face it provided something of a contrast as she approached me and said, "Of course. You are handmaiden to the queen. It is like unto giving it to the queen herself."

I took the tea carefully with both hands and sipped it cautiously. It was just like the one that Arthur had been drinking. For a moment I found myself recalling the poison taster who had worked in the employ of Uther and wondered if I was subjecting myself to the same hazards. But no, there was nothing poisonous about it. It was tea with honey, well made and enjoyable. Nor was there anything about Rowena that suggested the slightest interest in anything save a reaction to her endeavors.

"It is . . . quite good," I said.

The smile widened so that she was positively beaming. "I appreciate your saying so. I shall be happy to provide you with it anytime you wish." The expression on her face shifted and, contrite, she said, "War brings people together, you know. People whom one would have not expected to find common ground."

"Very true."

She started to walk away and, finding my voice, I said, "Rowena. The, uhm . . ." I cleared my throat, which was enjoying a smooth coating from the honey. "The stable master has been looking underfed lately. Perhaps you might wish to, uhm . . . attend to that?"

She did not comprehend at first, but after a moment she processed my words and then she did. She smiled gratefully and curtsied. The gesture looked awkward from one of her clearly rickety knees, but it was appreciated nevertheless. "Thank you, handmaiden."

"You are most welcome."

Odd how these things work out.

I reentered the queen's chamber. She looked at me curiously and asked to whom I had been speaking. I told her and asked if she would be interested in having some of the tea that I had started, or if she wished me to fetch back Rowena to inform her she desired some of her own. "Never much developed a taste for it," said Guinevere, "which is a shocking admission for a queen of the Britons to make, I suppose."

"None will hear it from me, highness."

"I do not suppose they will, no." She eyed me with what appeared amusement. "So are you going out this evening?"

"Out, highness?" I suddenly felt uncomfortable.

"Yes, Viviana, out. As you have every night lately when I am no longer in need of your services and you think I am paying no attention. Who is he?"

I could feel my cheeks stinging with embarrassment. I suppose I should have told her. But I remembered the way she had wrinkled her nose at the thought of an assignation with the mute stable hand. She did not know of his valor and of what she owed to him, but that again was because of my duplicity. There was no good way to respond to it except to lie yet again. "There is no one, highness."

She studied me for a long moment as if trying to see into my mind. "A pity. It would have been uplifting to know that, even in these trying times, young love can flourish."

"Young love?" Abashed as I am to admit it, the notion had not occurred to me.

"That is what I thought I was seeing in you. But if you assure me that I am mistaken . . ."

"Regrettably, highness, you are."

"Very well. Still, tomorrow is Sunday," said the queen. "I think it appropriate if, after mass, you spend the rest of the day in contemplation. Consider what you are missing by dwelling in solitude."

"But your needs, highness—"

"Can be well served by my sister. Fear not, Viviana. In the absolute worst case scenario, I am a grown woman and capable of tending to my needs."

I had no doubt that she was. Now I am only left to wonder if, as a grown woman myself, I am likewise capable of tending to my needs.

Day the One Hundred and Tenth

I AM A TERRIBLE WOMAN. A terrible and awful and evil slattern, and I know now without question that I am going to burn in hell. Hellfire, for all eternity, charring away my skin, boiling my innards, and then they will all regrow and it will start all over again.

Yet I find myself oddly indifferent to the prospect.

I was as imperious as I could be today when I went to the stables. The mute was there, as always. I strode up to him, and I had a sack slung over my shoulder in what I fancied was a casual manner. "The queen wishes to have her palfrey taken out for exercise," I said, "and she instructed me to accompany to make certain that nothing goes awry. So bring forth both her palfrey and my jennet and be quick about it." I clapped my hands briskly to accentuate my regal attitude, or at least what I fancied such to be.

The mute looked at me with what seemed mild confusion, but then shrugged and did as he was instructed. Within minutes both animals had been saddled and we were riding away from Camelot.

It was a beautiful Sunday. The air was warm and the sky was so blue that it almost hurt to look at it. We rode side by side. I spoke to him of how things were proceeding with the war, and the things that the queen had said to me. It was comforting to know that I had someone in whom I could confide, because naturally he would say nothing to anyone else. It was remarkable what a superb listener he was. Then again, perhaps it was not as remarkable as all that, since naturally all he could do was listen.

Even that, though, was not a wholly accurate thing to say. The mute and I had developed a means of communication that did not require speech. Instead we conveyed both meaning and intent through various hand gestures. Not spelling out letters and words so much as putting across broad thoughts, concepts and such. I would not have thought it possible, but I felt so . . . so connected to him in ways that I could not begin to express. Consequently I was able to understand him when he would ask me questions or convey his opinions.

And he did have opinions, lord, yes he did. There was no longer the slightest thought in my head that his silence marked some sort of mental deficiency. His mind was as blade-sharp as anyone else's and moreso than most. He could not write, but I was hoping that perhaps in time I might be able to teach him, thus expanding his horizons and options for communication. In the meantime, he was still able via gestures to make his thoughts known.

I told him that I had packed a picnic lunch in the sack and that I left it to him to select where we would go. He led us to a point deep in the woods and then veered off the beaten path. He dismounted and led the palfrey by the reins. I followed likewise on foot with the jennet. There continued to be no path, but it was passable as it was. I was curious to see where he was leading us.

Then the trees opened onto a secluded lake. It was beautiful, the surface smooth and as blue as the sky. We brought the horses to the edge and tied them off where there was a bountiful thicket of grass. I pulled the food from the sack and laid it out, and we sat on the ground and ate of what I had brought: two legs of mutton, a loaf of bread, some assorted cheeses, and a small skin of wine.

Potent stuff, the wine. I drank of it and felt more relaxed than I had in many a day.

I can only think that it was the wine that prompted me to my next actions. Loosened my tongue, loosened my inhibitions.

I leaned over toward him and smiled in what I can only imagine must have been a truly foolish manner. "The queen," I said, "spoke to me of young love. I have not thought myself capable of that for the longest time. Do you . . . think that I am?"

Very slowly the mute, this man who had risked his life and attacked armed villains in order to save the life of a lowly slave girl, nodded. He smiled, thumped his hand against his chest and then placed it against mine. He leaned forward and kissed me. Mute he may have been, but he knew how to utilize his tongue effectively in other ways.

His hands were upon me then, not roughly as I was accustomed to with other men, but soft, caressing. My mouth against his, I laughed delightedly. He withdrew his face from mine and he looked at me quizzically. "It feels nice," I said. Then I glanced mischievously at the lake and said, "And I will warrant I know what will feel even better."

I got to my feet without giving myself the opportunity to think upon what I was doing. A few quick movements, the undoing of some laces, and my dress fell around my feet. I stood naked as my day of birth in front of him. For a moment a wave of modesty tried to sweep through me as he eyed me hungrily. My hands drifted in a protective manner across my breasts, my loins, but then I abandoned all thought of proper decorum. Instead, with a crazed whoop of joy, like a madwoman newly freed from the asylum, I pivoted and sprinted for the water. I splashed into it, sending little waves cascading around me. I felt wanton and sluttish and alive.

I did not know how to swim, but that did not deter me from taking small, bounding steps. I descended into the water carefully, making certain that there were no abrupt drop-offs. When I reached a point where I felt it would not be wise for me to descend further, I halted my progress and spun slowly in place, laughing delightedly. Perhaps this was what sea nymphs as I had read about in mythologies would have felt like.

There was a splashing from behind me. I turned and saw that the mute had likewise stripped off his clothes and descended into the water. Unlike me, however, he could swim. He dove under and disappeared. There was only a faint rippling upon the surface to mark his passage. I waited, curious, and then he surfaced, blowing out water like a whale. I laughed again.

His long hair hung around his face. The dirt that normally cloaked his fine features was dissolving away in the wetness. He submerged again, then came up running his fingers through his hair, making an attempt to remove the copious tangles from it. I undulated through the water to him, wrapping my arms around him and reaching around to help him. He stopped in his endeavors and instead put his arms around me. Our naked bodies pressed up against each other. I was certain I could feel not only my own heart beating, but also his pressed against mine.

He continued to caress me, placing his hands with infinite care where other men had never bothered. He seemed as interested in my pleasure as in his own, which was a strange and heady sensation for me. Until that moment, I was unaware that a woman could even derive pleasure from the act.

We joined as a man and woman do, and I felt strange, bizarre sensations that were completely new for me. I barely know how to describe them and am not even certain that I can or should. They were unquestionably too exquisite not to be sinful, so writing of them would compound the sin. But it did not feel evil at the time . . . or perhaps it did, except it was too gratifying for me to notice it.

All I know is that the feelings built and built within me, beginning in my nethers and spreading to the rest of my body. Then the sensations exploded within me so intensely that I thought my eyes were going to leap right from the sockets. My legs were wrapped around the mute's hips at the time and my body shuddered and twitched with such force that the mute lost his balance and tumbled backwards, me atop him. We both went under, and since I was gasping for air at the time, water went down my throat and into my chest. I came up spluttering and coughing and, moments later, the mute did as well. I was totally mortified, not understanding anything that had just transpired, and I threw my arms around myself protectively, feeling vulnerable and shaken and utterly bewildered.

He drew me to him then, and I tried to pull away, but he would have none of it. Yet all he did at that point was hold me tightly against him until my trembling ceased. The warmth of his body was so comforting that it could not help but bring peace to me. I have no idea how long we remained there just that way, basking in the water, basking in each other.

A few minutes later we repeated what we had just done, and this time when the feelings arose within me, I was not afraid of them. Instead I moved slowly upon him, and when they finally built to their peak and erupted within me, I welcomed the sensations as I would the return of an old friend whom I had somehow just met.

He seemed satisfied as well. At least he did not seem to have any complaints.

We returned to the shore, wrapping ourselves together in blankets. We nestled against each other and when I felt his manhood stirring yet again, I was ready. So was he. I have no idea how much experience he had of such matters, but his stamina was formidable. Perhaps it is related to his being around horses so much, and their attributes have rubbed off on him.

Finally, reluctantly—at least on my part—we dressed and

sat together in comfortable silence. I ran my fingers under his chin, tracing the line of his jaw, and I said, "You should allow others to see you this way. I swan, you are unrecognizable when you are clean. Do you not wish to remain this way?"

He shook his head. As if to drive home the point, he picked up some loose dirt from the base of a tree and began to smear it in his face. I tried to pull his hand away but he resisted. "Why?" I said, ceasing my attempts to prevent him from dirtying himself once more. "Why do you wish to remain so? Why do you not speak? Are you someone who needs to remain hidden?" Instantly I took to flights of fancy, imagining him to be some sort of wayward prince who was secreted from foes.

But he simply shook his head and shrugged. He could have been lying, I suppose, but I do not think he was doing so. I think he was what he was, and wished to remain that, at least for the time being. I suppose it makes a degree of sense. He exists in an unappreciated job, in a hostile environment. Perhaps he considers it simply a matter of survival, of blending in with his surroundings. Yes. That does indeed sound most reasonable.

"Very well, then," I said, and joined him in soiling his skin once more. It became a sort of game and we even laughed together. Or rather I laughed, whereas his chest shook in amusement and he smiled widely. It took only minutes to return him to his previous dirty and disheveled look. The only thing missing was the distinctive aroma of manure and I had every confidence that it would be restored in short order upon his return to the stables.

We did not get back until late in the afternoon. We stood

together for a moment at the entrance to the stables, decorum firmly reestablished between we two. "Thank you," I said, and then added more softly, "for everything." He bowed slightly, and then walked the two horses into the stable.

I turned and started to walk away, feeling light on my feet, and suddenly I heard shouting from the stables. It was, of course, the stable master, since the mute was not exactly in any condition to verbalize. I realized instantly that the mute was the subject of the stable master's ire, bellowing at him, telling him that he had no business wandering off for the bulk of the day, and who did he think he was, and he was going to show the lad the foolishness of his actions.

I had no doubt that if the mute chose to fight back he would make short work of the stable master. Nevertheless, I bolted back to the stables and entered in time to see the stable master striking the mute with a short club. The mute was on the ground, writhing, offering no resistance to the pummeling.

Quickly I strode up behind the stable master and yanked the bludgeon from his hand as he raised it back for the purpose of bringing it down once more. He looked comically at his empty hand and then whirled to face me. His face turned a shade of umber as he said, "What do you here?"

"Leave him alone."

"What business be it of yours?"

"The queen's business. He was out with me, exercising the mounts."

His eyes narrowed as he stared at me. It almost seemed as if he were staring into my head, reading my thoughts. Then he looked back to the mute, who remained prone. But the mute was not looking at his tormentor. Instead he was staring at me and there was unmistakable gratitude in his eyes for my intervention. Gratitude and something more that, I suspect, was reflected in mine own face.

It must have been, because the stable master was able to discern it. "So that's the way of it, is it?" he said.

"There is no way of anything," I said, although I doubt I sounded especially convincing.

He merely grunted. Then he glanced down at the mute and said, "Get up," as if the mute had stumbled on his own. "Stop lying about. You look like a damned fool." He gave me one more disdainful look and then walked away.

The mute slowly got to his feet. I stepped in close to him and said softly, "You could have defended yourself. We both know what you are capable of. You could have given him a beating such as he would ne'er forget."

He just shook his head slowly and half-smiled as if I was discussing matters that I could not possibly understand. Maybe I could not, at that.

I look back now on the activities of the day, and again, I know beyond question that I am going to Hell.

But at least I will enjoy the ride.

Day the One Hundred and Twenty-Third

A RIOT BROKE OUT IN the town today and I was right in the middle of it.

I had gone to the apothecary to purchase some medication to help me with the headaches and nausea I have been experiencing of late. A pity that Merlin is still out with Arthur fighting the war, for he would certainly have been able to minister to my needs.

Two doors down from the apothecary was a tavern. I heard loud voices erupting from within even as I completed my transaction. I looked in the direction of the tavern and said, "Early in the day for a drunken brawl."

"The brawls come more and more frequently," said the apothecary with a grim expression.

"For what cause?"

"Why the king, of course," said the apothecary. "Odds blood, girl, you reside in the castle. You must be aware of it."

I was certainly aware that public opinion was becoming toxic insofar as the war was concerned. It had been well over a week since the queen had ventured out to be amongst the common folk. They had come perilously close to hurling ripe fruit at her, the only thing stopping them being the glowers from the armed guards that had accompanied us. As the apothecary told me of the recent unrest, it prompted me to think I would have been wise had I brought a guard with me myself.

More and more stories were reaching the local townships of the violent actions of Arthur's knights, a number of them courtesy of lower level foot soldiers who had decided that they were wasting their time and had deserted. One would have thought that the words of such men, betrayers of their oath and fealty, would carry no weight. Such was not the case. The things they said were given as much credence as if they were the most valiant of knights. According to the deserters, Maleagant had been found nowhere, and although there was much talk of how warriors of his had been captured and interrogated, apparently none of them had said anything useful. And the interrogations, by all accounts, had been brutal. Flame applied to body parts, stretching their bodies, holding them underwater for extended periods. All manner of things that civilized men simply did not do to one another.

"The people feel neglected, angry. Taxes are heavy upon them already to support the war and there is promise of more to come," said the apothecary. "There is a sense of hopelessness such as I have not seen in many a day, and I have many more days under my belt than most around here. Hopelessness breeds frustration, and frustration gives vent to itself in violent ways. I would take great care these days were I you, young Viviana."

I gave him thanks for his words of concern, hastily took

the medication from him and shoved it into the small leather bag attached to my belt. As I emerged from the street, I heard something break, and there was more yelling. Suddenly men came crashing out into the street from the tavern. They were pounding upon each other with drunken fury, and a handful were saying, "God save the king!" but most of the others were shouting vile desecrations of Arthur's name, calling him evil and a heartless bastard and other things so repellant that my hand trembles too much to write them here.

I fell back, watching with astonishment the ire that Arthur's actions had raised amongst the populace.

Other villagers poured forward then, driving a living wedge between the combatants and working to separate everyone from everyone else. That was a relief, I thought, for if the new arrivals had likewise been bellicose, a full blown riot might well have entailed.

As it turned out, my optimism was ill-founded. Harsh words were exchanged twixt the new arrivals and the still overheated battlers, and within seconds more fists were flying.

That was when one word soared above the tumult, and that word was "Her!"

It was nothing short of amazing that the declaration managed to rise above the melee, but it did, and heads turned to see who was being referred to. Mine was one of them as I turned around to see what poor, unfortunate "her" had suddenly become the focus of attention. There was no one standing behind me, and it was only then that I realized I was the "her" in question.

One surly man, clearly in his cups, staggered forth from

the crowd and pointed an angry finger at me, trembling with rage. "She is a handmaiden of the queen! She consorts with the royals who would destroy others with their brutality, and us with their taxes."

I could not believe the hideous luck that this person would have remembered me. Servants and slaves are generally invisible. None pay attention to us. This fellow did.

Slowly they advanced, with the foremost of them saying, "Use her to send a message back to the queen! Let her know what we think of her incompetent husband and his barbaric knights!" They were not forthcoming about how they intended to convey that message, but I could guess. Beat me, brutalize me, strip me, humiliate me in whatever means their besotted minds could conjure. I backed up, backed up . . . and fell in quite possibly the most awkward manner imaginable. My legs bumped into a horse trough, and I stumbled and fell in, landing on my backside. I sat there with no doubt a stunned and stupid expression on my face, with my legs sticking up and water splashing around me. I cannot imagine a moment when I must have looked more ridiculous.

As mortified as I was, that may well have been what saved me for the moment. The sight of me prompted raucous laughter. It is certain enough that too much drink makes virtually anything, no matter how mundane, seem funny. My situation was outright hilarious. Some of them were almost falling over, so seized were they with paroxysms of laughter.

I tried to pull together the tattered remains of whatever dignity I might have had as I stumbled to my feet, still in the trough, my sodden dress plastered against my body. I should have taken that moment to try and flee the area, but there were far too many of them for me to think I could elude them, even though a good number of them were inebriated.

Furthermore I was becoming angry myself, and not simply out of mortification for having plunged into the trough. Despite the way that the war was going, I knew that Arthur's heart was pure. Actually, perhaps pure is not the right word. Wounded. Wounded over the crime done against his mother, and yes, it may well have affected his judgment, but he was not the evil bastard as others were describing him to be. All I could think of were those times when I sat with him in an upper tower, and he was as open and vulnerable as any man could be. I felt growing outrage on his behalf. Arthur, I was convinced, was not the problem. It was those bloody bastards who were his knights, Lancelot and the rest of them.

"The king is not evil!" I said, mustering what nerve I had left. "As for his knights, all you hear are tales of misdeeds! In war, there are always misdeeds, but there are also great deeds as well! And you are not hearing any of those!"

"That's because there are none!" said the man who had first assailed me. He wiped his arm across his face and sneered. "There's not a single knight worth a damn in the lot of them!"

"That is not true!"

"Aye, is it not? Name one," he said challengingly.

And I said the first thing that popped into my mind, blurting it out ere I could give any thought to what I was saying: "Galahad!"

They looked at each other in confusion. "Which one's he, then?" asked one of them.

"The bravest, the purest, the most noble of Arthur's knights," I said quickly, feeling as if I were standing on a sheet of ice that was rapidly thawing and cracking beneath me. "Defender of women's virtue, protector of the weak. He is the right arm of the king."

"Isn't that Lancelot?"

"No," I said, trying to convey utter certainty. "It is Galahad. He is a knight so worthy, he is touched by God himself. He . . ." I paused, my mind racing. "Maleagant's warriors had taken hostages in a church in Gloucester. They were holding nuns hostages. They were threatening to rape them unless the king surrender himself, naked and unarmed."

"Rape nuns?" There were repulsed looks on their faces. I heard murmurs of "Brutes," among the crowd.

"Aye, nuns," I said, and continued, "and the king was prepared to do what needed to be done in order to save the sisters. But Galahad would not allow his liege to throw away his life needlessly. So Sir Galahad stripped to his skin and, taking Arthur's helm, he placed it upon his head so as to obscure his identity and approached the church."

"Naked save for the king's own helmet?" said the foremost man. I noticed several women in the crowd were smiling, obviously envisioning the scene. A couple of men were as well.

"Correct. He entered the church, and the door closed behind him. None saw what transpired next, save that there were screams and the sounds of bones crunching and bodies breaking. Then all was still. Finally Sir Galahad emerged, covered with blood, save it was the blood of his enemies. He said not a word, since Galahad was a man of few, but instead went straight to a nearby lake to wash clean of the blood. The nuns emerged, safe and whole, their virtue intact. When Arthur and the other knights entered the church, they found the bodies of Maleagant's men strewn everywhere. Galahad had slain them with his bare hands, every one."

"Balls!" shouted another man. "I've heard not this tale, nor of Galahad. Why have we not heard of him before?"

"Boundless modesty," I said. "He is not one for having tales of his deeds spread around."

"Anyone else hear of this 'Galahad?'" someone asked.

A deathly silence fell then, and I sensed impending misfortune for me wrapped in that silence.

Then a familiar voice spoke softly, but it carried nevertheless.

"I have," it said. "Saw him with my own eyes."

I turned and there, in the shadows of an alleyway between two buildings, was Modred. He was cloaked, with a hood, and he said, "I was at death's door. He laid hands upon me and brought me back."

"Balls!" the same man said, apparently having a limited means of expressing disbelief. "Back from the dead, you say? Prove it!"

"If you wish. But be not faint of heart, for I must warn you, a brush with the Reaper tends to leave its mark." He drew back his hood then, and although Modred was well enough known around the castle, none outside were aware of his existence. So his sallow skin, white hair and pale blue eyes came as a shock to all who could see him. The crowd gasped as one. Several crossed themselves. "Maleagant's men strangled me, left me for dead, and I nearly was," said Modred with eerie calm that even I found disconcerting. "Sir Galahad snatched me back from the brink. There was naught he could do to erase the evidence of the Reaper's touch, but still . . . at least air is still filling my lungs. In time, mayhap, my appearance will return to normal. In the meantime, I live every day thankful that I am here to see it at all, thanks to Sir Galahad the Pure."

"You know," another in the crowd said, "I think I have heard of this fellow, now that it is mentioned. Distant rumors is all."

"I did not know that his name was Galahad, but I have also heard tell of miraculous feats of a knight."

"It was probably he," I said, trying to keep the momentum shifted in favor of the nonexistent knight.

It was amazing to watch. The merest suggestion of Galahad's existence was enough to convince some that he truly did exist. The crowd rapidly began to degenerate into two groups: Those who claimed to have heard of Galahad, thus making themselves centers of attention, and those who had not the wit to fabricate or the conviction to convince themselves of Galahad's existence, but were eager to hear from those who knew of it, or claimed to know of it.

As this was happening, Modred gestured to me. I quickly went to him and together we made our way down the alley before any noticed that we were departing. I have no doubt that they became aware soon enough, but it would have been too late to hinder our departure.

"Your timing is amazing, Modred," I told him, gasping for breath as we ran.

Modred, by contrast, was not gasping for breath. He never seemed to tire. Not for the first time, I began to wonder if he was even human.

Suddenly a realization swept over me and it caused me to stop in my tracks. Modred overran me and then, realizing that I was no longer following him, retraced his steps and looked up at me with mild curiosity. "Problem?" he said.

I looked down at him and said, "It was not mere happenstance or timing. You followed me. Not enough that you keep appearing out of the very walls of the castle. Now you are following me into the streets?"

He regarded me with that same unearthly calm that he routinely bore. "You are interesting," he said at last.

"Interesting?"

"Yes. I find you interesting. Far more so than most others here. Would you rather that I had not been following you?"

"Of course I would rather!"

"And had I not been there, mayhap you would not have fared as well as you did with the crowd, eh?"

I was about to respond, and the only thing that prevented me from doing so was that I realized I had nothing to say.

"You may thank me at any time," he said.

Those words pushed me a bit too far. I stepped in close to him and said heatedly, "This must cease, Modred. Aye, you were of help just now, but I was handling matters. And you cannot continue to spy upon me as if I were your personal project."

"I cannot?"

"No. You cannot. It is horrid and invasive and if you do not cease immediately, I—"

And something changed with him then. Something in his face, in his tone, his manner, that frightened me for the first time since I had met him. He took a step toward me, just one step, and yet it almost seemed as those pale blue eyes had invaded my very soul, and he said in a low, cold voice, "You will what?" When I did not immediately reply, he went on, "You do not get to decide what I do. You never get to decide that. No one does except me. Do not presume to think for me, or speak for me, or to direct my actions. I am Modred, son of none, and I will answer to myself and myself only." I said nothing, and Modred seemed to step back into himself, to "become" the lad that I had known once more, as if he had transformed into someone else and was only now reasserting his normal appearance. "You will always have my gratitude," he said, "for intervening on my behalf that day with those boys. Still . . . do not press me. I would be loath to see something untoward happen to you, but unfortunately I am not always in control of such things. So please tread carefully, Viviana. Tell me you will?"

He genuinely sounded concerned for my welfare. My throat had tightened up, making it difficult for me to speak, probably due to substantial fear that had fallen upon me. A greater fear, I think, than I felt when faced with an angry mob. How it was that infuriated rabble was less daunting to me than one small, pale boy, I cannot begin to imagine. Yet it was

I managed a nod, and he seemed content with that. "Good," he said, and he pulled his hood up and turned away from me. I followed him contritely, almost like a whipped dog, back to the castle. Once we were within he turned, glanced back at me, and said, "We have started something this day. For good or ill, it has begun, and who knows where it will end?"

"Do you?" I said cautiously.

He did not smile. Instead he simply replied, "That would be telling," and then he headed off down a corridor, his cape swirling around him.

Day the One Hundred and Twenty-Seventh

THE MEDICATION PROVIDED ME BY the apothecary does not appear to be helping. The headaches are becoming more frequent, the nausea more prevalent. I have thus far managed to keep my condition hidden from the queen, but Guinevere seems to have her suspicions that something is wrong. The other day I was aiding her in dressing and actually fell asleep in doing so. That was mortifying. It is as if I do not know my body anymore.

The one consistent pleasure in my life is my continued assignations with the mute. I despise referring to him in that way, but I know not his name, and I do not feel it is my place to arbitrarily assign one to him.

Our times together are so fraught with lascivious activities that I cannot bring myself even to commit them to parchment. I have been trying to determine how I will possibly explain my actions when called to final account, presuming that I will even be allowed to face my maker and be given the opportunity. It is entirely likely that I will be dispatched directly to perdition for my actions.

Still . . .

I had come to realize that the congress I have had with men up until the mute was atypical. Most women were not, in fact, brutalized as part of their carnal relations with men. Granted, some men were likely better lovers than others, but I could not have been the first woman to actually find pleasure in the act, could I? And if that was the natural state of such intercourse, then how could it be sinful to enjoy it? How could our maker condemn us for it if He was the one who designed us in the first place? It did not make sense to me, and indeed offered some small hope that I might not have to spend eternity writhing in torment.

The mute and I have endeavored to keep our relations private. That has not always been an easy undertaking. Regular horseback rides out into the woods would certainly attract attention, sooner or later. As much as I hate to admit it, we have been making use of the stables during such times that the stable master is nowhere around. The armory has also served us nicely. It has been severely depleted since the war so there is not much activity there, and the vast majority of the knights are nowhere to be found.

It is regrettable that I must keep my relations with the mute as secret as possible. But I am too far into it now to confess the truth of it to the queen, especially after denying it. Plus she had made it clear that, as a handmaiden to the queen, it would be inappropriate somehow to engage in a relationship with a stable hand. Then again, I am a slave, about as low a rung on the social ladder as one can have. It is not as if I have a plethora of highborn suitors seeking my time and attention. However it would likely be a waste of time to point out to the queen that she is being unreasonable.

At least I have my books to keep me company during my rare off times.

My books. How odd that I would think of them in that manner. They are Merlin's books, his tomes and texts. The histories remain intriguing, yet I find myself lately drawn to matters of philosophy. Histories tell us of the world as it was, but philosophies explore the world as it might be, seeking reason in the face of irrationality. Religion teaches us that things happen because it is the will of our creator. Yet we are also taught that our creator has given us free will. Both cannot be true, for if our destinies are God's plan, then what meaning has free will, save as a cruel hoax to give us the impression that we are making decisions that have already been made for us? I thought I was alone in my confusion until I found philosophers, centuries gone, wrestling with much the same questions. It makes me feel connected to them, and I wish that I could have sat down with them and spoken to them. Such amazing lives they led, and so tragic the end of some. Socrates, in particular, forced to drink poison because, according to Plato, he had become a social gadfly to the state. Granted, supposedly Socrates welcomed the death sentence as a means of escaping the ravages of old age. Still, perhaps he only said that so as not to burden his friends and students with having to mourn his passing.

I feel there are so many things that I want to think about, to dwell upon, lurking just beyond the limits of my imagination. I can almost see them, touch them, but when my mind starts to reach out for them, they dance away from me.

I ache with longing to accomplish great things, and wish I had the wit and freedom to go about doing so. How limiting my previous concerns now seem to me. How narrow was my worldview. How much of my life I have already wasted.

Day the One Hundred and Thirty-Ninth

Arthur is returning.

A herald came riding to Camelot today, bearing tidings of Arthur's return. Arthur and his knights are claiming victory.

There are already rumblings amongst the court, though, that such claims are without foundation. Maleagant was never found. The story being spread now is that, on the verge of being captured by Arthur's forces, Maleagant took his own life and his body was buried in an unmarked grave. I do not know if it is true. Either way, it is a most unsatisfying conclusion to this entire business.

The warriors of Maleagant's desires are likewise difficult to locate. Rumors now abound that those who were captured and labeled as being among those warriors were just random sell-swords and free agents, or handfuls of Maleagant loyalists who were attempting to grab power for themselves in the name of their departed master. Either way, they hardly presented any sort of threat to Camelot or its peoples.

As a consequence, there is much discontent among the courtiers, particularly in relation to the considerable consumption of both taxes and manpower that have been consumed in pursuit of what many perceive as a feckless undertaking.

I miss going out into the village. I understand why Guinevere has forbidden me from doing so, especially in light of that day when the mob attacked me. Still, I did enjoy going out and about. Furthermore the ban has kept me away from the stables, away from the mute. He must be wondering what happened to me. Perhaps he believes that I grew tired of him and had no further use for him. That would sadden me tremendously, but I have no means of getting word to him of my restriction to the castle. There are none to run messages for me. I contemplated asking Rowena to do so since she has been so kind and supportive of late. It is as if those days past never happened. And if I could simply provide her with a written note and count on her discretion, perhaps I would do so. But I know the mute cannot write and have no idea if he is capable of reading, which means that I would have to entrust my sentiments to her to be passed along orally. I do not think I trust Rowena that much, that I am willing to take that chance and throw all discretion to the wind. Especially when one considers how she spoke of the mute on that day when she suggested I be subjected to his supposedly vile appetites.

How odd, the twists and turns of destiny's path, that I would have willingly given myself over to a fate previously described in the most unappetizing of terms.

Speaking of appetites, I have not eaten much of anything the past several days and have felt slightly better. I am hoping that whatever ill humours have lodged themselves within me, and have long overstayed their welcome, are in the process of departing. Guinevere noticed my poor health and suggested I have myself bled, but I politely declined the notion. I still remember my childhood friend, Cedric, who took ill and the local physicians bled him to allow the humours to depart. Roderick became sicker and sicker, and the worse he became, the more they bled him. He would beg me to find a way to stop the doctors from pouring the blood from him. He said the treatments made him feel worse than the disease. I pleaded with my father to intercede, but he pointed out that he was not Cedric's father and had no say in the matter. His parents had to do what was right. When Cedric died, the doctors claimed that the humours were particularly vicious and it was God's will that Cedric be taken from us. I refused to speak to God for a year after that, so angry was I, and I was furious with the doctors as well. I have since forgiven God, but my resentment for such treatments remain. I tend to think blood should remain within the body whenever possible.

And speaking of that as well, I have not had my womanly flow when normally I should. That, in and of itself, is not unusual, especially since the season is shifting and such changes in weather inexplicably cause my flow to arrive late or not at all. So I shall not worry about it and instead focus on fully reclaiming my health.

Day the One Hundred and Forty-Second

A CONFRONTATION TODAY THAT WAS both catastrophic and yet one of the headiest experiences I have ever had, with an outcome I could never have anticipated.

I emerged from my quarters this morning with the full intention of attending to the queen, but Guinevere was nowhere to be found. This was most puzzling as Guinevere was not typically an early riser, and it was usually left to me to aid her in beginning her day.

Before I could think to look for her, the doors to her chambers opened wide to reveal Morgan. I began to tell her that her sister was not there, but Morgan cut me off with a brisk, "I know where she is and thus came not seeking her, but you. You are to come with me."

"With you?" I was unsure what to make of such a summons. Certainly all my old fears and concerns about Morgan and her intentions for me swelled to the forefront of my consciousness. But I had no grounds upon which to disobey a direct order from her and so instead bowed my head meekly. "As you command."

I followed her down the corridor, curious as to where we were going. I could not have been more surprised when she stopped at the entrance to Merlin's study. She opened the door and stepped aside, gesturing for me to enter. I did so and stopped dead in my tracks.

Merlin was seated in his overlarge chair, the one with the dragon's heads carved ornately into the armrests. His face had lost the roundness it had previously possessed. His beard, always neatly trimmed, was now frayed and scraggly. His upper cheekbones stood out starkly against his face, and his eyes looked a bit more sunken. Nevertheless they glittered with power as they fixed on me and I sensed that I was in some manner of deep trouble.

Guinevere was standing to his right. To my surprise, she was still attired in her dressing gown. She never emerged from her chambers before she was dressed and ready to face the world as befit a queen, so I could not comprehend what she was doing there.

I said in quavering voice, "Milord Merlin . . . you have returned."

"Mastering the obvious, have you, Mistress Viviana?" he said with no trace of amusement in his voice. Before I could reply, he continued, "The king is en route and should be along within a few days. I went on ahead of the troops in order to ascertain what sort of reception he could encounter from his people. What sort would you anticipate, Mistress?"

"I do not know, milord. Certainly there are others who would be better qualified to answer—"

"I do not believe that to be the case. The queen has apprised me of a rather jarring encounter in the village. 'An angry mob' was her description. Kindly tell me what transpired that day."

"Milord, I—"

"Tell. Me." His voice was hard with a tint of anger to it.

I told him. What choice had I?

The one thing I did not mention in my description of those events was the presence of Modred. There was much about the lad that continued to unnerve me, and some instinct prompted me to keep him out of my narrative. I merely ascribed the role of Modred to a "random youth" in the crowd who, much like the adults, desired to bask in the reflected glory of the nonexistent Galahad.

I believe Morgan knew of the omission. When I mentioned the unnamed youth, something in her eyes flashed awareness. But she said nothing. If she was keeping track of the activities of her wayward son, she gave no indication beyond that momentary and silent acknowledgment.

Guinevere and Merlin did not react, so I had to think they were unaware of Modred's participation.

"So what you did," Merlin said slowly, "you did as a means of self-protection."

"Yes, milord."

"And you gave no consideration to the wider implications of your words."

I was feeling greatly confused at that point. I looked to Guinevere for aid in deciphering what Merlin was saying, but she provided none. She simply stood there with her arms folded, her face a mask. "Milord . . . with all respect . . . what 'wider implications?'"

"You are a handmaiden to the queen. What you say carries considerable weight among the populace."

I actually started to laugh at that point until I saw that no one else in the room was displaying the slightest hint of amusement. "Milord . . . I am but a slave. Even as a handmaiden to the queen . . ."

"There are no qualifiers to your status. Think you that the rank and file distinguishes between slave and freewoman when it comes to anyone associated with the royal family?"

"I . . ." I tried to rally. "Milord, I admit, I was simply trying to save myself from being humiliated or worse at the hands of a mob. I was not giving wider consideration to anything short of my own welfare. Truthfully, I am still unclear as to what I should have been considering. With all the respect—and I have a great deal—I have to think there is something transpiring here that I do not understand."

"Word has spread, Mistress Viviana, thanks to you."

"Spread, milord?"

"My entire trip home," said Merlin, "wherever I went, I heard tales of the mighty Galahad, the greatest of Arthur's knights. Indeed, he was often described as the one bright spot in a misbegotten and ill-advised venture. Unswerving in his loyalty to the king, preserver of the modesty of maidens, patron saint of nuns, widows, cripples and orphans. He even took time, I was told, to rescue a child's cat from a tree whilst simultaneously putting paid to an ogre."

"An ogre?"

"Aye. Even creatures of myth and legend surface to take on the incomparable Sir Galahad, and fall beneath the weight of his power."

"Milord, I—"

"You have set wheels into motion, Mistress Viviana, and now those wheels threaten to roll right over Arthur and his court. The people have built up a hero in their eyes where none exists."

To my surprise, Morgan spoke up. "With respect, Merlin, you sound as if you are blaming Viviana for this turn of events."

"Who else?" demanded Merlin.

And to my even greater surprise, Guinevere sided with her much-despised sister. "Arthur and his knights, Merlin. That is who else. The debauched and out-of-control activities of the knights, and my husband's inability to rein them in, are what instigated much of the anger in the populace in the first place. They are supposed to represent something great, something wonderful. Instead they represented power without the wisdom to guide it properly."

"And with respect to you, my queen, you were not there," Merlin said. His eyes darkened as if storm clouds were rolling in. "Brutal environs result in brutal responses. We opposed no organized foe. Everyplace we went, there were enemies who would attack us from hiding and then scurry back into their rat holes. And it was impossible to distinguish their supporters from innocent bystanders, at least not without taking extreme measures to separate one from the other. So Arthur's knights did what they had to do. Were some people who were blameless injured in the process? Yes. But what you do not hear about are all those who were not at all blameless. Who had either launched attacks against the forces of Camelot or supported those who had done so. We may have some blood on our hands, but they were up to their asses in it."

"And do you think," said Morgan, "that any of that matters to the common man?"

Merlin seemed prepared with a ready response, but he did not utter it. Instead he actually appeared to give thought to Morgan's question. Then he admitted, "Very likely not."

"I would say definitely not," said Guinevere.

Merlin nodded. "What they believe is what they hear from others, and what they think in their hearts is true. Reality does not objectively exist; instead it is shaped by perceptions. Whether our cause was righteous or not is secondary to whether the people believe it was righteous."

"So what does that mean?" said Morgan.

"It means," said Merlin, leaning back in his chair, steepling his fingers, "that we must shape their perceptions. Control the way they view things so that they are in accord with what we want them to believe."

"How?" said Guinevere.

"The war against Maleagant and the reasons that the knights did what they had to do are vast and difficult for the average man to comprehend. Since they cannot think grandly, we must think simply. We must give them symbols to rally around and we must boil down complex notions into a few words."

"Symbols," I said. "You mean symbols such as . . ."

Slowly he nodded. "Galahad," he said, a slow smile spreading across his face. "Putting aside the vastly irritation I felt whenever I heard the name of this fictional knight being bandied about, I could not help but notice the look of hope on the faces of the people whenever he was spoken of. Not dissimilar to the case, early in Uther's reign, when the people felt overtaxed and a brigand—Rabunhod—took to the woods with a band of yeomen. They robbed from any nobleman foolish enough to pass through the forest, relieved him of his money and then redistributed it amongst the poor."

"Everyone knows of Rabunhod," said Guinevere. "They sing songs of his deeds to this day. They were many and vast—"

"And wholly exaggerated," said Merlin dismissively. "He operated for a little under a month. Then Uther disguised himself as a traveler and rode into the woods. Rabunhod accosted him, as Uther assumed would be the case, and Uther dispatched him and most of his key yeomen within minutes. The rest of them fled, but obviously they'd be damned if they spoke of how their leader met so ignominious a demise. So the stories that everyone 'knows' to be fact are largely fabrications. In the grand scheme of things, he was a minor figure. But the ballads and tales built him up and now everyone knows of a certainty his mighty actions."

"Oh." Guinevere appeared to be rather disappointed at what Merlin had just told her. "Fact and fancy are oft' intertwined, it seems, and nigh unto inseparable."

"True, my queen. And that makes it something that we

can turn to our advantage."

"With Galahad?" I said.

"Aye. With Galahad," said Merlin. "I will gather the bards, the criers, the balladeers. They will be told tales of Galahad's bravery—tales that we will disseminate and tailor for maximum effect—and they will be instructed to spread those tales to all and sundry. They will, of course, be paid handsomely for their efforts. Coin buys reality rather handily."

"But whence will you draw these tales?" said Guinevere.

"From these," said Merlin. He reached into the folds of his cloak and withdrew parchment that he extended toward me. "Does this look at all familiar, Mistress Viviana?"

I gasped when I saw them. They were covered with my careful handwriting. It was the tales of Galahad that I had fabricated for Modred's entertainment. Dumbly I nodded.

"What are they?" said Guinevere.

"It seems that Galahad was not conceived off the top of Viviana's head, but rather already living a most exciting literary life," Merlin said to her.

"May I ask how you came by those, milord?" I said.

"You may ask, but answer, you will receive none. Have you not heard? We wizards are a crafty lot."

"You are no wizard, Merlin, no matter what others may think of you," said Morgan.

"As you should likewise be grateful for what you are not, Morgan, despite the beliefs of others about you," said Merlin, giving her a significant look. Morgan withered before it.

Guinevere, however, withered not. "Of what use will these

stories be, Merlin?" she demanded. "Stories only go so far. Sooner or later, will people not want to see this Galahad with their own eyes?"

"Why?" said Merlin reasonably. "Most have ne'er seen Rabunhod, but they believe in him."

"It is entirely different," said Guinevere. "Rabunhod represents a thought, a concept. But we are endeavoring to convince the people that there is at least one knight among Arthur's round table who is worthy of their adoration. If they are unable to see him, then the people will grow suspicious no matter how many tales are told."

"It would be impossible," Morgan now spoke up once more. "Even if an imposter were found to represent Galahad, the other knights would know him to be false. And they would never keep their tongues."

"Not necessarily," Merlin said, now appearing to give the matter serious consideration. He stroked his beard thoughtfully. "The knights did not move about the country en masse. There were a number of individual troops, operating independently of one another. That is, to be candid, why Arthur had such difficulties keeping control of them. He assigned lieutenants, but they did not always manage to keep order from descending into chaos. While this was happening, it was not unusual for troops to pick up recruits along the way. Assorted knights or would-be knights showed up to join the legions. Nor are all the legions returning together—they are making their way from various points. Arthur, with a small escort, will be arriving first. If Galahad is introduced to court as one of the knights who joined during the war, none will be able to gainsay it."

"If matters go anything the way that Viviana said they did in the public square," Guinevere said, "a number of them will swear that he was fighting by their side."

"I have no doubt," said Merlin. "Still, it leaves us with the problem of finding this non-existent Galahad. We may not be realistic in our expectations, since we require someone who looks handsome . . . is capable of handling himself in combat, because I assure you that the opportunity will arise . . . someone who is not known to the public nor would he be recognized as inhabiting the skin of someone who did not previously exist . . . and, most important of all, someone whose discretion could be counted upon."

I laughed.

My reaction startled the others, who looked at me in bewilderment. "May I ask, Mistress Viviana, just what precisely you find so amusing?" said Merlin.

"I know the exact individual. He fits all your prerequisites."

"Who?"

I paused, scarcely believing I was saying it. "The mute. The mute stable boy."

There was stunned silence for a moment, and then the three of them collectively bellowed in mirth. I ne'er would have thought there was one thing that could unite the three of them in merriment, but this was the case.

I wanted to feel angry with them, but I did not. I knew how they would react the moment I said it. How could it be any other way? They knew not the things that I did. So I merely stood there and waited for them to stop laughing.

Guinevere was the first to manage to compose herself sufficiently to say, "Viviana, you cannot be serious. That helpless, brain-addled creature . . . ?"

"He is not a creature save that he is one of God's creatures, and he is not brain-addled. And he is far from helpless. He is, in fact, remarkably formidable. He . . ."

"He what?"

I told her then. I could not withhold it from her any longer. I told her how it was the mute who had saved us on that day when Maleagant's men had endeavored to kidnap us. That we would indeed have been prisoners in a foreign land were it not for his intervention.

Guinevere's eyes went so wide that I thought they were going to burst out of her head. I would have thought her angry, but she appeared too stunned to react with anything other than shock. "And you thought it best not to tell me?" I tried to respond, but I could not, for right on top of that she said, "What else are you not telling me, Viviana?"

"He is her lover," Morgan said.

The queen's head snapped around and she gaped at her sister. "You know this of a certainty?"

"Merely a guess, but I suspect it is a correct one. It explains her silence. She was protecting him. And she wanted to keep him for herself."

"Nay!" I said with a bit more force than I intended. "It was not like that. Not at all. I . . . that is to say . . ."

"Is it true?" That was all Guinevere wished to know.

I have never so wanted to lie to someone as I did at that moment. But she was my queen, and she owned me, and I could not come close to obfuscating. I also could not bring myself to speak. I managed a nod.

Merlin and Morgan both began to speak at once, but Guinevere stopped them before they truly started with a sharp, "Quiet! Both of you!" As much to their surprise as anyone else's, they promptly lapsed into silence. I continued to look at the floor. I felt ashamed, not because of my choice of lover, but because I could feel the disappointment rolling off the queen in waves.

"Bring him here," she said at last.

"Highness, I—"

She interrupted me. "I was not speaking to you," she said imperiously. "I was speaking to my sister. Do my bidding, Morgan. Go cloaked. Let none see you. You skulk well; you always have. Bring him here straightaway."

"My queen . . ." Morgan started to say.

Guinevere had been looking at me as she had been speaking to Morgan, but now she whirled to face Morgan and she fairly bellowed, *"Do my bidding!"*

I believe that Morgan felt she was seeing her sister for the first time, or at least in a new manner for the first time. She hastened from the room.

I turned to the queen, about to address her, but she said, "Speak to me anon, Viviana, once I have given you leave to do so. Not before then. Speak to Merlin, if you wish."

Unsure of what I should do, I turned to Merlin. My thoughts were running riot, and I needed something to steady me. I had little hope that Merlin would provide it, for I assumed that he would be as put out with me as was Guinevere.

Instead he regarded me with what could only be described as open curiosity and said, "The stable boy, Mistress Viviana? Truly?"

"There is more to him than meets the eye, milord."

"As there is with you. Perhaps therein lies the attraction."

It could well be that he was correct. I am a creature of secrets, as is the mute. In our union, we celebrate our mutual ability to deceive the rest of the world.

Merlin moved closer to me and he spoke in a no-nonsense manner. "Let us be clear on this matter, Mistress Viviana. The game may provide great rewards. It may well serve to contribute to turning public opinion in a positive manner toward Arthur. It already seems to be doing that. The question is whether it can be perpetuated and built upon. But rewards cannot be attained without risk, and there is risk aplenty in this endeavor. Your taciturn lover must agree wholeheartedly to this charade. This cannot be undertaken in half measures. He dedicates himself fully or it does not proceed."

"I am sure that he will, sir," I said, which was less than truthful.

Merlin did not suffer prevarication. "No, you are not," he said frostily, "and if you lie to me one more time—"

He did not complete the sentence, but it was unnecessary for him to do so. There was danger in his voice such as I had never heard, and I knew then that nothing but complete candor would do. "My apologies, sir. It will not happen again."

"Be certain it does not." He appeared to be endeavoring to make up his mind whether to remain angry with me or not and decided, for the time being, not to do so. "The simple truth, Viviana, is that you have set this business into motion. It is upon you, then, to put it to rights."

The queen continued to say nothing to me, staring fixedly at nothing. Knowing that she could hear me but desirous to obey her edict that I not speak to her, I said to Merlin, "I hope the queen knows how much I regret keeping secrets from her."

Merlin shrugged, indifferent. "What she knows has very little to do with what she feels. At the moment she is governed entirely by the latter. Allow time for the former and all will be well." He glanced at the queen's icy exterior and added as an optimistic afterthought, "Eventually."

Some minutes later there was a knock at the door and Morgan entered with the stable hand. He reeked of horses and manure, and Merlin made a face the moment the mute drew within proximity. There was confusion in his mien; clearly Morgan had not told him why he was being summoned. Then he saw me, and the queen, and the way we were both regarding him, and I could see slow understanding dawning upon his face. He looked at me then with a clear sense of betrayal.

"I had to tell them," I said. "Matters have changed and . . ." My voice trailed off. How could I possibly summarize the situation we were about to present him?

I was saved the trouble when Guinevere said, "You are

needed to serve king and country. I myself have ordered you summoned here; your lover had no say in the matter." She watched carefully his reaction when she referred to me in that manner. She must have been disappointed, for he gave no reaction at all. He was a study in stoicism. Guinevere appeared to shrug mentally and continued, "Merlin here will tell you precisely what we are asking of you. Unlike Viviana, who was compelled to speak the truth against her will," and she fired me an annoyed look, "and my sister who brought you here, you will be given a choice in your subsequent actions. I am extending you this courtesy because you saved me from villains with evil intent, and I cannot find it within me to compel you to do what is about to be asked of you. However, should you commit to it, I expect you to do so fully. Is that understood?"

He hesitated a moment. I think he was considering playing the fool, looking blankly at the queen and pretending he lacked the wit to comprehend all that she had said. If that was indeed crossing his mind, it was a notion he promptly discarded, and he nodded.

"Very well, then. Merlin," and she gestured to him. "Tell our manure-covered bravo what we would of him."

Merlin did so in quick, concise sentences. The mute displayed neither emotion nor reaction as Merlin explained to him his role in what would be a massive fraud perpetrated upon the people of Camelot.

When Merlin concluded his recitation, the mute simply stared at him. It was impossible to determine whether he thought us deluded or reasonable or simply insane. Then, very slowly, he shook his head. Merlin appeared a bit crestfallen, as was Morgan, but the queen remained impassive.

"As you wish," she said. "You are excused, with the thanks of a grateful queen for your earlier service. If the stables are where you wish to remain, then I will accede to your wishes."

He bowed in a courtly manner and turned to head for the door.

I do not know why I then said what I did, for even now I am not certain if I believed it to be true. But say it I did as, before he could depart, I spat out, "Coward!"

The mute turned and stared at me, wide-eyed. He could not have been more shocked. Truthfully, neither could I. But I was caught up in an intense mix of emotions that were carrying me beyond anything approaching common sense or civility or even, God help me, love. "Yes! I call thee coward!" I said, and advanced upon him. There was a distant pounding in my ears; if the queen or anyone else was saying anything to me, telling me to hold my tongue, I heard it not. "Perhaps not in combat, no, for you have proven your worth mightily in that regard. But you are a coward when it comes to people. People who need you for emotional support, for commitment. Yes, commitment. You have no sense of it whatever. I am beginning to think that you are not silent from inability to speak, but from unwillingness. In your silence, you are able to control all interaction with others, and you are able to keep them at a distance. Even I, who should be closer to you than any. Now you are being offered the chance to rise up from the stables, to see your ability acknowledged. So what if the identity fashioned for you is fictional? You are every inch the Galahad that I created. Or at least that is what I had thought. Now," and I walked in a circle round him, "now I am beginning to think I misjudged you. That he has nobility and dedication to an ideal that you cannot begin to grasp because you are too afraid to try. Or maybe it is even simpler than that. Maybe you prefer to stay within that stable because it keeps you distant from me. If you were a knight, here in the castle, then you would see me all the time. We might, God forbid, become closer. Develop a true relationship as do a man and woman, rather than grasp stolen moments."

I stopped for breath, and Morgan interrupted before I could continue. "What makes you think, Viviana, that—should he become a knight—he will have the slightest interest in you? Should he assume the identity that we construct for him, he will be a valued catch by many ladies of highborn lineage. What makes you think he would carry on with a slave?"

That stopped me cold. Truthfully, I had not considered it. I felt my legs going weak from the emotion I had vented, and I slumped into a chair, the world suddenly seeming irrelevant to me. I had no idea what I was thinking anymore, or what I wanted on behalf of the mute or the queen or even myself. I was tired of thinking, tired of feeling.

"Well?" said Morgan, refusing to take no response for a response.

"I do not know that he would have an interest in me," I said. "But if it would mean a better station in life for one such as he, who saved my life and did me the service of loving me for at least a little while, then I am content."

I brought myself to look the mute full in the eyes then. He did not return my gaze. Instead he looked away from me and to the queen. He crossed the room to her, knelt before her and bowed his head, bringing his fist to rest against his chest. The gesture was unmistakable. He was putting his heart into her service.

"All right," she said. Guinevere was quite business like in her demeanor. "Morgan, you are certain that none saw you depart the stables with Galahad here?"

It was disconcerting to hear her refer to him in such a manner. I supposed I should be getting accustomed to it.

"None," said Morgan. Personally, I would not have been anxious to wager on that. It would not have surprised me if Modred had been a witness to it. He had the unnerving ability to be in the right place at the right time to observe all that transpired in Camelot. He might well be watching the proceedings at this very moment. I glanced toward the wall to see if I could spot his eyes peering through a small aperture, but was unable to perceive it. That meant nothing in and of itself.

"Good," said Guinevere. "Merlin, Galahad will stay here for the time being."

"Here? In my chambers?"

"If his departure was unobserved, so much the better. Let the stable master believe that he simply ran off, never to be seen again. A young grooms man absenting himself will attract no comment. I will enlist Eowyn's aid in transforming young Galahad here into something more akin to a warrior than a stable hand."

"Can we count on her discretion?" said Morgan.

"Eowyn served the late queen. When she learns that this young man was responsible for dispatching her murderers, she will crawl across jagged stones to serve him," said Guinevere confidently. Her mind was already moving on to other considerations. "Arthur will return—?" She looked questioningly to Merlin.

"A day. Two at most."

"We cannot proceed without his cooperation."

"Which he will give," said Merlin. "I am quite confident."

"You will see to it?" said Guinevere. He nodded. "Then we are agreed on this course, Merlin? Morgan? Galahad?" She added that last name with a trace of amusement, but she was clearly seeking the mute's agreement in the matter.

She did not ask me. The omission was pointed and if it was intended to hurt, then it succeeded.

Guinevere departed Merlin's chambers then. Morgan and I followed her dutifully as befitted our respective stations. We arrived at Guinevere's chambers and entered, and then Guinevere turned to me and said, "Wait here."

Naturally I did as I was bidden. She walked out, leaving Morgan and me alone together. An uneasy silence grew between us and finally I said, "I should have told her."

"Admitting that to me is hardly going to rectify matters, I would think," said Morgan, and I knew she spoke truly.

"Do you think expressing that sentiment to her will help?"

"I think," said Morgan, "that you sat in moral judgment upon me, and now such arrogance is being visited back upon you. You thought yourself to be better. A better aide to Guinevere, a better person. So how does it feel, Viviana, to be found wanting yourself?"

It felt terrible. I did not wish to say so, though. I did not want to give her the satisfaction.

"You do not wish to give me the satisfaction," said Morgan. The pronouncement startled me, since it seemed as if she had ripped the words out of my very head. "It matters not whether you admit it or not. We both know it to be true." Suddenly, very quickly, she strode forward, grabbed a fistful of my hair and shoved me back toward the wall. I slammed up against it and cried out as my skull thudded into the brick. "You know secrets of mine, things that I hide from my sister, and you have believed that that somehow makes you superior to me. But I have kept those secrets for my reasons, and you have kept them for yours, and now we see you have your own secrets as well. The mighty Viviana, having fallen from her high horse, rolling around down here in the mud with the rest of us. Are you enjoying being part of humanity rather than above it?"

"I have never believed myself above it," I gasped out. "I am a slave. Every day, all I need do is look upon my wrists, feel the weight around my throat, and I know that I am designated inferior to all."

"A happenstance of fate. It does not deter you from feeling the way you do, nor does it diminish your arrogance."

I tried to muster my nerve. "Do not presume to think to know my mind," I said and endeavored to push her away.

Without appearing to exert the slightest effort, she shoved

me back against the wall so hard that my teeth jarred in my skull. "Do not presume to think I do not know it," she said.

There was a sound at the door. Morgan, stepping back, shoved me aside and smoothed her dress. Guinevere entered. She frowned, looking from Morgan to me and back, aware that she had interrupted something but clearly uncertain what it might have been. Then she shrugged, dismissing it as something not worth pondering. "Viviana, come here," she said.

I did as she instructed. When I drew within several paces of her, she walked over to me and brought her hands toward my throat. My instinct was to flinch back, but I held my ground.

I heard a click. I was confused. Suddenly pressure relieved itself around my throat and I realized that Guinevere was removing my slave collar.

She stepped back and she was holding it in one hand. In the other was a key, a slaver's key. She lobbed the collar to the surprised Morgan, and then without a word took my left wrist and then my right, inserting the key into each manacle and unlocking it. I could not believe it. It was as if I was living a waking dream. The shackles fell to the floor. I knelt, picked them up, and stared at them. They had defined my life. Now, in my hands, they seemed small, even pathetic. Powerless.

"You are free. As queen of Camelot, I grant you leave to depart."

"I do not understand."

"Which word was unclear to you?"

"I comprehend the words, highness; simply not the deed."

She pursed her lips. "The reason you were of interest to me,

Viviana, was because of your scathing honesty. Most people are hesitant to speak truth to power. You felt no such hesitation. Yet now I see that you are no more honest than any others I have encountered. Since you are not, you are no longer of any use to me. But if I simply assign you to someone else in the castle, then I will have to keep looking at you, and that does not suit me either. I can either toss you in a cell until you rot or release you. I choose the latter. You are no longer a slave, Viviana. You are free to pursue your own destiny. I assume I can count on your discretion as to Galahad's true nature. Now go."

"But I—"

She never raised her voice, yet there was cold and anger and hurt in her voice as she said again, "Go."

"Where?"

She walked across the room, rummaged in a drawer, and removed a small purse. She tossed it across the room to me. When I caught it, it jingled slightly. There were coins within. "Wherever you wish. I care not. We are done, Viviana. Have a good life. But understand this: I am issuing the guards orders that, should you return to Camelot, you are to be thrown into the dungeons. Do not attempt to cross me on this, or I swear, it will go badly for you and any who accompany you."

I stared at the purse full of coins. I felt unworthy, dirty. "I . . . do not wish to leave, highness."

"Your wishes are not my concern. Now depart, before I have the guards escort you from the castle."

"I . . ." The words I wanted to say died in my throat, and instead I simply managed to say, "Thank you, highness."

She stepped in close to me and spoke in a tone so low that only I could hear. "There was much I wanted to share with you. My feelings about Arthur. My hopes for what we may be able to achieve together as king and queen. My decision about giving him an heir. But now . . ." She shook her head then and, straightening her shoulders, said in her normal tone, "If you truly wish to express your thanks, then depart immediately, before I change my mind and simply have you imprisoned for all time."

I did as she said, stopping only to gather my few possessions, including this journal.

And I fled.

I fled into the rapidly dwindling daylight. I ran across the drawbridge of Camelot castle, ran toward the forest and into it. I felt physically lighter than I had in years for there was no longer metal to weigh me down. I was feeling hunger pains because I had been eating almost nothing in the past days since I had been unable to keep any of it down. But I ignored them. I thought of nothing save the dizzying sensation of freedom coursing through my veins.

I ran into the forest, Camelot to my back. Once within the woods, I sagged against a tree, my breathing hard in my chest.

I began to laugh. And then I began to cry, great wracking sobs, and the sobs alternated with the laughter until I began to choke on my own breath.

And tears. My God, tears, after so long.

I was free. For the first time in years, for the first time in my adult life, I was free.

I turned and looked back toward Camelot, seeing distant torches burning in the uppermost corners of the parapets. I had arrived there less than a year ago, and yet it seemed I had spent an eternity there.

Free. Free to live my life, to pursue my destiny.

The problem was that I was certain that my destiny, whatever it was, lay within those very walls. How in the name of God could I fulfill it if I was departing from it?

I wanted to go back.

As insane as it sounded, even to my own thoughts, I wanted to go back there, to continue to serve the queen. I wanted to see what transpired with the mute. I was leaving before the story was ended, and every aspect of my being screamed that I was doing the wrong thing.

I had spent years thinking only of myself, and now the fate of everyone but myself was all that mattered to me.

But I was not being given a choice. The queen wanted nothing to do with me, and truthfully I could not blame her. I had had my reasons for keeping my business, my affairs, to myself, but now they seemed petty and pointless.

I began putting more distance between Camelot and myself, but walking rather than running. Evening tripped over into night, the shadows lengthened, and I began to grow more and more nervous. The prospect of animals coming from the woods—the two legged, human kind as well as the more standard four legged fur-bearing kind—became greater in my mind.

As the moon crawled higher in the sky, I saw something in

the distance. It was at that point I remembered that, on my way to Camelot, I had passed a roadside inn. Summoning strength to my flagging legs, I ran the rest of the way, imagining that thieves or wolves or both were hot on my heels.

None were and I reached the inn, sagging against the side of the building and trying to gather my breath. My emotions were still in turmoil, but the inn was at least someplace to provide sanctuary.

I went to the door and tried to open it. It was bolted. The inn was closed. I banged on the door. It shuddered beneath my pounding. Minutes seemed to crawl by and then the door was yanked open. A phlegmatic innkeeper filled the door, glaring at me through half-opened eyes. "What the hell, girl?" he demanded. "Is the devil himself upon your heels?"

"I seek shelter."

"We're closed."

"I beg you, kind sir."

"I am neither," growled the innkeeper.

I looked again and flushed with chagrin. "My apologies, madam," I said, "it is dark, I am exhausted and can scarce see straight." I did not add that her abundant chin hair had not helped matters. Instead, seeking to shift the situation more to my advantage, I said, "I have money." I jingled the purse so that she could both see and hear it.

Her pig eyes narrowed. She grunted then and stepped back from the door. "Let me see," she said.

I reached into the purse and removed a coin. "Will this suffice for a stay of a night?" I said. I had little idea of how much things cost since, as a slave, I never had money to spend. But from her reaction I discerned that the amount I was displaying was sufficient. I did not wait for her to reply, but simply said, "Good," with the air of one who did not gladly suffer fools. "Where is my room?"

"Up the stairs, to the right. It is the grandest room we have," she said with a deep bow that I suspected was intended to be mocking.

"Have you any food available?"

She shrugged. "Bread. Some cheese. Piece of fruit. Nothing else much at hand, and if you think I have any intention of cooking . . ."

"That will not be necessary. The bread and the rest of it will more than suffice."

I went to the place she had indicated while clutching to my bosom the simple foodstuffs she had provided me. I had been correct; mocking was certainly the intent since the room was hardly grand. A simple bed, a bureau, nothing more.

Yet it was mine. I had paid for it. Granted, it was not as if I had earned the money, but 'twas mine nevertheless.

I sat on the edge of the bed, devouring the mean repast. The bread was stale, the cheese had some mold I had to pluck from it, and the fruit was overripe. But it was the first meal I had ever had as a free adult, and that added immeasurably to the flavor.

Yet however much my belly might have been full, emotionally I felt strangely empty. This should have been the happiest day of my life, and yet I felt nothing but confusion, regrets, and a deep, abiding shame that I had let down the queen. Had I so thoroughly abrogated any interest in my own welfare?

I think I am a madwoman. It is the only explanation.

I pulled out my journal and inkwell and began to write. I kept on writing from that moment to this, and my hand aches and the sun is just beginning to creep over the horizon. It is the dawn of a new day.

A new day for a new woman.

My First and Second Day

I SLEPT THROUGH MY FIRST day of freedom.

I awoke briefly once or twice, albeit barely. The tavern owner thumped impatiently upon the door to my room, telling me it was time to be getting my things together and depart, or else pay for additional time. My eyes barely open, I rummaged in my coin purse, which I was keeping tightly against my body, wanting to take no chance of thievery. I withdrew a couple of coins, tossed them to her without looking and inquired sleepily if they were enough to purchase another night and some food besides. She muttered something that sounded like acquiescence and departed. I fell back to sleep and when I drifted awake again—this time on my own—I saw a plate of food and a wineskin had been left on the floor in front of me. The beef was gristly, the wine bordering on fermented, but it was enough to sate the beginnings of hunger. I fell back to sleep and dreamt of my father. I saw myself walking into his shop a free woman, and with anger he clapped slave bracelets upon me and sold me to the first slaver who walked in the door, shouting all the while, "How dare you defy my decision as to what's best for you!" I tried to cry out to him as I was hauled away, but no words emerged from my throat. I had become as mute as the stable hand.

It was then that I realized for the first time that I hated my father. Despised him. Loathed him for his betrayal. My pleasant memories were built on a total sham and complete denial of anger suddenly so suffocating that it was like bile on my tongue.

There, in the twilight place between sleep and waking, I heard noise and loud voices from downstairs and was unsure whether they were genuine or imagined. Then I realized that the voice was all too familiar, and all too French.

"The largest room must be made available for my liege. I do not care who is residing there at the moment. Inform the occupant he must be on his way."

I heard his feet pounding up the steps, with the innkeeper hustling up behind him calling out, "It is not a 'he,' sir knight, it is a woman—"

"All the more reason, then," he announced, and the door burst open to reveal the face and form of Sir Lancelot. The sleep falling from my eyes, I saw by the lengthening shadows that evening was crawling upon us.

Lancelot took one look at me and his eyes widened. He was dusty from the road, dressed in leathers rather than full armor, but he had a bastard sword dangling from his belt and apparently every willingness to employ it. "You!" he bellowed and yanked the sword from its sheathe at the same time.

He came at me, sword outthrust. I threw myself off the bed and, at the same time, shoved the mattress up at him. The sword went through the mattress, gutting it. The innkeeper let out a screech of protest as Lancelot made certain that was one mattress that would never harm another living soul. Good fortune, I think; my back was still sore from sleeping upon the lumpy thing.

I scrambled backward across the floor, trying to distance myself from him as he endeavored to extricate his sword from the mattress. I bumped up against the legs of the innkeeper, who was busy yelling at Lancelot to desist at once, and clambered to my feet. Lancelot turned to face me, still appearing incensed, and I slid past the angry innkeeper and onto the landing just outside my room.

Arthur was coming up the stairs. He stopped in his tracks when he saw me, looking no less surprised than Lancelot had been, but far less homicidal. I could scarce believe it when I saw him. He was thinner and haggard and world weary, and that was from a campaign that had been, relatively speaking, fairly short. Some kings spent months, years on such endeavors. Arthur looked as if he had had more than his fill after a relatively brief expedition.

"Viviana!" he said. "You here? And the queen as well?"

"Actually," I began to say, but then realized that Lancelot was coming up behind me. I quickly dashed down the stairs and shamelessly took refuge beyond Arthur. Lancelot appeared on the landing, still brandishing his sword in a threatening manner.

"Lancelot, are you insane?" said Arthur. "What do you think you are doing?"

Seeking to excuse his behavior, Lancelot displayed remarkable observational skills and quickly crafted an excuse. "I am endeavoring to apprehend an escaped slave," he said. "See? She has divested herself of her bonds to hide her status."

"The queen freed me," I said.

"Did she?" Arthur appeared surprised, but not overly so.

"She lies!" said Lancelot.

"And on what do you base that conclusion?" Arthur said.

Lancelot paused and then said, "She is a woman."

It was at that point I began to suspect that Lancelot had definite problems, not merely with me, but with my entire gender.

"That shall not be held against her. Leave us, please."

"But—"

As weary as he might have appeared, Arthur fired a glare at Lancelot that spoke volumes. Lancelot promptly backed down, bowing deeply, and stepped aside on the landing as he sheathed his sword. He swept his arm in a mocking gesture of civility. Not rising to the bait, I walked past him and curtsied slightly as I did so. Arthur followed and closed the door behind us.

He turned to face me. There was nowhere to sit in the room since Lancelot had gutted the bed. That did not appear to bother Arthur. He smiled that same, slightly vacuous smile I had come to know, and I did not realize until that moment how much I had missed it. "So . . . the queen has freed you. You must have done her a great service to prompt such generosity."

"I believe she simply felt it was time, majesty."

"I see." He sounded guarded, as if he did not truly see but

had no wish to admit it.

Hoping to turn the topic away from myself, I said, "I am puzzled you would be stopping here, majesty. You are not all that far from Camelot. On horseback, you could be there before midnight."

"True," said Arthur. "But that is hardly the return that I desired, arriving stealthily in the middle of the night. A messenger has been dispatched to Camelot to inform them of my imminent arrival. It is my hope that a proper reception will be prepared for when we get to the city gates tomorrow."

"Who precisely is 'we,' majesty? Are all your knights with you?"

"No, no. Lancelot. Bors. Palamedes. A handful of retainers and pages. The others will be following over the next week. We could have all found a common place to reconvene, I suppose, and arrive together. But frankly I was anxious to get home."

"And . . . was the mission a success, sire?"

"Yes, absolutely. We accomplished what we set out to do, which was to break the strangleholds that a number of independent tribal chieftains were placing upon various villages and territories."

"Is . . . that what we set out to do?" I said. "I thought we were specifically searching for Maleagant and the warriors of Maleagant's desires. Was that not the measure of the mission's accomplishment?"

"Things change once a mission has begun. New objectives have to be created."

"Why?"

"So they can be met," he said, making it all sound quite reasonable and me foolish for questioning it. "That is how Merlin explained it, in any event."

"Oh. Well . . . thank you for clarifying that, sire."

"I am pleased I could accommodate you, Viviana." He smiled wistfully. "Truth to tell, I cannot wait to sleep in my own bed or, even better, climb the stairs to my high tower and just look out in peace upon the realm. How some kings fight campaigns that stretch on for years, I cannot begin to fathom." He walked around the small room, his hands draped behind his back. "How fares the queen? Did she speak of me often? When did you see her last?"

"A day or so ago, and yes, very often."

"Good. Good," he said with a smile. "She is a remarkable woman, you know."

"Yes, majesty."

"She makes me want to be a better man and a better king." He looked at me with interest. "Would it be asking you to divulge a confidence if I inquired of you how she felt about having children? She never seems willing to discuss it with me."

"It is a matter to which she has given great thought."

"The odd thing is, I think I would like to have a child with her even if I were not king and having an heir were not a factor. I think I would just like to have a living embodiment of our love."

I smiled at that and said, "I believe if you put it just that way, she would find the notion appealing, majesty."

"Good," he nodded at that. "Good."

"Majesty," I said abruptly, "I think you should know . . . I believe I would be derelict if I did not tell you . . ."

"Tell me what?"

"The people have been . . . less than enthused about you . . . than has the queen. Were you aware of this?"

I have never seen someone look more surprised than did Arthur. Clearly he was unaware of the negative sentiment arrayed toward him. His advisors had likely isolated him from harsh truths. "No," he said, his voice barely above a whisper. "Are you certain?"

"Quite certain."

"You know this from first hand experience?"

"I was attacked by an angry mob because of it, majesty. I do not think my experience could be more first hand than that."

He seemed to grow taller at that moment, although I was likely imagining it. He squared his shoulders, his spine straightened somewhat, and then he said in a tone that would brook no defiance, "Tell me everything. Everything. Leave nothing out. As your king . . . dare I say it, as your friend . . . I charge you to be completely candid with me."

I was.

As if making confession, I told him everything: About my relationship with the mute, about my writings of Galahad, about the real reason that the queen had exiled me. All of it came spilling out in one great cleansing of my soul.

Arthur listened with astounding patience to every word. It was so much for him to hear and process at one time, and yet he did so calmly, barely reacting to any of it. Finally I sagged against the frame of the bed, exhausted, and looked up at him not knowing what to think or even what to say.

He did not respond immediately. Instead he paced the small room, hands draped behind his back, pondering all of it. Finally he turned and said, "Galahad, eh?"

"Yes, majesty."

He nodded as if that had answered a plethora of questions and continued to pace. Then he stopped, turned to me again and said, "If what you say is all true—and I have no reason to think otherwise—then I very much suspect my messenger will not return alone."

"That is entirely possible, majesty."

"Very well. We shall go downstairs and wait for him."

"And when he shows up and says what you obviously think you know he will say . . . what then, highness?"

"I am not certain of that. I am, however, certain of this: you will return to Camelot with us."

"No, sire," and I shook my head.

"You dare say no to a king?" He seemed more amused than put out.

"Under ordinary circumstances, of course not. But these are not they. The queen has made it abundantly clear that I am not to return."

"In the world of Viviana, does a queen outrank a king?"

"Not at all. Your word is the living law. But—"

"There is a 'but' attached to such a sentiment? How is that even possible?"

"Because for your sake, it is better to have the queen with

you than against you."

He seemed prepared with a ready response to that, but then did not reply quite so readily. "That . . . is true," he admitted. "Still, I want you to accompany me."

"If I may ask, majesty, why?"

"Because," he said, "I wish to learn to read."

I admit I was taken aback by that.

When he saw I did not reply, he went on. "Reports came to me from various fronts, and I was unable to read them. Others had to read them to me. I found that frustrating and humiliating. When I was in Camelot, accustomed to having others attend to my needs, reading seemed of little consequence. Out waging a campaign, on the other hand, it would seem that reading would greatly facilitate matters."

"Certainly there are others who can tutor you in that pursuit, majesty."

"I do not want others. I want you to attend to it." Then he seemed to step back mentally and gave a sad smile. "However, Viviana, you are a free woman now. And I do not think it meet that the very first thing you should experience as part of your liberty is having your free will taken from you. I have made clear my desires in this matter, but I leave the decision to you."

"I . . . need time to think upon it, majesty."

"Do you?" Arthur leaned his back against the wall and shrugged. "It has been my experience that thinking excessively can lead to second-guessing and over-caution. I prefer to think with my heart and my gut."

I suppose I should have complimented him on that, since

it had been my experience that most men tended to allow body parts situated somewhat lower in their anatomy to perform the majority of their thinking. Still, ultimately he was my king, and I decided to let myself be guided by his suggestions. I reached deep into my heart, into my gut, sought guidance therein, and let the first words that those noble organs generated spring uncensored from my mouth.

I was somewhat surprised to hear them as: "Very well, sire. I am with you, and serve at your pleasure."

"Good!" he said, clapping his hands together briskly even as I processed my own astonishment at my reaction.

"Still, majesty," I had to point out, "my willingness to accompany you does not resolve the problem of your wife's banning me from Camelot. I simply do not see any solution to the fact that the queen will react very, very badly to my presence, and neither of us, methinks, will enjoy being the recipient of her ire."

Arthur pondered the situation for a time and then said, matter-of-factly, "There will be no ire if she does not know you are there."

"Majesty, I have many valuable talents, but invisibility is not one of them."

"You do not need to be invisible. Merely disguised."

"Disguised? How so?"

He made his answer plain to me.

So it was that, within the hour, I was staring at the shorn chunks of my hair scattered about the floor. Naught was left upon my head but a short, boyish cut. My neck felt chilled and I had never felt more naked and exposed even when I had actually been naked and exposed.

Men's clothing, cobbled together from bits and pieces gathered from the squires, lay on the floor in front of me. It would hang loosely on me, which would certainly facilitate disguising my gender.

Still, I had to wonder how in the world I had gotten myself into this predicament. Now, with the passage of time, however brief, I was able to look back upon my from-the-heart, from-the-gut decision and determine why I had agreed to return to Camelot.

Freedom or no freedom, I hated the circumstances under which I had departed. I felt as if a cloud was still hanging over me. I felt loyalty to Guinevere, even if she felt only anger toward me. And Arthur was well-meaning and limited in vision, but desperately wanted to be liked by all, a goal that I had to think was an unreasonable one for a king. He seemed a man adrift at sea, and perhaps I could provide some degree of navigation. It might have been presumptuous to think so, but there it was just the same.

And I missed the mute.

There. Even as I write the words now, I shudder to think the truth of them. He awakened something within me, something ferocious, something hungry for more of the same. And the thought of never seeing him again, the man who was becoming the incarnation of Galahad, pained me beyond all reason.

After spending years thinking of naught but my own needs, my head was filled with nothing save thoughts of others. Is this what freedom is like? It is almost terrifying, this liberation of the mind as well as the body.

So it was that, with all those thoughts colliding within me, and the resulting noise drowning out the faint shouts of warning that my common sense was issuing, I stripped off my dress and pulled on the men's clothing. Having never worn breeches, I tripped and fell backwards trying to pull them on. It was one of the less dignified moments of my life. I wished now that I had paid more attention to how Guinevere went about it. Once I managed to deal with those, however, the rest was easily attended to.

I shook out my hair and ran my fingers through it repeatedly, making it look as disheveled as possible. My voice is normally low, so I was reasonably certain I could affect a tone that sounded at least vaguely male, but I resolved to try and be silent as much as possible.

I started to head for the door, and then caught myself. I realized my hips were swinging in the standard gait of a female. I practiced walking with what I thought was a fair imitation of a male swagger, squaring my hips and moving as if I had some sort of obstruction between my legs. It felt unnatural and ludicrous. Within seconds I was disoriented. I caught myself, took a few deep breaths, backed up, closed my eyes, and tried to remember how Guinevere moved. I figured I would have far greater luck approximating her mannish stride than that of an actual male. That gave me a closer feel for it, and in addition, I pretended that I was walking with five-pound weights strapped to each of my feet. This, I discovered, gave me the bearing I sought.

Then I heard hoof beats nearing the tavern. I looked out the window and saw two figures riding up. As they dismounted, I realized it was Merlin and the man who would be Galahad.

I scarcely recognized Galahad. Granted, it was night, but the full moon was providing adequate illumination. Eowyn had done a formidable job with his transformation. His hair was not only cut shorter and elegantly coiffed, but the color had been changed. His hair had been pale brown; now it was dark black. Even his eyebrows had been shaded to match his newly darkened hair.

Eowyn had certainly been resourceful. I wondered how she had done it, and remembered reading in one of the histories that the Romans had performed such changes in the coloring of tresses, utilizing a mixture of slaked lime and something called lead oxide. Obviously that which had worked centuries ago was still effective.

Merlin entered, Galahad directly behind him. I wanted to go down to them, to see them, to see him. Instead I remained where I was at first, frozen with indecision. Then, mustering my nerve, I emerged from the room and out onto the landing.

I crept down the stairs and heard their voices softly from the common area. Then the door to the tavern opened and closed again. When I got down there, Arthur, Merlin, and Galahad had departed. That did not surprise me. Merlin had to speak to Arthur of most unusual topics, and it was probably preferable to do so outside, away from prying eyes and eavesdropping ears.

Sir Palamedes and Sir Bors were at a corner table, deep in conversation. A couple of squires were attending to them, having taken over from the serving wench the responsibility of keeping their steins filled. The innkeeper kept a wary eye on the proceedings. Perhaps she had had earlier, unpleasant experiences with knights in the past and was anticipating possible problems.

Lancelot was nowhere to be seen. I felt a swell of relief over that. It was entirely likely that Lancelot, who had—as much as it appalled me—become Arthur's right arm had been included into the plan that Merlin was doubtlessly in the midst of explaining.

The knights and squires barely afforded me a glance, which was exactly what I was hoping for.

I took up a chair at the far end of the room and watched the men interacting in a different way than I had before. I was taking mental notes to see what of their actions I could apply to myself. I had no idea how long I was going to be adopting this guise, but for the time being, I was going to do as effective a job as possible.

A serving wench came by and asked if I wanted something to drink or eat. I dropped my voice to a growl and ordered some food. She did not so much as blink. There was nothing about me that appeared odd to her. Or if there was, she certainly did not let on. Minutes later she brought me food that was no more appetizing than anything else I had been served until now. One had to admire the consistency of the cuisine.

It was some time later that Arthur returned, accompanied by Lancelot, Merlin, and the man calling himself Galahad. Having an opportunity to inspect him more closely, I was further impressed by the quality of Eowyn's transformational powers upon him. As much as people claimed Merlin to be a wizard, I have to say that Eowyn had as much claim to magic as he.

"Good sirs," Arthur said, instantly capturing the attention of all within, "this fine young man is noble Sir Galahad," and he clapped a hand on the mute's shoulder.

"So this is Galahad," said Bors, rising from his chair. "The minstrels have sung songs of you on the road home, and it puzzled the hell out of me, for I had ne'er laid eyes upon you."

Merlin spoke up. "Galahad came to us highly recommended. He was responsible for carrying out assorted missions that required stealth that only a lone knight could have provided."

"Is that a fact?" said Palamedes, also rising. He appeared suspicious. "I have heard much the same tales as Bors. Hard to credit them as being rooted in reality."

"Yet here he is," said Lancelot. "I have long been watching Galahad's training and career. My heart is gladdened that he was able to serve our lord Arthur in our latest foray."

"And is he as formidable as they say?" said Bors, and before Lancelot or Arthur could respond, Bors was yanking out his sword.

And then Galahad was standing right in front of him, his own sword already drawn and out so quickly that it appeared a blur to me, and I was watching him the entire time. His face impassive, he had the cutting edge to the throat of Bors while Bors's sword was only half out of its scabbard. The pages and serving wench gasped, and Palamedes merely raised a single eyebrow, but it was clear that he was impressed.

Galahad's expression never wavered. His eyes were cold, empty. He looked prepared to cut Bors's throat or not; either way made no difference to him.

Bors did nothing for a long moment and then his fingers uncurled from his hilt. The sword slid back into its scabbard without ever having been fully drawn. "It would appear he is," said Bors. "An honor to meet you, Sir Galahad."

Galahad nodded and stepped back, sheathing his own blade. Palamedes introduced himself and the other pages as well. Galahad nodded to each of them but, naturally, said nothing. Palamedes—generally a more observant individual than the headstrong Bors—took note of the lapse. "Not particularly talkative, is he," said Palamedes.

"He has taken a vow of silence," Merlin said, obviously ready for such a comment. "He draws his strength from foreswearing conversation."

"I see," said Palamedes, still sounding a mite suspicious, but not so much so that he considered it worth pursuing.

Then Arthur turned and spotted me seated across the way. "You, boy!" he said in a preemptive manner. "Would you like to serve as page to a noble knight?"

I rose and looked nervously at Galahad. I nodded, not yet trusting my oral skills to fool those who knew me. Lancelot glanced at me, indifferent, as did Merlin, and Galahad seemed to gaze right through me. It was a look that I had known all too well as a slave.

"Excellent," said Arthur. "Gentlemen, the evening hours

stretch late. I suggest we get some sleep since we will be departing early tomorrow for Camelot where, I understand," and he glanced toward Merlin, "a stirring reception awaits us."

"Very much so," said Merlin.

The innkeeper was looking around at the gathering with annoyance. "With all deference, highness, I have not enough rooms to accommodate all of you."

Galahad pointed outdoors and Merlin immediately said, "Sir Galahad prefers to sleep under the stars, and I will be riding back to Camelot to assure that all is prepared for the return of the king. Will that allay your problems, woman?" The innkeeper nodded, although she seemed vaguely disappointed, as if she were more interested in quarreling over the matter.

Galahad gestured to me to follow him in a manner so preemptive I would have thought he had been born to it. I gathered up my belongings and followed him out.

We walked a distance into the woods and then Galahad found a clearing. The entire situation was bathed in unreality, my traipsing about in the woods with the incarnation of a knight drawn from my imagination. It was as if I had entered one of my own stories and become a character within.

Then Galahad turned to face me and before I could say a word, he grabbed me by the arms, drew me to him, and kissed me passionately. I gasped against his mouth, startled, but then practically melted into him. When our lips parted, I looked into his eyes that were glittering in the moonlight. "Either you have a fondness for young boys that does not befit you, or I did not fool you for a moment," I said.

He laughed silently. Then he touched my boyish hair and shook his head ruefully.

"I—" It was difficult for me to speak to him. "I thought you were furious with me for betraying you. I thought you would never wish to look upon me again."

He touched my cheek and smiled with what seemed infinite love and patience. It was as if he was becoming the man I had created before my very eyes. Either he had never been quite as angry as I originally thought, or else he had found it within his heart to forgive me. Or perhaps the prospect of never seeing me again had focused his feelings for me in much the same way that they had for me when I thought I would never again gaze upon him.

We pulled away each other's clothes, and he took me there in the woods, and I gave myself over to him.

He fell asleep against me, a blanket pulled from his saddlebag covering the both of us. I extracted my journal from my bag and inscribed the day's events. It is a fortunate thing that I am returning to Camelot, if for no other reason than that I am down to my last bottle of ink.

My Third Day

MADNESS. MADNESS AND TURMOIL AND death, all in a day that began as gloriously as this one did. I can scarcely credit it.

My return to Camelot could not have been more different from the first time I entered it. It was like a carnival as the citizenry assembled to welcome back its king.

I had been concerned about boos and catcalls and other hostile attitudes toward Arthur, but none seemed to be forthcoming. As Arthur led the small procession of knights, squires and pages—including myself—there were, however, repeated shouts, not for Arthur, or even Lancelot, but Galahad. Over and over was the chant of, "Galahad! Galahad!"

It was astounding to me, what I was witnessing. The public sentiment against Arthur had grown exponentially. But as word had spread of Galahad and his noble deeds, matters seemed to have turned around. It was difficult to comprehend that one person could have such an impact on the public.

It may well be that it was more than just one person. It may be what Galahad represented to the people: someone who cared about them, who performed great deeds on behalf of the common folk. It was not merely the existence of Galahad so much as the thinking behind him. People desperately wanted to believe in . . . well, to believe in something that was greater than they themselves. They wanted to believe in God, or the son of God, or the miracles that such deities performed, and perhaps most of all, they wanted to believe in God's spiritual heirs on earth. It was not that they were merely embracing Galahad; they were embracing the concept of Galahad. This was monumentally ironic, of course, since less than a week ago, Galahad had been nothing more than a concept. Yet now here he was, brought to flesh, fired by the collective imagination of the public. A mass delusion beaming at them from atop a magnificent white stallion, welcoming their adoration, giving them hope for a brighter future.

Galahad played his part beautifully. He sat astride his stallion, waving to the crowds, smiling, bowing his head in acknowledgment of their cheers. I walked alongside, as befit a page. Every so often, however, Galahad would steal a glance down at me and I would smile in return. I hope we did not look too much like lovers; it might have started rumors that would not have benefited anyone.

A podium had been erected in the midst of the town square. Guinevere was standing upon it, positively beaming. Morgan was to her right. They were both watching the progress of Arthur and the others, but they seemed particularly focused on Galahad. Neither of them appeared to notice me, which suited me quite well.

The cheers of the crowds thundered in our ears as Arthur

rode up to the podium, dismounted, and strode up the stairs to the platform. Guinevere extended her hand to him and he kissed her suavely upon the knuckles, which was about as much affection as would be appropriate for a king and queen to display in public.

Arthur then gestured for Galahad to take the podium with him. I noticed Lancelot glowering at him, but the Frenchman said nothing. Admittedly, that showed some element of restraint on Lancelot's part. Du Lac had not asked what had become of me since accosting me in my room at the inn. I have to think he believed that I fled the area. Certainly he had barely glanced at me since I had assumed my alternate identity, which was a blessing. Having Lancelot du Lac not looking at me was far preferable to the alternative.

Desiring to continue avoiding notice, I quietly distanced myself from Galahad as he rode forward toward the podium. Technically I should have gone with him and taken his horse from him, but I desired to take no chance of the queen somehow recognizing me and possibly raising a fuss.

A squire stepped forward and took the reins of Galahad's horse as he dismounted. He strode up onto the podium, offering a restrained wave to the crowd. There were even louder cheers, and people crying out his name. Arthur allowed it to continue for a time and then gestured for the crowd to rein itself in. The people did so reluctantly. Arthur began to speak to them.

He told them that he knew that the campaign had been a difficult one for all concerned. He spoke of getting justice in the name of the late queen, his mother. He said he knew that the taxes had been difficult upon the people, which garnered some grumbling from the onlookers. He went on to say that there had been claims of wrongdoings by various of his knights, which drew even more grumbling.

"Be aware," he said sternly, "that rumors can be spread by enemies very quickly as a means of destroying the spirits of the people. Is it possible that there were abuses? Yes. And I swear to you, as your king, that I shall investigate all such accusations and administer proper justice if they are found to be true. But do not discount the possibility that the enemies of this kingdom have spread calumnies precisely for the purpose of creating dissent amongst you."

I saw people nodding, looking at each other. Then I noticed that Arthur was glancing in the direction of Merlin, who was standing on the periphery of the assemblage. Merlin nodded once and Arthur beamed like a good student. I realized that it had been Merlin who had told him what to say. Merlin the puppeteer, pulling the strings that Arthur could feel and I could see.

I have to wonder how much of the public Arthur is truly him and how much is Merlin whispering in his ear, governing his words and deeds.

Arthur continued to press his advantage with the crowd, telling of Galahad's bravery and great deeds. The king was doing a superb job of carrying off the lie. Monumental, in fact. Varied emotions warred within me. Now that I was faced with the actuality of this fakery, I was appalled to have been a part of it. On the other hand, one had to admire the superb

efficiency with which it had been organized and was now being
perpetrated. And in the long run, all would benefit.

That was when I heard three words that threatened to bring
the entire affair crashing down.

"He's a mute!"

It was the stable master. He was standing not five feet away
from me, and even though he was a distance from Galahad, and
even though Galahad's appearance had changed dramatically,
he was not fooled for an instant.

The people on the podium were looking around, unable
to see whence the voice was originating. The stable master
continued to shout, "He's no knight, no man of nobility. He's
a lowborn runaway mute stable hand! It's a lie! 'Tis all a lie!"

The crowd seemed to be turning in an instant. I heard
cries of "A stable hand?" What trick is this?" "They believe
we're stupid!" "Don't trust the king!" Even Merlin appeared
disconcerted, which was never a good sign. Arthur seemed
flummoxed and it was Guinevere who stepped forward, raising
her hands in an effort to calm the people. "That is patent
nonsense. Galahad is of noble blood . . ."

"Have him speak!" It was not the stable master now, but
someone else in the crowd, a woman, her interest obviously
piqued. "If he's not the mute, have him speak! The mute can't
say a bloody word! Show us he's not!"

Others took up the cry now of "Speak! Speak!"

Trying to seize control of the situation, Arthur shouted
above the assemblage, "Naturally Sir Galahad can speak, but
he has taken an oath of silence to show his devotion to—"

He did not even get the entire sentence out. Instead he was greeted with hoots and moans of disbelief, and now the crowd was rapidly transforming into that which had threatened me many days ago: an angry mob. Arthur and Guinevere were clearly taken aback by the fury and vehemence of the people's ugly disposition. It was one thing to know in the abstract of people's hostility and quite another to experience it first hand.

And I was utterly responsible. I had set this mad chain of events into motion, and now I was standing there helpless. Matters could get even worse, I realized, because the crowd's mood was deteriorating with every passing second, and it was not as if Arthur was heavily guarded. Yes, granted, Lancelot and Galahad and the others were formidable fighters, but they were wildly outnumbered. If matters became bad enough—and I suspected they very much could—there was no telling what sort of horrific calamities I might be about to witness.

That was when Galahad stepped forward. He faced the crowd, looking down upon them with a gaze of such icy steel that one would have thought it was Uther Pendragon back from the dead. He said nothing, did nothing save stand there, and yet his very presence caused the crowd's voiced anger to drop in volume.

Then he opened his mouth.

The crowd instantly fell silent.

And he began to sing.

I could not believe it. No one could.

It was instantly recognizable: the Salve Regina. He was singing it in Latin, and at first he seemed hesitant, tentative.

But with each passing line his voice, pure and clean, grew in intensity and conviction.

> *Hail, holy Queen, Mother of Mercy,*
> *our life, our sweetness and our hope.*
> *To thee do we cry, poor banished children of Eve;*
> *to thee do we send up our sighs,*
> *mourning and weeping in this vale of tears.*

He continued into the second verse, all hesitancy long gone. If God on high had been speaking words of love to His son and the blessed virgin who bore him, that was what His voice would have sounded like.

My face was wet with tears, and I had not even realized I was crying. Nor was I the only one. The people around me were weeping, the men softly, the women unashamedly. Arthur drew his arm across his face, Guinevere sobbed openly, even Merlin appeared moved beyond anything I had ever seen. Everyone was affected . . .

. . . save for Morgan.

She merely stared at Galahad with what seemed distant curiosity. Then, noticing the reactions that others were experiencing, Morgan promptly began to wail.

> *Turn then, most gracious advocate,*
> *your eyes of mercy toward us.*
> *And after this our exile, show us*
> *the blessed fruit of thy womb, Jesus.*
> *O clement, O loving, O sweet Virgin Mary.*

There had been clouds in the sky, but now a section of them parted and rays of sunlight filtered down from above and shone upon him. God Himself had heard and was looking down, and I had to think that He found it to be good.

He reached the last several words of the hymn, the virgin's name, and by the time he did so his voice had dropped to a soft, reverential whisper that nevertheless carried across the town center, so quiet was the gathering. Then he lapsed into silence, and the only thing to be heard was the snuffling and sobbing of the people of Camelot.

Then someone began to clap, and another, and it broke the spell of silence and the square was filled with thunderous applause and cries of "Galahad!" and "God himself sent him to Arthur!" and "All hail Arthur!" and "Long live the king!"

All that adoration, all that love, because of one man who had touched their souls. Then again, I suppose it was not unprecedented, to have one man affect so many people merely with the power of his voice and his purity.

I looked to the stable master to see what his reaction was. To my astonishment he was not there. I tried to spot him and, seconds later, did.

He was not alone.

Rowena was with him. She was dragging him by the arm, and she looked nigh unto furious. The stable master was trying to sputter something at her but she wasn't hearing any of it.

In her case, that was by choice. In my case, I was consumed with curiosity.

Arthur, Guinevere, Galahad and the others were in the midst of their leave taking, basking in the crowd's adoration. My mind was still reeling, trying to grasp the concept of what I had just heard. He uttered not a spoken word, but he was capable of singing in a voice that was nothing less than a channel from the Almighty? It was unfathomable. I reasoned then that, that being the case, it was probably wisest for me not even to try to fathom it and instead concentrate on what was before me.

Rowena and the stable master entered the castle and I was right behind them. No one glanced my way. Why would they? I was a random page.

I watched as they headed off down a corridor that I knew, all too well, led to the kitchen. Ironic, indeed, that I had wound up there during my initial foray to Camelot, and now it was the first place that I was heading upon my return. But I could not simply follow the two of them down there. It was one thing not to attract much notice while in the corridors of the castle, but I could hardly stand there unobserved in the kitchen.

Fortunately I had other options.

I moved further down the hallway, past the juncture that led to the kitchen. I sought a telltale sign on the walls and, before too long, found one, conveniently situated behind a standing suit of armor. I pushed in on the off-sized brick and the wall slid aside. Stepping through, I closed it behind me and made my way through the walls. Whereas once I would have been unable to determine where I was heading, now I was able to make my way with confidence. At one point I did indeed lose my bearings, but I peered through a viewing hole to orient myself and then continued on my way.

Within minutes I heard the familiar voices of Rowena and the stable master. He sounded the angrier, which surprised me, for I thought that no one could be quite as angry as Rowena. I found a hole to view through the wall and could clearly see the stable master stomping back and forth in a white-hot fury. Rowena, the picture of calm, was preparing tea. None of the other kitchen servants were around. Doubtless they were still milling about in the crowd, trying to recover from the splendor that was Galahad.

"It's him! I know it is! I don't care what manner of dulcet tones emerged from his misbegotten mouth!" the stable master said. "And I am never going to stop telling people until I get someone to listen to me! And I'll manage it, you can wager your soul on that! You best believe it, Rowena—"

"I do believe it, Bernard. Softly. I do believe it," said Rowena, which surprised me since Rowena was not typically the voice of reason. Plus I realized that I had not known the stable master's name until that moment. "I share your sense of outrage, but your actions were precipitous. Here." She finished pouring in the honey that was her trademark and handed it to him.

He drank the tea, gulped it down rather than sipped it, as he continued to speak. "What is everyone's obsession with that damned mute? Bad enough that ye fancied him all these years. But now the king?"

My stomach near to sank into my legs. Rowena? Fancied the mute? The notion was repulsive. Surely the feelings were unrequited. The alternative was too horrific to consider.

"Bernard, don't be that way."

"What way do ye expect me to be?" said Bernard. He finished the tea and threw aside the glass angrily. "All these years, you know how I feel about ye. How I've craved you. And all you do is come down to the stables and spend time speaking soft, gentle words to that damned mute while keeping me at arm's length. I don't understand it. Not a bit of it."

Neither did I. When I had assumed that Rowena was having an affair with Bernard, I had been completely wrong. She had been courting the mute? The mute? It made no sense at all. Why, she was old enough to be his—

And that was when I realized.

I suppose I should take some degree of pride that it required only seconds for me to grasp what Bernard, in all those years, had never been able to. This was confirmed by Rowena's next words as she said, not unkindly, "Bernard, you never were the brightest of creatures, were you. He's my son, Bernard. The mute is my son."

"Your . . . your son?" he sputtered. "When the priest brought him to me as a lad, left him to be apprenticed to me as stable master, he . . . he said the parents were unknown . . . and you're a Moor! His skin is . . ."

"It is more reflective of his father's tone. As for the priest, I believe you will recall what he actually said was that he could not say. He could not, bound as he was by confession. The confession of a terrified young serving girl," and her voice grew hard, "impregnated her first day in Camelot by a vile king. Not that he remembered, of course. I was just another face, another body, another lowly creature to satisfy his drunken lusts before he tossed me aside. I hid my swelling belly under loose robes. My baby cooperated by being so small that he remained unnoticed until I fled to the church and gave birth to a prince. A prince, Bernard."

"A royal bastard," said Bernard dismissively. "God only knows how many of those are wandering around."

"I cared only about this one," she said. "I watched him from a distance, monitored his care as he was raised as an orphan. Always had an affinity for animals, he did. And when it was time for him to learn a trade, the priest brought him here, and I continued to watch him, befriend him. He never knew. Why should he? Why tell him his brutal origins, particularly when he was young and unable to understand?"

"Or speak. Why did he not speak?"

She shrugged. "I know not. God moves in mysterious ways."

"God can kiss my ass, Rowena," said Bernard angrily. "And so can you. Damnation, but you should have told me!"

"To what point and purpose?"

"So I would have known! Known of your past with Uther—!"

"Why would I want you to know that?" said Rowena as if it were the most reasonable thing in the world. "Why would I want anyone to know? So connections might be made? Conclusions drawn?"

That was when I realized where this was going. I gasped and Rowena, ears like a bat, heard it. Her head snapped around, her eyes lethal as a Medusa's, and clearly she thought her hearing must have played tricks upon her because she scanned the area but saw nothing. I had clapped my hand over my mouth and dared not breathe. Even my heart, pounding in my chest, sounded deafening to me.

"What conclusions?" said Bernard, who still had not grasped the enormity of what was being told him. He rubbed his eyes and his voice sounded muzzy.

"Uther was poisoned, Bernard," she said reasonably and with a grim smile. "Who else better to do it than she who makes his food? Who prepares everything just so?"

"Don't be ridiculous, you mad woman! Uther had a taster who checked for poison!"

"Yes, he did. Which was why it was necessary to feed it to him a small bit at a time, letting it build up in his system over months. The honey was particularly useful in that regard. You can make poison from honey, did you know that? Over the short term, it is not fatal, although it can make you quite ill. Over the long term, however, administered correctly, it will destroy the heart. The food taster, sampling only small parts, will never suffer any ill-effects. The king, the great glutton, devouring far more . . ." And she smiled.

The insane thing was, I did know about honey poisoning. I had read it in the writings of Pliney the Elder, in the *Naturalis Historia*. The tactic had been used against the armies of Xenophon and Pompey. But I had not made the association with the tea and honey that Rowena had prepared. And I realized that the symptoms I had been experiencing—nausea, dizziness, the headaches—were all as Pliney had described them. Uther had not been the only target of Rowena's schemes; she had been using the same tactic upon me. Had I not stopped eating, and had I remained at the castle, I might well have wound up dead.

Rowena was circling the kitchen, talking as much to herself as to Bernard. "It took me many years to reach a point of trust where I could be responsible for Uther's food preparation. But time favored me, as my son grew older, approaching an age where he could be positioned for greatness . . ."

"You're insane, woman!" said Bernard.

"Am I? I knew that destiny would favor my son if I helped tilt the odds toward him, and look what happened! Just look! Fate has conspired to elevate him to greatness, as I knew it would! Now it is merely a matter of disposing of Arthur and his bitch queen . . ."

Bernard shook his head so furiously that he nearly toppled over. "I'll not listen to any more of this . . . this blathering! This nonsense! Why, if any of this were true—"

"What if it were?"

"You would never tell me! Just blurt all this out!"

"Have you any idea how difficult it has been for me to keep this all to myself?" said Rowena. "I destroyed the brute who defiled me. Do you believe I didn't wish to shout it from the rooftops unto the heavens?"

"And you think to make me an ally in your delusions?"

"No," she said. "No, I do not think that. But I am certain you will tell no one all that I have told you."

"You believe you can stop me?" He snorted derisively.

"Actually, I believe I already have."

He stared at her in confusion and suddenly his eyes widened. He gagged, and white spittle spewed from between his lips as he clutched at his chest. Rowena watched impassively and said, "Poison drawn from the rhododendron can be used in far greater portions, of course. It is not subtle. And it does not provide for the prolonged deterioration of the victim, which, I have to admit, I enjoy watching. But it is nonetheless effective."

Bernard staggered to his feet, tried to get to Rowena, reached out. She never moved an inch. Then Bernard's legs gave out and he fell heavily to the floor. He made strangled, gurgling noises, spasmed, and then lay still.

She stood over him, surveying her handiwork.

I was paralyzed with fear over what I had just witnessed. And suddenly I realized there was someone at my right shoulder.

I turned and there was Modred, close in next to me, and a look of unspeakable fury upon his face. He brought his lips right up to my ear and whispered so softly that not even Rowena could have overheard.

"You left me. I did not say you could leave. As much as I love you, you must be punished for that."

Before I could fully process what he had just said, he tripped a release, and the wall swiveled open. I fell on my face right into the kitchen.

Rowena spun and her eyes widened in shock when she saw me. I scrambled to my feet, our gazes locked, and as much as my disguise might have fooled others, it did not deceive the murdering harridan for long. "You!" she shrieked.

There was a carving knife on the counter to her immediate left. She grabbed it and came straight at me.

I backpedaled and retreated into the wall. I grabbed at the door and she slashed forward with the knife. I yanked my hand away and the knife skidded against the brick. Had my hand still been there, it would have been minus fingers.

Modred, the little shite, had vanished back into the shadows that were his home. I did the only thing I could. I turned and ran.

She was right behind me, screaming profanities, as I sprinted up the steps, taking them two at a time. At one point I slipped and fell and she was right there, right behind me, and she lunged with her knife. I twisted my torso and she barely missed me. I brought my leg up, caught her in the stomach with my foot, and pushed as hard as I could. Rowena fell back and tumbled down the stairs into the darkness. I got to my feet and winced as pain shot through my left knee from my stumble. I felt around, trying to discern whether I was near an exit, and then I heard her footsteps as she came back up after me. I started running, or rather limping as quickly as I could.

I cannot even begin to imagine what people on the other side of the wall must have thought as they heard Rowena's banshee-like howling while she pursued me. At the very least, they must have thought that Castle Camelot was haunted.

I kept going, kept running, hoping to outdistance the shorter and older woman, but she was fired by her fury and her insanity, and she gave me no respite. Every second I expected the knife to lodge between my shoulder blades.

I glanced behind me to see if she had drawn closer and then I slammed into a wall. I staggered back, almost fell, and righted myself at the last instant. I shoved forward, found the release, and the wall swung open.

I stepped out onto the stairs, shutting the wall behind me, and started running upward. It was then that I realized where I was and, further, realized my mistake. I was in the high tower. There was no exit above; I had to head down the stairs.

I turned to retrace my steps and suddenly the wall swung open and Rowena was blocking my path to freedom.

"I should have killed you the instant I learned you were befouling my boy's precious body," she snarled and came at me, her knife drawn back. "But no, I had to be cautious! More fool I! Well, to hell with caution!"

I had no reply; I was too terrified of the insanity in the woman's eyes. I backed up and she advanced, brandishing the weapon. I tried to grab at it but she sliced with it expertly. I cried out, yanking my arm back, grabbing at the line of blood that was welling up on my forearm. My sleeve hung loosely, the cloth bisected.

The pain helped me find my voice. "You should be thanking me, you demented trollop! Were it not for me, your son would still be a stable hand. Now he is a knight, adored by the populace. I did that! I was responsible!"

"You lie. You will say anything to save your skin."

"I speak truly. Galahad was my creation and having your son impersonate him was my idea."

She hesitated.

"We have more in common than you are recognizing, Rowena," I said, speaking as quickly as I could. "We were both brutalized by Uther. I escaped; you did not. Who better than I to understand what you endured? We are more alike than different. And we both love your son . . ."

Her face softened. "You love him? Truly?"

I nodded. It was the truth, more so than I had been willing to admit, even to myself, much less to her.

Rowena considered that for a long moment, and then she screamed, "None can love him save me!" and, with her features twisted into an expression of demented ferocity, she came at me full speed with the blade.

The large window overlooking Camelot was to my left. I tried to twist away from her but the blade sank into my shoulder. I screamed, feeling it brush against the bone. Rowena yanked it clear, brought her arm back, ready to drive it fatally home. She expected me to retreat. Instead, desperately, I shoved against her. She tumbled back, clutching onto the front of my shirt, and together we fell out the window.

I twisted and grabbed at the sill with both hands, agony lancing through my shoulder where she had stabbed me. Rowena had both arms around my waist. We dangled there, my tenuous grip the only thing preventing us from plunging to our deaths, and I do not think she truly understood where she was. Instead she screeched, "We're nothing alike! You'd never have had the nerve to kill Uther! And I'll do the son like I did the father, but you first, you—!"

She brought the knife up and around, and I released my grip with one hand to try and bat her arm aside. But it was too much weight, and I lost my hold on the sill.

For a split second there was nothing stopping me from a fatal plunge, and the final thought that went through my head was that I had never learned what the mute's true name was, and was that not a great shame?

And then something gripped my wrist, halting my fall before it truly started.

The abrupt halt dislodged Rowena. She tried to grab at me once more, but the cloth of my tunic in her fingers tore away, and it was only then that she truly comprehended where she was and what was about to happen. But by then it was too late, for she was ten feet gone and falling fast. Insanely, she kept stabbing upward with her knife as if she could still plunge the blade into me. She tumbled end over end, shrieking the entire way, screams that I will carry with me unto my deathbed, although they paled compared to the muffled noise her body made when it hit the ground.

It was only then that I looked up.

King Arthur was leaning out the window. It was his hands around my arm that had halted my fall.

"She . . ." I began to sputter, pointing in the general direction of the fallen Rowena.

"I heard," he said grimly. "I heard her last words, may she rot in hell." He pulled me up as if I weighed nothing and seconds later I was in the tower next to him.

I sobbed with relief and threw my arms around him. He held me tightly as I shuddered from the nearness of my death. "Forgive me," I kept saying, "this is inappropriate, holding you, I am so sorry, majesty, I—"

"Think nothing of it," he said and patted me upon the back. Save for Galahad, I had never taken such pleasure in the nearness of any man, although naturally the circumstances were entirely different.

I lost all feeling in my legs and slowly sank to the stairs. Gently he lowered me and sat next to me. There was all manner of tumult from the courtyard below, but I paid it no mind. "Thank God you came up here . . ." I said.

"Well, I did tell you that I could not wait to come up to this place. Typically, though, I come here for contemplation. Trust you, Viviana, to make it far more exciting than I am accustomed to." There seemed the slightest trace of amusement in his eyes, but then it faded. He looked at the wound I had sustained and then removed his glove. He pressed the glove against the wound to stanch the flow. "This does not appear to be catastrophic," he said. "Lord knows I have had more experience of such things than I would have thought possible. One learns to adapt. Even Lancelot has developed a bit more nerve when it comes to dealing with the more sanguinary aspects of combat."

"That is . . . good to hear, sire. Or . . . sad to hear. I am not quite sure which."

"Truthfully, neither am I," he said. "And it was all a waste. All of it. Maleagant had nothing to do with it."

"No, majesty. It would seem not."

"I killed an innocent man."

There was nothing that I could say, and yet I found something. "I very much suspect that he was not innocent, majesty. Of your father's death, yes. But Maleagant was never going to be loyal to you. He was the type to plot and scheme, even if he purported to be an ally. In my opinion, he would have needed killing sooner or later."

Slowly he nodded. "You may well be right. Still . . . I think it best if knowledge of this does not become widespread."

"None shall hear it from me, majesty, I swear."

There were footsteps upon the stairs from just below us. We looked down and Guinevere approached, with Merlin right behind her. Guinevere was hiking up her skirt to maneuver her way up the stairs and when she saw the two of us, she gaped in bewilderment. "Arthur, how now? Who is this . . ." Then she stared more closely at me. "Is that . . . ?"

"Viviana," said Merlin. "Aye, 'tis her. She was at the tavern with Arthur when I rendezvoused with him."

"You recognized me?" I said in surprise.

"Of course I did. I am a wizard, you know." He said it with no trace of irony. I believed him. He turned to Arthur. "What the hell happened here? Did Rowena just fall out of here—?"

Arthur told them. Told them of what he had overheard. He then turned to me and I filled in all the details as I had witnessed them.

When I finished, they were silent for a time. Then Guinevere said, "We must tell no one else. Word of this does not go beyond we four."

"Excellent idea, my love," said Arthur, giving no indication that he had already said as much to me.

Guinevere returned her attention to me. "You returned." I nodded. "Despite my warning you what would happen if you did?" Again I nodded. "Why?"

"Because the king asked me to. And because I felt I could

do more good here than anyplace else in the world, highness."

"You have a very inflated sense of your own self-worth, Viviana."

"As you say, highness."

She looked at me with faint disapproval and then sighed as if greatly put upon. "Stay then. See if I care. But if you are to stay, in the name of God, dress properly. This boyish business simply will not do."

With those dismissive words, so drenched in irony considering who was speaking that I could scarce keep from laughing, she turned and headed back down the stairs.

"Highness," said Merlin, "if it is acceptable to you, it would please me if Mistress Viviana were fain to accompany me. Since she is apparently no longer a handmaiden to the queen, I have a task to which I think her talents could be well applied."

"If she so chooses," said Arthur.

I nodded.

"Will you accompany us down, Arthur?" Merlin said.

Arthur shook his head slowly. "I think . . . I shall remain here a time. I find it the best place to converse with God, since it puts me physically the closest to Him. And I think He and I . . . have a number of matters to discuss."

"As you wish, highness." Merlin bowed, as did I, and we left the king there.

I followed Merlin out of the tower. He led me without a word to a room I had not seen before. He opened the door and gestured for me to step in. I did so and looked around in surprise. It reminded me of Merlin's sanctum, but there were even more books and parchments and texts than there had been before.

At the far end was the biggest writing desk I had ever seen, with large quills and a copious ink bottle.

"What is this place?" I said.

"This," said Merlin, "is the chamber of the royal historian, Harold, son of Horace. Decent enough fellow, although annoyingly hard of hearing. If you wish, it will be your chamber."

"I do not understand."

"We are in need of a royal historian. Considering how vast your view of the world has become since I first encountered you, I cannot think of anyone more fitting for the position. Your job, Viviana, will be to record the adventures of Arthur for history to comment upon."

I could barely grasp it. "You mean . . . you wish me to record the details of all that goes on here in the castle . . . ?"

"Good God, no, of course not," said Merlin. "I want you to write stories that will inspire generations to come. Remove all the blemishes. Make the evil truly evil, the virtuous truly virtuous. I want you to shape the way that future generations view Arthur and his noble knights. Devil take the veracity of the details. Make it dramatic. Make it effective. Make it good."

"But . . . that is deceitful . . ."

"Nonsense. Historians write with agendas all the time. Yours will be to celebrate the greatness that is Arthur."

"Is it not evil to formalize lies?"

"What evil has come out of your lies that conceived Galahad, eh? The people have a new hero to worship. A truly evil woman has been dispatched. Arthur's reign is reinvigorated." He stroked his great beard. "You continue to underestimate the power of fiction, Viviana. You should not do so. Fiction can change the world, especially when it masquerades as fact."

I could not argue with that.

Slowly I walked around the chamber. I inhaled deeply. It smelled musty, the odor of scholarship.

"Well?" said Merlin.

"I . . . would be honored, sir. Except . . ."

"Except what?" He sounded impatient.

"Well . . . will not Harold, son of Horace, have something to say in the matter?"

"I very much doubt it. He is dead."

"Oh! Was it unexpected?"

"I would say so. Rowena landed on him. Apparently the poor bastard never heard her coming. Ah well. There is a reason for everything, I suppose. I shall convey the good news of your appointment to their majesties." He turned and walked out before I could respond.

I sank down into the chair next to the writing desk. I stared at it, then slowly ran my hand across its smooth surface.

I smiled.

I was home.

Later that night, I was awakened by the sound of the wall scraping open. I was not surprised. I suspected it would happen sooner or later.

Galahad lay next to me sleeping deeply. I had worn him out,

the poor dear. I wondered if I would ever learn the mystery of his silence, but did not dwell on it overlong. We had learned to communicate in other ways.

I eased myself out of bed, never waking him. Fortunately I was wearing a shift, for it was cold in the castle, even under the blanket with my knight. I stood and faced Modred, who was standing at the far end of the room. He was holding a sack, which I immediately recognized as my own.

"You dropped this," he said softly, "when you were fleeing Rowena."

He set it down upon the writing desk. I went to it and checked the contents. My journal was still within. "I would not have had to flee her if it were not for you," I pointed out.

"True. I am sorry for that."

"I suspect you, in fact, are not sorry."

"You suspect correctly. But it seemed the thing to say."

I paused and then asked, "Did you hear the things Rowena said to the stable master? In the kitchen?"

"Of course I did."

"You must tell no one. Not even Morgan, presuming you have not done so already."

"I have not, and I shan't. I rather like secrets. I am learning that the only thing more powerful than the spoken word is the unspoken word."

"There is much truth in that."

"And there is much truth in there," said Modred, pointing at my journal. "I suggest you continue to maintain it, even while inscribing the histories that Merlin wants you to write.

History always has two sides. It is rare, though, that the same person gets to record both of them."

"I shall do so," I said.

He turned, about to step back into the wall, then paused and said, "I expect you to do a superb job of writing me. If you do not, I shall be very cross."

"I will keep that in mind."

He stepped into the wall and slid it shut.

I sat down at the writing desk and inscribed in my journal all the events of this day. At least I do not have to worry about running out of ink.

I wonder if my father is still alive. I must find a way to get word to him if he is. I hope he will be proud of me. Certainly he will be surprised.

And when I next speak with Guinevere and ask her of her plans for a child and how she and Arthur plan to guide the kingdom, we will speak . . . well, not as equals, certainly. But as less unequals, if that makes any sense.

I must also be certain to plug whatever seeing hole Modred has into this room. I do not need him spying upon my adult activities with Galahad.

Speaking of whom, he stirs in bed. He is looking up at me now, smiling. He gestures.

I shall attend to his needs and to mine. But his first.

Enough writing for now, Viviana. More on the morrow.

About the Author

PETER DAVID IS A PROLIFIC author whose career, and continued popularity, spans nearly two decades. He has worked in every conceivable media: Television, film, books (fiction, non-fiction and audio), short stories, and comic books, and acquired followings in all of them.

In the literary field, Peter has had over seventy novels published, including numerous appearances on the *New York Times* Bestsellers List. His novels include *Tigerheart*, *Darkness of the Light*, *Sir Apropos of Nothing* and the sequel *The Woad to Wuin*, *Knight Life*, *Howling Mad*, and the Psi-Man adventure series. He is the co-creator and author of the bestselling *Star Trek: New Frontier* series for Pocket Books, and has also written such Trek novels as *Q-Squared*, *The Siege*, *Q-in-Law*, *Vendetta*, *I, Q* (with John deLancie), *A Rock and a Hard Place* and *Imzadi*. He produced the three *Babylon 5* Centauri Prime novels, and has also had his short fiction published in such collections as *Shock Rock*, *Shock Rock II*, and *Otherwere*, as well as *Isaac Asimov's Science Fiction Magazine* and *The Magazine of Fantasy and Science Fiction*.

Peter's comic book resume includes an award-winning twelve-year run on *The Incredible Hulk*, and he has also worked on such varied and popular titles as *Supergirl*, *Young Justice*, *Soulsearchers and Company*, *Aquaman*, *Spider-Man*, *Spider-Man 2099*, *X-Factor*, *Star Trek*, *Wolverine*, *The Phantom*, *Sachs & Violens*, *The Dark Tower*, and many others. He has also written comic book related novels, such as *The Incredible Hulk: What Savage Beast*, and co-edited *The Ultimate Hulk* short story collection.

Furthermore, his opinion column, "But I Digress . . . ," has been running in the industry trade newspaper *The Comic Buyers's Guide* for nearly a decade, and in that time has been the paper's consistently most popular feature and was also collected into a trade paperback edition.

Peter is also the writer for two popular video games: *Shadow Complex* and *Spider-Man: Edge of Time*.

Peter is the co-creator, with popular science fiction icon Bill Mumy (of *Lost in Space* and *Babylon 5* fame) of the Cable Ace Award-nominated science fiction series *Space Cases*, which ran for two seasons on Nickelodeon. He has written several scripts for the Hugo Award winning TV series *Babylon 5*, and the sequel series, *Crusade*. He has also written several films for Full Moon Entertainment and co-produced two of them, including two installments in the popular *Trancers* series, as well as the science fiction western spoof *Oblivion*, which won the Gold Award at the 1994 Houston International Film Festival for best Theatrical Feature Film, Fantasy/Horror category.

Peter's awards and citations include: the Haxtur Award 1996 (Spain), Best Comic script; OZCon 1995 award (Australia), Favorite International Writer; Comic Buyers Guide 1995 Fan Awards, Favorite writer; Wizard Fan Award Winner 1993; Golden Duck Award for Young Adult Series (*Starfleet Academy*), 1994; UK Comic Art Award, 1993; Will Eisner Comic Industry Award, 1993. He lives in New York with his wife, Kathleen, and his four children, Shana, Gwen, Ariel, and Caroline.

If you liked
Crazy 8's first offering,
you'd be *crazy* to miss this next book!
Check out the first chapter of
the hilarious science fiction adventure

Can fowl play save the universe?

NO SMALL BILLS

by award-winning author
AARON ROSENBERG

Chapter One

DuckBob, meet the Universe.
Universe, meet DuckBob.

Ever have one of those days where nothing ever seems to go quite right? Where you miss the train by seconds each time, fumble your change at the snack machine, click away from the porn site too slow to fool your supervisor, kick yourself in the head when you're trying to tie your shoe, take a swig of your beer only to realize it's a canister of baking soda instead?

That's pretty much every day for me.

The name's DuckBob. DuckBob Spinowitz. No, that's not a nickname or a pet name or any of that other funny stuff. It's my name. I had it legally changed. Figured it was easier to join 'em than try to beat 'em. Why? Well, okay, here's the thing—

—I've got the head of a duck.

I know, right now you're thinking "oh, he's got a flat nose" or "he's got a weak chin and a high forehead" or "he must have feathery blond hair." No. That's not it at all.

I.

Have.

The head.

Of.

A.

Duck.

Really. My head? It's that of a mallard—a Wood Duck, to be precise. Complete with black-tipped red-and-white bill, white below the bill and down the front of the neck, a touch of yellow rising up from the bill and leading to a white streaks above red eyes, and emerald green feathers covering the rest, with a few white streaks mixed in.

A duck.

Only, y'know, man-sized.

I've also got webbed feet. And feathers instead of hair. All over. Soft downy feathers, looks just like fine hair until you feel it. Speckled brown down the chest and on the feet, tan across the arms and hands, emerald green on the back (yes, all the way down!), and white on the belly, groin, and legs.

It's pretty slick-looking, actually. If I were a crazed xenobiologist with leanings toward ornithology, I'd say I was an impressive specimen. I even won a few awards at bird shows, before I was disqualified—seems

the entry and the owner can't be the same person. Purists.

On the plus side, I can walk in the rain and not get wet. And

swimming? Fuggedaboutit.

No, I wasn't born this way. And no, I don't want to talk about it.

Just another example of the colossal bad luck that routinely plagues my

life. Because that's what it was—bad luck. I mean, was it my fault I was

hiking through a restricted area in the Catskills in the dead of night,

waving a lighter in one hand and a neon-orange fishing pole in the

other? While naked?

Long story. There was a girl involved. At least I certainly hope so,

because otherwise I've got no excuse.

Beyond that—let's just say that, all those stories about alien

abductions and crazy experiments? They don't know the half of it.

Those little gray buggers are downright cruel.

So you're probably thinking, "Okay, this guy's half man, half duck.

That's weird. I'll bet he's a superhero, with a face like that—DuckBob

the Avenger. Or a mad scientist. Or at least a sunglasses model.

Nope. Sorry. I'm just your ordinary average guy, and when I'm

dressed I look completely normal, 'cept for the whole duck-head thing.

I'm no superhero. I work at—aw hell, does it even matter what the name is, really? It's an office job, okay? I'm a pencil pusher, and not even a glorified one. I shuffle papers and push buttons in a little cubicle all day. Then I leave.

Whee.

Some life, huh? Well, it beats the alternatives. At least that's what I like to tell myself. Hey, whatever it takes to get through the day. For me that usually includes watching a few minutes from old Donald Duck cartoons at some point. It's about the only way I can convince myself things could be worse. Look like this, not be able to talk straight, and be forced to walk around with my butt and my business hanging out all the time? Yeah, that would pretty much be the last straw.

Anyway, I'm used to being the butt of some cosmic joke. That being said, I was still surprised when I walked into work one Tuesday and two guys grabbed me by the arms. Big guys, too—they lifted me right off my feet, and I'm not small myself. Plus the bill weighs a lot—I've got amazing neck muscles.

"Hey, what's the big idea?" I demanded as they turned and carried me back out the door. "I've gotta punch in!"

"Mr. Spinowitz?" One of them asked. He had a face like a microwaved potato—squishy and overflowing—and a voice like a hoarse bulldog. He was wearing a suit, a dark one, and I was pretty sure I heard fabric tear each time he shifted.

"Yeah. Who the hell are you guys?"

"We need to speak with you about an urgent matter of national security," the other guy said. He was taller than his buddy, athletic where Mr. Potato Head was just squat. (I'm big-boned and slightly rotund, by the way. It's the slacker lifestyle that does it.) Matching suit, though. I thought that was sweet. Like jewelry but washable.

"National security? I was just curious what sort of brownie recipes it had," I said quickly. "I didn't try any of the other stuff, and even if I did Missus Gries down the hall had it coming! I'm sure the twitching will stop soon!"

The shorter guy raised an eyebrow but shook his head. "That's not why we're here."

"What, then?" I thought for a second, then gasped. "Oh, come on! I know the porn was from Yugoslavia but I only traded an old Steve McQueen movie for it! It's not like I was selling state secrets! It's not even a clean copy!"

By this time we'd reached the curb, and a big black sedan idling there. Mr. Potato Head opened the passenger door and slid in, then Mr. Tall shoved me in after him. I've never understood the whole "dark sedan with government plates" thing, actually. Why that kind of car? Why not those crazy monster SUVs, so the agents can drive over anyone who gets in their way? And nobody'd escape custody—it's not like you can get out of one of those without a ladder and some pitons. Or go for sports cars, classy and great in a car chase. Or the old kidnapper classic, the white Econoline van—cheap, ubiquitous, and now with faster sliding doors! Or maybe something to counteract their whole "we're not really on your side after all" image. I bet government agencies wouldn't seem half as scary if they all drove brightly colored compact cars or minivans with "My Kid's a Soccer Star" bumper stickers.

Instead, there I was in the back of a dark sedan. The windows were tinted—I could have made faces at my co-workers and they'd never have known. Not that I can do many faces anymore—duckbills are not very versatile. I'm great at Charades, though. As long as it involves water fowl.

"Where're we going?" I asked as the car pulled away—there must have been a third guy driving but I couldn't see him. "Who are you? What do you want from me? Say, what's that?" That last one I asked while pointing at the Empire State Building, just to get a reaction. I did. They looked at me like I was a moron.

With a head like mine, it's hard getting people to take you seriously.

"Our superiors want to speak with you," the taller guy answered.

"They never heard of the phone?"

He glared at me. "It's a matter of national security."

"Yeah, you said that already. Couldn't they have used a nationally secure phone?"

That got snorts from both of them, and I think from the driver as well. "No such thing," Mr. Potato Head said. "You have any idea how easy it is to tap into a cell phone conversation?"

"No. Could you show me? I'd love to know what my boss says about me." Though actually I think I have a pretty good idea. "Quack, quack" is surprisingly easy to lip read.

They didn't answer, and we spent the rest of the ride in silence. I hate silence. It gives me time to think.

Finally we pulled into a building down near the south piers. A warehouse, it looked like, on a narrow street full of warehouses. I didn't see a sign or a street number or anything. Which I guess was the point.

"Out," Mr. Tall demanded once we'd stopped and the garage door clanked shut again. He got out first and Mr. Potato Head shoved me from behind to make me move, then clambered out after me. Maybe his door was broken. I looked around as I got out but it just looked like a warehouse. There was a guy standing there watching us, though.

Average height, skinny as a razor blade, with features to match and glossy black hair that looked painted on. Same suit as my escorts but his looked better on him.

"Mr. Spinowitz? I'm Mr. Smith," he said, offering his hand. "Thank you for joining us."

"I didn't really have a choice," I pointed out, but I shook hands with him anyway. Hell, I was in a nondescript warehouse somewhere in Manhattan with at least four guys, all of them probably armed. Being rude didn't sound like a good idea.

"I apologize for our insistence," Smith explained. "But this is an urgent matter and we couldn't risk you refusing our invitation."

"Okay, so I'm here." I glanced around again. Nothing to see but rusty walls and stairs and railings, concrete floor, the car we'd pulled up in, and us. "What's this all about?"

Smith started to say something, stopped, and started again. "We have a situation, and we think you may be uniquely qualified to handle it for us," he said finally.

"Qualified? Me? You haven't read my performance reviews. What makes me so qualified?"

Smith pointed at my head. "That."

"Oh."

"Yes. You see, we've been approached by extraterrestrials. We have no idea what they want, and none of our attempts to communicate have worked. But you've encountered them before—we hoped that might have granted you some rapport with them."

I stared at him, at the guys behind me, and then back at him again. "Let me get this straight—you've got some aliens you want to talk to, and you want me to do the talking because I got abducted and given a duck head so you figure I can relate to them better? Are you mental?" Okay, I forgot about the whole not-pissing-off-the-men-with-guns thing.

"You may be correct," Smith admitted. "But we have little to lose at this point, and it seemed an avenue worth exploring. Would you be willing to make the attempt? For the good of your country?" Man, this guy was good! Those callers from the Fraternal Order of Police had nothing on him!

I took time to think about it, though. I didn't want to just jump into anything. "Yeah, okay, sure."

"Excellent!" He actually rubbed his hands together. I thought they only did that in cheesy movies. "Come along, it's right this way." I followed him to the back of the warehouse, which had several doors. The floor above continued back past this point so I was looking at the doors to several rooms rather than a whole set of back doors. Which makes sense because why would anyone need more than one back door, especially all in a row? Why not just have one great big giant door? Smith gestured toward the door to the left. "After you."

"Oh, the alien's in there?" He nodded. "And you want me to talk to it?" Another nod. "Alone?" Nod number three—one more and I walked. "But you just said 'after you'—doesn't that mean you're going in with me?"

Smith smiled then, which looked like something you'd see on a buzzard that suddenly found itself at a breakfast buffet. "I lied." He indicated the door again, and rested one hand on his side. Right below the bulge I suspected was his gun—either that or he's got a hideous growth under his left arm. Either way I figured I'd better do what he wanted.

"Okay, okay, I'm going." I turned the knob and pulled the door halfway open. At least it looked dark on the other side, no blinding lights and sets of examining tables and rows of glistening tools. Not that I think about such things. Much. Ever.

"Right." I took a deep breath. "Here goes." And I stepped inside.

And promptly screamed as the door slammed shut behind me. Then the lights came on, showing me four plain metal chairs and a small folding table—and the little figure sitting in one of the chairs facing the table.

Short, skinny, gray skin, huge head, huge eyes, no hair. An alien. Just like the ones who . . . anyway, an alien.

Though I wondered where he'd gotten the Halloween-themed footy pajamas. Those didn't seem like standard issue. At least the black-bat pattern went with his skin tone and his eyes.

"Uh, hi." I walked over to the table and leaned over it so we were roughly face-to-face. "I'm Bob. DuckBob. Have we met?"

CRAZY 8 PRESS ™

Peter David
Michael Jan Friedman
Robert Greenberger
Glenn Hauman
Aaron Rosenberg
Howard Weinstein

Go to http://www.crazy8press.com
to check out more CRAZY books
from our collection of crazy-talented authors!

Twitter: @crazy8press
Facebook: http://www.facebook.com/crazy8press